THE
WOLVES
OF
FREYDIS

JC RYAN

vinci
BOOKS

By JC Ryan

Carter Devereux Mystery Thriller Series

Nothing New Under The Sun
The Wolves Of Freydis
The Alboran Codex
The Nabatean Secret
The Labyrinth of Minos

Vinci Books

vinci-books.com

Published by Vinci Books Ltd in 2025

1

Copyright © JC Ryan 2016

The author has asserted their moral right to be identified as the author of this work in accordance with the Copyright, Designs and Patents Act 1988.
This work is a work of fiction. Names, characters, places and incidents are the product of the author's imagination or are used fictitiously. Any resemblance to actual persons, living or dead, places and incidents is entirely coincidental.
All rights reserved. No part of this publication may be copied, reproduced, distributed, stored in any retrieval system, or transmitted in any form or by any means, including photocopying, recording, or other electronic or mechanical methods, nor used as a source for any form of machine learning including AI datasets, without the prior written permission of the publisher.
The publisher and the author have made every effort to obtain permissions for any third party material used in this book and to comply with copyright law. Any queries in this respect should be brought to the attention of the publisher and any omissions will be corrected in future editions.
A CIP catalogue record for this book is available from the British Library.
Paperback ISBN: 9781036703288

Printed and bound in Great Britain by Clays Ltd, Elcograf S.p.A.

Prologue

Ahote turned over in the dark and lay on his back. He considered turning the bedside light on but didn't want to disturb Bly.

Something had woken him, but he couldn't identify what. He frowned. For some reason, he felt uneasy. Bly stirred beside him, "Ahote? You okay?"

"I suppose so."

She leaned up on her elbow, "That's a strange answer."

"Hmm…"

He got out of bed and restlessly went over to the double glazed window to look out over the snow-covered landscape. High above, the full moon caused the trees to cast their shadows towards the house.

He put his head against the cold glass and rested there a moment as Bly got out of bed "Well dear, whatever it is, you will need a nice warm drink to get you back to sleep." She pulled on her slippers that matched her floor-length pink flannel nightgown and wandered off into the open plan living quarters looking like a waif in the light cast by the glowing embers of the fire.

A moment later the light in the kitchen came on, and he could hear her fixing a saucepan of hot milk for them both.

What was it? Something's wrong; I can feel it; but what? He shifted uneasily in the dark.

Moments later, he heard wolves howling; was that it? Is that what woke him? No, he was used to the wolves howling, he'd know something was wrong if they didn't howl.

He gave up and wandered into the kitchen. "The wolves are giving voice tonight, must be the full moon."

"Maybe it's them who woke you."

"No. Well, they might have, but they aren't what's giving me this presentiment of something being seriously wrong."

The wolves' howls came closer, and Bly went to open the upper half of a Dutch door and peer outside. "Now, that's odd. Those are Mackie's wolves."

"How do you know? We don't usually see them while Mackie and Carter are away. In fact, come to think of it, they haven't been here for a couple of months."

"Well, we're seeing them now. They are actually in the compound near the barn, staring up at the house. They've never done that before. Come and see."

He got up and moved to her side. "Are you sure they're Mackie's wolves?"

"Oh yes. I'd know their howl anywhere; it's different from the others. They howl to get Mackie's attention. I'll bet if you check around Carter's house and buildings in the morning, you'll find their footprints. They're looking for her."

Ahote sighed, "Oh hell Bly I hope you're wrong. If they are looking for her, then something bad has happened."

The next morning, they took off on the snow sled and covered the mile to the Devereux homestead in a short time. There they dismounted and walked around the buildings.

Sure enough, there were wolf prints in the snow up to the main house door and the windows. There were even signs the wolves had stood on hind legs to look inside.

"This just isn't normal wolf behavior, Bly." Ahote was disturbed.

"No, but these are not ordinary wolves Pet. They know and love Mackie, and they know something we don't."

"How on earth can they do that?"

"Perhaps the same way you woke up last night feeling something was wrong." Bly shrugged, "There's no way they'd come into close contact with the buildings here or at home if there were nothing wrong. We wouldn't normally see them until Mackie returned; you know that."

When they arrived back at their house, the wolves were waiting for them.

Bly told Ahote to wait for her and started to walk towards them. "Don't do that Bly; they may not be all that friendly while Mackie's away."

She turned back, "Don't worry, we've been introduced. I know their names." She smiled mysteriously at him.

She drew closer, "Keeva, Loki, come." She beckoned with her hand, and they moved closer. They stared into her deep brown eyes with their equally dark gold ones. She put out a hand and placed it on Loki's head. "You're looking for Mackie, eh? Something's wrong, isn't it? Keeva moved in and welcomed Bly's touch with a soft whine as if both of them were feeling lost and needed some reassurance.

Bly smiled to herself. Ever since the Wolves met Mackie,

and indeed even before that, they'd been around. They never caused any trouble but if Carter took a horse out for the day or chose to camp out for a while, they would go with him. When Mackie arrived, they seemed drawn to her, and she to them. She had never been afraid of them, and they came in close to walk side by side with her.

Bly spent a few minutes just patting them and crooning a little Indian song, the sort she used to sing to her babies before they grew up.

Eventually, they moved away and quietly vanished into the trees.

She returned to the back porch and accepted a cup of hot coffee from Ahote, then settled down next to him on a bench, hunching deep into her all weather poncho.

"Will you tell me their names?"

Bly smiled, "Of course. The female is Keeva, which means beautiful and gentle, and the male is Loki, which means Wolf Spirit."

Ahote nodded and asked. "So, do you think they will come back?"

"No, they don't need to. They've done their bit; told us something is wrong. Now we have to worry about it." She sipped her coffee.

Ahote was silent for a moment. "You're right though aren't you? Their instinct for things goes far beyond what we can see, hear, and touch. Animals have instincts – no, they have knowledge about this world we live in – knowledge that we just don't understand, although it's not as though people haven't tried."

Bly nodded, "Yes they have, but people want it all to be so cut and dried and it isn't. Look at you; you feel something's wrong, you can't explain it but you know it's real.

They do too, they may even know what it is, but could never tell us how they know."

"Like the elephants in Indonesia that knew about the Tsunami days before it hit and moved up into the mountains for safety."

"Or birds that vanish before an earthquake."

They fell silent again then Ahote added "Like dog owners who claim that their pets know when they are due to come home even if they change their routine and arrived at different times. Still, without fail, the dogs go and wait for them at a door or window ten to twenty minutes before they come home just as always."

Bly giggled, "Do you remember that little dog we had when the children were small – the one who always knew when a visitor was due even though we weren't expecting one?"

Ahote laughed, "She was always right. So we just accept that Loki and Keeva know. No scientist on earth can explain how, all we can be sure of is there's a link – an invisible cord – between them and the family. So something is wrong, and they came to tell us. Now that we know, they trust us to sort it out. Is that how it goes?"

Bly nodded "I'm afraid so. We are now sure something is wrong, and the wolves expect us to fix it. It would help to know what it was."

A phone call to the Andersons went unanswered so there was nothing more they could do.

It was two days later, when James Rhodes called, that their presentiments became real.

Chapter One

BREAKING NEWS

United Airlines flight 7 hours out of Tel Aviv, 5 hours after the bomb explosion in Jerusalem's Downtown Triangle

James Rhodes tried to stretch his long legs to ease the discomfort of being cramped for so long in the airline seat. His thoughts briefly turned to his friend Carter and his family, well into the first day of their six-week holiday, as he flipped through the channels on the small TV screen in front of him.

Carter had accompanied him to the airport to see him off and to wait for the arrival of his family on a flight from Boston, which was scheduled to land within an hour after James' departure.

He found the CNN channel just as a red, flashing, breaking news banner flashed on the screen ….

Bomb explosion in Jerusalem. 15 killed, 35 injured.

News about bombs killing and maiming people in the

Middle East, especially countries such as Iraq, Afghanistan, and Syria, was an almost daily event. However, bomb blasts in Israel were not such a regular occurrence, even more so in Jerusalem. But that was not what set the alarm bells off in James' brain. Those stomach-churning sounds in his brain were triggered by the thought of his friends, Carter and Mackenzie Devereux with their six-year-old son Liam, who were on holiday in Jerusalem.

Oh God, please don't let them be part of this, was his first thought as he grabbed the earphones out of the seat pocket, plugged them in and started pushing buttons to find the one that controlled the volume.

He'd set out from Tel Aviv's Ben Gurion International airport seven hours earlier. He and Carter had just finished a research expedition to India and Egypt, and he was on his way back home. Carter and his family were getting a six-week holiday under way, starting with two days in Jerusalem and the rest of the time on a luxury Mediterranean Cruise ship. Carter had accompanied him to the airport to see him off and to wait for the arrival of his family on a flight from Boston, which was scheduled to land shortly after James' departure.

Finally, he found the right button and raised the volume to hear the news. As the facts were announced, a nauseating foreboding started to wash over him. The bomb explosion happened about five hours after he departed from Tel Aviv. It happened in the Downtown Triangle of Jerusalem – that was very close to the hotel where he and Carter stayed for the last two days before he left. The two of them had visited the Triangle the night before, and Carter told him that he was planning to take his family there on the first night after their arrival.

The Triangle is a big place; he kept telling himself. *Maybe they weren't even in the Triangle when the bomb exploded.*

The fact that thus far four American citizens were amongst the dead and injured did not help to alleviate his disquiet. Neither did the notice that the final death and injury toll was still unknown but would undoubtedly increase over the next 24 hours, as rescue teams sifted through the rubble to locate additional victims. No names or details would be released until next-of-kin were notified.

James spent the remaining hours of the flight looking out the window, torn between hope and fear for his friend and his family. After hours that seemed like an eternity, the plane finally landed at Dulles International in Washington, DC. As it touched down, he had his cell phone ready in his hand, waiting for the announcement, which would allow passengers to switch on their mobile devices. The announcement came as soon as the plane started taxiing to the main building. He could not switch his phone on quick enough to suit him.

The moment the phone connected to the cellphone network a series of loud beeps sounded, there were two messages – a voice mail notification and a text message. He read the text message first. It was from Hunter Patrick, the Director of A-Echelon, where he worked: *Contact me the moment you land. It's critical.* He pushed the speed dial button to retrieve his voicemail messages. It was Hunter Patrick's voice – "Jim, *I know you will still be en route when I leave this message, but I just want to make sure that you contact me the moment you get my messages.*"

His hands were slightly trembling when he pushed the speed dial button for Director Patrick's cellphone. Hunter answered on the second ring.

"James here, we've just landed, and I'm still on the plane. I can listen but can't say much."

"I can't talk much either." Hunter's tone was somber. "I'm afraid it's dreadful news. I can't tell you more over the open line. I have arranged for airport security to meet you and escort you through customs immediately. Give them your ticket and boarding pass; your luggage will be delivered later. A driver is waiting to bring you directly to the office."

"Okay. I'll see you there." He replied. He didn't require more information to know they were dealing with a severe situation. He had seen enough of those in his line of work to know there was a tsunami of trouble waiting at the office.

James was a former CIA field operative working on special assignment for A-Echelon - a small but top-secret organization consisting of a limited number of specialists who were tasked to investigate global archeological anomalies that might have a bearing on national security. The A in the name was for Archeology. Their covert workspace and offices were hidden in some of the secret underground facilities below the Smithsonian Institution Building known as The Castle. The Institution hosted many different research centers, involved in a broad range of top-secret initiatives and programs across the globe.

On the way to the office, he phoned his wife, Carolyn, to let her know something had come up and that he would probably be home much later than planned. He would let her know as soon as he had more information. He and Carolyn had married when they were 25 and were still madly in love with each other after 31 years. Carolyn was an exceptional woman who understood what she got herself into, the day she said, "I do" while looking into the eyes of the CIA spook she loved. Over the years Carolyn learned the meaning of all those code words – 'something came up,' 'I'm going to be late,' 'don't worry I'm okay.' She also learned to value and make the most of, every moment of the time she and her James were together. And with the same fervor, she would switch her mind to her gardening and writing when they were not together.

James had a tender smile on his face when he ended the call with Carolyn. *What would my life have been without that beautiful angel of a woman who understands the work I do, and me, so well?*

His mind returned to the news and the conversation with Hunter. There were two, or maybe three, possibilities. It could be related to the bomb explosion in Jerusalem and Hunter's words, 'I'm afraid it's dreadful news' led him to expect the worst news about Carter and his family. The other option was that it could have something to do with the ancient nuke project that he and Carter had been working on, and the reason for their visits to India and Egypt. Or it could be nothing to do with any of that, but then, he had no idea what that could be.

It was 3:00 am when he approached Hunter's office and saw the door was closed, but light was seeping through the line underneath. He knocked and entered when he heard Hunter's voice call him in. His heart dropped to the floor the moment he set eyes on Hunter's face and Irene O'Connell's tear filled eyes. He hesitated, his breath trapped in his chest, "This is about Carter and his family, isn't it?"

Patrick nodded slowly. Irene was wiping the tears from her eyes with a tissue. "I'm sorry Jim; it's dreadful news. Please take a seat." Hunter's voice was quivering as he struggled to contain his emotions.

Irene O'Connell had a Ph.D. in Human Biology and was an employee of DARPA on special assignment with A-

Echelon to assist Mackenzie Devereux with her respirocyte research. Without asking, she got up and poured James a cup of coffee, black without milk or sugar, and handed it to him. That's how he always had his coffee. He reached for a chair, as he accepted the cup with shaking hands.

While James stared at them, Hunter gave him the information he'd collected from various security agencies in contact with their counterparts in Israel. They'd learned through those channels that Carter was alive and in the hospital. He was the only one inside the restaurant at the time of the explosion who survived, and it was assumed that Makenzie and Liam were killed in the blast. The death toll was 25 with 56 injured. Carter was in the critical care unit of the Shaare Zedek Medical Center, Jerusalem, in very serious but stable condition.

As soon as he'd learned what had happened, the President made a personal call to Mackenzie's parents to inform them of the tragedy.

"Has anyone claimed responsibility for this?" James asked with an ashen face as he looked at Director Patrick.

"No one so far," Hunter was shaking his head, "that's according to the Director of the CIA who has been in direct contact with his counterpart in the Mossad."

"I'm going back to Israel," James said in a solemn tone. "I have to be there for Carter." He raised his eyebrows while looking at Hunter as if to say, '*and don't you try and stop me.*'

"Of course you are, and thank you." Hunter nodded. "I made arrangements for Steven and Mary Anderson, Mackenzie's parents to go with you. As soon as they arrive from Boston there is a private charter ready to fly you all over to Tel Aviv."

"Thank you for that, Hunter. I appreciate your understanding."

"Okay, the Andersons should arrive at Dulles by 9:00 am. I suggest you go home and spend some time with Carolyn. You'll have time on the flight to get some sleep."

James stood to leave. He moved towards the door but turned back to Hunter and Irene and started to say something then stopped.

"What is it, Jim? It looked like you were going to say something?" Irene asked.

James shook his head slightly, almost as if he did not believe what he was about to say but decided to continue. "Do you think this could somehow be related to either of the projects Carter and Mackenzie have been working on for us?"

Hunter and Irene looked at each other and shook their heads. None of them had given that any consideration. "I won't rule out anything at this stage Jim. Ruthless lunatics who don't care about killing and mutilating innocent people committed this senseless massacre, so anything is possible. But I would say it's highly unlikely there is any connection to those projects. I would go so far as to say that you could definitely rule out Mackenzie's respirocyte project."

James didn't reply. He just nodded his head slowly and turned back to the door. There was nothing more to say – for now.

Chapter Two

IN THREE DAYS

Riyadh, Saudi Arabia, 10 hours after the bomb explosion

Xavier Algosaibi was usually a very calm and confident man. He was a man who listened more than he spoke for he had learned long ago that information and knowledge could be gained by his silence. These were personality traits that had served him well all his life and part of how he succeeded in becoming one of the wealthiest and most influential men in Saudi Arabia. Information and knowledge were powerful and profitable commodities.

However, he was on the verge of exploding into a rage of fury with the man sitting in front of him, Youssef Bin-Bandar. Youssef was a prominent member of the Saudi establishment. He was the third highest-ranking member of the General Intelligence Presidency, directly beneath the director and deputy director. The two men shared an absolute hatred of the Saud royal family, and over the past 35 years, they had formed a close friendship. They were united in their desire to bring down the House of Saud and unify the world under a new Islamic caliphate, or as Westerners would term it, an Islamic State. Youssef was one of the very few of Xavier's confidants.

"Youssef," Algosaibi spoke softly and slowly, trying his best to suppress the rage, which had been building inside him. "This is the second time in just a few short weeks that an operation has not been completed successfully. I hate loose ends and sloppy work. I have become one of the most successful men in this country through diligence and precision. Why did this happen?"

"Xavier," Bin-Bandar's voice was trembling. In the 35 years they had known each other, he had witnessed the consequences of Algosaibi's wrath on two occasions, but the memory of those two occasions gave him reason to be shivering in fear. "Please accept my sincere apologies. I am ashamedly responsible for the failure, and it hurts me to have disappointed you."

"Not just me Youssef." Algosaibi's voice rose. He was about to tell him that he had also disappointed the Foundation of the Real Princes of Saud, but Bin-Bandar didn't know of their existence. Instead, he said, "Worst of all is that you have disappointed Allah!" Bin-Bandar flinched when he heard those words.

Algosaibi stopped and drew breath. His anger had driven him almost to exposing the Foundation of the Real Princes of Saud.

It rattled him; how could this happen? Was he so angry that he had forgotten the secret cabal of five men who, with him, planned the final destruction of the House of Saud?

His black eyes stared at Bin-Bandar as he took a sip of water he'd poured from a carafe. He breathed deeply, drawing on his inner reserves to find his core of peace once more.

Bin Bandar waited. He had no choice; he'd wait until Algosaibi released him, and there was no way Algosaibi would do that yet.

With another sip of water, his mind went over the five men whom he'd carefully selected.

Each of them hated with a passion the House of Saud. It had taken five long years of seeking, selecting, and then checking and rechecking each one of them until he was convinced they were indeed trustworthy.

His choices were not based solely on their wealth, standing in society, their businesses or families, nor on how influential they were, although all that mattered. One of them was even a drug dealer, an occupation Algosaibi loathed, even though the money was excellent. The choice was made by the quiet and silent tests he carefully crafted and presented to each of them, without their knowledge, to discover if they were honest, loyal, fierce in their courage, and silent - above all silent.

It took a long time to approach them and he never did this himself. First, an intermediary would seek them out and sow the seeds to pave the way for him. It took patience.

The final result was a foundation that consisted of five exclusive members who, between them, had access to revenue from 250,000 barrels of oil a day.

The Foundation was well planned and organized such as a terrorist group might be set up. It was impossible to infiltrate as it was set up as isolated and independent cells that only one person knew the extent of, and that person was Algosaibi himself.

The members were smart and never met in public. There was nothing to connect them to each other, and all meetings were held underground, in places very few people knew existed.

Bin-Bandar's gaze was fixed on the floor in front of him. He didn't dare look up at Algosaibi; he thought that would be seen as an act of defiance, which would be an assurance of death for him.

"Youssef, a few days ago you sat here in that same chair, and I asked you to give me the assurance that you had everything ready to execute the operation in Jerusalem. Is that correct?"

Youssef was unable to speak he just nodded.

"Look at me when I talk to you and answer me!" Algosaibi yelled.

The man's head snapped up, "Yes that's correct. I am … I am … very sorry."

"Did you not put your hand on your heart and say these exact words: 'everything has been planned in minute detail. Now I only wait for you to say the word and the operation will kick into action.'"

"Yes Sir, I did." Bin-Bandar felt an icy chill slip down his spine.

"Youssef it is only our friendship of the past 35 years that is preventing me from killing you here and now." Algosaibi's voice had gone soft and measured - deadly. "What exactly happened? And don't leave anything out. I don't have to tell you what will happen if I find out you have lied to me."

"Yes, sir," he nodded. "We had a team of three people following Devereux and his family from the airport in Tel Aviv to their hotel in Jerusalem. In the background, we had two vehicles ready, one with the martyr and the other with the three Special Forces soldiers. With our electronic surveillance equipment, we overheard that they were planning to visit the Triangle and have dinner at a corner café. When they left the hotel, they were again followed, and we kept tabs on their conversations with the parabolic directional microphones. When we heard that they were heading for the restaurant, two of our collaborators took up their places in the restaurant and kept a watch on the family to see when would be the right time to strike." Bin-Bandar's throat was dry, and he was shaking. He paused to take a sip of water.

"Continue Youssef." Algosaibi snapped at him. "I am waiting."

"The family took their seats at an outside table, and shortly after that, our people inside reported that the woman had gone to the restroom. The mission leader told everyone to wait until she got back. Minutes later, our agents inside said that the woman had returned, and the mission leader gave the order for the extraction to commence.

One of our agents started a fight with another man across the street from the café to draw attention away from the restaurant and allow the van with the extraction team to drive up to the building unnoticed. They were to grab the family and take off before the truck with the bomb arrived." He paused again to take a few deep breaths.

"Don't make me wait, Youssef. You are angering me."

Youssef drew in a shaky breath and continued, "As soon as the mission leader gave the order, the extraction vehicle was on the way. Just when the 'fight' was about to start, Devereux left the table and went to the restroom. The agents inside said they reported this to the mission leader, but the mission leader told me that he never received the text message."

"And that's where everything went wrong," Algosaibi stated.

"Yes, sir," he answered miserably.

"Youssef, I think I've heard enough. I'm not even going to ask you how many loose ends are hanging out there. You will make sure they are all tied up in the next 24 hours and report back to me."

Youssef nodded vehemently, "Yes sir, I will."

"When will the team arrive?"

"In three days' sir, they are already in Gaza."

Algosaibi waved his hand at Bin-Bandar as if he were shooing a fly away. He had already made up his mind. He would have to find a new director of operations for the Foundation of the Real Princes of Saud.

Chapter Three

WILL HE GET THROUGH THIS?

Thirteen hours after the bomb explosion

At the Dulles airport, a still shattered Irene met Mackenzie's shocked and grief-stricken parents, Steven and Mary. Their son - Mackenzie's brother- Ray Anderson had arranged for emergency leave and accompanied them. Irene escorted them to the chartered Gulfstream jet where James was waiting. Other than conveying their deepest and heartfelt condolences, there was not a lot either of the agents could say to the devastated family.

During the flight to Israel, James tried to share with the Anderson's as much information as he could about his relationship with Mackenzie, Carter, and Liam. There was so much more he wanted to tell them but was unable to, due to the secrecy of the Institute and the projects Mackenzie and Carter had been working on.

Steven, Mary, and Ray were quiet most of the time, reliving the last day they had seen Mackenzie and Liam. They'd lost track of time since they received the dreadful

The Wolves of Freydis

news. It was just two days ago when Steven and Mary accompanied their daughter and grandson to Boston's Logan International Airport. Both of them were so full of life and excited to see Carter again after six weeks. There was so much for them to look forward to; two days in Jerusalem, and then on to a luxury cruise ship sailing the Mediterranean for six weeks, and visiting ports in Turkey, Cyprus, Malta, Greece, Italy, France, and Spain.

Mary just smiled when she remembered Liam's final instructions to her about how to take care of his little four-legged friend, Jeha. Jeha was a Cavoodle, a cross between a King Charles Cavalier Spaniel and a miniature Poodle. The two of them were inseparable. Jeha even slept with him in his bed at night. She had been a birthday present from his grandparents.

"Jim I know this is unfair to ask you but," Mary stopped unable to continue for a moment. "Is it too unrealistic to hold out hope that Mackenzie and Liam could still be alive? I mean as far as we know their bodies haven't been recovered."

James found it difficult to look at her. He took her hands. "No, I don't think that's unrealistic. I promise you, as soon as we get there, I will get in touch with the authorities to get more information." He took a deep breath and continued. "The President has made arrangements for me to meet with some high-ranking officials in the Israeli government."

"Thank you, Jim," She whispered.

Steven was staring silently out the window, not seeing the view. He nodded slowly as he quietly resolved *until I have seen the bodies of my daughter and grandson they will remain alive for me.*

About four hours into the flight, the effects of the sedatives and the stress of the trauma during the past 24 hours took its toll on everyone, and they all fell into an exhausted and troubled sleep.

On arrival at Ben-Gurion International Airport in Tel Aviv, they were met by Joseph Carry, a staff member of the Consulate General of the United States in Jerusalem. He greeted them solemnly and drove them to their hotel where their rooms had already been booked. The hotel was close to the Shaare Zedek Medical Center in Jerusalem where Carter was hospitalized. They signed in and went to their rooms, took quick showers, and then met with Joseph, who accompanied them to the hospital to see Carter. They were scheduled to meet with a senior member of the Consulate General's office early the next morning where they would get a full briefing on what happened.

The hospital staff proved both kind and helpful. Steven, Mary, Ray, and James were all allowed to see Carter and were directed to his Unit. Although he was still in a coma, he was not in the critical care unit anymore. He had been moved to a private room earlier in the day where he was still under close observation.

The Nursing Unit Manager led them to Carter's room while giving them an update on his condition. He was making steady progress, and they expected him to come out of the coma within the next 10 to 15 hours. Although they tried to steel themselves for what they were about to see, they were again traumatized when they looked down on his pale form under the white sheet on the hospital bed. There seemed to be tubes and wires everywhere, and he was so still that the beeping monitors and barely noticeable breaths were the only signs of life. The mask on his bruised and lacerated face, the cast on his arm, and a leg in traction were just too much for all of them. They looked at him in horror; none of them had expected things to look as bad as they did. They all struggled to contain their emotions.

The Charge Sister told them that the doctor who operated on Carter was busy in surgery, but would come to see them as soon as he was finished.

They pulled up chairs and sat down, facing Carter's bed. What else could they do but watch and wait, and hope, and pray?

James was quiet and pensive. *How am I going to tell Carter?*

When James got to the hotel earlier, he contacted Director Patrick on the secure satellite phone to let him know they had arrived and to get the latest news. Hunter told him that the death and injury toll had been completed. It was established that several of the victims would never be found because their bodies instantly disintegrated in the explosion. Mackenzie and Liam's bodies were not among those that had been retrieved from the rubble. Therefore, the dread was that they were among those that had vanished with the impact of the explosion.

Carter won't even have his family to bury. There is nothing left. Jim grieved silently for his friend.

He decided to wait until he had official confirmation before telling the Andersons. For now, it would be better not to add to their sorrow.

A soft groaning sound escaped from Carter's lips. They jumped up and approached his bed. Could it have been their imagination? The monitors kept their regular rhythms; nothing appeared to have changed.

The Charge Sister told them it was clear he'd been blown backward and apparently his head had smashed against a wall, or door, or some other solid object. The impact cracked his skull and caused severe bruising of his brain as it hit the bone. The force of impact was not just to the back of the brain, but also to the front as it bounced forward. James still wondered if somehow Carter already knew Mackenzie and Liam were dead and wasn't prepared to come out of the coma to face it. He couldn't blame him if that were the case.

There were questions that had to be asked and answered, and James had no idea where to start. His thoughts raced, but he had no answers. The reality was, this was Israel, it was the Middle East, the breeding ground for the worlds' most vicious and barbaric terrorists, and most of them had only one aim – to destroy the state of Israel.

He'd gone over everything he and Carter had been working on. They were both aware it could prove dangerous, but there had been no indication of any threat.

The same was true for Mackenzie. Yes, she too could be in some danger, but again there had been no sign of danger.

While James and Ray slowly paced the room, Mary got up and washed Carter's face and hands with a cold cloth.

A strange but vaguely familiar smell registered in Carter's brain. *What is it? Where have I smelled this scent before? The hospital! Mackenzie was in the hospital. It was when Liam was born.*

He tried to open his eyes. *I've been dreaming.* His eyes were open. People were standing by talking quietly. There was something over his mouth and nose, his throat was dry, and no sound came out of his mouth when he tried to talk. He struggled to sit up, but couldn't.

I have to wake up. He moved his arm and blinding pain

shot through his head and body. He couldn't move. A wheezing sound escaping his lungs brought the four people in the room close to the side of his bed. They all looked shocked, pale, and shaky. *What's wrong?*

"Mary, Steven, Ray … Jim?" His voice was hoarse and muffled. His head was spinning, and confusion was distorting his thoughts. They couldn't hear him. He tried to look around the room, but couldn't move his head.

Mary pushed the call button for the nurse. Seconds later a doctor and two nurses arrived. Carter was struggling to sit up, to wake up out of his dream, but every time he tried, agony forced him back. His arms and legs wouldn't move. His right arm was held in a cast and his left leg anchored by traction. A neck brace prevented him from moving his head. Panic and claustrophobia were rapidly taking over as full consciousness drew near.

Mary saw the anguish in his eyes when he realized that he was awake, and this was real. He closed his eyes again.

"Professor Devereux! Can you hear me?" He didn't open his eyes. He didn't want to answer. The nurse had a hand on his shoulder. "Professor Devereux! Can you hear me?" If you can hear me, move your fingers, please."

The doctor took over. He opened Carter's eyelids, and shone a bright light into his eyes to check for pupil reaction; it hurt. "He's awake." He removed the oxygen mask.

Carter opened his eyes again and managed to turn his head slightly to the right to look at Mary, Steven, Ray and James. His lips formed words, and a faint whisper followed, "Where am I? What happened?"

"You're in the hospital Carter. You'll be alright." Mary said.

He frowned "Alright? What happened?" He whispered.

Mary's face was drawn with grief as she looked at him.

"There was a bomb, an explosion …" Her whole body started shaking; she buried her face in her hands and turned away.

Carter saw tears on Steven's cheeks, hollowness in Ray's eyes, and Jim looked ghastly as well. Then he remembered. He tried to see past them. "Mackie! Liam! Where are they? Oh God please!"

Steven stepped close to the bed and took Carter's hands in his; he looked deep into Carter's eyes and quietly shook his head.

Carter's whole body convulsed and his scream echoed through the hospital, "Nooooo!" The excruciating pain that exploded through his body and soul sent him back into a coma. He didn't feel the stab of the needle that entered his arm sending him back into blessed oblivion.

"We'll keep him sedated for a few days." The doctor said, "Right now his body is too fragile to handle the emotional stress of the loss. We need to give his body a chance to get stronger before he will be able to face and deal with the horror of it all."

"Will he get through this?" James asked. "Will he recover?"

The doctor took off his glasses and polished them. James decided it was what the doctor did whenever he was faced with a difficult question. "It's too early to say, Mr. Rhodes. "He will survive the injuries, yes. The scans showed internal bleeding, and that has been stopped. His arm and leg are fractured, but they will heal with time. He has a severe concussion, which will slowly reduce over time, and the hairline fracture at the back of his skull will also eventually heal. He is young and fit, and I'm confident his body will recover completely. What I can't give you is any prognosis for his psychological and emotional wellbeing. That might take years, and even then he could be left with invisible scars."

"Thank you, doctor," Steven murmured.

"Mr. and Mrs. Anderson," The doctor said as he walked around the bed to them, "you have my heartfelt sympathy for your daughter and grandson. I wish there were more I could do." He held on to their hands for a moment and then left the room. The two nurses remained at Carter's bedside adjusting and recording readings from the beeping equipment.

Mary, Steven, Ray, and James said nothing; they just nodded slowly while they stared at Carter's broken body.

Chapter Four

UNTIL I SEE THEIR DEAD BODIES

Three days after the bomb explosion

The next morning, shortly after breakfast, they were picked up by Joseph Carry and transported to the offices of the Consulate General of the United States where they would meet with Mathew Thompson, one of the senior staff members.

The U.S. Consulate in Jerusalem, an independent diplomatic mission, functioned similarly to an embassy in that it reported directly to the United States Department of State rather than an ambassador. The Jerusalem office was located in the Arnona neighborhood of Jerusalem and served Jerusalem, the West Bank, and the Gaza Strip.

On the way to the office, Steven, Mary, and Ray half-heartedly listened as Joseph gave them a brief history of the Consulate.

"It first opened in 1844. Back then it was in the Old City of Jerusalem, inside Jaffa Gate, but now that is the Swedish Christian Study Center," he informed them. "The office has moved several times over the years, but in 2010, it was finally established in the Arnona neighborhood of Jerusalem. During the First World War, this area was a 'no man's land,' an area neither of the warring sides wanted to enter for fear of causing a retaliating attack. It's also very close to the 'Green Line.'"

"Green Line?" Mary responded absently.

"Yeah. After the 1948 Arab-Israeli War, when they were drawing demarcation lines on the map during the talks for the Armistice agreements between Israel, Egypt, Jordan, Syria, and Lebanon, they used a pen with green ink."

"Mmmh," Mary responded.

On arrival at the consulate, they were immediately escorted to Thompson's office. He was a tall man, in his early sixties, with salt and pepper hair, wearing gold frame glasses. He met them at the door and extended his condolences, assuring them of the full cooperation and support of the consulate.

Thompson guided them to a corner of his large office and encouraged them to sit in the comfortable chairs. He offered them something to drink before he sat down with them.

Looking at them he asked; "I trust it will be in order if I start by giving you all the information we have gathered thus far?"

They all nodded their heads in agreement.

"If you have any questions, please feel free to ask them."

"Thank you," James responded on behalf of them all.

Thomson continued and gave them the details. The rescue teams had completed their searches of the site and had retrieved 25 bodies. The injured amounted to 60. Mackenzie and Liam were not among the dead or wounded.

Steven and Mary stared at each other and then at Thompson. "Is there any chance they weren't at the site when the bomb went off?" Steven inquired.

"It's impossible to rule that out at this stage Mr. Anderson. I am sorry; I wish I could be more precise. The investigation team is still busy. They are in the process of attempting to identify eyewitnesses and gather information from them. It will take days, maybe weeks before they complete their work.

Steven nodded. *Until I see their dead bodies, they are alive.*

Thompson looked uneasy when he cleared his throat to continue. "The next bit is hard to tell you." He hesitated for a moment and then continued. "A team of forensic experts is now fine-combing the site for DNA evidence." He paused to see if they understood the implications of what he just said.

"Why?" Mary asked. She was way past tears now and needed answers. Her daughter and grandson were dead, and she had to know why. She felt anger growing deep down inside her

"A few reasons Mrs. Anderson," Thompson replied. "They have to find out what type of explosives and triggering devices were used. That's information that could lead them to the perpetrators. The next reason is that the bodies of the victims closest to the explosion have disintegrated due to the severity of the blast. DNA tests are the only way to …"

He was unable to continue as Steven let out a deep groan, "Oh my God! No!"

"I'm so sorry …" Thompson whispered. He waited in silence for a minute before continuing, "What I need to ask you both is if you are willing to give us a DNA sample? It could help a lot and possibly eliminate them both from the primary explosion site."

James remained quiet. He had been listening carefully to Thompson and studying his body language to see if the man was hiding anything from them. When the meeting ended, James was sure that Thompson was hiding nothing.

Just before they stood to leave, Thompson told them that consulate staff had collected the Devereux family's belongings from the hotel where they stayed and placed in it all in safe storage in the consulate's vaults. "Would you like us to make arrangements for it to be shipped back to the States?"

The Anderson's thanked him for that but suggested it be kept at the consulate until Carter could make a decision.

James had already arranged, the night before, with Director Patrick to ensure that Carter's laptop and the contents of the hotel safe were separated from the rest of the belongings and delivered to him. He had to make sure that all classified information was removed and secured after which he would return it to the consulate.

Joseph drove them back to their hotel where he dropped the Andersons off. Later they would return to the hospital to be with Carter. James remained with Joseph, who would take him to a meeting he needed to attend in Tel Aviv.

James had two hours before his meeting in Tel Aviv and asked Joseph to take him to the site of the explosion. Although he knew that he wouldn't be allowed to set foot on the site itself, he might still be able to get an idea of the location and damage.

As expected, police had cordoned off the site, and it was

heavily guarded. A team of forensic experts was meticulously sifting through the rubble and collecting information. He was able to get right up to the secured perimeter, about 20 yards from the site where he was able to view it from different angles while moving along the barricades.

The Downtown Triangle, also known as 'The Triangle,' was the central commercial and entertainment district of Jerusalem. It was Jerusalem's most famous area and covered more than three hundred thousand square feet with an open-air pedestrian mall, many outdoor cafes, souvenir shops, and the Zion Square.

The explosion happened at a corner café on the ground floor of a four-story building.

The last bomb explosion was fifteen years ago in 2001. Before that, various terror groups had targeted the area on numerous occasions, due to its central location and the high number of visitors it received.

In 1948, three British Army trucks driven by British deserters, led by an armored car driven by Arab irregulars exploded on Ben Yehuda Street killing 58 Jewish civilians and injuring 140 others. Since then, many more had been killed and maimed in subsequent attacks in the Triangle.

However, since the last attack in 2001 when the Israeli government placed security measures in the area, it was believed to be one of the safest places in Jerusalem to visit – until three days ago.

James shook his head as he took pictures with his cell phone from different angles. The place resembled a mini version of the Twin Towers' ground zero after the 9/11 terrorist attacks in New York.

Seeing the devastation and trying to reconstruct the explosion in his mind as best he could, he concluded that the death and injury toll was surprisingly low. The only reason he could think of was that it was still early in the evening when the bomb exploded, and there were not many people around the restaurant at the time. He had no doubt in his mind that no one inside the establishment at the time of the explosion would have escaped alive. Where was Carter when the bomb went off? And where were Mackenzie and Liam?

Maybe his meeting in Tel Aviv would provide the answers.

Half an hour later, he returned to the car where Joseph was patiently waiting for him.

Chapter Five

A VERY UNUSUAL REQUEST

James watched the main entrance of the coffee shop. Seated with his back to the wall, he had a view of the entire place, and he studied everyone inside as well as everyone coming and going.

He was five minutes early for his meeting with the man from The Institute. 'The Institute' was the short and the literal English translation for the Hebrew word Mossad. The full Hebrew name HaMossad leModi'in uleTafkidim Meyuḥadim translated to mean 'The Israeli Institute for Intelligence and Special Operations' – the most feared secret service agency in the world. Along with Aman, military intelligence, and Shin Bet, internal security, Mossad was one of the three key units of the Israeli Intelligence Community. Mossad was tasked with intelligence collection, covert operations, and counterterrorism.

Ben Friedman, the man who had just walked through the door, was an old acquaintance from James' days as a CIA operative. He owed James a huge favor that James was about to call in.

Ben, five ten and a bit overweight, was in his mid-fifties - about the same age as James. He was dressed casually in jeans and a t-shirt, with a baseball cap on his bald head. There was nothing in his demeanor or clothing that would give away the fact that he was one of the Mossad's senior secret agents. In the past five years, he had been promoted out of the field to lead a team of field agents out of an office in Mossad's headquarters in Tel Aviv.

"Jim, my friend, it has been too long!" Ben smiled as he approached and extended his hand. After shaking hands with James, he took a step back and looked at his old friend who saved his life many years ago during a covert operation in South America. "Jim, I see the years have been kind to you. It must be that lovely wife of yours that you always told me about that is keeping you in such good shape."

"Yeah Ben," James laughed, "there is that, and I can see you haven't lost your touch for flattery; either that or your eyesight must have taken a turn for the worse." Laughing, Ben took a seat next to James; he also wanted to keep watch on everything. They ordered coffee and food and got all the niceties about family and health out of the way before they got to the main reason for their rendezvous.

"Jim, let me guess," Ben started. "This has something to do with the bomb explosion in Jerusalem the other day?"

James nodded.

"Our intel says there were four Americans involved, the Devereux family of three and a young single woman, Sally Johnson, who was backpacking through Israel. Which of those is the subject of your interest? Or is it someone else?"

"It's the Devereux family."

"Jim, are you here on a personal or official mission?"

"Official, but you know what it's like; you work closely

with people, and sometimes you become friends. In this case, it was both of them."

"Yes I know, and I understand. Are you saying Devereux and his wife were working for you?"

James nodded yes.

"I take it you will tell me when I need to know, what type of work they were involved in." Ben had a questioning frown on his face.

James nodded again.

"Okay. Let me tell you what I know." Ben took a sip of his coffee and continued. "As you probably know, the investigation is still in progress, and there is a lot we still don't know yet. What we can be sure of is that everyone who was inside that restaurant is dead, except for Professor Devereux. He only escaped death because he was in the restroom at the back of the building when the bomb went off. He was discovered there by the first response rescue team, and if it were not for their swift actions, he would have been dead as well."

James nodded. That answered one of his questions. "How did it happen?"

"We are still questioning eyewitnesses. So far, we've established that shortly before the explosion a fight broke out across the street from the restaurant. A crowd gathered quickly; security personnel rushed in to disperse the crowd and stop the fighting when a van drove into the restaurant, and the bomb exploded."

Ben's explanation answered another James' questions from earlier about why more people had not been killed. They were on the other side of the street and dispersing when the bomb was triggered. "Has your forensics team been able to identify the type of explosives used?"

Ben licked his lips and looked around almost nervously.

He dropped his head and whispered, "Jim, what I'm about to tell you is extremely sensitive, and until I tell you otherwise you cannot discuss it with anyone. I trust that you will honor this request?" He raised his eyebrows to get James' agreement.

"You have my word, Ben."

"They used a mini thermobaric bomb of Russian origin. We've known for some time that Russian Spetsnaz forces had these bombs in their arsenal, but it's the first time it's been used by terrorists as far as we know. As you can imagine, we are more than worried by this turn of events."

"Oh – my – God." James was shaking his head slowly.

The Russians had developed and tested a thermobaric bomb in September 2007. They called it the FOAB, which was an acronym for 'Father of All Bombs.' After the first tests, the deputy chief of the Russian general staff, Alexander Rukshin was quoted as saying; *'all that is alive merely evaporates.'*

The bomb was said to be the most powerful conventional, non-nuclear, weapon in the world - four times more powerful than the US military's GBU-43/B MOAB – 'Massive Ordnance Air Blast Bomb.'

The Russian thermobaric device yielded six to seven times more explosive power than TNT of the same weight and produced twice the blast radius of the USA's MOAB, which yielded only 50 percent more blast power than equivalent weight TNT.

A supersonic shockwave and extremely high temperatures inflicted most of the FOAB's damage.

"And now they have created a mini version, which has landed in the hands of terrorists?" Jim responded.

Ben nodded. "I guess you can understand our concern.

The problem is, these bombs are so small they are easy to hide and transport, and extremely difficult to detect."

A long silence followed while James considered the impact of what he just heard.

"Ben I appreciate your openness and the information you've shared with me. Do you know; do you have any idea who is behind this attack? Is there any reason to believe that the Devereux's were somehow connected to this?"

Ben was shaking his head. "We have no idea who did it, Jim. Our moles and agents have not been able to pick up anything. Our electronic surveillance hasn't picked up even one single lead so far. There isn't any chatter on the wires. This is not going to be easy to unravel."

James looked at Ben intently. "Ben, you haven't answered my other question. What about the Devereux's."

"I haven't answered because I don't have an answer for you. I first learned from you just a few minutes ago, that they were doing undercover work for the US government. As far as I know, no one in the Mossad even knows that much."

"Okay then; can we please keep this between the two of us until I tell you differently?"

Ben nodded his agreement. "What else can I help with, Jim?"

"Ben, I need to see every shred of evidence that your teams have collected; every report, all the tests with the results, statements, everything," James said.

Freidman frowned. "This is a very unusual request, my friend."

James noted the look on his friend's face, "Ben, this is of the utmost importance to both our countries. I can assure you that the Devereuxs were on a family holiday here in Israel. They were only going to spend two days in Jerusalem and then they were going on a six-week Mediterranean cruise. They were not spies. They were researchers; working on two very different, but significant projects. Carter's project has potential global security implications. Unfortunately, I can't tell you more at the moment, but I promise you, if you are willing to cooperate with me on this, I'll get the necessary authorization to tell you everything. In the meantime, please, will you just trust me?"

Ben looked at James. "Jim, we've come a long way. I trust you; I owe you my life, man. I will make sure that you get the information you asked for."

"Can you pull some strings to make sure that Carter Devereux is kept safe in that hospital and, if necessary, that he is moved to a safe place as soon as possible?"

"Absolutely. I will attend to that as soon as we are done here."

"Thanks for that. Finally, we need to establish as quickly as possible, whether Dr. Mackenzie Devereux and her son were killed in that explosion or not. I don't have to tell you how important it is in our line of work to verify facts."

"Leave it with me and I'll see what I can do to speed up the process. But, I have to remind you that the forensic analysis is a long and tedious process. And as you know from 9/11, forensic testing does not always reveal everything." Ben replied.

A stab of pain for his friend went through James' heart, and he nodded sadly, "Yes, I know."

James was all too familiar with the shortcomings of forensic testing in scenarios like these. High-powered thermobaric bomb explosions such as the one at the Triangle could literally vaporize human bodies and convert building material and human tissue into homogeneous dust that could render DNA and other forensic tests useless.

Of the estimated 2,780 people killed during the 9/11 destruction of the Twin Towers World Trade Center, more than 1,000 remained unidentified and missing to this day.

On his way back to Jerusalem, James reviewed the conversation with Ben Friedman in his mind. He was absolutely sure he could trust Ben and that his friend had not withheld any information from him. The fact that no one had claimed responsibility for the attack, and that the world's most efficient intelligence agency had no clue who was behind it, posed a problem.

As James was working through the information in his mind, he just couldn't shake the feeling that the attack was connected to the Devereuxs' work. That thought scared him immeasurably.

If Carter or Mackenzie's work was the motive for the attack, it meant A-*Echelon has been infiltrated!* His whole body filled with tension and dread as the thought resonated through his brain.

Chapter Six

ON YOUR SHOULDERS

Three days after the bomb explosion

She woke with a throbbing ache in her head and blinked her eyes against the bright light in the room. Her mouth was dry, and she was thirsty. *Where am I?* Her foggy mind questioned as she looked around. *What happened?* She turned her head to the left and nearly screamed when she saw a veiled face next to her bed. She could only see dark, unreadable, emotionless eyes.

"What …? Who are …?" She stuttered. She wanted to bring her hands to her face but she couldn't; they were tied to the bed, as were her legs. *Why am I tied to a bed?* She became aware of the drip stand next to her bed. Her eyes followed a tube leading from a bag of fluid hanging from the stand and ending in a cannula secured to her left arm with a piece of tape.

The figure was dressed in black from head to toe; a niqab covered the head and face revealing only two big dark brown eyes. The figure got up from the chair and moved to the bed.

"Dr. Devereux my name is Seema."

A woman Mackenzie thought. *And she speaks perfect English but with a thick accent.*

"I am here to take care of you and make sure that you are comfortable," The woman continued. "Would you like something to drink? You must be thirsty." She turned and busied herself at a table pouring water into a glass.

Mackenzie didn't answer – her memory returned like a flash of lightning. *Jerusalem. Restaurant. Liam. Carter.* "Where are my son and my husband?" She demanded with as much force as a dry, whispering, voice could produce.

"Don't worry about them, Dr. Devereux." Seema placed her hand on Mackenzie's arm. "They are both alive and well. You will see them soon."

Mackenzie let out a big sigh. *Thank God.* She paused and closed her eyes. "Where am I? Why am I here? What is this place?"

Seema lowered her eyes and replied quietly, "I am not permitted to talk to you about any of that. My orders are to take care of you, feed you, and make sure you are comfortable. The Director will see you later and explain everything to you."

"What Director? Where am I? Why am I tied to the bed?"

Seema ignored Mackenzie's questions and shook her head. "I already told you I will not discuss any of that with you. Don't waste your breath asking again." Her eyes were shooting darts as she spoke. "I'm going to give you water now and then I will feed you. After that, I will wash and dress you for your meeting with the director."

Somewhere in her befuddled mind, Mackenzie was

amazed that just a set of eyes in a hidden face could express so much anger.

Wash and dress me? I think not! Mackenzie pulled at the restraints on her arms and legs, but she couldn't get them free. She rested back on the pillow. There was nothing she could do. It was hard to think, to assign meaning to all of this. For now, she knew that her head hurt, she was thirsty and hungry, she was tied to a bed with a drip in her arm, and she didn't know why. Her only consolation was that Liam and Carter were okay.

She closed her eyes trying to return to the past. The last thing she remembered was being at a restaurant in the Downtown Triangle in Jerusalem with her husband, Carter, and their six-year-old son, Liam. Carter had gone to the restroom, and there was a noise and disturbance across the street. A fight had broken out, and she stood to watch, her arm around Liam, who was standing on his chair. And then there was nothing, no images, only a blank.

"Good morning sir," Seema greeted when Daiyan Nasser answered the phone in his office. "Dr. Devereux is awake; if you would like to see her, I will have her ready for you within the hour."

"Thank you. An hour from now will be good. Take her to the interview room and let me know when you're ready."

"Yes, sir, I will let you know."

Daiyan Nasser was the Director of the Institute of Scientific Research and Development – ISRD. It was a private organization, owned by a group of wealthy Saudi Arabians.

The ISRD was located about six miles south of Mecca,

in the mountains of Jabal Thawr (Mount Bull). It was very close to the famous cave, Ghar al-Thawr, the Cave of the Bull where Muhammad and his companion Abu Bakr, stayed hidden from the Quraish, their persecutors, during the migration to Medina in 622 CE.

It is said that with the help of Abu Bakr's family and slave, Muhammad and Abu Bakr took refuge in this cave. When the Quraish came seeking them, Abu Bakr was worried and told Muhammad, but Muhammad assured him that Allah was in the cave with them. When the Quraish reached the cave, it was clear to them no one was in the cave because there was a spider web spread across the mouth and birds nesting nearby.

The ISRD conducted two types of research, overt and covert.

Their overt operations were housed in a six-story building above ground where they performed various medical and technical research projects. These were related to the business operations of the institute's financial benefactors.

The covert operations were housed six levels underground, directly beneath the building of the overt operations. The building on the surface was the spider web that was hiding the subsurface facility. Except for two people, no one working above ground knew about the underground facilities. They had no clue about the activities going on beneath their feet. There was only one way into the underground facility from above. It was a small lift and staircase hidden behind a bookcase in the director's office. He was the only one who knew about it and used it.

Staff working on the secret projects entered the facility from a parking garage located about 300 yards away. From there they took an elevator down to an underground access tunnel that led to their workplace.

The handpicked and carefully vetted covert operations staff members were specialists in a variety of scientific disciplines from across the globe, and they were sworn to secrecy. Their research projects covered chemical warfare, human performance enhancement, medical research, nanotechnology, and nuclear physics.

Many of them did it for the money. They were paid exorbitant contract rates to work and keep their mouths shut. Some of them, as Mackenzie was about to find out, were unpaid, 'compulsory volunteers.'

Mackenzie had furiously protested when Seema approached her bringing the traditional attire of a Muslin woman for her to wear. "I am not a Muslim; I won't wear this clothing!" She shouted. But Seema ignored her.

"Dr. Devereux, please don't test our patience. You are now in a Muslim country, and you will wear what every woman wears." Seema stopped what she was doing fixed her dark, angry eyes on Mackenzie, "Let me give you some advice. The quicker you accept your situation and cooperate the quicker you will see your husband and son."

After fifteen minutes of arguing, Mackenzie realized the futility of her protests and decided that if she were to discover what was going on, she would have to cooperate.

Within a few minutes, Mackenzie was dressed in black from head to toe, with a niqab covering her head and face. The only part of her body that could be seen was her two emerald green eyes.

Before she knew it, she was seated at a big oval table in a large room; there was a dark tinted window behind her. She was handcuffed, and Seema sat beside her on the right.

They waited in silence for several minutes. Mackenzie was still seething and thought it best not to antagonize her captors further for the moment. The door opened, and Seema stood when a middle-aged Arab man walked into the room. Mackenzie remained seated. The man wore a business suit; his dark hair was neatly combed. His dark eyes and skin spoke of Arab ancestry. He smiled when he looked at Mackenzie.

"Dr. Devereux." The man started. "You will have many questions, no doubt, and I will be happy to answer as many as I can."

"You underestimate my thoughts; I can assure you." Although Mackenzie kept her voice low, it vibrated with anger, and fiery sparks flashed in her eyes. "What is this? Why am I here? I'm sure you know this is an outrage! I am a United States Citizen, handcuffed and held hostage."

The man smiled and held his hand up. "Dr. Devereux, I appreciate your restraint."

Mackenzie was angrier than she'd ever been in her life and this alone was making her very precise and correct in her use of language. "I'm glad that I please you. Now, I insist you remove these filthy things and that I be allowed to see my family. Immediately!"

"All in good time Doctor, I will answer all of your questions. My name is Daiyan Nasser, and I am the Director of this Institute …

"I don't give a damn who you are or what the Institute is; I want to know about my family," she kept her shaking hands in her lap out of sight. So far, she was keeping things pretty equal. "I demand to see my family and that you also remove these handcuffs. There is nothing you can make me do unless I am prepared to cooperate, and at present, I'm not prepared." She held her head high in defiance.

"You have to understand Doctor, that I hold the reins here. You do not. I can see that further explanation is needed. In the interest of clarification, I will show you something that will help you understand."

"Give it your best shot," Mackenzie intoned under her breath.

"What was that Dr. Devereux?"

Mackenzie cleared her throat and replied, "Nothing."

A tight smile twitched at the corners of his mouth, and he inclined his head to her, "of course."

He stood and pushed his chair aside, and then walked to the door where he whispered something to the guard. He turned around and spoke to Seema. "Stay here and keep an eye on her. I will be back shortly."

A few minutes later Nasser returned and said. "Turn her around so that she faces the window," He said indicating the window behind her.

"You should have taken my advice," Seema whispered as she turned Mackenzie's chair around. A light went on beyond the window to reveal a small room with a long narrow table in the middle. There was a door to the left, which opened and a tall masked man, dressed in black, stepped into the room. He was holding the hand of a small child with a black bag over its head; he led the child to the table. When they reached the table, he removed the bag.

"Liam!" Mackenzie jumped to her feet and started pounding on the window with her fists. "Liam, can you hear me?"

Seema grabbed her by the shoulders and pushed her back into the chair.

"It's a soundproof room and a one-way window. He can't see or hear you. So stop!" Nasser said.

He stepped next to the window and flipped a switch on the wall. "Proceed," he told the man in the room.

Mackenzie watched in sheer horror as the man effortlessly picked Liam up and placed him face down on the table where he tied the little boy's hands and feet with leather straps attached to the table.

Nasser stepped in front of her, leaned forward to look her in the eyes and continued, pointing toward Liam, "You hold the safety of this child in your hands. Do you understand?" He asked.

Mackenzie, cringing with terror she could not fathom, slumped into her chair, defeated and began to plummet into a bottomless pit of fear and panic.

Nasser stepped aside so she could see into the room again.

She watched as the man walked to the window, flipped a switch on his side of the wall, and said. "I am ready, sir." His words came over a speaker in the room where Mackenzie was. Then he walked back to the table - taking a cane about four feet in length and half an inch thick with him in his hand.

Mackenzie swiveled her seat around and looked at Nasser with hate-filled eyes. "You utter bastard!"

Nasser fixed a hard gaze on her and spoke again. "Here is what is going to happen. You will make no further demands. You will be quiet, and you will listen. I will ask you questions; you will answer. Every time you hesitate or fail to answer, your little boy is going to receive one lash with the cane in that man's hands. Have I made myself perfectly clear?"

Mackenzie nodded, her cuffed hands straining against the restraints. "Please don't hurt him; he is only an innocent little boy. Please?"

The Wolves of Freydis

"The only person who can hurt your child now, Dr. Devereux, is you. Answer my questions and he is safe. Hesitate or fail to answer and he is not. And by the way, my friend in the room does not differentiate between a man and a boy when it comes to the strength of his strikes."

"I will do whatever you say." Her whole body was trembling in fear for her child.

"Good. I wish it hadn't come to this, but you have given me no choice. You are not a citizen of the United States here, and that has to be made clear. I own you, and you will do what I wish. No one is going to find you. No one is going to magically appear and whisk you away. You are unreachable." Nasser walked around the table and stood to the left side of the window facing Mackenzie.

"I will repeat; my name is Daiyan Nasser I am the director of this Institute. You are now a guest at this institute. You have no need to know the name of the Institute, and you don't need to know which country you are in. We also have your husband in custody. You and your husband are now in our employment."

Mackenzie was staring at Liam's little body stretched out and tied to the table; she only caught a few words of what Nasser was saying. Nothing was registering in her brain.

Nasser saw that she was not paying attention. He walked to her and pivoted her chair away from the window. "I can see you are not listening to me. This is important. I suggest you pay close attention. Or do I need to tell that man to strike your boy to get your full attention?"

Torn and trembling with fury and fear, Mackenzie shook her head. "Please don't do that. I will listen carefully."

"Good. Let's continue." Nasser started again. "As I have

said before, you and your husband are now working for us. We have some vital projects that require your expertise. Our facilities and equipment are the best in the world, and we hope that you'll be able to make rapid progress. I'm sure that once you start working in our laboratories and see what has already been achieved, you will enjoy the work." Nasser paused when he saw the question on her face.

"I understand." She nodded. "What is it that I - we, I mean my husband and I - will be working on?"

"I'm a bit surprised that you haven't figured that out already," Nasser grinned. "You, of course, will be working on respirocytes, and your husband on ancient nuclear weapons."

Mackenzie's eyebrows shot up in surprise. *Who are these people? How do they know about the top-secret work Carter and I have been working on?*

"We have all of your research available here at the Institute, along with your husband's research as well. This is good, no? It means you won't have to start all over again." Nasser said, amused at her surprise.

When Mackenzie heard that, she came to the same conclusion that James had a few hours earlier. *A-Echelon had been compromised!*

"Do you have any questions?"

"Yes I have, and many more for later, but for now, my only question is when can I see my family?"

"Your husband is working in a different location, and you won't see him soon, or even very often. You will live here at the Institute where you will be taken care of. Your son will be moved to a different location where he will be taken care of. You will see your child only with my permission, and you must understand that my approval will be based on your performance, behavior, and progress."

Mackenzie nodded and rotated her chair back to the window. "Please, will you allow me to see him now, even if it's just for a few minutes? Please." She begged as the tears gathered in her eyes.

Nasser looked at her for a long time as he was contemplating what to do. Finally, he nodded slowly. "You have been cooperative. I will allow five minutes," he said as he walked to the intercom and told the man on the other side of the window to release the boy and bring him to the meeting room.

When Liam, accompanied by the man in black came into the room, he looked fearful and unsure of what to expect.

Mackenzie pulled her veil off and rushed to him. Sinking to the floor, she gathered him in behind the handcuffs to her heart. For moments, they clung together just feeling the assurance that they were both still alive and together.

Slowly Mackenzie moved away from him enough so he could look into her eyes and see the love and support he so desperately needed.

"Liam, my love, we've come to a time in our lives that is going to be very hard for us. We are going to have to be very brave and full of courage."

He nodded, "Where's daddy?"

"He's here, but we aren't allowed to see him yet; we will later, though. Can you trust me enough, Liam, to believe I will do everything I can to get us to see daddy and to return home? Whether you see me or not, can you know that I have you in my heart every minute of every day?"

He nodded "I know Mummy," he was silent a moment, "What about Jeha? Will she be alright while I'm gone?"

"Now Liam, you know your grandparents love that little

dog as much as you do. They will take very special care of her while they wait for you to return." *Dear God, Jeha is all they have left of us for now; I just hope it's enough to give them hope.*

He nodded and snuggled back to her shoulder and chest.

Mackenzie glanced up over his head at Nasser, who nodded and allowed them a bit more time. He was pleased with how both of them had behaved and how they'd calmed each other down. This was going to work.

Mackenzie held Liam close for another couple of minutes and then said, "You must go now, you have places to go and things to do while I stay here and work. Is that okay?"

"Yes, will you be alright?"

"I'll be just fine, I promise." She smiled, kissing him on both cheeks, and then let him loose from her handcuffed arms. It tore her heart out to watch him walk away with the man in black. For a few more moments she stayed on the floor, calming herself, wrestling with her fear and trying to take her own advice.

Nasser came over to her, helped her stand, and unlocked the handcuffs. "You handled that beautifully, I can see you are a devoted mother."

Inwardly, Mackenzie fumed at his words. She didn't care what he thought of her and had several choice words she would like to unleash on him, but knew that she had to hold her tongue for Liam's sake.

He led her back to the table where a cup of strong black coffee was waiting for her. She tentatively held it in her shaking hands.

"If you can continue in this vein and work with me, I think that before long I could arrange for Liam to live with you. But…" he held up his hands, "you understand this is entirely dependent on your behavior and work."

Mackenzie's relief for palpable, she nodded, thankful she hadn't lost her cool with the man. Despite everything, she had gained some of his respect, and this was going to be important in the coming weeks.

Chapter Seven

HOW DID IT HAPPEN?

It was late afternoon when Joseph dropped James off at the hotel where he and the Andersons were staying. James had two things to do – report to Director Patrick, and phone Ahote and Bly, who were still unaware of the tragedy.

Pulling out the secure satellite phone, he punched in his passcode when told to do so, and then listened to the electronic sounds as the call was directed to the A-Echelon exchange that would encrypt the call. Director Patrick answered almost immediately.

Their call lasted for about 10 minutes. During that time, James provided his Director with the latest information. He recounted the morning's meeting at the Consulate General's offices in detail but kept the particulars of the meeting with Ben Friedman to himself. Hunter had no new information from his side.

When the call with Hunter ended, James sat staring at the floor for a long time. He mulled over how he was going to break the news to Ahote and Bly. They loved Carter as if he was their son. Mackenzie was their favorite 'daughter in law' and Liam their favorite 'grandson'. Ahote taught Liam how to ride his pony, went on camping trips with him, and taught him everything about nature, fishing, and hunting. When the Devereux's were on Freydis Liam practically lived with Uncle Ahote and Auntie Bly.

As those thoughts went through his mind, James murmured softly, *"How am I going to give them this devastating news?"*

At one stage he wondered if it would be better to ask the minister of the church in Saguenay, the little town close to Freydis, to deliver the news to Ahote and Bly. In the end, he realized he was only trying to take the easy way out. He had to call them. His hands were shaking as he dialed their number.

Bly answered, and James asked her if she could call Ahote to the phone and then put it on speaker, as he would like to talk to both of them.

"Is this bad news, Jim?" Bly asked. The tension in her voice was obvious. "It's about Carter, isn't it?"

"Yes Bly, I'm afraid it's terrible news. Please, get Ahote on the phone and then I can tell both of you."

James could hear Bly calling Ahote. "Come quickly! Jim Rhodes is on the phone; something's up with Carter!"

"Jim, Ahote here. Something serious has happened hasn't it?"

James was taken aback and paused for a moment, "Yes. How did you know?"

"Just tell us; is he alive? Are Mackie and Liam okay?"

"Carter is alive but in the hospital. He's severely injured, but will live. We don't know about Mackenzie and Liam."

There was silence on their end. "What do you mean you don't know about Mackenzie and Liam?"

"There was an explosion in The Triangle, a large shopping mall and entertainment center in Jerusalem. Many people were killed and injured. Somehow Carter survived it, but there's no sign of Mackenzie and Liam."

"How can that be Jim?" Bly asked with a shaky voice.

James' heart hit the pit of his stomach as he answered, "They ... they might have been vaporized in the explosion."

Another long silence followed. James could just imagine the emotions flooding Bly and Ahote.

"Jim, how's Carter coping?" Ahote asked with deep concern in his voice.

"He's not Ahote; they are keeping him sedated at the moment so his body can do some healing until he's strong enough to face the worst of it."

"Which hospital is he in?"

James told them and answered a few other pertinent questions before he had one of his own. "Tell me; you already knew didn't you? How?"

"It was Mackie's wolves, Jim, they never come near the houses or the farm buildings when she and Carter aren't here, but two nights ago they turned up and wouldn't stop howling. We knew then something was badly wrong. We've been waiting ever since to hear what it was."

James felt guilty. They should have been told at the same time as the Andersons. They were the nearest Carter had to family since his grandfather died a couple of years ago.

"Jim, what can we do to help?" Ahote asked.

"Carter will probably be in the hospital for another month or more. Let's see when he gets out of the coma what would be the best course of action. The Andersons and I are with him at the moment. I will phone you every day from now on. You also have my number now so please, don't hesitate to call anytime you want."

"Thank you, Jim. I will make sure our passports are in

order so that we are ready to travel on short notice." Ahote said.

Jim's other phone began to ring; it was the duty nurse attending to Carter. He'd emerged from the coma, and he was asking to see Jim alone.

Jim passed this information on the Ahote and Bly and told them he'd keep them closely informed, and then he hung up.

He quickly washed his face and then left for the hospital.

Carter became aware of the hospital smell again and opened his eyes. In that fleeting split second, he remembered where he was, and why. He shut his eyes again trying to erase the memory, but it was impossible. An image of Mackenzie appeared in the darkness before him. Her beautiful face and green eyes smiled at him as she reached out to take his hand. Liam appeared next to her holding his arms out inviting Carter to pick him up.

"Mackie, Liam," he whispered as tears trickled from his eyes.

He opened his eyes again; the image remained. He moved his head to see if the vision was real, and pain shot through his neck forcing a groan of agony and vanquishing the image. They were gone, and he was left alone, staring at the white ceiling above him; more alone and empty than he had ever been.

Mackie and Liam are dead. I will never see them again. God, why have you done this to me? My parents, my brother, my sister, and now my wife and my son. Why? What have I done to you? His mind went blank, his vision glazed over, and he just stared into emptiness. There was nothing; no answer; only pain and silence.

The nurse standing beside his bed checking the monitors saw the tears running from Carter's eyes over his cheeks and onto the pillow. She placed her hand softly on his shoulder. "Professor Devereux, can you hear me?"

"Yes, I can," Carter whispered through dry lips.

She poured some water from a jug into a glass, placed a straw in it, and brought it to his lips without saying a word.

Carter took a few small sips and thanked her.

"You must be hungry. Can I get you something to eat?"

"No. I'm not hungry, thank you," He whispered. "Can I have more water please?"

She brought the straw to his lips again, and while he was sipping slowly she said, "Professor do you remember that your in-laws, Mr. and Mrs. Anderson, their son Ray, and your friend Mr. James were here before?"

Carter nodded slightly. He moved the straw out of his mouth with his tongue. "Yes, I remember. How long have I been here?"

"Three days."

Carter didn't respond. He just looked at her.

"They have asked that we contact them when you wake up; they're staying at a hotel very close. Is it okay if I let them know?"

"I would like to see Jim Rhodes first. We need to talk before I see the Andersons."

She gave him a brief smile as she left the room.

James arrived ten minutes later and was let in past the guards Ben had put in place at his request. He looked at

The Wolves of Freydis

Carter, who still had oxygen supplied by a tube near his nose, but the mask was off and to Rhode's relief his eyes were aware although shadowed with sadness.

"Come, Jim, sit down." He whispered.

James sat and just stared at Carter as if fearful he would vanish. The last hour had broken the reserves he'd held in place over the past few days as he tried to get everything sorted out and also look after the Andersons.

"What?" Carter asked.

"I don't think I can explain it, Carter. I feared I'd lose you too."

Carter looked at him for a long moment, "They're dead aren't they."

James nodded slowly. There was no way around it, "Yes my friend. I'm so sorry, but there is no other conclusion we can reach. There are no bodies, no sign of them at all. You were the only person who came out of that place alive. Several others are missing as well – all of them were in the restaurant at the time."

Carter stared at the roof and spoke very softly. "They could have been vaporized."

James nodded again. "Forensics is working on that now. We should know more in the next few days."

Carter let out a long sigh.

James hesitated, "What can you remember?"

"We'd taken a pavement table at the restaurant. Mackie went to the ladies' room while I stayed with Liam. She returned, we ordered our food, and then I went to the men's room. As I was about to open the door of the gents on my way out, I was hit and blasted backward."

He stopped and frowned, "I can't get past that point, Jim."

James' eyebrows rose, "I'm stunned you can recall so

much. So they were out on the pavement and would be, to your knowledge, there when you returned."

Carter shrugged. "Well… yes."

James was silent as he took this in and reorganized his thinking. "So how long were you gone? Three or four minutes, maybe?"

"Yes, it could've been that long, maybe a bit more. I don't know."

James didn't say anything; he didn't want to tell Carter what was going through his mind yet.

"Can you give me some water please?" Carter asked.

They fell silent for a little while, each lost in thoughts that were his alone. Then Carter asked, "Have you told Ahote and Bly?"

James winced, "Yes I did, just a few minutes before I came over here today. I'm sorry it took so long to let them know."

Carter waved his hand as if to say, "Don't worry about that."

"They are waiting for me to let them know how you are doing. They want to come over to be with you."

Carter took a few breaths. "Let's give it a day or two. Maybe I will be able to talk to them on the phone and then we can decide if they should come now or later."

"Okay, I'll let them know."

James stood up and placed his hand on Carter's shoulder and said, "Carter, Winston Churchill once said, '*If you're going through hell, keep going.*'"

Carter listened, nodded his head slightly, and whispered, "Thank you, Jim. I will try to remember that."

Carter watched as his friend left the room and the door closed quietly behind him.

After seeing James leave, the nurse entered to check up on Carter and see if he was hungry, "A little bit of soup maybe?" She enticed him.

He agreed soup might be nice with a bit of bread and butter. She left him to organize this, wanting him to have some space between visitors and also to get some sustenance.

An hour later, when she was satisfied he was well enough, she rang the Andersons.

The relief that showed on Steven, Mary, and Ray's faces as they entered the room gave Carter some idea of what they'd been through. Mary had flowers for him. She put them on the bed and came over and kissed him.

"Carter, we're so thankful that you are back with us dear."

He put his free arm around her and held her close, "Mary I'm so sorry, so terribly sorry. Oh my God, this is so horrific."

"Hey, Carter, my son," Steven stepped forward and held his shoulder, "This is not *your* fault. Don't blame yourself for it."

Ray took Carter's hand in his and said through a tight throat, "I love ya, bro."

Carter nodded, reduced to silence. What do you say to such wonderful people who'd raise the most wonderful woman in his life? "Thanks," He whispered, "how are you bearing up?"

Half an hour later he was showing signs of tiring, and they left him to sleep, promising to return in the morning. They knew how much rest he needed and understood their presence for too long at a time would only hinder his recovery.

Outside the doctor caught up with them and gave his assurances that Carter was doing well but did need time and peace to get past this stage of his recovery. He was satisfied with his progress so far, but he was not about to rush anything.

"In about a month's time Carter will be more mobile and you can begin to consider how to get him home.

Chapter Eight

TYING UP THE LOOSE ENDS

Youssef Bin-Bandar's instructions were clear; get the entire Devereux family, alive, and deliver them to the underground facility in the Jabal Thawr Mountains south of Mecca. But now Carter Devereux was dead, and Algosaibi was furious.

When they'd planned the Devereux's abduction in collaboration with Hassan Al-Suleiman's Special Forces it all seemed perfect. And in fact, everything worked out exactly as it was expected to, except for Carter Devereux's trip to the restroom.

Professor Carter Devereux was the primary target of the mission. He was the man who Algosaibi most wanted, the man who would lead Algosaibi to the ancient nuclear weapons that would give Algosaibi the power to destroy the House of Saud and unite Islam into one mighty force that would control the world.

Two days ago, when Youssef Bin-Bandar walked out of the meeting with Xavier Algosaibi, he had an intense feeling of doom. If he could make sure the loose ends of the Devereux mission were tied up, maybe he would win back the trust of Algosaibi. Although he doubted that would be enough to appease Algosaibi's rage, he was going to try.

He was given 48 hours to make it all happen, and he did exactly that. The two men who were working in the restaurant, reporting to the mission leader about the Devereux's movements were both dead. One was involved in a terrible single car accident, and the other unfortunate man hanged himself.

The three men who had followed and reported on the Devereuxs from the airport right up to the Triangle were also dead. They'd safely extracted the operations team back to their base in Syria. Everything that could lead investigators back to him and Algosaibi had been wiped out. No more loose ends, he had tied them up; in 48 hours.

Nevertheless, Bin-Bandar still had an uneasy feeling it was not going to be enough for Algosaibi. He feared the meeting he was scheduled to have with the man during early morning prayers the next day. But then Allah smiled upon him. He was looking at the classified report on his desk; it was the list of the missing and the survivors of the bomb explosion.

Carter Devereux was one of the survivors! How the man escaped that explosion was a mystery, but it didn't matter. He had escaped with injuries but was alive, and that was all that mattered to Bin-Bandar.

He went to work immediately, and within two hours he had verification from his agents in Israel. Carter Devereux was indeed alive and receiving treatment at the Shaare Zedek Medical Center, Jerusalem.

As long as Carter Devereux is alive I have a chance to escape death as well.

The meeting with Algosaibi went well, better in fact than Bin-Bandar would have expected. Algosaibi praised him for tying up the loose ends and was elated to hear the news that his most wanted archeologist was still alive. What he'd considered a major fiasco before, was now seen only as a setback. Bin-Bandar sat back and relaxed as he took a sip of his coffee. Preparation, information gathering, and planning for Carter Devereux's abduction had to start immediately. Bin-Bandar gave his friend the assurance that he would not fail him again; ever.

Algosaibi knew Carter was heavily guarded by the police and could not be abducted from the hospital, nor, most likely while he was still in Israel. He kept his thoughts to himself and didn't mention this to Bin-Bandar; in fact, he didn't pay much attention to Bin-Bandar's babbling at all. There were many other sources from which he could gain the required information; he had never relied on Bin-Bandar alone. He was, however, 100% sure that Bin-Bandar would never fail him again; never.

Carter was still alive, but not at his facility in the Jabal Thawr Mountains; this had become a major issue. Algosaibi knew that, given time, the opportunity for an abduction operation would present itself again. The problem was, at some point Carter could discover that his wife and child were not dead. The chances of him making that discovery on his own were remote, but with the former CIA man, James Rhodes, around it was a different ballgame altogether.

When Bin-Bandar walked out onto the street outside the mosque where his meeting with Algosaibi had been in a secret underground room, he looked up and let the sun shine warm on his face, as he thanked Allah. He stood there for a minute with his head raised to the sky, his bodyguards around him, and then he collapsed. He was dead before his body hit the ground. According to the coroner's report issued a few days later, he'd suffered a massive heart attack.

In Jerusalem, 850 miles away, at about the time Bin-Bandar's dead body hit the pavement outside the mosque in Riyadh, James was in his hotel room studying the first reports of the explosion.

Ben had called the night before, to arrange for the delivery of a flash drive. Shortly after James left Carter's bedside and was walking out the main doors of the hospital, a stranger bumped into him.

"Pardon me, sir," the man said, "I'm very sorry. Are you alright?"

"I'm fine," James replied. "No harm done."

They both continued their separate ways. As James entered the lobby of the hotel where he was staying, reached into his pocket for his room key and felt a small rectangular box in his pocket. He had received the flash drive containing the first information about the explosion.

James had a lot of compassion for Carter and Carter's in-laws; this was a tragedy of immeasurable proportions. He had lost friends and close family during his life but nothing as traumatic as this.

Trying to comprehend Carter's emotional suffering was beyond him. However, when he left Carter's room, it was with a conviction that his friend was capable of getting through this hell. He knew that Carter would have many nightmares in the months and years to come, but over time, he would be able to move away from them. He had learned a lot about Carter's psyche during his orientation course, and he knew the man was unbreakable and had the strength to conquer.

He looked at the list of dead again and then at the aerial photo of the site showing the exact location where each body had been found. According to the report, 24 of the 25 bodies were found inside the building or just a few yards away on the outside. Only one body was found on the road where the fight took place. Many people on that side of the street received minor wounds from the flying debris, but only one of them died.

James looked at the number of the lone body on the photo and pulled up the person's name and details from the files. He drew a sudden deep breath when he saw the cause of death – a single gunshot wound to the head. The ballistic report showed it was a subsonic .45 hollow point bullet, fired at very close range, probably with a silenced gun, which blew half of the man's head away. The dead man had been identified as one of those involved in the fight. According to one of the witness statements, he was the one who started the fight.

Assassinated. This street fight was part of the plan. It was to cause a distraction, and the terrorists were leaving no loose ends. The first rule of assassination is; kill the assassins. These killers were professionals.

James looked at the numbers again; 25 dead, 16 bodies had been identified, and nine remained missing. The forensics team had collected almost 3,000 pieces of human tissue and was busy matching that to the DNA samples they had. So far no matches for Mackenzie and Liam had been identified.

Of the 60 people who were wounded, 50 had already been questioned. The others were in conditions that still needed to stabilize before they could be questioned.

Reading through the statements James slowly got a better picture of what had transpired. Many eyewitness reports confirmed that an old gray van with dark windows was seen driving up the road at high speed just before it suddenly swerved to the left crashing into the restaurant. The explosion followed one to two seconds later. A few witnesses recalled seeing a few vehicles drive past the restaurant before the gray van arrived. One witness said she saw a white van coming up the street towards the restaurant just as the fight broke out. After that, the fight and the people gathering distracted her, and she didn't see where the white van had gone.

James poured his second cup of coffee while he was going over the information in his head again.

Ben had reassured him the night before, that there were no Israeli intelligence assets in the restaurant that evening, no politicians, and no other targets of potential value to terrorists. Ben admitted they were still scratching their heads as none of the more than 50 terrorist groups in the Middle East had claimed responsibility for the attack. Usually, terrorist groups were quick to trumpet their barbaric victories, especially when they were able to penetrate an area as secure as the Triangle and cause as much death, destruction and commercial damage as this explosion did.

James took a sip of his coffee and strolled over to the window overlooking the street in front of the hotel. He immediately took a step back and to the left, hiding in the shadow behind the curtains when he noticed a dark blue Toyota Camry with two men sitting in the front. *That car was parked there last night.* He had noticed it but hadn't paid much attention to it at the time, but now he was on alert.

He watched them carefully and soon he had confirmation. When the man in the passenger seat scanned the hotel with small binoculars, he knew they were on a stakeout, no doubt about that. But who was their target? This was a big hotel. Their target could be any one of the more than 200 guests.

He stood for a few minutes watching them. Then he walked over, turned out the bedside light he'd been using and retrieved a small flashlight from his travel bag. He unzipped one of the side pockets and withdrew a small but powerful high-resolution camera with a hyper-zoom lens. Then he carefully returned to the window but remained hidden.

Zooming in on the car and its occupants he spotted both men's earpieces. Were the earpieces for them to listen to sounds from hidden microphones in someone's room or were they to communicate with someone else?

Since the day he arrived, he had been using the scanning feature built into his satellite phone to scan his hotel room for hidden microphones every time he returned. He was fairly certain his room was secure. But he had been in the covert business far too long to know not to make any assumptions, and that words such as 'coincidence,' 'maybe,' and 'probably' didn't exist in the vocabulary of a field agent who wanted to stay alive.

He studied and photographed the car and the two men very carefully. Later he'd ask Ben to have a look at the photos and try to ID the men.

Chapter Nine

FIRST DAY ON THE NEW JOB

Mackenzie's day started early when Seema unchained her from her bed. After yesterday's meeting, Nasser had given instructions that Mackenzie be kept in the clinic room and chained to the bed for one more night to reinforce his message to her. He wanted her to understand that he was in charge, and she was going to do exactly as he ordered.

Mackenzie didn't get much sleep. She lost all sense of time and had no idea if it was morning or night. Once the full reality of the hopelessness of her situation became apparent, she wasn't even sure what day it was. She spent most of the night, or what she thought must have been night, thinking about Liam, Carter, and her situation. She finally drifted into a troubled sleep, and when she opened her eyes, Seema was sitting next to the bed. The woman had become her ever-present shadow.

She had been assessing her situation and found it discouraging. She knew escape was not an option; there was no escape without Liam.

She knew Seema was there watching her and now

understood that her highest priority was to cooperate in hopes that Liam would be allowed to stay with her. Once that was accomplished, then there would time to think about her situation again. Another decision she made was that she was not going to lie to Liam. She was going to tell him that they were being held captive.

Seema led her to the quarters where she was told she would be staying while working at the Institute. It was barely more than a cell with a bed, a cupboard holding three sets of black jilbabs – long, black garments to hide the shape of her body, as well as two niqabs, a small table, and a chair. There was a door leading to a shower and toilet.

Seema told her the jilbabs and niqabs had to be worn at all times when she was outside her room. There were a few basic toiletries provided: soap, shampoo, and towels. The door leading into the room was made of steel and had a lock on the outside. *A prison cell*, Mackenzie thought, *not even a window with bars through which I can look outside.*

Once Seema had shown her everything, she turned to Mackenzie and said, "Dr. Devereux, I know you are upset and troubled by the events of the past few days. And I know you might not believe me, but I would like to help you make your stay as tolerable as possible for you. We have a few other people here at the Institute in the same position as you. In other words, they also are not here of their own free will. Over the past few years, I have seen many of them. The ones who are still alive are those who accepted their situation and cooperated. The choice is yours; you can make it hell, or you can make it bearable. I trust that for the sake of your son you will choose the latter."

Mackenzie was listening very carefully and nodded but didn't say a word. *Psychology: Lesson one: to get captives to cooperate, break their spirit.*

When Seema left, and Mackenzie heard the lock clicking from the outside, she slowly sat down on the bed. *How long is this nightmare going to last?*

She leaned back against the wall for a while and studied the grim little room. Two surveillance cameras and a few microphones were clearly visible. *No attempt to hide them; obviously they want to let me know I'm being watched.* She got up and inspected the bathroom and toilet. They too had surveillance cameras and microphones. It was humiliating to the nth degree. She would have to cover the cameras up when she wanted to take a shower or use the toilet.

She sat down on the bed again and made a promise to herself, her son, and her husband. *Mackenzie Devereux's spirit will not be broken. I'm going to keep my mind and body healthy and sound. When the time comes, I will be ready.* Her thoughts turned to her son and her husband, her parents, Jeha, Liam's little dog and his pony. *Freydis.* She also thought of her wolves, Keeva and Loki loping free through the forest they called home. That is when she realized that although her body was incarcerated in this unknown place and country, her spirit would always be free and that she would be able to visit Freydis with her family, Ahote and Bly, and her wolves whenever she wanted.

After what felt to her like hours, she heard the lock on the door click again, and Seema appeared carrying a tray with food and a cup of coffee. These she placed on the table and told Mackenzie to eat. After that, she would show Mackenzie the workplace and let her meet her new colleagues. She didn't feel hungry. In fact, she had been feeling a bit nauseous since she woke up, but it was important to get food into her body to keep her going and her mind working properly.

As she and Seema were walking down the brightly light

hallways, Mackenzie tried to get an idea of the size of the place and the activities going on. But that was limited to what she could see while passing closed doors with small windows. She had glimpses of people in small offices and some in laboratories but she was not allowed to stop to see more. Seema refused to answer any questions. By the time they reached a big steel sliding door, she was sure she was underground. Nowhere had there been a glimpse of the outside world, and the place was huge.

Seema swiped the security badge, hanging around her neck through the slot on the wall, walked up to the steel door and peeped into a retina scanner for a few seconds. The door slid away revealing a large room about the size of a basketball court.

A glass wall separated the back half where people in masks and white coats worked in a laboratory. Two of these workers were women; they wore white lab coats over their black jilbabs. In the front half, Mackenzie could see people at desks working with computers. She noted that there was only one woman among them.

Daiyan Nasser smiled as he stepped forward when she and Seema entered. "Good morning Dr. Devereux. Welcome to your new workplace."

Mackenzie had to bite her lip for a second before she responded; luckily the niqab hid the odium on her face. She would have preferred to tell the man what she thought of him and his 'new workplace.' *Labor camp* was one of the words that came to mind, and another had to do with the part of his anatomy where she would like to have him shove this job. But she managed to respond with a polite sounding "good morning."

Nasser nodded slightly. "Please, follow me so that I can

introduce you to your new colleagues and then we will discuss your project."

Over the next 15 minutes, she was introduced to everyone but when it was over she could only remember three names. Those of the three scientists with whom she would be working closely on the respirocyte project. They were: Andon, a Bulgarian a professor of medical nanotechnology; Rameez, a Pakistani medical doctor, and professor of human respiratory sciences; and Duyi, a Chinese professor of microbiology.

Nasser led her and Seema to a small glass-walled breakout area in the corner of the room where he switched on a wall mounted screen. He asked them to sit down at the table while he started the laptop and brought a PowerPoint presentation up on the monitor.

This gave her a high-level overview of the respirocyte project that the current team had achieved, and what their objectives were. The arrogant smirk on his face made it obvious to Mackenzie that he was taking great delight in opening a folder that contained all her research work. It even included the last presentation she gave to Irene O'Connell, Director Hunter Patrick of A-Echelon, and the two DARPA scientists Drs. Cate Nelson and Scott Watson.

It was the second time in about half an hour that Mackenzie was actually glad she was forced to wear a niqab behind which she could hide her facial expressions. It was the treachery by someone in the midst of A-Echelon that was causing her absolute shock and horror. She noticed that Nasser was studying her carefully as he opened the files and she made sure that he would be none the wiser about her emotions. She kept her hands hidden in the black folds of the hijab and gazed, immobile and emotionless, up at the screen

"Dr. Devereux, I want you to have a good look at these files. I have already loaded them onto your computer here in the lab. If there is something amiss, we can retrieve it from the A-Echelon servers," Nasser advised her.

Mackenzie nodded. "I will have a look and let you know," she said calmly. She was struggling with another jolt of disgust to hear that not only did he know the name of the top secret organization, but it also sounded as if he had complete freedom to roam through their 'impenetrable' servers to copy data from there as if he was doing it on his own computer.

So much for securing my research.

Nasser was also very proud to let her know that he was able to get access to research from almost anywhere in the world. If she were aware of research that could help with this project she just had to say so and he would get it.

It left Mackenzie with no doubt that the Institute had their fingers deep into the filth of industrial espionage.

The next part of Mackenzie's induction was a round table meeting and discussion with the Andon, Rameez, and Duyi. When they entered the room, it was the third time she was glad to be wearing the niqab because it hid the smile playing on her lips when the thought; *the three stooges* entered her mind. And she was soon to discover that the name was befitting.

The three of them took turns to tell her about their backgrounds and expertise and then showed her what they'd been working on. It included a trip to the lab where they showed her some of the animal experiments.

The demonstrations and explanations while they walked past cages with animals kept in a room adjacent to the lab almost reduced Mackenzie to tears. It took a lot of willpower not to start screaming at them and ripping the cages open to set the helpless and bewildered animals free; only the thought of Liam prevented such an outburst from her.

Four hours after she walked into the room Nasser called a halt and told them all to break for lunch. The lunchroom was on the other side of the steel doors through which Seema had to escort her. During lunch, the female coworkers all sat at the same table. No one was willing to talk about anything other than his or her work.

The afternoon session of Mackenzie's induction started with a video of a marathon. It was sickening. The three stooges were so excited to show and tell Mackenzie how close they came with this human experiment they didn't even notice that she had her eyes closed most of the time.

It was already difficult, to the point of revulsion, to see the animals suffering from their callous experiments. To see another human being suffering from it was driving her to the brim of an eruption.

She watched as the athlete coughed up a frothy pink blob of phlegm and fell to his knees before he started vomiting a pool of bright-red blood. The man's face was distorted with pain.

She whispered, "He's drowning."

Andon stopped the video and looked at her. "What was that?"

"I said," Mackenzie fought to keep the outrage and anger out of her voice, "the man is drowning."

"Why do you say that?" He asked. The Stooges were looking at her skeptically.

Mackenzie spoke slowly and measuredly, controlling fury as best she could. "The pressure in the vessels in his lungs has augmented to the point where the fluid has begun to leak back into the air bags inside his lungs."

From the dumbfounded expressions on their faces, she felt as if she was lecturing a bunch of sophomore students and she had to check herself not to turn sarcastic in her tone. "He is suffering from pulmonary edema. Those little sacks where the oxygen transfer is supposed to happen have been flooded with fluid. His lungs are unable to provide oxygen to his blood, which is causing hypoxia - oxygen deprivation. He will be dead in minutes."

The three men looked astounded and turned to look at each other, and then slowly back to Mackenzie. "I guess I don't have to see the rest of the video to know I am right? Is that it? He died a few minutes later?"

Andon and Rameez failed to meet her gaze; Duyi was the first to acknowledge when he nodded without saying a word.

Nasser had a depreciative frown on his face when he turned his glare to the three men. "It looks like we will have to go back to the drawing board," he growled. He waved for the men to leave and then turned to Mackenzie.

"Dr. Devereux do you know how to fix this problem?" He held his hand up to stop her from responding immediately. "I want you to think very carefully before you answer me."

Mackenzie could see Nasser was a worried man. It didn't take much for her to add two and two together. She had been paying close attention to what she heard from the Stooges and Nasser since that morning. They had overspent their resources on this project, and it was a dismal failure. They were fooling around with something they didn't have the expertise for, and it was obvious that she had more knowledge of the subject than the three stooges combined. She would use that to her advantage.

"I would be lying if I told you I can fix this. Respirocytes and the improvement of human red blood cells have been my field of study for many years. I can assure you that I am not aware of anyone who is even close to the point of human trials."

Nasser nodded slowly. Up till this morning, he had been so sure that it would take just a little bit more work to produce the desired result. They'd spent more than 50-million dollars on this project over the past two years, and so far they had produced a mountain of dead animals and killed nearly 50 people, possibly more. This had to be reported to his superiors; he tried to subdue the chill that was running down his spine. The directors of this institute didn't take kindly to failures.

Mackenzie was watching him carefully and for the first time in 24 hours she felt a glimmer of hope igniting somewhere inside her as she detected the signs of anxiety on his face.

"If this was your project to run, where would you start?" Nasser asked and again he held up his hand. "And if I also say that I will make immediate arrangements for you to move to larger quarters and allow your son to be with you?"

Mackenzie kept her poise, although her smile behind the niqab must have filtered through to her eyes. "I will immediately stop all animal and human trials. It must be obvious that we are not ready for that yet."

She was selecting her words with great care, making sure he could hear her using the word 'we,' indicating that she accepted she was part of a team, and she was enthusiastic, but not overly so. "I will sit down with Andon, Rameez, and Duyi and create a new approach and plan. As you already know from my research, which you have here, I have discovered how in ancient times oxygen-filled microparticles covered with a layer of fatty molecules were used as a transport medium to carry oxygen to the blood. Each molecule encapsulated a tiny pocket of oxygen. The microparticles were injected into patients in a liquid solution."

Nasser stared at Mackenzie and slowly nodded. He didn't like it that the day before he held all the trump cards in his hands, and now the roles had reversed. The only card he had now was her son and the lie about her husband. For now, those were two good cards. But it didn't negate the fact that all of the sudden this woman was holding his future in her hands. No, he didn't like this at all.

"Good. The job is yours. I will let the others know that you are the project leader. You will sit down with them and start planning. I want to see the first draft on my desk within four days. Is there anything you will need?"

"The first thing I will need is a translation of the Sirralnnudam; it's a book of ancient medicine, specifically …"

Nasser held his hand up and stopped her midsentence. Mackenzie saw the look of defeat in his eyes. "I know. It's a book in proto-Arabic, 'Scroll of Secrets of blood' and was kept at the Mesrop Mashtots Institute of Ancient Manuscripts in Yerevan, the capital of Armenia." He was shaking his head by the time he finished talking. "It was recently lost, shortly after you left Armenia, in fact." He was rubbing his nose when he said that last part and Mackenzie knew he was lying.

Mackenzie took a deep breath when she realized that she was being watched while she was in Armenia. *How long had that been going on?* She shrugged; there was nothing she could do about it now. *Why is he lying? What did he have to do with the book's disappearance?* Then she smiled as she remembered, *I will not tell you what I have. That might just become my son's and my ticket out of this place at some stage.*

She acted surprised. "Oh no! How did that happen? That book is crucial for our project." The niqab was turning out to be a real blessing in disguise.

Nasser didn't look at her. "Yes, I believe it was going to be a precious resource."

Mackenzie threw him another lifeline. "Well, I guess we have enough to make a start. At least, we know where to start; it might just take a bit longer than it would have if we had the Sirralnnudam. There might also be other resources available. I trust you will be able to locate them for us when we need them?"

"Yes of course. The directors of the Institute have wide influence across the globe. You just have to let me know what you need."

"Thank you; that could be very helpful," She replied with a hidden grin of satisfaction. She took some pleasure out of seeing him experience the shoe on the other foot.

"Is there anything else you need?"

"No not for now. Thank you for allowing my son to be with me." She just wanted to make sure he didn't forget his promise. "But if I may, I would like to ask for two favors, please?"

He raised his eyebrows.

"Can I please have my watch back, and could you please arrange for the removal of the surveillance cameras in my bathroom? Please."

Nasser smiled as he tapped his fingers on the table for a few moments. He smiled, "Yes of course. No problem, Seema will take care of everything."

He stood and started walking to the door and then stopped short. "Dr. Devereux, I am very happy with your change in attitude and your willingness to cooperate with us. You will be well rewarded."

Chapter Ten

MOVING HIM OUT

James sent Ben Friedman the photos he took of the suspicious looking car and its occupants outside his hotel. Later the same day, he got a call from Freidman on his secure phone.

"Jim, my friend, I see you haven't lost your touch yet. Good catch." Ben laughed. "I will be over in the next hour or so. I have more information for you."

About two hours later Ben turned up at James' hotel and knocked on his door. As always Freidman was dressed casually and looked like a tourist with his small backpack.

James started the coffee machine in the room and prepared two mugs of coffee. Freidman took a little scanning device out of his backpack and walked around the room checking for any microphones while he made small talk. He nodded and gave James a 'thumbs-up;' the room was clean. Only one thing remained. He took a box about the size of a pack of cigarettes from his backpack, flipped on a switch, and then placed it on the windowsill. It was an electromagnetic pulse generator, which would neutralize any directional parabolic microphones aimed at the window.

"Jim, let's first talk about your two friends outside." Ben started. "They are Saudi's. My agents have planted a GPS tracker on their car and have been trying to drop in on their conversations with a directional parabolic microphone, but it seems they have the equipment to counter that. They are not on our list of bad guys, so we don't have enough reason to move on them yet."

James grinned. "What do you say we walk out there and have a chat with them? He knew what Ben was going to say.

Ben started to speak, but Jim held his hand up. "Don't worry Ben I won't do it." He laughed. "I know it's better to follow and monitor them – we will learn a lot more that way. But believe me, at this stage it wouldn't take much to persuade me to go over there, pull their asses out of that car and have a nice quiet word with them in private."

"Okay good, I was getting a bit worried there for a moment," Ben grinned as he remembered the destruction and pain James could cause when he lost his temper. All he could hope for was that James had learned to control his temper a bit better with age.

James nodded. "Okay. In that case, I'm not taking any chances. I'm going to make arrangements to move Devereux out of here and back home immediately. And let me tell you; if I find anyone of those clowns near Devereux when he is back in the States they are going to be the sorriest Saudi's in the universe."

"Agreed," Ben said. "In the meantime," he paused and reached into his bag again and pulled out a 9 millimeter SIG Sauer P938, and three six round magazines, "you can carry this."

James thanked him. He didn't need any instructions –

the P938 had been one of his hand weapons of choice for many years. It was a compact but lethal weapon, and due to its size, easy to conceal on the body.

"I've arranged for a few of my people to keep a close watch on those two jokers out there and to make sure you and the Andersons are safe."

"Thanks, Ben. You have gone above and beyond. I owe you big time." James smiled.

Ben waved his hand. "It's the least I can do for the man who saved my life."

"Ben, I've been in this business long enough to know I shouldn't ignore my intuitions." James had a slight frown between his eyes. "I know we don't have much, or in fact anything, that can corroborate what I am suspecting but I just can't shake the feeling that this has something to do with the work my friends were doing. And those guys out there in the car have not helped to make the feeling go away."

Ben thought for a moment, "Jim I have always believed that instinct is the result of a partnership between my emotions and my brain. It is a reality, and it's not to be ignored." He hesitated for a moment more to look at James. "Let's go over the latest reports I brought with me; maybe we'll find something there."

James nodded. "If you have more information let's see it."

James and Ben studied the latest reports. The numbers were still the same, 25 dead. However, 20 bodies had now been identified, and five remained missing or unidentifiable. The forensics report stated that they had matched all the collected human tissue to samples they had. There were no matches for Mackenzie and Liam. Their conclusion was that the remaining five people were either not onsite at the time of the explosion or had been vaporized.

James sat back after reading the report. "This doesn't take us much further. All we know now is that Mackenzie and Liam were either vaporized or were not on site. It's just a forensic confirmation of what we already knew," he said with frustration in his voice. Ben nodded his agreement. "Easy, Jim." It needed no further discussion, the only way to establish whether they were onsite or not would be an eyewitness report. "Let's keep looking."

They continued looking at the new reports. There were now 61 reports, but none of them contained the information they were looking for. A few more people who were wounded and could give statements were still in the hospital and medically unfit to be questioned.

"Thanks again for the help, Ben, it is really highly appreciated." James stood. "I need to get over to the hospital and talk to the doctor, to see if we can transport Carter back home."

Ben got up, but James waved him down. "Before I do that, however, I'm going to tell you what the Devereux's were working on." James had made up his mind; he was not going to ask anyone at A-Echelon for permission. Ben Friedman was one of only a very few people he truly trusted.

For the next hour, James gave him every bit of information about A-Echelon and the Devereux's projects. At some points, Ben went totally slack-jawed and stopped him to ask questions.

When James stopped talking, Ben was on his feet, pacing around the room. "Shit Jim, and I thought we had a problem with thermobaric bombs. Now you're telling me we are looking at nuclear obliteration."

"Yes my friend, and, unfortunately, there seems to be more than a distinct possibility that those damn ancient nukes are real, not just internet conspiracy theories. The problem is we don't know who else is out there looking for them."

"This is giving an entirely new meaning to the term 'nuclear arms race.'" Ben muttered.

"Now Ben, here's the rap." James' face looked as if he was in pain. "You cannot talk to anyone in Mossad about this."

"Shit man! You've got to be kidding!" Ben exploded. "You can't be serious; you can't expect me not to talk to my bosses. This is a cluster-fuck. We'll have to put people on this right away. We have to find those fuckin nukes and quick."

James held his hand up for Ben to stop and listen. "Ben, the predicament we have is that A-Echelon has a mole problem."

"What? ... Oh shit on top of all this we have to deal with a fuckin mole?"

James smiled inwardly despite the situation. It amused him how quickly his easy going, fun-loving, polite friend could become such an efficient user of profane language when the occasion called for it.

"Yes, unfortunately, that seems to be the case. I have no idea how deep or how far it goes, or how many are involved. You, my friend, are the only person I trust at the moment."

"You sound a bit unsure. Do you indeed know you have a mole problem or do you just think you have one?"

"At the moment its suspicion only, but if this bomb explosion is connected to the Devereuxs, then it is definitely the case."

Ben plucked his baseball cap off and started scratching his head. After a while he looked at James and grinned. "Okay. I will let MI6 know to pull James Bond off the streets and get out of our way – Ben and James are about to get to work."

James smiled. Ben always had the weirdest things to say in the direst of circumstances. That was his stress coping mechanism, and most of the time it helped to break the tension for everyone – like now.

"You phone that doctor and find out when you can see him regarding getting your Professor Indiana Jones back home. Getting him back to the States will take at least one worry off our minds."

James grinned, picked up his phone, and called the hospital. He felt very lucky when he reached the doctor's secretary, and she told him the doctor would be able to meet with him within the hour.

Ben called his men outside and told them that he and James were on their way to the hospital. Ben waited in the hospital lobby while James spoke to the doctor who was uneasy with the idea of moving Carter so soon. James could not tell him the reason, but in the end, he was persuasive enough, and the doctor agreed. However, the agreement came with a long list of provisos.

All that remained was for James to make the necessary arrangements with Director Patrick, which was not too difficult once he explained that Carter needed better treatment that he could only get if he was back home. Also, being home where family and friends could visit him easily would help speed his emotional and physical recovery. James didn't give Hunter the real reason for the necessity to move Carter.

With Hunter's approval in hand, he went to Carter and

told him about the plan to move him. He didn't tell Carter the real reason either.

Carter, although still hazy most of the time from the cocktail of drugs dripping into his system, knew James was not being entirely honest with him. James' explanation about security concerns for all of the survivors did not convince him. He suspected something more than that was afoot.

His first reaction was to resist the idea. Leaving Jerusalem alone felt as if he was abandoning Mackenzie and Liam. He was still blaming himself for going to the restroom; it didn't make sense, but he could not get past the thought that he was not there for them when they needed him. After a few minutes of arguing and thought, reality got the upper hand, and he agreed.

James also convinced him that it was important not to discuss it with anyone including his in-laws. That request had him on high alert again, but he decided not to ask for an explanation yet. He trusted James would explain things to him later.

James and Ben went to work immediately, to plan how Carter and the Andersons could be moved to the airport and kept safe at the same time. Hunter had agreed to the use of a private charter again to transport everyone back home. Part of the doctor's orders included that a nurse was to accompany them and that Carter was to be sedated for the duration of the trip.

James and Ben made the necessary arrangements for secure communications between them before they said their goodbyes. Eighteen hours later the group was safely in the air en route to Boston where Carter's room at Massachusetts General Hospital – one of the best hospitals in the USA, was ready for him.

At Massachusetts General Hospital James made arrangements for Carter to be guarded again. This time, there was a lot of explaining to do. Carter was extremely suspicious when he realized that his room was under guard. James explained that it was precaution more than anything else because they still didn't know who was responsible for the attack and so all survivors were being watched.

Carter just listened to James and when he finished the explanation Carter looked at him and said, "Bull. That explanation has more shit in it than a stockyard, Jim. As soon as I've recovered from the trip here, you will have to come back here and tell me the truth."

James raised his eyebrows and grinned, thinking; *I knew I wouldn't be able to keep it away from you.* He stayed over in Boston for a few days until he was sure his friend was in good hands and then returned to DC.

The thoughts about the security breach at A-Echelon continued to haunt him and he was still thinking about how to approach the issue. At best it was unsettling to think of everyone as a potential quisling or traitor. But until he could find out more that's how he had to handle all interaction with co-workers at A-Echelon.

Two days after Carter's arrival in Boston the doors to his hospital room swung open and to his relief and pleasure, Bly and Ahote put their heads around it. "Oh yes!" He reached out his good arm, and Bly moved in close to give him a kiss as Ahote gently took his other hand and just hung on as if never to let it go.

For moments there was silence between them, something too big had happened - it felt as if there was a yawning gap in front of them, where to start? What to say?

"God I'm so thankful to see you both, you have no idea." Carter's voice was wobbly, and the hand Ahote was holding shook badly.

"I just wish we'd known sooner, it's been a nightmare, one we don't seem to be able to wake up from.

"One we may never wake up from," Carter whispered.

Ahote pulled a chair up for Bly to sit on, but she gingerly settled on the bed beside Carter, she couldn't put the distance a chair would invoke between them.

Ahote tilted his head to one side as if considering, "Maybe we will Carter, and maybe we won't, but we're in it together, all three of us, and we'll see it through somehow."

Bly nodded, firmly holding Carter's good arm.

"They told you about… about what happened?"

"Bly nodded and whispered. "Yes, they did," tears ran down her face, "It's awful darling, so awful."

Carter closed his eyes against the pain.

"Ahote squeezed his hand "We'll get through this lad, your Grandfather Will would insist on it now, wouldn't he."

Carter nodded silently

Bly wiped at her tears and sat straighter, "Tell us all about your injuries and how you are progressing and what the doctors plan next."

She could see Carter's effort to push the pain away as he described all he knew and how much better he was already after coming home.

Watching him carefully, Bly could see he was not in any way defeated and so put forward an idea she wanted him to consider.

"When you are ready to come home, we want you to

come and live with us until you are healthy enough to return to your own homestead. Freydis misses you, and I want you where I can make sure you return to full health."

Ahote interrupted at that point, "Better say yes Carter, you know what a force she is to be reckoned with. There's no way I'm going to continue to live with her if you refuse."

That drew a smile from Carter at long last, and he nodded his head. "You two take the cake," his voice shook with a tiny tremor.

Later that afternoon he had two more visitors. Not expecting anyone after Bly and Ahote left, Carter had drifted into a daze that was full of jumbled movement and misery. When the door swung open yet again, and he found himself looking into the eyes of two of his dearest friends, Carter almost cried in relief.

He sat forward and raised his good arm "Jacob, Pete, I can't believe it! How did you guys get past the guards? I'm sure they wouldn't have let you both in, did you bribe or overpower them?"

"They didn't see us," Jacob laughed, "we came in undercover with these." Flowers and grapes landed on the bed table. "We were ordered to bring these from everyone at Uni," he said.

"But," interrupted Pete, no one believed us when we said men don't take flowers to hospitals. They threatened all sorts of awful things if we reneged."

"Yeah, they were going to pull the power on Pete's computers and then lock him in a room without them…"

"And," Pete responded, "They said they'd shove Jacob behind a desk and never let him out to do field work again - even if he found a dozen more gold birds."

Carter was chuckling at their enthusiasm, "Well I still reckon you bribed the guards."

The atmosphere suddenly turned somber when they stopped talking.

"Man, I'm so sorry about Mackenzie and Liam," Jacob said, "I just can't believe they're gone."

Pete was struggling to say something but ended up just looking at Carter as he nodded his head in agreement with Jacob.

"Thank you guys, I'm glad to see you two." Carter whispered.

Chapter Eleven

COMPETITIVE RESPONSE SOLUTIONS

Dwayne Miller, the CEO of Competitive Response Solutions – CRS – stood in the boardroom pointing at the big screen on the wall while explaining the company's quarterly financial performance to the five members of the board of directors.

CRS had more than 500 employees working in offices located on every continent across the globe, except Antarctica.

The company was in the information business, the most profitable commodity of the modern age. Throughout human history, information had always been the most valuable and profitable commodity, but very few people recognized it.

Gathering and analyzing commercial information for clients was CRS' specialty. Customers from across the globe paid CRS exorbitant amounts of money and kept them on retainer to know everything about their competitors and the market. It was called 'competitive intelligence,' and entailed the gathering and evaluation, in a legal and ethical manner, of commercial information regarding their opposition's strengths and weaknesses to enhance business decision-making.

CRS's competitive intelligence activities provided their clients with short-term tactical advantages enabling them to capture bigger market shares and increased revenues. It also provided long-term strategic value by pointing out key risks and opportunities to their clients that helped them make better decisions and enhance organizational performance.

Competitive intelligence did much more than simply trawl the internet to find information about a client's competitors. Valuable information was rarely, if ever, easily found online. A diligent study that would produce good results for a customer required the gathering of information and analysis from a multitude of sources, which included customer and competitor interviews, news media, industry experts, government records, trade shows, conferences and public filings.

CRS's competitive analysis activities were all legal. In fact, CRS was one of the founding members of the watchdog body for this industry known as the Strategic Competitive Intelligence Professionals, and Dwayne Miller was the chairperson of the board of the SCIP.

There were four directors attentively listening to Dwayne Miller. They were happy and impressed. The company just had another record quarter, showing a $300 million profit.

The five men in the room, however, knew that the sterling performance of their company over the past few years had very little to do with their legal, competitive intelligence activities. More than 80% of their profits, skillfully hidden in those figures by their accountant, came from their illegal industrial espionage business.

CRS's legal activities were the ideal front to conceal their industrial espionage pursuits. It was, as Miller had pointed out to them a while ago, like a spider web covering a cave entry. It was an analogy he got from the director of their best and most lucrative client, Daiyan Nasser of the Institute of Scientific Research and Development in Saudi Arabia.

Industrial espionage was as old as humanity. Père d'Entrecolles, a French Jesuit missionary in the early 1700's, learned the secret techniques for manufacturing ceramics while in China. He passed this information back to France in his letters.

In the 1800's, the British hired a Scottish botanist and adventurer Robert Fortune to smuggle tea plants, seeds, and the secrets for growing tea, out of China into India. The result was that 40 years later India's tea production surpassed China's.

In modern times, General Motors, the IT giants – Oracle, Hewlett-Packard, and Google, - and oil companies such as Royal Dutch Shell, Exxon Mobil, and British Petroleum were all victims of industrial espionage. The military industrial complex, pharmaceutical companies, and technology companies, were some of the highest value targets of industrial spies.

Acquisition of trade secrets was big business for CRS. In the shady world of industrial espionage, the removal, copying or recording of confidential or valuable information by any means, which included theft, bribery, blackmail, and technological surveillance, earned them the dubious reputation of the world's leading industrial spy organization. As long as the world believed that China was the only perpetrator of this type of crime, CRS was flourishing, and no one would ever suspect them of any wrongdoing.

Industrial spies used many of the same tools and methods that intelligence and security agencies across the world such as the CIA and FBI as well as terrorist organizations used.

CRS was very careful to make sure that knowledge about their industrial espionage projects was not shared between directors. The five directors each took responsibility for one or more projects and hired his own contractors. He never discussed any of his projects with anyone other than Dwayne Miller. Some of the world's most notorious, but anonymous, computer hackers and experts could be found among the contractors commonly hired by the CRS directors. Also in the service of CRS were a number of ex-Special Forces from America, Russia, Israel, Britain, France, South Africa and various Middle Eastern countries.

All projects were run as independent operations, very much like terrorist cells.

The board meeting was over, and Miller invited everyone for lunch at the Corduroy on 9th Street. Later he had an appointment scheduled with one of the directors of the CRS board, Nate Gordon, to discuss his project. Gordon was the project manager for all projects related to the Institute of Scientific Research and Development in Saudi Arabia.

Chapter Twelve

WE HAVE TO CONTINUE THE WORK

A-Echelon's director, Hunter Patrick was having his second coffee of the morning while waiting for Irene O' Connor and James Rhodes, two of his special agents, to turn up for a meeting. Recently, while discussing the results of his latest annual physical with him, Hunter's doctor had told him to cut down on the coffee, start exercising and reduce stress. His high blood pressure coupled with an arrhythmia, an irregular heartbeat, made Hunter Patrick a mobile massive stroke waiting to happen.

Hunter had grimaced as he walked out of the doctor's office. *Now, doctor, why don't you tell me how I'm supposed to do that?* He wondered. *Maybe he should come and fill my shoes for a week and show me.* But in the back of his mind, he knew the doctor was right. He had to do something, and with his sixty-seventh birthday a few months away it would probably be a good time to call it a day and retire.

He had requested six weeks' leave that would begin in three days' time. His idea was to get away with his wife to a quiet place and think through his plans for the future. And in that regard, he had a little surprise he planned on giving James at this meeting.

When Irene and James arrived, he showed them to their seats and got straight to the point. "We need to talk about the Devereuxs' projects. I know it is very soon after the tragedy, but they were working on important matters, and we have to discuss how the projects should be continued." He looked over the rim of his glasses at them. "Do you agree?"

They both nodded.

Hunter continued. "I understand that Carter will be hospitalized and out of action for several months at least, and that is only taking into account his physical injuries. I'm sure he is strong enough to overcome those and make a full recovery, but what worries me is his emotional health." Hunter paused for a few breaths. "How he will ever get over the loss of his family I don't know. If it happened to me, I would lose my mind."

"Yes, Hunter I have to agree with you," James said. Carter is a strong man physically and psychologically – I can testify to that, but to get over a loss like this is going to take a miracle." James paused, "At this stage I'm not sure that he will even want to continue working for us, and no one can blame him if he makes that decision. In any event, I wouldn't even think of discussing that with him for at least the next six months."

Hunter and Irene agreed.

"And of the two projects Carter's is the more important one," Hunter noted. "My suggestion is that we find another person to take his place and continue the work until we know if Carter is coming back or not. It's too important to let it sit in limbo."

James nodded in agreement. "I have to agree and have

come up with a few names. Give me a day or two to check them out and get back to you."

Hunter smiled, James was by far his best and most senior agent, and he'd already decided he would recommend to his superiors that James be his replacement when he announced his retirement. "Thanks, Jim, let me know when you're ready."

Hunter turned to Irene O'Connell. "Now Mackenzie's work. I think the same goes for her project. It is, of course, not as mission critical as Carter's; nevertheless, I believe it is important. I would hate for all the work she has done to go to waste. What do you think?

"I agree with you, Hunter," she said. "I'm very glad to hear you would like her work to continue. I feel like I have a moral obligation to her and her legacy, to make sure the project goes on."

James nodded his agreement. "Yes, that's how I feel too."

"Good, we're in agreement then." Hunter continued, "So Irene I assume you have given this some thought?"

"Yes indeed, I certainly have."

Hunter waved for her to continue.

"I want to start by getting that Sirralnnudam text in Armenia translated first. For that, I need to assemble a team of linguists who can do it, and obtain the assistance from our embassy in Armenia again to get the necessary permissions for access to the document. I take it you would be able to help me arrange that like you did last time?"

Hunter smiled and shook his head. "No, I won't." He paused and enjoyed the flabbergasted look on Irene and James' faces.

"Wha ... how do you ... ah," Irene stuttered in confusion.

"You'll have to ask Jim here to help you with that." He was still smiling. He was starting to get an idea of what he had to do to relieve stress.

Now both James and Irene looked confused, and Hunter enjoyed it.

"Okay, let me put the two of you out of your misery. I'm going on six weeks leave starting this Friday, and Jim is going to hold down the fort while I'm gone."

James was surprised. Hunter hadn't discussed this with him at all. "Well, ah, mhh ... what can I say. Do I have the option to turn down the appointment?" James grinned.

"Nope, comes with the territory. Check your employment contract, there's a paragraph that says something about accepting and diligently executing all reasonable tasks assigned to you by your manager." Hunter laughed.

"I have no contract. Agents like me don't have contracts, and you know that." James retorted in good spirits.

"Yeah well, in that case, it's even worse for you. That means you'll have to do *anything* I tell you to do."

James shrugged. "Okay then, but be warned I'm going on leave the moment you walk back in here. You can pick up the pieces while I'm gone."

A few more good-natured comments and chatter followed before Irene and James left to get started on their work.

Two days after Hunter left, James was sitting in the big office when Irene rapped her knuckles on his open door. She had a troubled look on her face.

"Come on in, Irene; what's up. You appear a bit concerned."

"Deeply worried is more like it, Jim. I'm not sure what to make of it. Let me give you the details."

James invited her to sit down. "What is it?"

"This morning I phoned the Director of the Mesrop Mashtots Institute of Ancient Manuscripts in Armenia to let her know we are planning to send a team of linguists over. That was just to make sure we still had her goodwill and cooperation as we did a few weeks ago during Mackenzie and Harry's visit. That's when she gave me the shocking news. The Sirralnnudam has somehow disappeared from their vaults!"

"What!" James exclaimed. He felt the hair rising on the back of his neck. "When did they realize it was gone? Do they know what happened?"

"The Director told me they discovered the disappearance of the manuscript about a week after Mackenzie and Harry left. The Armenian police are investigating, but so far there are no leads. The text is gone."

James stared at her. "You don't think …" He shook his head. "No, she would never."

"No, Mackenzie would never have taken it," Irene replied. Besides, the library assistant who was assigned to Mackenzie and Harry has already confirmed to the police and the Director that Mackenzie gave the book back to her before she left on the last day. She also reported seeing the book on the shelves the day after. Mackenzie is definitely not on the suspects list."

Irene was a bit more paranoid than the average person because of the fieldwork she'd done during her time as a CIA agent.

"Jim, since I heard this I can't stop thinking about your question to Hunter and me that night when you first came back from Israel."

James knew what she was referring to but wanted her to say it. He frowned as if he didn't know what she was talking about.

"Remember, you were standing there," she pointed to a spot halfway to the door, "and you asked if we thought the explosion could somehow be related to either of the projects Carter and Mackenzie have been working for us.

"Yeah, I remember," James replied.

"Well, I know this doesn't prove anything, but here is what's going through my head." She took a deep breath. "My understanding was that Mackenzie and that assistant were the last two people to handle that book. Harry wasn't there on the last day; when Mackenzie went back to the Institute, he was on a guided tour of Yerevan accompanied by one of the US embassy staff members. There were, as far as I can reconstruct the events, only four people who knew Mackenzie was interested in the Sirralnnudam. Those were Mackenzie, Harry, the assistant, and the Director.

On the top of my list of suspects, at the moment, would be the assistant and the director. Although, anyone who had access to the Institute's computer systems could have discovered Mackenzie's interest in the text and then stole it." She paused.

James nodded. "I see what you're getting at. The one sure thing is someone other than A-Echelon took an interest in Mackenzie's work."

"Exactly," Irene nodded. "If that is true, the question then becomes, what was in the text that was so important it warranted killing Mackenzie, her son, and 23 others plus wounding 60 more?"

James sat back and went quiet for a few moments. He had decided, before he arrived back in DC, not to trust anyone at A-Echelon. Now he wondered if he should make an exception with Irene. He decided not to for the moment. Instead, he got up and walked over to close the door to his office.

He returned to his seat at the desk and looked carefully at Irene. "Let's assume someone knew about Mackenzie's work. What do you think that infers?" James knew of course, but he wanted to see Irene's face as he led her to the conclusion.

"My first question would be. How did they come to know about it?" James saw the genuine shock and disgust erupt on her face when the answer to her own question flashed through her mind. "Oh – my – God! Jim. That means A-Echelon has a mole or moles." She was shaking her head. "How …" she didn't continue; she knew it was possible.

Studying her face carefully as she responded, James became convinced he could make the exception he considered a few minutes ago. Irene could be trusted. That is what he needed, an ally inside A-Echelon, to help him trap the mole.

The news Irene had just brought him, confirmed a mole existed in A-Echelon. He had worked with Irene before, at A-Echelon, and also during the time when they both served the CIA. She was an intelligent person, loyal, and he had just reconfirmed she was also trustworthy.

James nodded with raised eyebrows. "There are two possibilities. The first is that whoever knew about her work killed her to prevent her from continuing with it, or …" James had one more revelation, and she was going to be the first person to hear it.

"Or what?" She asked as she leaned forward when he paused.

"… or Mackenzie and Liam were kidnapped and"

He didn't get to finish his sentence. Irene interrupted, "Are you kidding? No one came out of that restaurant alive except Carter. You can't possibly be serious. What evidence do you have for your theory?"

"It's not so much evidence for my theory that's driving my thinking, but rather the lack thereof," He replied.

Irene held up her hand. "Wait. You mean the five missing people for whom there were no DNA matches?"

James nodded, "Right."

"But their bodies would have been vaporized."

"Yes that's true, but then it's also possible that one or more of them were not vaporized and were simply not present when the bomb went off."

She nodded slowly. "I see. We need to talk to that assistant and the Director. Don't we?"

"We sure do," agreed James. "Leave it to me, I'll make arrangements."

Irene nodded. James then told her more about his suspicions and included a report of the men who had been watching his hotel in Jerusalem. He didn't tell her about his contact with Ben Friedman; it could wait until it became necessary for her to know. He asked her to keep everything they had discussed a secret until he told her otherwise. Irene understood the importance and agreed.

James went on to discuss his speculation that both Mackenzie and Carter were targeted and that the terrorists' plans didn't work out exactly as they hoped. Carter's trip to the restroom had kept them from capturing him along with his family. The implication of that quickly registered with Irene.

"That means, not only did someone know about Mackenzie's project, but that same someone also knew about Carter's research," she said with an ashen face.

James nodded. "And that, Irene, scares the hell out of me. In the wrong hands, Mackenzie's project can't do a fraction of the damage that Carter's is capable of. And the nightmare is that it means someone out there, other than us, is also on the hunt for an ancient nuke. And we have just experienced how cold-blooded they are."

After a few more minutes of discussion, they returned to the respirocyte project and the impact of the loss of the Sirralnnudam.

"It's a setback, of course, but I'd like to believe that there are other sources of the information we are seeking." Irene mentioned. "At least, we know the ancients had the knowledge and used it. There must be more information out there somewhere."

"Agreed," James nodded. "I'm glad you have such a pragmatic view of the matter. So I guess the next step will be to find someone who could continue Mackenzie's work and bring that person on board?"

"Yes, I will start on that right away. I will also get hold of Liu Cheun to see if she has any information that we don't have about Mackenzie's work."

When Irene left, James got ahold of Harry and asked him to come and see him. During the meeting, James had to be very careful not to raise any suspicions. He explained to Harry that he just wanted to get a good idea of Mackenzie's project now that they had to look for a replacement for her. They went over the work Harry and Mackenzie did in detail during the time they were working together, especially during their visit to Armenia. By the end of the conversation James had all the information he required, and Harry was none the wiser. In fact, Harry was quite excited about the prospect of visiting Armenia again.

James made his daily call to Carter, who was still at

Massachusetts General Hospital in Boston. They had a long talk, and Carter told him that the doctors expected him to be able to go home in four weeks. Carter was apparently doing extremely well physically, but James could detect that his friend was going through hell on an emotional level.

His next call was to Ben Friedman on the secure phone. He wanted to know if Ben had any assets in Armenia who could make a few urgent, but discreet, inquiries and perhaps conduct a private interview or two on his behalf.

Chapter Thirteen

A FEW INQUIRIES AND A PRIVATE INTERVIEW

Ben Friedman had somehow wangled things with his bosses at the Mossad to put him in charge of their investigation into the latest Triangle explosion. He was, therefore, more than happy to oblige James when his request came through for assistance with the inquiries that had to be done in Armenia.

James provided Ben with all the details he had, and Ben went to work. He contacted his senior agent in Armenia, Vartan Chagoyan, and arranged for surveillance to be placed on the Director of the Mesrop Mashtots Institute of Ancient Manuscripts as well as Meryl, the woman who'd assisted Mackenzie and Harry when they were there.

Ben required as much highly detailed information as possible about the personal lives and routines of the two people under surveillance before he would make the next move. Vartan Chagoyan was a native Armenian, who spoke the language, understood the culture, and blended in perfectly with everyone. It took him seven days to collect all the information required by Ben and pass it on to him.

A few days later, Ben landed at Zvartnots International Airport in Yerevan. Posing as an Israeli businessman on a short trip to the capital to meet with a business colleague, he went through Armenian customs without any problems

The Ural Airlines flight from Tel Aviv was smooth, and Ben had used the six-hour flight time to consider various strategies. He had made the decision to work his way from the bottom up, and would have a private interview with Taline 'Meryl' Jafarian first. Then he'd approach the Director of the Mesrop Mashtots Institute of Ancient Manuscripts.

Vartan Chagoyan met him when he arrived at the airport shortly after 8:00 that night. They drove straight to Meryl's apartment and waited for her in the car. She had gone out to dinner with friends and was expected to return about 10:00 pm according to Vartan's information.

At almost 10:45 pm, just when Ben was getting tired of waiting, Meryl was dropped off at her apartment by a car with several other women in it. Ben and Vartan made sure the car was gone, and then waited for Meryl's apartment lights to go on before they moved.

Varatan had studied the lock on the backdoor to the ground floor apartment a few days before and had made a copy of the key, which he now handed to Ben. Once Ben was out of the car, Vartan drove a block away and parked on a side street. From here he would wait and listen. He and Ben were both wearing earpieces and microphones to keep in touch.

Ben slipped unnoticed, through the backdoor. Once inside, he pulled a black balaclava over his face and moved quietly through the apartment. It was important to get close enough to Meryl to put his hand over her mouth to stifle any scream. Indeed, he didn't like the idea of doing what he was about to do, sneak up on a defenseless, unsuspecting young woman and most likely scare her half to death, but there weren't any other options. He couldn't approach her in the open, in a public place, or at her workplace. He had to keep his face hidden. Still he couldn't shake the morality of the attack from his conscience. Unfortunately, it came as part of his job. There were 25 people dead, and 60 wounded; their family and loved ones wanted to know who committed this terrible act, and this girl or her boss could be holding information that would help him answer that question.

He saw the light in the bedroom; the door was ajar. He approached slowly and carefully; she was standing with her back to him in front of the cupboard less than two paces away. He moved quickly, placing his right hand over her mouth from behind and his left arm around her neck. A jolt of shock coursed through her body. She was screaming, but his hand muffled the sound.

"Meryl, I'm very sorry to sneak up on you like this," Ben spoke in a very calm voice. "I won't hurt you, I promise. I only want to talk to you. It is vital that I ask you a few questions. All you have to do is answer me honestly, and nothing else will happen."

He could feel her relaxing a bit but knew it wasn't over yet. He kept his hand over her mouth and his arm around her neck but let her feel him relax just a bit. He kept talking to her, assuring her that no harm would come to her and kept on apologizing for scaring her. Slowly she calmed down and finally he felt safe to say, "Okay Meryl, I'm going to remove my hand from your mouth. Please don't scream or make any noise. Okay?"

She nodded slowly, and he removed his hand from her

mouth but kept his arm around her neck. "What … what is it … you want from me?" She stuttered.

Ben felt like the lowest of heels when he turned her around and saw her tear-filled eyes. He apologized again. "Let's go and get you a drink of water." He took her hand and led her to the kitchen "You sit down while I get it." She was still shaking.

He started slowly, "I know you understand English. Are you comfortable speaking in English, or would it help if I get someone who can speak Armenian to interpret for us?"

She nodded; "English I not speak well" Ben's Armenian was non-existent, so he pushed the button on his throat mic and asked Vartan to join them. He explained to her that Vartan was a good friend of his who was coming to interpret for them, and she had nothing to fear from him.

While they waited for Vartan to arrive, Ben continued to talk to her to keep her calm, asking fundamental questions. Where do you work? What do you do? How old are you? Her English was broken, but she answered as best she could.

When Vartan arrived a few minutes later, Ben could see that his covered face had frightened her again. He tried to reassure her that neither one of them was going to hurt her; they only wanted to talk, to ask her a few questions. As Vartan translated, adding a few assurances of his own, the fear left her eyes, but Ben could see the doubt in them and got straight to the point. "Meryl," he said. "I know you were involved in the disappearance of the Sirralnnudam from the Mesrop Mashtots Institute of Ancient Manuscripts." He held his hand up when she started shaking her head. "Meryl, it's imperative that you tell me the truth. You should not lie to me. We know you took that book. All we want to know is what you did with it?"

She started crying softly and shook her head.

Ben leaned forward and took her hand. "Meryl, I won't tell anyone that you took the book, I promise. You will keep your job. I just need to know the truth."

After listening to Vartan's translation, she shrugged her shoulders and started talking. Ben and Vartan listened carefully and did not interrupt while she told them what happened.

Over the next hour they learned that the man who contacted her and offered her money was probably of Arabic ancestry but she had no idea from which country. They met twice and spoke English on both occasions. The description she gave Ben: dark hair, medium build, about thirty or so, and olive skin, matched almost any young Arabic-looking male on the planet. She had no idea if he had accomplices or if he was working for anyone else. All she knew was that the day when she lost the book, there was another man with him. He was the one who ripped her laptop bag with the laptop in it out of her hand when she was on the ground.

Ben also discovered that she had been recording Mackenzie and Harry's conversations while they were working and stored it on the laptop, so those conversations were now in the hands of someone else.

James sat back in his chair, sipping a cup of bitter, black coffee while he considered the conversation he'd just had with Ben. He allowed his mind to review Ben's report on his trip to Armenia and the meeting with Taline 'Meryl' Jafarian.

Well, now we know we're right about our suspicions that a third party is also interested in Mackenzie's respi- thingamajigs. He was about to call Irene to discuss the latest development when she walked into his office. She had another worried look on her face, the same as a few days before.

"Irene, I saw that look a few days ago, and it wasn't good," James grinned. "I was about to call you, but I think you have something more pressing on your mind than what I have to say."

Irene walked over to the coffee machine and made herself a mug of coffee while she started talking. "It's Liu Cheun," she said. "Something isn't right."

James had a frown on his forehead. "What's up with her?"

"Well I'm not sure, but here is what I've managed to find out so far." The coffee was ready, and she took the mug and sat down in the chair opposite James' desk.

"After our discussion the other day I tried to get hold of Liu at the University in Boston, but they told me she took a few weeks leave to visit family in China. I rang her secretary and asked when Liu was expected to be back. She told me that Liu was supposed to be back a week ago."

James was shaking his head. He was beginning to understand why this job had destroyed Hunter Patrick's health.

Irene continued, "The secretary told me she had been in contact with Liu's family in China through some of Liu's Chinese friends in Boston, and the family told her that Liu went back to America as planned. They are worried about her because they haven't heard anything from her since she left.

I just got off the phone with border control, and they confirmed that they have a record of her leaving the USA for China, but no record of her re-entering the country."

"So she's been missing for a week already?" James asked.

"Yes," Irene nodded. "In fact, it's been eight days by my calculations."

Jim stared into space as he tried to put some sort of reasonable hypothesis in place that would explain her absence.

"She's a senior lecturer at the University. She has an unblemished work record there." James was talking slowly as he went through the facts. "I personally vetted her to work for A-Echelon with Will Devereux years ago. I know her. She wouldn't just up and leave without telling someone. Something is wrong here."

"I agree. I've read her file. She has always been a reliable and trustworthy worker, beyond any reproach. The fact that she didn't turn up for work means either she is in some sort of trouble or her family is lying."

James closed his eyes as he let out a sigh. Another red light on his Devereux's dashboard just started flickering.

Chapter Fourteen

SHE CALLED SILENTLY INTO THE NIGHT

When Mackenzie and Liam were reunited, she felt truly blessed. Even though their living quarters left a lot to be desired, it was acceptable, all that mattered was that she had her son with her.

Having two bedrooms made her feel as if they were living in the lap of luxury after the cramped one-room prison cell. They even had a kitchen where she could make tea or coffee, and prepare meals. The available food wasn't much as they were supplied by whatever someone felt like delivering to them, but cooking for her son returned a small feeling of normality and control to her, so she wasn't going to complain.

There was a total of seven people living in this part of the floor, two other women with children, Liam, and her. The other women were friendly, and the children got along, as children always do no matter the circumstances.

When they had first arrived, Mackenzie told Liam the truth about their situation; at least as much as a six-year-old could comprehend. It was the only way he would understand just how much their lives had changed.

"But Mommy, we can still think about the people we love can't we?"

She nodded, "Of course we can, dear. That will never change!"

"Good! Because I talk to Dad and Jeha, and Bly and Ahote, and Nelly, my pony all the time and I know they can hear me, can't they?"

She smiled, "Well, I can't imagine for one moment they couldn't hear you, darling; they've never had any trouble before have they?" Her own joke gave her cause to smile.

"Don't you talk to them, Mommy?"

"Yes, I do all the time, and Grandma and Pops too." She didn't add how often she communicated with her wolves, so often, in fact, that she felt they were standing right beside her every night, guarding her and keeping her strong.

Some nights she'd frown in the darkness thinking, *I must be imagining this surely? I can almost feel their fur in my fingers and their breath on my cheek.*

Then she'd turn over and mutter, *wouldn't the scientific community love to know that a woman who is working her guts out to discover a way to bring hope to the ill with a new souped-up blood speaks to wolves every night. I must remember never to say anything.* Then she'd smile to herself and went back to sleep.

Mornings were always busy, as she had to get herself ready for work and Liam ready for school. They frequently ate breakfast with the other women and children in the compound. A daily vitamin D supplement was provided to make up for the lack of sunlight they suffered from being underground all the time, but when Liam wasn't with her, she worried whether he was being given the proper food a small boy needs to grow. However, he seemed happy and healthy, so maybe the vitamin D supplement was sufficient. *It's still not the same as fresh air and sunshine.* At least, it prevented rickets in the children and provided them with the essentials found in liver and fish oils. She tried to console herself thinking that there were many children in the world whose lives were nowhere near as good as Liam's.

In recent mornings, she tried to eat breakfast but often felt nauseous so she'd skip the meal and eat later in the day. After their morning meal together, she'd get Liam ready to go to another section of the compound before showering and getting herself ready for the day. She had to force herself to dress in the black garments. Oh, how she hated them, and the niqab that covered her face made her feel as if she was losing her identity, she felt like she was becoming a non-person. *I am NOT Johnny Cash, and if we ever get out of here, I will never wear so much as even black socks ever again!*

One afternoon Liam came home excited, it seemed the children would be taught to speak Arabic. There were ten children altogether in the building, and although they were not allowed to talk about their families, they went to school and played together. For Liam things were so busy in his world, he barely noticed as the days slipped by.

Mackenzie began to learn Arabic with Liam, and they also started doing exercises every day. Every morning, when they woke up the two of them would do the Five Tibetan Rites. It was an ancient exercise routine that originated amongst Tibetan monks and took about fifteen minutes to complete. Carter had taught it to Mackenzie years ago, and she had been following it ever since.

The Five Rites had been touted by many as the 'secret' to memory improvement, sleeping soundly, waking up refreshed and energized, improving physical strength, endurance, and vigor, and improving emotional and mental health. Some even claimed it cured medical problems such as back and arthritis pain.

The first few days Liam was not too enthusiastic about the idea of waking up in the mornings and having to do exercises while still half asleep. He didn't want to disappoint his mother, though, and joined her in doing the exercises. To his surprise, he soon found that he actually came to like it and looked forward to it.

For Mackenzie, the nights were the hardest. No matter how much she tried to draw close to Carter, she couldn't feel him near at all. She put it down to the idea that wherever he was and whatever he was doing must be wearing him out. Nevertheless, she was worried sick about him. Since there was nothing she could do about it, she'd mentally take herself back to Freydis and the land, visiting the creeks and trees in her mind, enjoying the golden colors of autumn and the blanketed world of a snow covered winter. Snow, how she missed it. Here below the ground, there was just one season – FARCE: Florescent, Air-conditioned, Regulated, Confined, Environment. All of it was artificial: air, temperature, lights, friends, even the day time and night time cycle, and there was no sunshine. As someone who loved nature and was used to four seasons, living in this artificial environment was severely depressing.

At night, she could smell the pine scent from the mountains surrounding Freydis, hear the birds in the trees, see the eagles as they lazily soared on the air currents high in the blue sky and even laughed at Liam's pony as she tried to trick Liam into falling off.

Mackenzie occasionally caught the scent of Bly's cakes and craved for Ahote's kind, warm treacle brown eyes as he carved small animals out of bits of wood he'd pick up on his rambles.

She visited the cave, swam in the river, watched salmon leap in the stream as the bears fished for them.

Then she'd turn over in bed and sob quietly into the emptiness in her soul, longing for her home. She wished her mind would stay in Freydis and not bring her back to the laboratory and the complexities of her work. She wished she didn't have to deal with the three stooges.

No one deserved three stooges in their life. Then she would dream of them all falling into a deep hole, as the floor of the laboratory opened up with a thundering crack. There she'd be standing on the edge watching them as they tumbled over and over, finally disappearing into a fog.

"Carter, where are you? Will I ever see you again?" She cried silently into the night.

Chapter Fifteen

OUT OF THE HOSPITAL

While Hunter Patrick was away on stress leave, James and Irene had their hands full. They not only had to find replacements for the Devereuxs' project, but also had to continue the investigation into the perpetrators of the explosion, the loss of the Sirralnnudam and their growing suspicion that Mackenzie and Liam might still be alive. And there was the mole issue to contend with as well.

They'd used all their contacts with the Department of State to raise the issue of Liu Cheun's disappearance through diplomatic channels with the Chinese government. But it was as if they were hitting a brick wall at every turn. Although it was not official Chinese policy, it quickly became apparent to James and Irene that Chinese officials did not take kindly to any of their citizens taking up residence in other countries.

After three weeks of back and forth, and miles of red tape, they had only one piece of information. Liu Cheun had not left China. As far as China was concerned she was still in the country and if she wanted to remain in China and not return to her job at the University in Boston that was her prerogative.

They left out the part that should have been said, *and we would be delighted if she didn't return,* James thought when he read the latest message from the embassy.

The phone on the secure line started ringing, and he answered, it was Ben Friedman.

"Jim, how are you holding up in the new job my friend?"

"Only by the skin of my teeth, Ben," James chuckled. "Hunter had better get his ass back in this chair soon. In the past few weeks, I've done enough desk-jockeying to last me a lifetime."

"I know the feeling. Since they brought me in and tied me to a damn desk, all the fun is gone," Ben lamented. "Jim, I'm sending you the latest tidbits of information we've collected. You already know it all, except for one bit. Anyway, you'll get it after we're done with this call."

"So what is this new bit you've got? I guess that's why you called?"

"There was an old man, early eighties, who was injured in the explosion and taken to the hospital," Ben explained. "The injuries he sustained during the blast were moderate, but unfortunately, he was already pretty fragile. Shortly after his admission, he had a stroke. It's a miracle that the poor man didn't succumb to all the trauma. However, he got through it, and the investigators were able to get a statement from him."

"I'm all ears, Ben. Continue."

According to his statement, this guy was walking up the street towards the restaurant, and he noticed a white van pass him. He says it stopped right on the sidewalk in front of the restaurant, and he saw three men with stockings over their faces jumped out, grab two people, and bundle them into the van. Then the van took off. The old man says he was hurrying towards the scene, but suddenly another van came from the same direction as the white van and drove right into the restaurant. He remembered the explosion, but nothing after that until he woke up in the hospital."

James could feel the excitement starting to bubble within, but he kept it under control. "Ben, you said this guy is in his eighties, his health was not good before he was wounded, then he sustains all these injuries and on top of that he suffered a stroke which incapacitated him for weeks. How reliable do you think his memories of the events are?"

"Jim, I had the same concerns and phoned the investigator who took the man's statement. He said it was difficult to understand him for two reasons; one the man's native language is Yiddish, and his ability to speak Hebrew is not that good. Secondly, his speech is still moderately impaired from the stroke. But the investigator assured me that although he had difficulty understanding the guy, his mind was lucid."

"Okay. Let's assume for the moment that is the case." James replied. "Was the old man able to get a look at the people who were hustled into the van?"

"According to his statement, he could see one of them was a woman…" James could feel his heart racing with anticipation. He said she had long blond hair." James felt his heart drop to the floor. If there was one feature about Mackenzie that no one could ever miss, it was her stunning red hair. "He said that he couldn't see the other person clearly – he has no idea if it was a man woman or child."

James heaved a long pain-laden sigh. "I guess that accounts for two of the missing people then, but unfortunately not the two I'm looking for."

"I'm sorry Jim. You needed to know that bit of information before I send you the documents."

They said their goodbyes. James got up and walked down the corridor to Irene's office to share the latest bit of information with her. It was as if a black blanket had been dropped over him. *Maybe it's time to make peace with the facts. Mackenzie and Liam are dead. We will have to move on.*

It was taking weeks, but slowly Carter was beginning to recover, physically anyway. Spiritually and emotionally he was a mess; he was fully aware of the fact, but there was little he could do about it.

He tried to put his thoughts aside as he worked in the hospital's rehabilitation gym. Under the watchful eyes of the physiotherapist, he was regaining his strength and learning to walk again. His arm was out of plaster, and his leg had a partial cast up to his knee, so he was free to hobble around with a walking stick.

The physical pain was a something he could master, but not the awful, haunting, agony, deep within that he had no idea how to let out.

A Grief Counselor visited Carter every few days, and although he was knowledgeable and did his best, he had no personal experience with such a loss as this. He did have lots of experience helping people who were going through the grieving process of losing a loved one, so Carter tried to work with him. In his moments of raging anger, he considered the man full of 'psycho-babble' as Carter had screamed at him one day. But, from the depths of his despair, he reached out to and welcomed the man's wisdom and compassion.

His in-laws, Mary and Steven, visited him almost every day. He knew they were suffering deep pain just as he was. Some days it drew them together in comfort; other days it brought a sullen silence between them that none of them understood.

In the first days after Carter was moved to Boston, they had discussed a funeral, but the idea ran out of impetus. How could they have a funeral with no bodies?

"Maybe we could have a Memorial Service," Mary suggested.

He nodded but let the idea slide. *I don't want a funeral or a memorial service!* He screamed inwardly; *I want my wife and son back!* A pretend 'lay them to rest' ceremony was just more than he could bear to think about.

It might be very different if I had their bodies he pondered, but I don't, and I've never been one to pretend. Then he'd berate himself as he realized that what Mary and Steven required was closure. They needed something, a point in time, to signify it was time to move on.

In those early days back in Boston, he'd toss and turn in the dead of night trying to accept that closure was necessary, yet dreading even the thought of any kind of ceremony designed to say goodbye to Mackie and Liam. They all needed closure, and he knew it, but the whole idea was revolting to him. *I can't say goodbye to them; not here, not now. I need to go home; I need time to myself; I need Freydis.*

He finally suggested to the Andersons they have their own Memorial Service for their daughter and grandson and allow him to do something for them when he was ready. *Maybe when I'm back at Freydis where we were a family.*

It was the best he could do to help resolve the issue. He saw the puzzlement in their eyes, and then the anger followed by hurt which gave way to partial understanding as they talked. In the end, he believed, like it or not, they accepted it. The subject never came up again.

On one of their visits, they said they felt he should have Jeha, who was growing up, and needed to know his permanent home. They were not his family, Carter was, and it was right that Jeha should return to Freydis with him. He had some misgivings as he realized the little dog would bring back memories of Mackenzie and Liam that would be painful. However, he did love the little pooch and, in the end, decided they needed each other and told Mary and Steven he was happy to accept. And so they began the regulatory red tape game to get Jeha over the Canadian border.

As the weeks passed, he started to feel a bit more like his old self. Of course, he wasn't that man any longer, and the mere thought of picking up the reins of his work for A-Echelon sickened him. After all, it was that work which killed his wife and son. How could he ever return to it? If he'd never taken on that job, they'd still be alive; he was convinced of that.

The Dean of Faculty from the archeology department at the University started paying him regular visits as did several of his colleagues.

They brought news of what was happening in the outside world; of events at the University, new findings and information from the underground city he'd discovered. None of it interested him anymore, and sometimes he was glad when they went away again. He had nothing to add to their conversations and felt stilted and trapped by them most of the times.

A few days before he was due to leave for Freydis, the Dean came by for another visit, and Carter finally told him he is resigning.

"Carter, my friend, I figured you were going to do something like this."

"Good, then you understand, and there won't be any problem."

"That's not quite the case. I've been waiting for you to hand in your resignation so I could hit you over the head with it."

The new approach picked up Carter's interest; this was the first time someone was threatening to become firm with him instead of being sympathetic.

"Well, it's what I have to do," Carter said before the Dean could continue. "I can't see myself ever picking up the reins again, and of course, financially, I don't have to."

The Dean nodded, "I see, so this is how you are thinking. You lose one side of your life to a ghastly tragedy so you will destroy the other side of your life to balance things up, is that it?" The Dean's voice rang with an anger Carter wasn't used to.

"You don't understand."

"I don't understand? Just where the hell do you think I've been all my life? Locked up in that damnable office, never having anything bad happen to me? Do you think I've never experienced the pain and agony of loss? Do you really think your brand of suffering is unique?"

Carter had never heard the Dean expound so graphically before, and it had the effect of pulling him out of his deep sinking determination to let go of everything. He'd underestimated the Dean. He softened and spoke quietly, "No, of course not, I'm sorry. Of course, you've suffered loss too, even if I don't know about it."

"No, you don't know about it young man, and that is your mistake." His voice was trembling with emotion, "Now, first and foremost understand this: you are not on your own. You may feel like you're an island in a vast ocean, but you're not special. Life is hard, damn near impossible sometimes, and there's no such thing as 'Happily Ever After." If you can get that through your head, I will have at least served some purpose in this life."

He stopped and drew a breath before Carter said, "I don't know what to say. I can't ever imagine wanting to go back to work, not the sort of work I was doing anyway. I believe it is what killed Mackie and Liam, and I can't face it."

"Okay Carter, I can understand that, but time changes many things, and as you are still officially on sabbatical, I insist you ride out that time before you do anything rash. Will you, at least, do that for me?"

Carter gave a half-hearted smile and shrugged, "I can't really say 'No' now, can I?"

"Good! My day is made. I've had one win; that is a rare thing in my life Carter, and don't you forget it."

With that, the Dean whisked out the door and was gone leaving Carter feeling like a puppy who'd wet on the carpet – small, shamed, and out of favor.

However, it had done him no harm, and the adrenalin from the confrontation, quite apart from the realization that the Dean would fight tooth and nail to keep him, began to put some building blocks in place. Blocks he could use to clamber slowly up.

At last, Carter was released from the hospital and, carrying Jeha in a case, along with his ticket, they boarded the plane to Quebec where Ahote would be waiting for them.

When they landed, Ahote greeted them warmly, hugging Carter and rescuing Jeha from her confinement. The little dog was excited to have gained freedom and wiggled wildly in his arms. Ahote helped Carter transfer his luggage, and the squirming furball, into the small private plane.

As Ahote lifted the plane off the ground and turned toward Freydis, an enormous load slid from Carter's shoulders. Freydis, where his Grandfather Will had lived out his life and where Carter grew up, was home. Even though it was now empty of his loved ones, he would be able to grieve properly. Here was the place where he, Mackenzie and Liam had the most precious moments of their short time together.

A few weeks of Bly's home cooking and common sense, plus some fishing and riding around with Ahote began to work its magic. The wolves turned up on Carter's first day back and looked at Jeha with disdain. In the end, she was far too 'cute' for them to take her seriously, so they more or less ignored her.

Watching the interaction of the wolves and the little dog, Carter came to realize that pups understand 'ignore.' He watched with amusement as Jeha behaved with an attempt at great dignity when she was within sight of the two wolves.

He was intrigued by the fact that the wolves were never far away. If he went out, they were with him, if he was inside he would catch sight of them lurking near a building or sitting near the edge of the tree line. He was telling Bly and Ahote about it over dinner one evening. "I've never known wolves to behave like this. They are wild; there's nothing domesticated about them and yet they, of their own free, won't let me out of their sight. I don't understand it."

Bly and Ahote smiled and nodded, "It makes sense Carter. I don't think we ever told you, but the night of the explosion they sat just outside our barn and howled all night."

Carter looked at Bly inquisitively.

"It's true. The next morning," Ahote continued, "we went to look around your place. They'd done a great spying job there, even looking in windows."

"You're kidding me, surely."

"No, you could see where they'd stood on their back legs to see into the house."

"Then, when we got back here," Bly continued, "they were waiting for us. I went over to them and patted them."

"They accepted that?"

"More than that, Carter, they needed it; they were severely disturbed. However, after I'd sung them an Indian lullaby, they returned quietly to the woods."

"Two days later Jim called and told us what had happened," Ahote finished.

Carter shook his head, "Well there's no understanding that unless they could feel something."

"I believe they did Carter; animals have senses and intuition that we can't even begin to understand."

Carter finally felt he was ready to take up residence in his own home again and made plans to return there. He asked Bly to take care of Jeha for a few more days as he had a trip in mind that he wanted to make alone. Bly agreed, and Carter packed a sleeping bag, food, and water, and headed for the cave.

It was here he had first made love to Mackenzie,

proposed marriage to her and watched Liam grow in her tummy. It was their place, and he knew it was where he needed to be if he was ever going to pick up the reins of his life again and be more than a hindrance to all the people who had given him their love and support.

When he left the hospital and arrived at home, the snows had melted away, and spring was already in full bloom. Now Freydis was in the height of late summer. Before long, autumn would turn everything to amber and gold, but for now, it couldn't have been a better time to return to the cave.

Keeva and Loki still accompanied him everywhere, and the attention of the two wolves bemused him. If he went riding, they would suddenly appear and go with him no matter where he went.

By the time he reached the cave, settled the horse, and unpacked his provisions, the scents and peace of the place was seeping deep into his bones; bones that were raw with bruising, the agony of loss, and new healing. He had come to understand that profound loss affected every part of his body as well as his mind and soul, and the sense of being out here away from everything and everyone gave him a release he'd thought would never happen.

He stood for a long time, staring out over the grasslands down to the river, across the valley to the mountains on the other side, and watching the eagles ride the currents in the summer sky above. He was, at last, alone and able to be himself. He didn't know who he was anymore, or who he would be in the future, but it would be here that he'd find himself again.

That night as he sat by the fire watching the embers climb their way to the stars, his mind began to unravel, the tight knots he had fastened around himself fell loose, and he began to cry in earnest, huge wrenching sobs from deep within his soul.

Keeva and Loki moved in close and lay down on either side of him, supporting him as the pain poured out and out and out, seemingly without end.

Never in his life had Carter understood tears. He'd cried over losing Will when he was alone, but nothing like this. There was no stopping this. His body wouldn't let him stop until it had turned him inside out, releasing all the grief, and then he collapsed into a state of sheer exhaustion.

He didn't even know he'd finally curled up with the wolves. It wasn't until the next morning when he found them still there, pressed close against his body that he knew what they'd done for him.

They'd taken his pain and sent it to the stars.

He spent the rest of his time at the cave swimming in the icy waters of the river, running wild and naked through the long dry grasses, chasing anything that moved, shouting and yelling and then returning to the cave completely worn out ready for a meal and good night's rest. Keeva and Loki remained ever present.

A week later Carter returned home, picking Jeha up on his way. Bly sensed a change in him, but kept it to herself, allowing only a smile to surface on her face.

He began his morning Thai Chi rituals again, registering how much of the poise and keenness he'd once had was gone and determined to regain it as soon as possible.

There were big differences in him now, that was clear. This new man was a stranger to him, but he felt it was an improvement over his old self. There was a greater sense of awe and mystery; things he'd always chased in his profession, but never knew could be part of his own life as well.

Something had shifted, and now he was ready to begin

again. It would be difficult hoeing the hard row, but he knew he was now able.

What he wasn't yet ready to do was pack Mackie's and Liam's things away. There was no need to, they weren't haunting him as he expected, they were just there, as they should be. Maybe sometime in the future, he'd pack them away, but not now.

Jeha jumped into bed with him every night, and Carter found he liked the company. A small living creature breathing and snuffling nearby was better than a big empty bed all on his own. The little dog had wormed her way into his heart and was clearly going to stay there.

Chapter Sixteen

THE NEXT MISSION

With Youssef Bin-Bandar's sudden and tragic death, the King of Saudi Arabia sought the wise counsel of his old time confidant, Xavier Algosaibi. The astute King knew it would be in the best interest of the House of Saud to appoint another member of the Wahhabi community in Bin-Bandar's place. After all, the Wahhabis were his power base, and he had to make sure that he appeased them. Algosaibi was a highly respected and revered man amongst the Wahhabis and if he supported the King's appointment of the deputy director of the General Intelligence Presidency, then the King was assured of the support of the Wahhabis.

Algosaibi was extremely pleased and honored by the Kings request for his advice and had no hesitation in recommending Ibrahimi El Fadl as the new deputy director.

Algosaibi had known El Fadl and his family for nearly 40 years. El Fadl was an educated and intelligent man with a Ph.D. in International Relations and Strategy from Princeton University He started working at the General

Intelligence Presidency shortly after he completed his Ph.D. and had been noted by his superiors for his diligence and loyalty. Algosaibi knew El Fadl had been steadily rising through the ranks over the years and was ready for a top position.

The most pleasing aspect of El Fadl's profile, something which didn't appear anywhere on his record and which the King didn't know, was his devoted loyalty to Xavier Algosaibi and his unwavering commitment to destroy the House of Saud.

Although El Fadl was unaware of the existence of the Foundation of the Real Princes of Saud, he would not have had any hesitation to swear allegiance to them. He would have been very pleased to know that he had, unknowingly, actually done quite a bit of work for them already.

Once El Fadl's appointment as Deputy Director of the GIP became official through royal decree, Algosaibi would reveal to him what was expected of him in the plot to bring down the House of Saud.

Algosaibi was satisfied that his plans were slowly but surely getting back on track since the setbacks of the two half-baked missions planned and controlled by that inept Youssef Bin Bandar.

He was confident that El Fadl would do a much better job than his predecessor and that it would, hopefully, not be necessary to get rid of him, as he was forced to do with Bin Bandar. Algosaibi was still intensely angry and felt like killing Bin Bandar again every time he thought of how the man had missed the golden opportunity to abduct Professor Carter Devereux, as well as the loss of that irreplaceable text, the Sirralnnudam.

He grinned to himself when his thoughts turned to

Hassan Al-Suleiman, also known as the Sultan of Syria, and his True Sons of the Prophet. If ever there was a wise business decision he had made, it was going into partnership with Hassan. As Algosaibi sat staring at the luxurious Persian carpet on the floor of his lounge, sipping his coffee, he wished it was physically possible to pat himself on the back.

It was his foresight to study and follow Hassan's rise to power, to research him and his men and pick the time to engage with him that enhanced the power he felt within himself. The allegiance with True Sons of the Prophet was going to play a vital role in his plans. Hassan was a worthy leader, an intelligent man but unfortunately, he had a very limited vision. However, that was not an issue yet. All that counted, for now, was that the Sultan of Syria's influence was rapidly expanding.

Hassan was shrewd – he made sure that the True Sons of the Prophet maintained excellent relations with ISIS. His forces would never oppose ISIS, and he ensured that they understood that both groups subscribed to the same Wahhabi ideology.

The difference was ISIS conquered and ruled by fear while the True Sons of the Prophet won over the hearts and the minds of the people. They brought peace and prosperity to the war-weary populace. Therefore, Hassan was adored and respected wherever he and his armies set foot. He and his men received a hero's welcome in every city and town where they showed up. Those who lived under ISIS rule implored him on a daily basis to come and liberate them from the fear and oppression incurred at the will of ISIS.

Algosaibi knew that the day was fast approaching when ISIS would wake up and realize that Hassan had swept the country from under their feet. He also realized that it was probably going to be too late for ISIS to rectify their mistake.

With their endless posturing about their barbaric atrocities, which was leaving a trail of blood and destruction across Syria and Iraq, ISIS had been inviting their own destruction. It was just a matter of time until the world would have enough of ISIS tyranny and join him to wipe them out.

Hassan's military forces had the best trained and disciplined soldiers in the Middle Eastern theater of war, and his unit of highly skilled, secret, Special-Forces could be counted among the best of all the armies of the Middle Eastern countries.

Syria would soon be under Hassan's complete control, and he had already commenced top-secret exploratory missions into Iraq and Egypt.

Algosaibi was confident that he was betting on the right horse in this race. It was only a pity that the horse would have to be eliminated later. But, until then, he still had a lot of important races to run.

His thoughts were interrupted by his secretary informing him that his emissary, Wasif Tahan, had returned from his visit to the Institute of Scientific Research and Development south of Mecca. Algosaibi was one of the investors and directors of the Institute and as such had sent Tahan on a tour of inspection on his behalf. Now he was here to report his findings.

Tahan was shown into the lounge and welcomed by Algosaibi, who offered him something to eat and drink while inviting him to take a seat. For the next two hours, Tahan gave him a detailed account of his visit and the status of the projects in progress.

Algosaibi's interest spiked when the conversation turned

to the respirocyte project. Tahan narrated about the good work Dr. Devereux was doing, the change of approach, and the rapid progress they had made since she took control of the project. Algosaibi was pleased; at least one part of the late Bin Bandar's otherwise failed missions was starting to show promising results.

However, with the mention of Dr. Devereux's name, Algosaibi couldn't help but feel the anger rising within him again when he thought of her husband, Professor Carter Devereux, who would also be at the Institute were it not for Bin Bandar's incompetence.

"Wasif," Algosaibi started. "What is the real state of affairs in the search for the ancient nuclear weapons?"

"Sir, unfortunately, that is the part of my report which is not as encouraging as the preceding. The researchers have many ancient texts they are studying, but I believe they are feeling their way around in the dark. Since the stream of information from Professor Devereux has dried up, they seem to have become directionless."

Algosaibi shook his head and muttered. "If only Youssef had done a better job when he had the chance …" He had his hands in a steeple under his chin. "We have to get that project back on track. It is a matter of urgency."

"Yes sir, I agree. Is there anything in particular that you want me to do about that?"

Algosaibi waved his hand. "No, don't worry about that now; I will take care of it. Thank you very much for your report. You have done a good job."

Tahan stood, bowed slightly towards Algosaibi and left.

Ibrahimi El Fadl just got his first assignment. I just need to inform him about it. Algosaibi thought with a grin on his face.

He would get Ibrahimi El Fadl and Daiyan Nasser, the Director of the ISRD, to work together to make contact with Nate Gordon of Competitive Response Solutions again. They would have to start collecting information and help them plan the next mission.

The nuclear project was dead in the water without the expertise of Professor Devereux. He had to be captured and moved to the ISRD.

Chapter Seventeen

SHE WILLED HIM TO FIND IT

Mackenzie was a bit nervous the first few days after Nasser put her in charge of the respirocyte research. It wasn't that she was uncertain about what had to be done; she had a firm handle on that. No, she was concerned about the reaction from her colleagues, the Three Stooges: Andon, Rameez, and Duyi. Heaven only knew what was to be expected from them.

However, she'd worked with invidious colleagues before and knew it was best not to confront them, but rather to try and get their cooperation. As expected, the three stooges were quite stiff-necked the first few days, but with her professional and friendly approach, she had them wrapped around her little finger within a week or two. Part of their amenable attitude could be ascribed to the fact that they also knew it would take only one word from Mackenzie to have Nasser come down on them like a ton of bricks.

All animal and human experiments were halted immediately, and the animals were removed from their cages. Nasser told her that the animals would be taken good care of and, where possible, set free. Mackenzie doubted that he was truthful but, at least, she wouldn't have them on her conscience anymore.

She and her new team went back to the drawing board. They started by looking at the texts that Mackenzie found in the Books of the Elders of Medicine. They had to figure out, through trial and error, how to create oxygen-filled microparticles covered with a layer of fatty molecules to use as a transport medium to carry oxygen to the blood. Each molecule had to encapsulate a pocket of oxygen.

There would be significant obstacles to overcome. One of the most challenging was the body's rejection response to foreign matter, something that was one of the main reasons that the previous experiments didn't work. It killed the subjects without fail, every time the artificial respirocytes were injected.

Mackenzie insisted that they map out the entire process and document everything. She had them consider every possible angle and side effect before they proceeded. Every now and then one of the stooges would comment about the slow and tedious process. Mackenzie ignored it most of the times but occasionally she had to remind them of the end results of their previous methods and Nasser's displeasure with them.

Nasser paid them daily visits to find out about their progress and from time to time he would praise Mackenzie and her team for the excellent work they were doing. Nasser was beginning to feel confident that they were now on the right track and that they would produce a pleasing result to the board of directors.

The work and Liam kept Mackenzie's mind occupied, but thoughts about Carter were never far from her. As the days and weeks passed without seeing or hearing any word of Carter, she began to be plagued by thoughts that threatened to send her into a crippling depressive state. *Was Carter still alive? Did they kill him when they captured Liam and me and they aren't telling me?*

Mackenzie had already deduced from Nasser's vague and evasive answers and body language, whenever she asked when she would be able to see her husband again, that Carter was not at the Institute. That did nothing to relieve her anxiety or help her fight the idea that Carter might be dead. One thing she knew was that she could not allow those thoughts to control her life. It was vital to survive and remain positive for Liam.

Part of her research work was to continue digging in ancient texts to find more information and maybe even the breakthrough she was hoping for since she set out on this quest a few years ago. In this regard, Nasser kept his promise to locate and supply her with copies and in some instances the original texts she wanted.

Someone Mackenzie was not allowed to meet did the translation of the documents. She explained to Nasser that it would be much more productive if she could have the person with her, but Nasser refused, actually getting visibly upset when she asked. Mackenzie knew he was intelligent enough to see the logic of her request, but it was obvious there was another reason for his strange behavior.

Mackenzie's brain never stopped working on finding a way to get a message out about the fact that she and Liam were alive. But the answer remained elusive. She had no idea where they were, nor had she seen a way to communicate with anyone on the outside. She realized that she could not risk talking to any of her coworkers about it. If she were discovered doing so, Nasser would immediately take Liam away from her.

She was surprised to find a reference to the Sirralnnudam while reading the translations of some ancient Sanskrit texts. Something stirred in her mind when she saw the reference to the book. At first, she didn't know what her mind was trying to tell her, but as she pondered on it, everything fell into place. *I might just have found a way to get a message out of this prison.* Her hands were shaking when she filed the document away.

That afternoon, or what her watch was telling her was afternoon; Nasser arrived at her desk for his daily progress report.

"Dr. Nasser I made a fascinating discovery today," she said. "I found a reference in one of those Sanskrit texts to the Sirralnnudam." She paused to allow her words to register.

"So it's back to haunt us again." Nasser was shaking his head. "The loss of the Sirralnnudam is such a tragedy. I just wish there was something we could do about it."

"I have an idea. It is a very longshot, but I think it's worth a try."

"What would that be Dr. Devereux?"

"There is the remote chance that the book kept in Armenia was not the only one. I suggest you launch a global search for another copy of it. And by global search I mean get the word out to rare book collectors, libraries, universities, archeologist, private collectors, artifact dealers, and such. Put a big price on a copy of the book. We don't need the original we only need a readable copy. Who knows, the person who stole the one in Armenia might even come forward for the right price?"

She was glad her smile was hidden behind the niqab when she saw Nasser nodded slowly. "I guess it's worth a try." He said. "We don't lose anything and have everything to gain. Let me see what I can organize. But don't get your hopes up too high yet." He smiled as he got up.

Mackenzie could feel her hands shaking again with excitement. It was not much, but it was a glimmer of light. She knew a lot of things would have to fall in place for her plan to work, but as Nasser said, it was worth a try. There was nothing to lose and everything to gain.

Nasser was also excited. Maybe, just maybe, Dr. Devereux's plan could produce results. He would have to get permission to contract Competitive Response Solutions to do the work for them. He needed to speak with Nate Gordon.

That night, after Liam was asleep when she ordinarily set her mind free to wander around Freydis, Mackenzie instead prayed that Carter was alive and that he would discover the copy of the Sirralnnudam on that golden key ring with the hidden flash drive.

She willed him to find it.

Chapter Eighteen

WHAT HAVE YOU GOT THERE GIRL?

The six weeks away from the office did Hunter Patrick a world of good. He felt rested and energized when he took his seat behind his desk again. James gave him a detailed overview of what had transpired during his absence and handed the wheel back to him. James left out the details of the suspicions he and Irene had about the mole inside A-Echelon.

Hunter was glad to hear that Carter was doing well, under the circumstances, and would be returning to Freydis shortly.

James gave him an update on the progress they'd made to find replacements for Mackenzie and Carter. For the latter it proved to be a challenge. James had a few people in mind, but he had to talk to Carter first, to see if he would be prepared to be involved, even if only in an advisory capacity.

When James finished his report, Hunter was satisfied that James had done a sterling job. He ended the meeting with, "Well done good and faithful slave."

James was glad he could move the burden off to Hunter and get back to work. His first stop was at Irene's office where they discussed Mackenzie's and Carter's replacements. They agreed that James should go and visit Carter at Freydis. He would give Ahote a call first to get an independent opinion of how Carter was actually holding up and if it would be a good time to talk to him about work.

Carter made a habit returning to the cave whenever he felt the loss of Mackenzie and Liam beginning to drag him down. He knew that once there, away from everyone, he always gained a clearer insight into how he was feeling and how to move forward again.

Seeking that insight and direction, he was once again visiting the cave, but this time, it was different. This visit left him with a lot more mystery than he'd ever imagined could exist, and he'd known a fair bit in his time.

Having set up his camp, he left the horse free to wander around, knowing it wouldn't go far and would come when he whistled, he went down to the river for a long and power-inducing swim. Swimming was now part of his routine at the cave, and once more it was followed by the complete freedom he felt without clothes as he raced up and down the grasslands shouting and yelling and forcing his lungs to take in great gasps of pure, untainted air.

Tired out, yet exhilarated, he returned to his camp and settled down to cook something. Later he would meditate.

Strangely it was in these times that he felt closest to Mackenzie and wondered if her ghost was nearby. Although he believed it was nigh on impossible, he sometimes talked to her anyway, hoping that somehow she could hear him, was there with him. But sadly, he never heard an answer, not even a hint of a feeling.

Usually, Keeva and Loki would fall into his routine with him, but things were different this time. He had yet to learn how different.

The first thing Carter discovered when he patted Keeva's flanks was a small bulge there that had not been present before. He looked carefully at her "Keeva, are you going to have babies?"

She returned his look and moved around a bit so he could feel the other side and under her tummy, yes the bulge was real. The thrill that ran through Carter was incredible. *How is it I can feel such joy at Keeva and Loki's expected family? But I do, and I won't deny it.*

He settled back, leaning against a log he'd brought forward and spread his sleeping bag over. For the moment, all felt right with the world.

Keeva nudged his shoulder; looking up he saw she had something in her mouth. He frowned, "What have you got there girl?"

She dropped it in his lap, turned and went into the cave. Returning a few minutes later with another item, she also dropped this in his lap.

He picked them up. To his surprise one of the things was a favorite hair clasp Mackie thought she'd lost, and the other was a small stuffed teddy bear, somewhat worse for wear, it was Liam's, also believed to be lost.

He put them on the ground at Keeva's feet, "You can have them lass, you need something to remember them by too."

Once again she put them in his lap and stared at him. Loki joined her, watching with deep intent. Carter frowned, what was going on? To see if he could understand more, he once again put the items on the ground further away. Keeva, just as determined, picked them up and gave them back to him, this time licking his hand as she dropped them in his lap, and stopped him from picking them up again.

"Okay, you want me to keep these?" Both wolves stepped back and lay down in their usual place. It occurred to him they were using the cave as their own, which felt right, no doubt Keeva would give birth there when her time came.

A couple of days later after his return from the cave, he went over to Bly and Ahote's for lunch, taking the curious items with him. Curious, not in themselves, but that Keeva had given them to him.

Putting them on the table after dinner, he told Bly and Ahote about them and asked what they made of the 'gifts,' as he was calling them.

Bly picked them up and held them for a moment; her hands tingled ever so slightly. She stood and went out onto the back porch where she could see the wolves. They had followed Carter from his place.

"Don't they usually go away once you get home, Carter?"

He nodded, "Yes, usually they just go back to being wolves again. Why?"

"Well, they are here now and look as if they have no intention of retiring to the wild just yet."

Carter and Ahote joined her on the porch. "I haven't told you yet; Keeva's pregnant."

Bly could hear the excitement in Carters voice and nudged Ahote, "Listen to him; you'd think he was going to be a grandfather."

Had that statement been from anyone else Carter would

have shriveled up inside, but Bly saying it just made him grin.

"I'm going to try something, Carter. Take a seat and don't move okay? Pet, can you go back inside, so Carter is on his own?"

With the arrangement as she wanted it, Bly picked up the two gifts and went over to the wolves. "So, would you like to tell me about these?"

Dark gold eyes sought out her almost black ones as they watched and assessed her. She put the gifts down on the ground, and instantly Keeva picked them up and put them back in Bly's hands.

"Hmm, so there is more to this than you just wanting a keepsake isn't there." She put them on the ground again and stepped back.

Keeva looked long and hard at her; then her attention went to Carter. Several minutes passed before the wolf carefully picked up both items and, breaking every rule in the wolf codebook, went over to the house, up the steps and firmly put them in Carter's hands.

Once done, she stared at him intently for a moment, then turned, and firmly left, gathering Loki on the way back to the wild.

Carter stared down at his gifts more than a little stunned by the experience. Ahote, who had watched the proceedings from a window, came outside just as Bly sat down on the porch beside Carter.

"Well, I don't know what to make of this. I would never have believed it had I not seen it happen." Carter paused thoughtfully. "What does it mean?"

Bly took a deep breath; she didn't want to tell Carter what she thought. How could she give him any false hope when he seemed to be getting better every day?

Instead, she said. "How will we ever know? I think they feel your pain and sorrow, and this is their way of giving comfort. Trying to tell you they also miss Mackenzie and Liam."

Carter slowly nodded as he stared out at the trees where the wolves had disappeared.

Ahote stood up "I think it's time we have something stronger than coffee and give a salute to those magnificent creatures."

The next day James called Ahote and inquired after Carter "How's he doing, Ahote? Is there any change in him? Is he getting stronger?"

"Jim you wouldn't believe how much better he is. He's been working on his physical fitness program, his meditation, and is walking like he could carry the world on his shoulders."

"So you reckon he could stand a visit from me?"

"I think he'd welcome it."

"That's great news. I'll call him now and arrange to spend a few days with him this coming week."

Chapter Nineteen

YOU CAN DO THE MATH

There was a small mirror in Mackenzie's bathroom that she used to fix her hair or make sure she was looking acceptable, not that anyone saw under the jilbab and niqab. She could have painted her face blue, and no one would notice. It was hard seeing the changes in herself as the weeks went by; she was looking tired and stressed, and her red hair looked lank and tired. *I suppose it's to be expected since it's constantly covered in black and never sees the sunshine anymore,* Mackenzie sighed. She didn't feel well either; she lacked energy and had a sense of having put on weight, although she very much doubted it given the limited diet she was afforded.

This morning as she dried herself after her shower she ran her hands over her body, noting its lack of muscle strength, but when looking in the mirror, she was also concerned to see that her nipples were much darker. She frowned then moved the mirror down and saw the brown stain from her navel to her pubis, signifying pregnancy. "That's ridiculous; of course, I'm not," she whispered to herself. As the realization deepened within her, she thought to herself with horror. *I can't be! Not here, not now, not without Carter here to share this with!* Then she recalled she hadn't had a period in all her weeks of incarceration, and the nausea was only now beginning to abate.

"But that's normal enough, given the circumstances, I'm sure," she ran her hands over her lower tummy and realized it was not as flat as she was used to.

As her racing mind calmed, she looked at herself in the mirror again, "Good Grief! I'm pregnant." She quickly recalled the last time she and Carter had been together and then counted the weeks since then. It was three months. "Okay, I'm in my second trimester. Well, Little One, now what are we going to do about you? Here I've been thinking you were just bad food and stress, and all the time you were hiding there and not telling me."

A sudden thrill ran through her even as she had to consider the difficulties she would be facing in the next few months. *Unless something happens and we escape.* "Hmm… well now, this sort of puts a stop to that doesn't it, eh?" She told her image in the mirror, "I can't see myself clambering over walls and running anywhere once this little bundle begins to make its presence known."

She shook her head with mock severity. She could hear Carter saying, *"Mackie you chose the damnedest time to do this. After all, we've been trying for almost a year, and I was beginning to worry you would never become pregnant again, and yet here you are, doing it the hard way."*

She pulled her black jilbab over her head and dropped it to the floor, then pulled it out from her body, laughing, well I won't have to worry about pregnancy clothing will I, this will cover us very nicely. Putting on her niqab, she set forth to find Seema and tell her what she'd discovered.

Seema was never far away, after all, she was her guard, but they had also become friends. She was the only woman Mackenzie felt comfortable with, so it seemed giving the news to Seema was the best thing to do. It also meant that Seema could organize an obstetrician for her when the time came.

To her relief, when she was called away from her work a few days later, it was to be introduced to Dr. Gabor, Ameera Gabor, and Mackenzie liked her immediately.

A thorough check-up confirmed Mackenzie was indeed pregnant, but also stressed and tired, and would need more rest than she had been getting. Dr. Gabor also insisted Mackenzie called her Ameera, which Mackenzie liked - it felt friendly.

Seema had told Nasser of course, and he was distantly pleasant about it, but it was made clear it wasn't men's business. Only women get excited over a baby, at least until it was born, and if it was a boy, then things changed.

Mackenzie didn't care, she had a new life inside her, and that very afternoon she told Liam. Maybe Liam just needed something a little bit extra in his life, for his eyes lit up like sparklers as he hugged her in delight. "Do you think it will be a girl?" he asked. "Mom, I seriously need a little sister."

"Well, you can do the math Liam, there's a fifty percent chance it will be."

"Oh Mommy, very funny. When will you have it? Will we still be here?"

We have about six more months to wait, and I suppose it will be born here, I can't imagine us being able to get home in time for it."

He shook his head, "No I suppose not," He sighed and turned away, tears welling up in his eyes.

"Liam?" she held his arm.

"Oh Mom, I miss them all so badly. Dad and Bly, Ahote and my pets, I can't believe we'll never see them again."

"I miss them too, Liam, but don't think that way. I know we will see them again; it's just that it's not going to happen quite yet." Liam had grown a lot over the past three months, gone was the little boy. He'd grown tall and lean, and in many ways looked a lot like her with his bronze hair, but his character was so much like his father's that it made Mackenzie's heart lurch at times to see Carter's image flit across his son's face.

Chapter Twenty

WHERE DO WE START?

Carter met James at Quebec City's Jean Lesage International Airport, and soon they were in the air again on their way to Freydis in the Piper Seminole. James peered out the windows, once again stunned by the beauty of the landscape below as they spoke of Carter's physical and emotional health and what he was doing to keep himself busy.

Carter got the espresso machine going while James unpacked his bags and settled into his room, and then they sat down to relax with their coffee on the deck outside the cabin. Jeha, who stayed with Bly and Ahote while Carter went to fetch James, must have heard the plane return for she came charging up the stairs of the deck towards Carter and leaped onto his lap, soon after they sat down.

"Where did this little pup come from?" Rhodes inquired in surprise.

"It's Jeha, Liam's dog. She was with my in-laws all this time and came home with me when I left the hospital. The little bugger has crept into my heart, Jim. I can't tell you how much comfort she has brought me the last few months," Carter was scratching Jeha's ears and back.

Jeha jumped off Carter's lap, ran over to James, gave him one look, and jumped right onto his lap without any invitation. James just laughed as he patted the little animal. He loved dogs. His wife Carolyn kept three of them, and they were like children in their house.

While they were enjoying their coffee, James gave Carter an update on matters at A-Echelon and then got to the main reason for his visit.

"Carter, I guess there is no easy way to approach the subject, so I will just get right to the point."

Carter nodded for James to continue. "Other than wanting to see you and spend a bit of time with you, I'm here to talk to you about the nuclear project and also Mackenzie's project. Is it okay with you if we talk about that?"

"No problem Jim. I sort of expected that to be on the agenda."

"Okay, that's good," James smiled. "I'll start with Mackenzie's project first. A few months ago, shortly before Hunter went on stress leave, we - Hunter, Irene and I - discussed her project and decided her work is too important not to continue what she started. We agreed it was necessary to find a replacement who can continue her research."

"I'm pleased to hear that," Carter said, "and I think she would want that." A dark shadow of sadness passed through his eyes, and he paused briefly before continuing, "Although Mackie's research didn't fall into my area of expertise, I would like to help in any way I can to progress what she started."

"Thank you for that Carter. It's good to hear you talk like that."

"I owe it to her and Liam, Jim." Carter's voice trembled a little, and he turned his face away. "Continuing her work and being part of it is one way I can honor her memory."

James nodded his head and gave his friend a few moments of silence to regroup. "The second matter is the ancient nuclear project. I'm sure I don't have to bring up the critical nature of that project again. The problem is, since you've been injured, the project has come to a complete stop, and that has become a big worry not only to me, but also to Hunter and the President.

"We've been trying to identify someone we can approach to carry on from where you and I left off, but that has not been an easy task. However, I have to admit that part of the delay is because I wanted to talk to you first." Rhodes took a deep breath and continued, "The thing is Carter, I need you badly; you are about all I have, and trying to find a replacement is proving impossible, and believe me, I've tried."

James didn't get a chance to continue. Carter was shaking his head vehemently. "No, Jim. Count me out. I will not get involved in that again," he said emphatically. "My involvement in that project is what caused the death of my family. I'm done, and that's final." Carter had risen from his chair and was shaking, clearly very upset.

James was taken aback by Carter's extreme reaction. It was the first time he understood that Carter was blaming himself and felt guilty for the death of his wife and son. He held his hands up in surrender. "Easy, my friend, I'm sorry. I apologize. I won't pursue this any further. But please, will you allow me to make just one more comment before we step off the topic?"

Carter's face was pale, and he hesitated. Finally, he nodded for James to continue.

"I'm not going to tell you that I understand your pain and suffering because I don't. I can't even begin to imagine it. But there is one thing I do know, and that is you are wrong to blame yourself for what happened to your family." Carter started shaking his head again, but James held his hand up again, "Just hear me out. I don't want to argue with you about it Carter, but there is no valid reason whatsoever to blame yourself."

"Stop!" Carter said. He opened his mouth to respond further, but instead, turned his back to James and remained quiet, staring at the mountains and trees in the distance. James knew the subject was closed, and he would have to find another scientist.

James got up, gathered their empty mugs, and went inside to make them each another cup coffee. When he returned to the deck, Carter was once again seated and appeared to have gained a measure of control over his raw emotions. Handing him the cup of fresh coffee, James took his seat, and they drank in silence for a few minutes before Carter told him Ahote and Bly had invited them to dinner and asked if he would like to walk over instead of riding in the cart.

James agreed to the walk, and they were on their way. Jeha bounded ahead of them, chasing grasshoppers and barking at butterflies. They laughed at her antics, and the comfortable companionship descended between them once again.

Seeing Ahote and Bly again was good for James, and during the meal, the three men decided it was time for James to experience trout fishing on Freydis.

The sun was just touching the horizon the following morning when they set out on horseback to Ahote and Liam's favorite fishing spot. Bly made sure they had enough food and drink for a day out in the wild.

Not long after they unsaddled near a patch of trees at a bend in the river, James spotted two wolves and whispered to Carter, "My friend, we've got ourselves a problem." He nodded his head in the direction of the wolves, which were standing about 20 yards away.

Carter immediately saw an opportunity to have a bit of fun at James' expense. He winked at Ahote, who got the message and played along.

"Don't move guys. Keep your eyes on them, don't show them you're scared, or you could be dead," Ahote whispered, his eyes sparkling with humor that James couldn't see.

Planting his two feet shoulder width apart, James folded his arms and tried his best to stare the wolves into retreat. It was clear the man was severely scared.

Ahote had to chuckle at James' pose. He spoke quietly, "Okay listen to me carefully. You two stay here, keep looking at them, and I will go and talk to them."

"Shit man! Are you crazy? They'll rip you apart," James whispered fiercely.

"Don't worry James my ancestors were renowned wolf whisperers," Ahote replied, deadpan. "It's in my genes as well. This is the only hope we have."

"Man, I don't know about that," Carter played along. "I think that's a stupid idea."

Ahote ignored them and started moving forward slowly. The wolves looked perplexed. They must have been wondering what was wrong with their two-legged friends.

Loki had turned his head sideways as if to ask, *what is wrong with you?*

Ahote got to about two yards from them and spoke very softly while he went down on one knee. "Don't worry we are just having fun with our friend, that new man," he smiled.

The wolves sat down and looked at Ahote with their heads on one side.

"I'll be damned!" James exclaimed as quietly as he could while looking at Carter. "Have you ever seen anything like that?"

Carter could not hold it in anymore and fell onto the grass rolling with laughter to James' considerable consternation.

"Shit man! Stop that before they attack us! If you …" James paused a moment to reconsider the situation. "Carter, what the hell is going on here?" James shouted as he realized he was the center of the joke.

Ahote got up, shaking with laughter as he walked back. The wolves followed him but stopped a few yards away from James and Carter, and sat down again.

When Carter got off the ground and managed to stop laughing, he explained, "Jim those are Mackie's wolves. Keeva and Loki. They won't attack us. You can relax …" Carter started laughing again, "I wish I'd had a camera to film what just happened."

Ahote had a big grin on his face. This was the first time since Carter had returned to Freydis that he'd seen him laugh. It was good to see and hear that again.

James was still a bit wary, and he kept glancing at the two animals. He stepped back to put a little more space between himself and them. When he was about five yards away, he stopped. "Mackie's wolves? You're not going to try and tell me she managed to domesticate them?"

"No, Jim they aren't domesticated," Carter said "but I will have to give you the history. I'm sure you won't believe half of what I'm going to tell you, but Ahote is my witness, it's all true."

Carter told him about the night when he asked Mackenzie to marry him while they were camped at the cave and the wolves suddenly appeared and didn't leave, but spent the night a little distance from them. He recounted how he woke up one morning on their honeymoon, and Mackenzie was gone from his side, but before he could start searching for her, she came walking out of the woods with the two wolves keeping pace next to her. "She actually patted them before they went back into the forest."

James stopped him, "Carter, you're not pulling another fast one on me, are you?"

"No, Jim, it's all true. But wait, there's a lot more."

James nodded and Carter continued to tell him how the wolves appeared, every time, shortly after they arrived on Freydis. "When we leave, they disappear again.

"That was until the night of the bomb explosion when they turned up at Ahote's place. I'll let Ahote tell you about that."

By now they were sitting in the shade of one of the big trees, the fishing expedition entirely forgotten. James listened with an open mouth as Ahote told him everything that happened that fateful night.

"What do you think it means, Ahote?" James asked. "I know animals have senses that humans don't have, and I've heard some incredible stories about animal intuition in my time, but this is weird, fantastic even."

Ahote just shook his head. "All I can think of is that they

were trying to tell us something had gone wrong with Carter, Mackie and Liam. And as you know, we only found out about the tragedy two days later, when you phoned us."

"I still owe you and Bly a sincere apology for not calling earlier. It's impossible to express how embarrassed I still feel about it," James looked at Ahote.

Ahote waved his hand. "That's water under the bridge Jim, water under the bridge. I might have done the same had fate reversed our situations."

They fell quiet for a bit before Carter spoke again, "Now let me tell you about my most recent experience with Keeva and Loki."

James looked up to see Carter smiling again. So the story of the gifts was told, and how Keeva had put aside her 'wolf code' and taken the gifts up on the porch and put them back into Carter's hands.

By the time Carter finished his narrative, James was on his feet. His face had paled. While he had been listening to Carter and Ahote, unbeknown to him, his subconscious mind had been working overtime connecting the dots and now all of a sudden it flooded into his conscious mind. He was breathless and overawed.

"Carter, Ahote, we have to get back home now. Please don't ask me why. I will not tell you until I have spoken to someone I know. No matter the outcome of that conversation I will tell you, but for now, please don't ask me. Can we go now?"

Carter and Ahote were dumbfounded. They exchanged a look, shrugged, and started saddling the horses. James was almost feverish in his haste to get back to the homestead, and they took off at a gallop, leaving the wolves behind.

Carter and Ahote were worried. They spent the ride

wondering, and trying to figure out what was going on in James' mind.

When they brought the horses to a walk so that the animals could get a breather, James attempted to break the tension.

"Carter, how do the wolves handle Jeha? I would have thought they would see her as a tasty little snack."

"In the wolf world, they ignore the young unless they are training them. These two don't recognize her; they ignore her and she, as you will see, behaves so well around them you have to believe she's terribly impressed with being ignored by such big animals," he laughed.

James smiled, "You will have to talk me through that again sometime. It sounds a lot like psychological mumbo-jumbo to me."

"So what's your take on this strange behavior of the wolves?" James continued, trying to divert their minds away from his sudden urgency to get back home.

"It's difficult to describe it, Jim. Sometimes I just stand in awe; sometimes I attempt to figure it out, but most of the time I am frustrated with my inability to communicate with them or understand what they are trying to tell me. Humans have shared the planet with animals for hundreds of thousands of years, if not millions. We're supposed to be the advanced ones, yet we haven't even begun to understand them. In fact, I am convinced they comprehend us much better than we do them."

Ahote nodded. "I can tell you Jim, animals are far more intelligent than we have ever given them credit for."

While they were talking, they had covered the last few miles to the homestead, and James left them to unsaddle the horses while he went straight to the study and connected his satellite phone to the secure line, which A-Echelon had installed for Carter and Mackenzie when they became part of the team.

As Carter and Ahote cared for the horses, they exchanged their thoughts and feelings about the events of the past hour.

James waited impatiently for the phone to connect and once he was sure it was safe to make the call, he punched in Ben Friedman's speed dial number. It was 6:00 pm in Tel Aviv, seven hours ahead.

Ben answered almost immediately.

"Ben, sorry to trouble you after hours," James teased. "I know you work regular office hours these days and don't like to be disturbed after five, but I have an extremely urgent request for you."

"James, you know in our line of work there is no such thing as regular office hours. What's the urgency, my friend?"

James explained what he wanted Ben to do for him and Ben told him to keep his phone with him. He would call him back within the hour.

When the call ended, James looked at his watch. An hour can be a very long time when you have to sit and watch every second tick by. He collected his laptop from his bedroom and connected it to the second secure line to check his work email. At the 60-minute mark, he looked at his watch for the hundredth time, groaned, and got up to make himself a coffee. Carter and Ahote were sitting outside on the deck and didn't notice him enter the kitchen. *Good. I'm not ready to answer questions yet.*

He had just returned from the kitchen with the mug of coffee in his hand when his satellite phone started ringing. It was Ben. James' voice was quivering with anticipation when he answered.

"Ben, are you absolutely sure? Have you personally checked and double-checked this? There can be no mistakes, Ben. You know what the impact of that would be to my friend. He had to go through it once; it was hell, and it is not over yet. I just can't put him through it again."

James listened and asked a few more questions. He was trying to write something down on the piece of paper in front of him, but his hand was shaking so much he dropped the pen, so he decided to leave it where it was and just listen.

"Okay, Ben. Thank you very much. I can't begin to thank you for all your help with this."

They said their goodbyes and James got up, paced the room for a few minutes to regain his composure, and walked out to the deck where Carter and Ahote were waiting for him.

"Ahote, can we go over to your place? Bly will want to hear what I have to say too."

Bly was surprised when she saw the men coming back from fishing so early. She was even more surprised when she realized they weren't carrying any fish, and they were coming straight to the house. Carter and Ahote both looked puzzled, but James's face wore an expression she couldn't read, and she felt her stomach clench with anxiety. When they entered the kitchen, she invited them so sit at the table and took a seat next to her husband.

James shook his head slightly, wondering where to begin. He realized he had kept everyone in suspense for long enough. *But where to start?* At the beginning was not the right approach in these circumstances.

He took a deep breath, focused his eyes directly on Carter alone, and said, "I have good reason to believe that Mackenzie and Liam are still alive."

Bly jumped up shouting, "I knew it! I knew it! That's what Loki and Keeva were telling us! I knew it!" Then she started crying.

Ahote was on his feet trying to calm his wife down, but then James' statement struck him like a ten-pound hammer right between the eyes and he slumped back into his chair and started laughing. "Mackie! Liam! You're coming back. Oh my God. You're coming back. You're alive!"

All of a sudden the two of them stopped and looked at Carter. He looked as if he had seen a ghost. He was motionless, staring into nothingness. Then they saw a tear slowly dribbling down his cheek. He opened his mouth to say something, but no sound came out. His mouth closed again.

James and the other two waited for Carter to speak.

Finally, his voice tight with emotion, he said one word, "How?"

"Okay Carter, I have to start at the beginning, and I hope you won't despise me for what you are about to hear. I've had my doubts about their death from the very first day. Even before I arrived back in Israel. Don't ask me why; there is no rhyme or reason to it. It was just this deep-seated, gut feeling that they weren't dead." He stopped and drew breath, "Maybe I was on the same wavelength as Keeva and Loki, I don't know." He stopped again, shook his head and continued, "I couldn't tell you what I was thinking. If I were wrong, I would put you through the terrible sorrow of the death of your loved ones twice, and I just wouldn't do that to you."

Carter kept his dark eyes on James and remained silent.

"Right from the beginning I had my doubts about this being just a random attack, I couldn't believe that either you or Mackenzie had been compromised, but it had to stay up on the board as a possibility. Both of you were working on some highly important stuff, and yours more dangerous than anything we have ever worked on. I had to consider, right from the beginning, that you might have been the target of the attack, but now I am convinced both you and Mackenzie were the targets. That's why I arranged guards to be placed outside your door at the hospital.

In the days that followed, as people were recovering from their wounds and others came forward, statements were collected, and a picture slowly unfolded. One of the descriptions that was of particular interest to me was by a woman who said she'd seen a white van with tinted windows draw up at the restaurant and pull away again just before the explosion. She had no other information and was the only one out of more than fifty witnesses who saw that van.

Then the forensic results came in, showing that none of the DNA results matched Mackenzie or Liam. With those results, the only logical conclusion was to assume that the two of them were vaporized in the explosion."

Carter was slowly recovering from the shock of the news, "Go on."

"A very fragile, old man in his 80's who survived his injuries in the blast only to sustain a stroke a day later was in critical condition for a long time, but he did recover enough to give a statement about a week ago. In his statement, he told the investigators he'd seen the white van too. He was just steps away when he saw it pull up in front of the restaurant, three men jumped out, grabbed two people and put black bags over their heads and pushed them into the van before it drove off again. Seconds later a gray van drove into the restaurant, and the bomb exploded. As you already know, everyone thinks it's a miracle that you came out alive while everyone else inside perished."

James stopped to draw breath, "What my contact told me about the old man's statement, had me in a heat of excitement, and then the depths of complete despair. The old man said that one of the people they captured had long blond hair. Well, that ruled out Mackenzie with her red hair. I thought that was conclusive evidence that Mackenzie and Liam were dead."

The man is old and fragile, and Yiddish is his mother tongue. His Hebrew apparently was not that good. However, my contact assured me that the investigator was confident that the old man's mind was lucid and that he understood him well enough during the questioning."

"Okay, so something has now changed. What is it?" Carter prodded.

"The story that you and Ahote told me about the wolves triggered it, Carter. While I was listening to you and Ahote, I looked at those two wolves sitting there, and I had the strangest feeling they were listening and understood every word we said. Then I recalled the telephone conversation I had with my contact in Israel and remembered the old man's statement. That's when I realized no one had shown that old man a photo of Mackenzie and Liam."

Carter had paled, and his eyes had turned almost black with the intensity of emotion he was feeling.

"Those phone calls I just had in your study were with my contact in Israel. He personally went to see the old man who is still in the hospital and showed him photos of Mackenzie and Liam. The old man was unable to explain why his statement said the woman pushed into the van had blond hair. He was sure he said red hair. When he was shown Mackenzie's photo, he was absolutely positive that was the woman he saw before they put a bag over her head and she was pushed into the van along with someone else. He didn't recognize Liam from the photo he was shown, and that remains consistent with his previous statement. He said he couldn't see what the second person looked like." James fell silent.

Bly spoke first. "They are alive somewhere out there Jim, and we must find them."

Carter nodded but didn't say a word.

Ahote got up, took four bottles of cold beer out of the fridge, and placed a bottle in front of everyone. He was still shaking his head. "Mackie and Liam are alive," he kept on mumbling.

Bly was still struggling to contain her tears of joy. "Thank you Keeva and Loki. You did it. You finally got through to our stupid brains."

Carter turned to James again. "You've been to hell and back haven't you Jim? Here was I thinking I was the only one suffering, apart from Mary, Steven, and Ray. I'm so sorry."

"No apologies required my friend. None at all."

Carter nodded. "Thank you, Jim. I will never forget this as long as I live. Oh, and forget about what I told you yesterday. I've changed my mind; I'm back on board with A-Echelon."

James leaned over and shook Carter's hand. "Thank you, my friend; I'm glad to have you back."

Carter smiled. "So, where do we start?"

Chapter Twenty-One

I WAS CAPTURED

Mackenzie put her pen down and stared at the words they'd sent her from her unknown translator. She frowned in frustration. Not all of the translation was clear, a lot of it wasn't making any sense, and without the person sitting next to her for on-the-spot interaction, it was turning into a very long, tedious, and aggravating task.

These were the moments she longed for Liu and Harry. She missed them, and not only their expertise but also their friendship.

That Nasser would not allow her to work directly with the translator was more than just irritating, it was infuriating. She was sure he knew it was more than just an inconvenience; it made the situation much harder and, consequently it slowed down progress. She was equally sure he understood that, in the end, unless he capitulated and brought the translator to work with her, he would be the loser since there was nothing more she could do to make things move faster.

The three stooges were worse than useless. Unless she

practically stood over them, guiding their work, they could be considered a hindrance. She frequently had to stop what she was doing to go over and recheck something that was done incorrectly because one or other of them had become lazy or negligent.

She sat up and rubbed her eyes; *I'll need glasses next*; she thought as she stood and stretched. She smiled as she ran her hands over the small bump that had grown a bit since its discovery.

Just then the door opened and Nasser entered, indicating he wanted a word with her, so she joined him in another part of the room away from the three stooges, as was their custom. She had pondered at how insignificant they'd become since her arrival and wondered at the mystery that none of them had attempted to poison her coffee.

"How is the work progressing, Mackenzie?" he had dropped the Dr. Devereux name over the preceding weeks since he'd heard of the baby and was almost paternal with her. She wasn't quite sure how to treat this change but decided it had to be to her advantage, so she played along. *Maybe he feels he will be a surrogate grandfather,* she thought and then added, *especially if it's a boy.*

"It's not coming along well at all. There is so little I can do since I have to wait for translations only to find they are not adequate, and I have to send them back and wait again for another report. We are wasting needless time this way, and I'm sure you know it."

He nodded, accepting her irritation, "Yes, you are right; so I have decided, against my better judgment, to bring the translator here to work with you. However, there will be rules you will both have to abide by."

Mackenzie wasn't sure what she had put herself into

with her determination to get him to relent about the translator, "I'm sure both of us can manage whatever rules you wish to impose, Nasser, after all, it's the work that concerns me, not needless chatter." She was admonishing him and recognized it. Still he continued to stay calm.

"The translator will arrive this afternoon. Let me make this abundantly clear: neither of you will discuss anything outside the work you will be doing together. If there is even a hint of unrelated topics, we will return the translator, and you will lose your son. Have I made myself clear?"

"Translucent as always, Nasser." They stared hard at each other for a moment; he might have the upper hand about Liam, but she had the upper hand about her research, so, in fact, they were on par, each of them trying to unbalance the other just to score points.

He swept out of the room, and she returned to her desk, picked up her pen and began again.

Later that afternoon she was interrupted again and this time it was Seema bringing the welcome assistance of the new translator. As the person was dressed all in black like herself, Mackenzie recognized immediately that although this person was a stranger to her, she was another woman.

Mackenzie stood up to greet her, "Hello, I'm Doctor Devereux," she said extending her arm to shake hands with the other woman.

"I know who you are, Doctor Devereux." The voice was familiar, but it took Mackenzie a moment to realize whose it was, and when she did, she nearly fainted from shock. *Liu Cheun!*

"Liu, is that you?" Mackenzie asked.

"It is I, Mackenzie; it's nice to see you again."

Aware that Seema was watching, Mackenzie stepped

forward to hug Liu. "You a traitor?" Mackenzie whispered as they gave each other a hug.

"No," Liu whispered savagely, "I'm not."

They stepped back each staring into the other's eyes as Nasser appeared in the doorway.

"I see you ladies have been reunited. Now, it's back to work. You both know the rules and the consequences for breaking them. Do not break them," and with that, he was gone.

Mackenzie gathered her wits after such a shock and guided Liu to her desk. Seema stood in the background as their guard. Regardless of how friendly they'd become; Mackenzie knew without a doubt that Seema would report anything either she or Liu said that was out of line. More than that, Mackenzie had slowly come to realize that Nasser had a hold over Seema too, although she never spoke of it.

Liu pulled up a chair and joined Mackenzie at the computer screen where the recent translations were waiting. Each of them was edgy, unsure of their situation with the other. Mackenzie was shocked to her core that Liu was here, and couldn't believe it wasn't of her own volition. Her trust in her friend was severely rattled.

Liu was tongue tied, reduced to silence with shock. She'd been through so much, and to find it was Mackenzie she had been translating for reduced her to a heap of emotions impossible to express. The last thing she'd heard was that her friend and the little boy had both been killed in that terrible explosion. Silently tears ran down her cheeks, and she was thankful for the niqab that hid them from everyone. She longed to be able to explain to Mackenzie that she'd been captured and brought here against her will, but that was impossible given the rules they had to abide by.

She could feel Mackenzie's antagonism toward her, and it was breaking her heart.

"Okay then, I suppose we'd better make a start." Mackenzie's voice was business-like and hard.

Liu quelled under its impact. She drew a deep breath, "yes, okay, what do you need, I'm here for you Mackenzie, let's make this work." She hoped Mackenzie would recognize the secondary meaning her words carried.

She said she's not a traitor, and now she's telling me she's here for me? Is this true? Is she a prisoner as well? Mackenzie's doubts about Liu's voluntary involvement caused her to relax just a bit. *Maybe, over the months ahead we can get some sort of communication going,* Mackenzie thought.

Liu sensed the lessening of tension, and so they got down to business, trying to pretend all was well. Thoughts similar to those of Mackenzie's were going through Liu's mind, *neither of us is slow, or lacking in ingenuity, we'll find a way to talk that they won't know about.*

By the following morning, Liu had a plan. It entailed using their translations to pass messages to each other. It might take a little while for Mackenzie to catch on, but Liu knew she would in the end.

The day began just as every other one did. Both women were in the laboratory, the three men on Mackenzie's team were in place, and Seema has already taken a seat not far from them. Liu looked around a second time, took a deep breath, and went to work putting her plan from the night before into action.

It required taking words from the translations she knew Mackenzie was familiar with and then discussing them as if it were part of the work they were translating. Thankfully, Mackenzie had become familiar with many words that no one, other than the two of them, would be able to translate.

Liu, therefore, considered it was safe to proceed with caution.

"I was captured," were the first words she put on the screen.

Mackenzie had been deep into a part of the work that was beginning to shed some light on her research when she looked up and saw Liu's message. She did a quick double take and was, once again, thankful for the niqab.

"When?" she responded in like manner.

"Not long after you."

They stopped it there and went back to their work but over the course of the day Liu was able to relay to Mackenzie how she had been taken from an airport in Hong Kong and held captive somewhere with no idea of what was going on. All she could gather was someone wanted her for something and when the moment arrived she would understand.

Mackenzie said how sorry she was that she'd thought her a turncoat and Liu accepted her apology.

A few days later, Liu had just related to Mackenzie that she'd heard she and Liam were dead. Mackenzie asked if she had heard any news about Carter.

Liu said no, but that she'd heard there was one man who survived the explosion. He had been in the restroom inside the restaurant at the time of the explosion. She was captured before she could learn anymore.

Mackenzie's heart erupted with joy when she learned that. *Carter was alive and free! Thank you, God.*

Mackenzie told Liu what she thought. "He'll find us, I'm sure."

After Liu's arrival, the research moved a lot faster, and Nasser began to relax. Apparently both women were abiding by his rules, and that pleased him. The thing he had feared most was Liu telling Mackenzie that Carter was alive; that was a trump card he wanted to hang on to.

Hunter dropped his head into his hands and inwardly collapsed. He was feeling decidedly ill, finding it hard to breathe and his heart was racing, making him gasp for air. Sweat was beading on his forehead; he finally managed to call his secretary.

She quickly helped him out of his chair and onto the floor, called for an ambulance, and then called Irene.

Irene's advanced first aid training helped her to quickly assess the situation. She made Hunter as comfortable as possible as she helped him to sit up, "That will help, okay?"

He nodded, "Thanks, that's better."

She went on to check for other symptoms, noting his swollen legs, racing pulse, and she detected an uneven heartbeat, in his pulse. And, she realized, it's becoming even more erratic.

She said nothing until the paramedics arrived and then suggested to them he might be suffering from hypertrophic cardiomyopathy. Upon their examination, they agreed that her assessment was highly likely. They placed oxygen firmly over his nose and mouth and attached an EKG machine to his chest in case of heart failure. Then they quickly vanished down the corridor and transported him to hospital

A little later when she had the information she needed from the doctors, Irene rang James at Freydis and told him the news. "The doctors have confirmed that he had an enlarged heart, which is serious James. It's one of those things you don't recover from; it slowly kills you. It will be impossible for him to return to work, this is retirement time for Hunter."

"Oh hell, poor man. You want me back immediately, right?"

"Right James."

"I'm on my way."

Several days later, Hunter was firmly established in the hospital and now knew there would be no more workdays for him. The doctors had made it abundantly clear that, in fact, his days were severely shortened unless he adopted a relaxed and sedentary lifestyle. That included properly supervised exercise, proper food, no alcohol, and definitely no stress; only then could they say he would be able to live out his days for maybe a few more of years. It was made so clear to him, he instantly agreed to all the doctor's recommendations, and gladly handed the reins to Rhodes.

"Almost like a hot potato." James thought when he went in to visit him.

James wasn't all that sure how he felt about the radical change from being a mobile agent, as he needed to be, to Acting Director for some weeks and then quickly to Director, but figured he'd better get used to it. Nevertheless, there was a condition. He would not take the job if he couldn't have Irene appointed as his second in command, in other words, Deputy Director; he was not going to 'do a Hunter' and try to carry the burden on his own.

Luckily for him, Irene agreed, and the new management structure was immediately deployed at A-Echelon.

Chapter Twenty-Two

THEY MUST BE DESPERATE

Soon after the King made the official announcement about Ibrahimi El Fadl's appointment as the new deputy director of the General Intelligence Presidency, Xavier Algosaibi met with him to brief him about what would be expected of him during his tenure in that position.

Algosaibi lifted the veil for El Fadl and told him about the undercover operations going on at the Institute of Scientific Research and Development – ISRD - located in the Jabal Thawr Mountains, six miles south of Mecca.

El Fadl's first major assignment was to launch a new project to capture Professor Carter Devereux and transport him to the ISRD.

Algosaibi told him to secure the services of Competitive Response Solutions – CRS – to conduct all the surveillance and intelligence gathering for the mission. He explained to El Fadl that CRS had provided excellent services to them in the past and that the information they provided about the Devereux's research and movements had been precise. They were not to blame for the failure of the Armenian and

Jerusalem operations, that had been Bin Bandar's failure and he had suffered the consequences

El Fadl learned that Nate Gordon was the CRS contact person responsible for all Saudi Arabian projects and that Daiyan Nasser, Director of ISRD would facilitate his introduction to Gordon.

El Fadl was pleased and honored by Algosaibi's personal interest, support, and trust in him. He and Algosaibi saw eye to eye about the future of Saudi Arabia and the expansion of Wahhabism across the globe. By the end of the meeting, El Fadl understood the significance of the new Devereux mission entrusted to him and had no illusions about the consequences of failure.

Nasser was still contemplating Mackenzie's idea of launching a global hunt for a copy of the Sirralnnudam. This was one of those decisions that he felt was above his pay grade, and which he had always referred to Youssef Bin Bandar in the past. Nasser was not a security or intelligence expert, and it made him very uncomfortable and reluctant to make a decision like that without the authorization of someone higher up the food chain. In the end, he decided he was not going to take the risk. He would give it more time to see if someone with the necessary authority would emerge or wait for the next quarterly board meeting, two months away, to table the matter.

Nasser's problem turned out to be short-lived. He received instructions to travel to Riyadh to meet with some of the members of the ISRD Board. While attending a dinner at Algosaibi's mansion one evening, he was introduced to the new Deputy Director of GIP, Ibrahimi El Fadl.

Later that night, after dinner while all the men were gathered in the lounge, drinking coffee, smoking, and talking politics, El Fadl indicated that Nasser should follow him to Algosaibi's study for a private discussion.

In the study, El Fadl asked Nasser to make the necessary arrangements to meet with Nate Gordon and also solved Nasser's problem by authorizing the global hunt for a copy of the Sirralnnudam. It was agreed that El Fadl would discuss their requirements with Gordon when they met and contract CRS to get it for them.

Two weeks later El Fadl and his family traveled to Dubai for a short holiday before he would assume his duties as deputy director of GIP. Daiyan Nasser had persuaded Nate Gordon to make a small change in his travel plans so as to include a two-day visit to Dubai on his business trip to India.

Gordon was more than happy to accommodate the request. Since he had become the Saudi Arabia account manager, he had doubled the CRS's projects and almost tripled the income from the Kingdom. His Saudi portfolio accounted for close to thirty percent of CRS's total revenue.

The Saudi's never hesitated to pay well as long as they got results and CRS was good at producing results. CRS almost never got involved in the operational side of their clients' businesses; it was not their area of expertise, but when it came to providing substantial, timely and actionable information, CRS was unmatched. For the privilege of having that kind of information, the Saudi's didn't mind putting their hands deep into their pockets.

The room where Gordon and El Fadl would meet late at night was in a hotel where neither of them stayed. The room was booked in the name of a local resident and was swept for bugs at least three times before El Fadl arrived.

Once he was given assurance that the room was secured, he was on his own and used the service elevator from the basement to reach the room.

As arranged, Gordon turned up ten minutes after El Fadl. They recognized each other from their photographs and, thanks to Nasser acting as a mediator to set the meeting up and his glowing character reference for both of them, they trusted each other.

Gordon struck an imposing figure. He was about six five, in his mid-forties, had curly blond hair, and blue eyes. El Fadl thought Gordon's appearance spoke of Germanic or Scandinavian origins rather than English or French as his surname suggested. On Nasser's request Gordon was dressed very informally, wearing jeans, a T-shirt, Nike running shoes and New York Yankees baseball cap.

El Fadl, who wore a suit and tie every day, felt a bit out of sorts with his informal attire, but he knew it was important that he not be recognized by anyone other than Gordon. Gordon's large frame dwarfed him. He stood about five-ten in his socks, was in his late 50's, had salt and pepper hair and wore a neatly trimmed beard on his olive-skinned face.

"Mr. Gordon," El Fadl started. "Please allow me to convey greetings from a mutual friend, Daiyan Nasser of the ISRD, and also his gratitude for the outstanding job your organization did in collecting and providing information about the research and movements of the Devereuxs. Since Dr. Devereux started working for the ISRD, the respirocyte project has been moving forward in leaps and bounds."

"Thank you for that," Gordon smiled. "But please, call me Nate. Youssef and I were on a first name basis as long as we knew each other."

"Thank you, Nate," El Fadl nodded. "You may call me Ibrahimi."

With the formalities out of the way the two men sat down, each with a cup of strong Arabica coffee, and talked business.

"So Ibrahimi, I understood from Daiyan that you might have a need for our services again. Is that correct?"

Although he had an American education, El Fadl hasn't been in the USA for many years, and he had to remind himself that the American's direct, no-nonsense approach was not rudeness, but rather, efficiency.

"Yes, that is indeed the case," he stated. "As you know the Devereux mission was not as entirely successful as we had hoped it would be."

"Let's call it fifty percent successful," Gordon grinned. "It was definitely not the outcome you wanted, but I wouldn't call it a complete failure."

El Fadl was a little embarrassed but managed to hide it well, and he appreciated the fact that Gordon didn't make any derogatory comments about the botched mission. He was still contemplating how to approach the subject of the failed Armenian mission with Gordon, without making his colleagues look like a bunch of amateurs.

"So the first new assignment we have for CRS is to start a new surveillance and information gathering project on Professor Devereux. We *have* to get him to come to work for us."

Gordon managed to suppress the smile that threatened to break across his face when he heard what El Fadl said and the desperation in his voice. No sales talk would be necessary; this was going to be an easy deal. The client was desperate, and it didn't escape him that El Fadl used the words 'first new assignment' which meant there was going to be more than one assignment coming out of this meeting.

Two hours later, after at least four cups of the extra strong Arabica coffee, and few more cigars, the deal was complete. CRS would take on two projects for the ISRD. The contract price and payment plan were agreed on, and the paperwork would be handled by the lawyers and accountants over the course of the next few days. As soon as the usual 50% deposit cleared in CRS's bank account in Switzerland the projects would kick off.

The two men wished each other well, expressed their mutual gratitude for a good meeting, shook hands, and said their good-byes.

Dwayne Miller almost fell out his chair when he saw the paperwork coming across his desk a few days later. *Fifty million dollars!* He had to use all his self-control not to jump up and run around the office shouting out the amount for everyone to hear. It was the biggest single contract in the history of CRS's existence. And that was achieved during a two-hour meeting while on vacation in Dubai.

They must be desperate.

Chapter Twenty-Three

I HAVE TO FIND THEM

In his new role, James' world rapidly turned into near chaos. He took on the responsibility for all of A-Echelon's operations while having to give top priority to launching a mission to rescue Mackenzie and Liam. Coupled with that was the equally important issue of saving the world from the threat of annihilation by an ancient nuclear weapon.

His decision to appoint Irene as his second in command turned out to be a brilliant one. Irene was an excellent planner and administrator, as well as a highly skilled intelligence expert, and an experienced operator. As such, she quickly became James' confidant and right hand. She quickly expanded her already vast network of connections throughout the political and government officials' labyrinth in Washington to become James' eyes and ears in the capital.

James decided to have her assume control of both Devereux projects. As soon as he informed Carter that Irene would be stepping into his role as Carter's handler and contact at A-Echelon, she arranged with Carter to fly down to DC for a few days so that they could plan and launch the mission to find Mackenzie and Liam and reignite the search for the ancient nukes.

When Carter arrived, he was escorted to Hunter's office which James now occupied as acting Director of A-Echelon. James and Irene were waiting for him, and after the three of them exchanged the usual how-are-you's and other pleasantries, they filled their coffee cups, took their seats and Carter looked at James and Irene, in turn, waiting for one of them to start the conversation.

The first thing James noticed when Carter walked in was the change in his demeanor, the light in his eyes and the new energy radiating out of him. It was gratifying to see the positive change and new zest in his friend.

More than a week had passed since James left Freydis, and Carter had used that time to think through and analyze all the information that James had shared with him. Neither one of them spoke, so Carter started the conversation. "Okay James, Irene, here I am; ready, willing, able and more motivated than I have ever been in my entire life." He had a little smile playing on his lips as he continued. "I think you'll understand when I say I'm a lot more than just a little eager to track down my family and bring them back home."

Irene smiled, "We're just as eager, Carter. But I probably don't have to tell you that we have almost no leads to follow. I've gone through every scrap of information we have available, again and again, and I can't find anything we can follow up on. That doesn't mean it's the end of the road; it just means it's going to be much more of a challenge to track them down."

"I understand that," Carter nodded. "What about those people who were watching James' hotel in Jerusalem and the people who were so keen to take pictures of us in India?"

"As for the photographers in India, we're working on that already, but it's not going to be easy. We have to get the cooperation of India's Intelligence Bureau and for that, I have to go through the CIA. I've already made contact with them and am waiting for an answer," Irene replied. "I still have some good contacts there, right up to the Director if necessary."

"Okay." Carter nodded.

"As for the people outside the hotel in Jerusalem, our Mossad contacts have already questioned them, but they couldn't get much out of them. Apparently the two men were instructed to watch the hotel and record the guests coming and going, and photograph everyone. They didn't know who they were working for except that they were paid well to deliver the information to an internet dead letter box at the end of every day. Again, there is nothing that points specifically to you or James or that could lead us to the next bit of information."

"Okay, I get the picture. It's a familiar concept for me as an archeologist to go on a hunt for something that I know exists but without much, or sometimes any evidence of its existence. I usually overcome that problem by continuing to dig until I find what I am looking for." Carter grinned.

James and Irene smiled. Carter's positive attitude was contagious and inspiring.

Carter paused, and a grim look came over his face as he spoke again. "Now, the next thing that hit me like a ton of bricks, while I was reading and thinking through everything, was the realization that someone in A-Echelon has been leaking information out to those killers. Am I right about that?"

"Yes Carter," Irene confirmed, "unfortunately, that is the case." Irene became serious, "James and I have been speculating about it for weeks already, but now we are convinced. As you already know, both of us are ex-CIA field agents. We have firsthand experience of how awkward it is to operate in an environment where you know a mole is on the loose."

Carter sat back and took a sip of his coffee. "I imagine that must be like living with a constant fear that you are about to feel the stab of a knife between your shoulder blades."

"That's exactly how it feels," James grimaced.

Irene continued, "But that doesn't have to cripple us to the point of inaction. A mole situation can sometimes be used to advantage if you handle it correctly."

Carter frowned. "How?"

Irene and James smiled. "By creating havoc amongst the enemy by feeding them false information or luring them out of hiding," James said. "Sometimes a mole is your only lead to the enemy, and this could be one of those cases."

Carter leaned back, "Ah so!" he smiled, "and how do you want to go about it in this case?

"Well, first we'll have to get the two projects going again," James explained. "We won't replace Mackenzie; you'll have to take on that work, Carter."

Carter nodded.

James continued, "We'll have to make absolutely sure your work is kept secure at all times. I'll leave it to you and Irene to work out those details. Irene's had a lot of experience with that from her CIA days. There can be no slip-ups at all. The three of us will be the only ones who will have access to that information, and we will decide what is released, when, and to whom. When information is released, we will put tabs on who we release it to and track where the information goes."

Irene joined in. "That means nothing can be stored on our servers, and nothing can be sent or discussed over our so called 'secure links;' they are not secure."

"Okay," Carter replied.

"To start off with," Irene continued, "we will work on the assumption that the people who were behind the theft of the Sirralnnudam are the same people who are holding Mackenzie and Liam."

"Yes, I had reached the same conclusion," Carter agreed.

"James and I are of the opinion that they might be forcing Mackenzie to work for them, holding Liam as leverage."

"What I find odd is there have been no ransom demands," Carter said. "I would have expected they would try and swap the nuclear research information for Mackenzie and Liam."

"No," James shook his head. "I think they have more brains than that. A ransom demand could lead us to them; they would know that. What's more, you also have to assume that they already have every bit of information you've collected on the nuke project so far, so there is no need for it. They already know as much as you do, thanks to the work of the scumbag of a traitor – whoever he or she is."

Carter's voice was quivering with fury when he spoke again. "Jim, you know me by now. I'm normally a patient and peaceful man, but let me assure you and Irene of one thing today; if we ever find that mole, I'm going to make sure he will regret the day he was born. That's not an idle threat; it's a sincere promise that I intend to keep."

James grinned. "You can have him right after I'm done with him, Carter. I've known about the mole longer than the two of you, so I'm first in the line."

Irene laughed, "I get the impression there's only going to be tatters left for me when the two of you are through doing whatever it is you have in mind."

Carter responded with a grin, "You can add the 'insult' to the injuries we inflict, Irene."

"I'll take it!" she said as she and Carter left James and went outside to get themselves take-out coffee and sandwiches before they made their way to her office to start the planning.

Shutting the door firmly and indicating that Carter should remain silent; Irene closed the shutters, scanned the room for surveillance bugs, unplugged her phone, and shut down her computer. Carter watched in silent amazement, and growing anger as Irene completed the whole routine. She was thorough, no question about that, but it was infuriating to witness what had to be done to sidestep someone who was supposed to be trustworthy - someone who had betrayed America and didn't care about the killing, wounding, and abduction of people.

"Carter," Irene started as she sat down and took a sip of her coffee. "The first thing we have to discuss is your safety. I guess I don't have to explain to you that the people who are holding your family were most likely planning to abduct you as well, but were frustrated in their attempt?"

"Yes, I figured that out over the last few days. What do you have in mind?"

"James and I have discussed it and have a few ideas. While in the CIA and also here at A-Echelon James and I have, from time to time, used the services of a private security company to undertake some 'off-the-record' assignments for us. We think this situation calls for another engagement with them." Irene paused for a moment.

"Can you tell me more about them?"

"The name of the organization is Executive Advantage. The CEO is Sean Walker, a former SEAL Team Six commander. When he left the military, he set up this private security company and recruited a core group of highly skilled ex-Special Forces, electronics, and computer experts from around the world. He and his group have built quite a reputation for themselves in the security and intelligence community. They are one of the few 'go to' trusted private contractors we use whenever we have a mission that requires work that has to be executed totally off the radar, in other words, unofficial."

"Sounds like a good outfit to have on our side," Carter smiled. "So how do you see their role in our projects?"

"They are definitely a good team to have on our side when the going gets rough," Irene nodded. "I speak from personal experience. So our plan is that we contract them to take responsibility for your safety and the security of the research. We don't want anyone in A-Echelon to know anything other than what we decide they should know."

"Good, when do I get to meet with Walker?"

"James has arranged a meeting for tomorrow afternoon at a secret location, and he's already given Sean a high-level briefing."

"I'm looking forward to meeting him," Carter responded. "One more thing," Irene indicated for him to continue. "I haven't told Mackenzie's parents about our discovery yet, mainly because I thought the fewer people that know about it, the better. Much as I would like to tell them, and they deserve to know, I also realize that it could put Mackenzie and Liam at risk."

"Yes, absolutely; no one else must know. And it's not that I don't care about their feelings, God knows I do, but it is more important that we keep the risks to an absolute minimum by limiting those in the know."

After that, the rest of the day was spent planning the relaunch of the ancient nuke project.

Irene agreed with Carter's suggestion to send a small team of well-equipped and duly vetted experts out to Professor Chandra Pillay's dig in North India to conduct proper underground surveys with powerful GPR equipment.

Carter told Irene that he still believed the City of Lights in Egypt might hold the key to many of their questions. It was the oldest known antediluvian human civilization on the planet. By his last assessment, less than fifty percent of that site had been uncovered. There were still many unanswered questions and mysteries hidden below the sand in the city where giants once lived. And the most intriguing question in Carter's mind remained; *where are their written records?*

Any civilization as advanced as that must *have had a written language and records of their history. I have to find them.*

Chapter Twenty-Four

FIFTY MILLION ON THE TABLE

Nate Gordon was the top performer of the five members on the board of directors of CRS. This was partly due to his relentless search for new opportunities and new contracts, but mostly because of his networking skills, 'Social Capital,' as he liked to call it. He didn't have a Facebook or Twitter following, in fact, he didn't even have any social media accounts. Rubbing shoulders with the political and social elite on Capitol Hill, right up into the halls of White House created his network of contacts.

His network was not a large group; nothing like celebrities would have, but they were the most powerful and influential people in the country. Nate Gordon believed in quality over quantity. He was on first name basis with the chairperson of every oversight committee in Congress, and he had the names of some carefully selected, very powerful lobbyists on the speed dial of his smartphone.

Over the years, and with the help CRS's covert surveillance teams, Nate had collected some very useful information about some of his contacts. He'd never had to publish any of it, not that he would have any scruples about doing so if it was necessary, but it came in very handy now and then to help secure a new and lucrative contract, turn a vote or get access to privileged information.

On his return from the trip to India, with the quick stopover in Dubai, there had been a lot of urgent work to attend to. It was necessary to meet with Dwayne Miller, the CEO of CRS to plan and prioritize the execution of the two Saudi contracts. The 50 million dollars on the table would make it the largest and most lucrative contract in the history of CRS if they were successful.

When Miller saw the draft heads of the agreement come through from Gordon after his meeting with El Fadl in Dubai was over, he went to work immediately. He knew Gordon would want to see him as soon as he set foot on American soil again. Therefore, he got in touch with the lead analyst on the CRS IT team and instructed him to conduct a very discreet preliminary inquiry about Professor Carter Devereux and supply him with the information within the next twelve hours.

For the analyst, it was like a walk in the park on a lovely sunny spring day. Professor Devereux was a famous man; he was not trying to hide his existence. Thanks to one of Gordon's contacts, CRS had access to the NSA database, and running CRS' customized data analysis algorithm on the NSA database produced a 20-page report on Devereux in less than an hour.

Miller smiled when he looked it over before Gordon arrived for their meeting. It was mind boggling just how much information about people was available in electronic format, and how easy it was to get the most private of information if you had the benefit of access to the NSA database.

"Fruitful trip you had, Nate," Miller complimented Gordon when they shook hands.

"Yes, I would say so," Gordon laughed.

The secretary brought them drinks, and they got down to business.

"Nate, I hope you don't mind, but I took the liberty to collect a bit of information about Devereux in anticipation of our meeting." Miller handed him a copy of the report.

Gordon smiled. "I would've been disappointed if you hadn't, Dwayne. I'll read it later, just give me the highlights."

"Well, Carter Devereux is almost 40. He lost his entire family in a nasty car accident when he was eight and was brought up by his grandfather on his father's side, William Devereux, who passed away a few years ago. When he was about 23, during a summer break from his Master's Degree studies at a Boston University, he and a friend discovered an ancient Viking longship off the coast of Florida which netted Carter about 20 million."

Gordon whistled.

As you know, he married Dr. Mackenzie Anderson, and they had a son William, whom they called Liam. When his grandfather passed away he inherited everything – we are still looking into the details, but we already know it's more than a billion."

"Holy crap!" Gordon exclaimed. "I could get used to that sort of money!"

Miller continued. "He owns a house in Boston, and an enormous ranch of 50,000 acres in the mountains of Canada, north of Quebec City. There's also a four-seater Piper Seminole that he uses for transport between the ranch, DC, and also Boston where his in-laws, Mary and Steven Anderson, live.

He is currently on sabbatical from the University and works for A-Echelon, as you obviously already know.

Since he left the hospital, he has based himself on the ranch, which they call Freydis. He lives there on his own. The closest neighbors, Ahote and Bly Loloma, who are long-time friends of the family, are about a mile away from the Freydis Homestead."

"I thought you said a bit of information," Gordon laughed. "This sounds more like the whole ensemble to me."

"No, not really, Nate; that was just the overview. I won't bore you any further; you'll find all the rest of it in that report. His telephone numbers, Internet connection, social media accounts, passwords, bank accounts, blood type, fingerprints, DNA, and a whole lot more. Thanks to the access to A-Echelon's servers, which you so kindly provided, we also have a copy of the security checks on him and his wife."

"Shit!" Gordon exclaimed. "I'm glad I'm working on this side of the fence. I would hate to think what those NSA people are holding on me."

"Yeah, it's terrifying isn't it? There's no such thing as privacy and secrecy anymore."

"That's good for our business I reckon, Dwayne."

"Yes, of course," Miller nodded, "as long as one of us don't become the subject of such an inquiry."

"Okay, Dwayne, thanks for that. I'll have a good look at this report and get back to you so we can work out a plan of action to get the information the Saudi's need to plan and launch their operation."

"Just let me know when you're ready, Nate."

"Now, let's talk about that weirdly named book," Gordon said. "I don't suppose you have another 20-page report available for me on that?"

"No, unfortunately, the NSA database is of no use when it comes to ancient documents," Miller laughed. "But I've looked at Mackenzie Devereux's report about the book and what I've learned is that it was discovered at a dig in Çatalhöyük, Turkey about 50 years ago. A German archeologist, Karsten Rischmüller, was working a dig sponsored by the Armenian government at the time he found the book and that's how it landed in the Mesrop Mashtots Institute of Ancient Manuscripts in Yerevan, Armenia," Miller paused.

"That's it?" Gordon looked surprised, "nothing else?"

"Unfortunately, yes, that's it," Miller nodded. "I have one of the IT people on it already, but so far nothing else has turned up. There are no references to the Sirralnnudam whatsoever on the Internet."

"Bummer," Gordon muttered. "I thought it was going to be an easy one. Well, let's keep on digging for another day or two. If we can't get anything, we'll have to look at the alternative suggested by El Fadl."

"What alternative was that?"

"He suggested we launch an international search for a copy of the book, contacting rare book collectors, libraries, universities, archeologists, private collectors, artifact dealers, et cetera. If that doesn't produce results, he suggested putting an enormous price on the book and advertise in the right places that we are looking for a copy. We don't need the original; we only need to be able to make a decent and readable copy."

Miller was quiet for a while. "For obvious reasons, I'm not very excited about those options as they involve too much exposure for us."

"Agreed. We will have to think through the consequences very carefully before we do anything like that," Gordon replied.

Chapter Twenty-Five

EXECUTIVE ADVANTAGE

Carter and Irene met with James to report on the outcome of their planning sessions over the past two days. James agreed with their approach and authorized them to go ahead. Later that afternoon James drove the three of them to one of Executive Advantage's safe houses in Herndon, Virginia, about an hour and a half from Capitol Hill.

On the way, James and Irene gave Carter some more background information about Executive Advantage. They had a core group of about ten people who were highly skilled specialists in the various disciplines of modern day warfare and intelligence operations. They also had access to a large number of subcontractors with a variety of skills and expertise, whom they called on from time to time as circumstances dictated.

Executive Advantage was an organization of last resort whose services were called for whenever security and intelligence agencies found themselves with an intractable problem that had to be dealt with when commercial, diplomatic, and political solutions were not an option.

They offered specialist services in covert surveillance, information gathering in hostile and friendly environments, counter terrorism, prime target elimination, hostage rescue, demolitions, weapons training, tactics, and VIP protection.

Sean Walker, a former SEAL Team Six commander, was one of the military's most highly decorated soldiers when he received his honorable discharge from the Navy. There were a few rumors that he was headhunted by the CIA at the time, and that was the reason he left the military and setup Executive Advantage, an independent group of international Special Forces operators. It was one of those scenarios where those who talked about it didn't really know anything at all, and those who *did* know weren't talking.

The truth was that Executive Advantage was established when leaders of a few likeminded security agencies from around the world got together and agreed to form an independent global Special Forces unit with a deep pool of expertise. It was a unit that consisted of specialists who could assure swift and successful clandestine missions anywhere in the world. The result was that Executive Advantage had access to the skills of former Special Forces members from around the globe. These members included former: Navy SEALS, Delta Force, British and Australian SAS, Canadian Joint Task Force 2 - JTF2, French Foreign Legion, Israel's Kidon (part of Mossad), Oman's Desert Phantoms, and others. Political leaders of the member countries made sure they didn't have any knowledge about the members or activities of this group – plausible deniability.

With all the background information about Executive Advantage and its CEO, Carter was almost disappointed when he shook hands with Sean Walker. To the casual observer, there would not have been much to the man. He was in his late 40's, Carter estimated. He had dark hair with a few strands of gray showing here and there, was a little taller than average - maybe five ten or so, and a little slimmer than average for someone his size - about 150 pounds. There was nothing special about his looks. With his olive skin, dark eyes and hair, he could easily disappear into the crowds of any Middle Eastern country. Nevertheless, a close look at the man's eyes revealed there was something different. Something in his dark, almost black, eyes was enough to give anyone reason to pause and think about things.

Carter realized that the saying was true; *don't judge a book by its cover* and smiled when he remembered the modern version; *don't judge a book by its movie.*

James and Irene gave Sean the details of the type of services they required from Sean's organization without going into any of the details of Carter and Mackenzie's projects, or the fact that she and Liam had been abducted. First, they wanted to make sure that Carter would be kept safe at all times, and not only that; they also required extensive counter surveillance measures to protect his research and detect anyone who had surveillance tabs on him.

Sean remained quiet most of the time while James and Irene were talking, listening attentively, and asking few questions. It struck Carter as odd that Sean was not taking any notes; at least until he realized that he was now in a world where no records existed. It was a world where you had to rely on a superior memory and trust the people with whom you work.

Sean smiled when they discussed the details of Carter's safety and James told him about Carter's ranch north of Quebec City and the need to extend their protection to include the times when Carter was there.

"That's going to make two of our sub-contractors euphoric. They are ex-JTF2 - Joint Task Force 2 - one of the Special Forces units of the Canadian Special Operations Forces Command. One of them is from Quebec and the other from Saskatchewan. I take it you want his protection detail in place right away?"

"Yes, if that's possible," James replied.

"No problem," Sean replied, "I placed two people on standby after our telephone conversation. When we've finished this meeting, I'll call them in, and we can go into the details."

James nodded.

"Carter what are your plans? How much longer are you going to be in DC?" Sean asked.

"I am flexible," Carter replied. "My plan was to stay here for another five days or so, but I am happy to fit in with whatever you want."

"Are you planning to go back to Freydis from here?" Sean asked.

"Yes, unless you have something else in mind for me."

"No problem," Sean smiled. "I'll just have to give the two Canucks notice to prepare themselves for a gig in their homeland."

"Sean, have you ever been up that way?" James wanted to know.

"I've been in all the provinces of Canada quite a few times except for Quebec. Why?"

"Do yourself a favor; go and have a look at Carter's place one day. It was a life-changing experience for me," James smiled.

"You're welcome anytime Sean." Carter smiled." My family and I believe it's the most beautiful place on earth."

Despite Carter's smile, Irene noted the shadow in Carter's eyes when he spoke about his family.

Sean nodded. "Sounds like I will have to go and see it then."

Next they discussed the electronic security requirements.

Irene explained. "Sean, we want to keep most of Carter's research off the A-Echelon record. I say most because from time to time we will allow selected bits and pieces to pass through the network, servers, and computers."

Sean didn't have to ask; it was clear, A-Echelon had an internal security problem. At the very least, James and Irene were just being extremely cautious, and that was never a bad idea.

"Okay, I'll get our IT guru, Rick Winslow, to get in touch with you tomorrow morning to set it all up for you."

Sean called in his VIP protection expert, Norma MacMillan. Norma was a decorated former senior Secret Service agent assigned to the protection detail of a previous President of the United States.

She was in her mid-40's, about five eight, with shoulder length auburn hair, which she kept in a ponytail and lively, brown eyes. She was dressed in a dark gray pantsuit.

Sean introduced her to his visitors and asked her to take a seat. He gave her a brief overview of Carter's protection requirements.

Within an hour of listening and questioning James, Irene, and Carter she had enough information and said, "If you give me an hour there will be two people ready to accompany you when you leave. I'll work out a protection plan overnight and meet with you again tomorrow morning to finalize the details if that suits you, Professor Devereux."

"That will be fine, but since you're going to be responsible for my safety, it would be best that you call me Carter." He smiled.

"Thank you, Carter, I'll do that. You may call me Norma. What time tomorrow and where?"

Despite her friendly smile, she was a quiet, no-nonsense person. Carter could see in her demeanor that she was efficient and every bit as professional as he always believed the Secret Service agents to be.

"0900 hours at the A-Echelon offices?" Carter asked while looking at Irene. She nodded.

Thank you, I'll see you there.

About 40 minutes later Norma returned with two men whom she introduced as Jack Simms and Peter Roderick. They were Carter's bodyguards for the next 24 hours until the detailed plan had been worked out and approved by James and Irene.

Chapter Twenty-Six

I HAD A DREAM

Mackenzie sat on the edge of her bed. Liam was off somewhere playing, and it wasn't quite dinner time. She was tired and depressed. It had been months since they'd arrived here and each day was the same as the rest.

She pushed her hands through her long red hair; it was dry and listless. It was months since she'd been outside in the sun and fresh air. Her body was suffering just as her mind was.

Having Liu working alongside her had been a real boost to her morale, but the constant care they had to take not to be seen talking about anything other than work was bringing her down. Indeed, the code Liu had developed from the language of the ancient texts they were working on helped a lot, but Nasser kept Liu in a different part of the facility, and she and Mackenzie were not allowed contact outside work hours.

Discovering that there had been an explosion she knew nothing about, and knowing that Carter was inside the restaurant when it happened gave her cause for concern.

And yet, if he was the man who had been found alive after the bomb detonated, it was likely he had survived, and that gave her hope. At least, she had some information, but it wasn't nearly enough.

Had he been injured? Did he survive? Somewhere deep inside her, she felt sure he had and maybe even now was back at Freydis. But how did he feel believing they had been killed? Was there any chance at all he would learn they were alive; how could he possibly know?

This was a question that haunted her every night. Sometimes she would lie awake and try to imagine being on Freydis with him. She would try to recall the sun and the fresh air, the smell of the trees, the snow in winter, the autumn gold, but for all that, she was losing the battle because one of the most fundamental things humans need to know was denied her; where was she? Was it day or night? Not even that was known. Living underground, reduced to work and being controlled was having its effect on her.

It was ongoing without end, laboring over the ancient texts, and trying to survive. The monotony was appalling, go to bed, sleep, get up, eat, work, go back to her two-room cell, eat, sleep and do the same again the next day.

Indeed, her time with Liam was good; he brought the only brightness into her day and made her feel alive again. Their mutual study of Arabic was interesting and also helped break up the monotony a little. Each of them had reached a stage where they could make a basic conversation in the language, and it made her think of Carter and his long list of languages he studied as a hobby.

She sighed, smoothed her hands over her swelling tummy, "Hello little one. How are you down here?" Talking to the new life inside her reminded her she had a lot to live for, and all she had to do was hang in and keep the days busy. If Carter were alive he would find them; she knew that without a doubt, and it was the only thing that stopped her from giving up. Surely, without that hope, she would slowly shrivel up and die.

Liu had made a significant difference to their work; she was able to ignite some fire into Mackie's thinking when she felt beyond tired and unable to keep going.

Maybe for Liu, not having to be afraid of losing a child here, and not having someone she believed could be dead made things easier, although she didn't underestimate how hard it was for Liu as well. The confinement was pulling Liu down too. There were days they would barely code-talk to each other. They just sat side-by-side; working to translate the ancient texts in the hope of discovering something more that would move the work along.

Mackenzie sighed and pulled herself to her feet; it was time to make some dinner for her and Liam. Afterward, as usual, they would settle down and study more Arabic before going to bed.

Bed, another long night of lying in the dark trying to imagine being on Freydis. Sometimes she was fearful she was forgetting the place, afraid she would never see it again. Not Freydis, or Ahote and Bly, not her wolves, Keeva and Loki, would they even remember her? When her mind went to that point the tears would fall and her pillow became damp as she tried to wipe them away. She couldn't cry, for Liam's sake she must believe even when all belief seemed suspended.

By the time dinner was over, Liam had recounted all he'd done during the day and provided news of each of his friends. They had spoken in Arabic the whole evening long, and now it was time for bed.

Liam was happily tucked in and kissed goodnight, but as she left him he said, "Mummy, do you ever think of Freydis and all our loved ones there?"

She paused in the doorway and leaned her head on the timber frame sighing quietly to herself.

"Mommy?"

She looked up and tried to smile, "Oh Liam darling, of course, I do, just as you do; it's what keeps me going here. I can't imagine we will be here forever, and when we leave it will be to go back to Freydis, you know that." She smiled and moved over to kiss him again, "Just keep those thoughts in your mind; it's what will make them come true."

Back in her own room, she undressed and slipped on another black gown - *God, I'm so sick of black*, - a soft light cotton, and climbed into her bed.

Lying on her back with her arms folded above her head, she tried to cast off the day and move onto Freydis, but for some reason it was extra hard, maybe she was just too tired.

With that thought, she turned over and dropped into a deep sleep.

The first thing she was aware of was a cold nose pushing against her cheek. She tried to push it away, but it persisted, so she opened her eyes and found herself mirrored in the dark gold of Keeva's eyes.

"Keeva? What are you doing here?" she sat up and found Loki lying beside her.

Looking around it was clear she was outside the cave on Freydis. She blinked her eyes trying to remember how she'd gotten here, but the memory simply didn't exist.

Around her, the air sparkled with a crisp spring freshness she had all but forgotten. The trees in their spring coats were lime green, and down the hill, the river ran fresh and cold. The dawn was coming up, and she watched the pink sky with awe and wonder as a new day began. This was something she had not seen for months.

Turning to the wolves, she spoke to them, "How are you both?" she threw her arms around Loki and hugged him, reveling in the soft deep fur and the sense of strength in his body. His wolfy smell was magic, and she breathed deep, holding it to her.

Keeva moved closer and then rolled on her back stretching her legs.

Mackie gaped in sheer delight, "Keeva, you're pregnant too. Oh, you clever couple." And she burst into tears.

Warm tongues dried her damp cheeks and for a long while, she just lay back against Loki's body stroking Keeva's ears.

She could feel exhaustion drain away as she lay there, a sense of vigor moving into her body as if rising from the grounds of Freydis to feed her.

"Mom. Mommy?"

"No, no please, I don't want to leave, not yet."

"Mommy? Wake up, please."

Reluctantly she stirred and opened her eyes, letting the dream go, "Liam? Are you alright?"

"Yes I am, but you were calling out, and I couldn't hear what you were saying, I thought something might be wrong."

She smiled at the child and assured him nothing was wrong. Not one thing was wrong; it was all going to be all right.

"Liam, I had a dream…."

Chapter Twenty-Seven

VIP PROTECTION

James, Carter, and Irene were gathered in James' office once again, a preliminary meeting between the three of them before Carter and Irene met with Norma to wrap up the details of Carter's protection. Carter was pacing restlessly. He was finding it more and more difficult to control his growing impatience with all the planning and security arrangements. If it depended on him, he would issue orders to the American armed forces to invade the entire Middle East and do a house-to-house search for his family. It was frustrating to know that none of that would happen; no one knew where his family was.

It was only a gut feeling that they might be somewhere in the Middle East, but by the same token, they could be in any country in the world, even in the United States. No one knew. That was if they were still alive; maybe that too was just another gut feeling. His emotions oscillated between excitement, hope, and belief one moment to doubt and despair the next.

James and Irene could see his suffering and tried their best to help him to be pragmatic about it.

"Carter, it would be an insult to say I know what you're going through, I don't," Irene told him, "All I can say is; I can see you are suffering, and I'll do everything possible to help you get through this."

James joined in. "Same from me Carter. I can't even begin to imagine how you must feel and what is going through your mind, but you must believe one thing; Irene and I will stand by you and help you see this thing through."

"Thanks, you two, I appreciate that." Carter quit pacing and sat down. "It helps a lot to know I have people around me that I can trust and lean on for support."

They all went quiet for a few moments, sipping their coffee before they continued.

"Okay Carter," Irene said. "Although it might be frustrating to have to go through all these security measures, it's crucial that we get it in place as quickly as possible. We can't take any steps forward in this case until we know that you are safe."

"Understood and agreed." Carter nodded.

"Okay. Our first priority is the meeting with Norma MacMillan so that we can finalize all the details and requirements for your protection. That will include not only your personal safety but also the security and secrecy of your research and communications."

Carter nodded.

"Once we have that in place, we will meet with Sean Walker again to kick off the next phase which is to find Mackenzie and Liam."

Carter smiled. "I trust you and James will understand if I say that is the phase I'm most interested in."

"Yes, of course," Irene smiled.

James' desk phone rang, it was his secretary letting him know Norma had arrived and was waiting at the security desk in the foyer for someone to sign her in.

Carter and Irene went to meet her, and after taking her through the Airlock, they all went down to Irene's office. Irene went through the entire office securing process, closing the blinds, scanning the room, unplugging and switching off the computers, desk, and cell phones.

Once Irene was happy that the office was secure, Norma presented an overview of the plan. Irene had worked with the Secret Service on numerous occasions in the past and was familiar with how they operated. Carter, of course, had no idea what a complex operation VIP protection was.

She explained at a high level how the security array would be setup and then went into more details about protection in different surroundings such as at home, a hotel, a restaurant, a conference, et cetera. She covered the basic principles of having a break in routine, identifying suspects, use of technical equipment, sabotage awareness, planning and using escape routes, driving and shooting.

Notwithstanding Irene and Carter's varied levels of experience and knowledge of the subject of VIP protection, they were both highly impressed by Norma's plan. There was no doubt that she knew what she was talking about.

"After having said all of that," she looked at Carter, "rule number one is always; the best personal protection we can provide will fail if our client is not cooperating."

Carter frowned.

"Sorry, I don't mean to offend you; it's just that I need you to understand that we can only be as efficient as you will allow us to be. If you don't tell us what your plans are, where you're going, when, and how, we can't help you," she smiled, "in other words, we can't read your mind; don't surprise us."

Carter gave a slight shake of his head. "I won't."

Norma continued. "Rule number two, an informed client is much easier to protect than an ignorant one. That means we will give you some training in our processes so that you know what to do at all times."

"Makes a lot of sense to me," Carter agreed. "I'm in your hands now Norma; you just tell me what you want me to do."

"That's a great start, Carter," She laughed. "I wish all of our clients could hear what you just said. Some of them just don't understand that it is a joint responsibility between them and us to make it work. The worst of the worst are politicians with their inflated egos. Sometimes it feels like I'm herding cats."

Irene exploded in laughter when Norma explained about the problem she had with some of her clients. Irene knew all too well how obstinate some politicians could be.

After lunch, Norma described the new technical security measures she and their IT security expert, Rick Winslow, had in mind. She had made arrangements for him to join them for this part of the meeting.

Irene fetched Rick from the security desk and brought him to her office. He was a young guy, in his early thirties at the most, Carter guessed. He was tall - maybe six two or so, slim, with unkempt dark hair, silver wire-frame glasses, and dressed in the standard geek uniform of jeans, flip-flops, and a T-shirt with a slogan which only another geek would understand.

Norma had given them a heads-up before his arrival. "Don't be fooled by his appearance," she said. "He is a professional when it comes to his work, and everything else, including his clothes, is of no significance to him. He is the most brilliant mind I've ever seen behind a computer."

"How did you get hold of him?" Irene asked.

"Well, I won't give you all the details, but I can tell you he got into a bit of trouble one night when he demonstrated to a few friends how he could hack into one of the FBI servers with his Samsung smartphone. The CIA heard about his stunt when the FBI had him in custody and was contemplating criminal charges. They pulled him out of there and got the charges quashed. So now he works for the CIA and us."

Carter and Irene were just shaking their heads. The modern day action heroes were in cyberspace.

Norma had them rolling with laughter when she told them how Rick, not too long ago, explained to her how to copy data from a flash drive to a computer. Apparently when she stopped him and told him that she knew what a flash drive was and how to use it. He responded with, "Well I am just making sure. You're about eight to ten years older than I am and in my world, that is about the same as being on the Ark with Noah."

Once the introductions had been made and Rick was settled, he explained to Carter, Irene, and James that they were to be issued with new, secure, phones that would not be connected to A-Echelon in any way. They would also be supplied with tablet PC's that he would install and configure with special software.

He then continued to describe how he'd created a VPN – Virtual Private Network - between the three of them that could not be penetrated. It was built with new technology he had developed for the CIA, using unique ephemeral (temporary) key exchanges, not available to anyone else anywhere in the world.

When he said that Irene and Carter both looked at him with frowns on their faces. Rick saw their puzzled looks and responded. "Yes, I know people always say no communications are secure, and they are right. But let me just ease your minds about that."

They nodded for him to continue. Not that they would understand much, but it did bring a certain level of comfort to have him say it.

He went on to explain that all data going through the VPN would be encrypted and that the key length determined how long it would take to break using a brute force attack, also known as exhaustive key search, which involved trying every possible combination until the correct one was found.

"So to put that in perspective," he said. "To break a 128-bit key cipher would require 3.4×10^{38} operations. The NSA can break 1028-bit encryptions. My algorithms are using 4096-bit encryption. If anyone were able to have the same computer processing power as the NSA, it would take them just shy of two billion years. That's if they were running those machines at full capacity 24/7, to break my algorithm. In other words, yes, your VPN can be compromised, but it's not something you have to worry about in your lifetime."

That settled it for Carter and Irene. They were satisfied that they would be able to communicate with each other without having to worry about the mole eavesdropping on them.

"Thanks for the reassurance, Rick, I feel a lot better." Carter chuckled. "We'll make sure that we get this work done before anyone breaks your encryption keys."

The next morning Carter was introduced to the team who was assigned to his protection detail and spent the next three days with them in training. Learning what was expected of him at all times and practicing the various mock scenarios, which they created. It was a welcome distraction for his anxious mind that was continually wandering back to Mackenzie and Liam.

It was during those three days that Carter made a firm resolution that when the day dawned for Mackenzie and Liam to be rescued from wherever they were; he was going to be there.

There was nothing, and no one, who could stop him. If he had to acquire Special Forces skills to do it, then he would acquire them. He was not going to ask James or Irene's opinion or permission; he would inform them.

Chapter Twenty-Eight

NO BUTS, JIM

With Carter under the constant care of bodyguards and Rick's technology measures deployed, Executive Advantage's security was in place, and they could turn their full attention to Mackenzie and Liam's rescue.

James kept in touch with his friend from the Mossad, Ben Friedman. He had confided in Ben, telling him of Carter's work with the ancient nukes and giving him updates on Carter's progress. Understandably, Ben was in a hurry to go after the ancient nukes. No one had to tell him that the terrorists who abducted Mackenzie and Liam had also been after Carter and his research. Carter was lucky to have escaped them. He knew he had no evidence to suggest the terrorists were from the Middle East, but it would have been a big mistake to ignore the possibility and not act accordingly. It was no secret that the terrorist groups in the Middle East would give anything and everything to get their hands on a nuclear weapon. And there was no doubt that they all had the same, single primary target: Israel. Once Israel was wiped off the face of the earth, they would go after each other, but Israel had to go first.

Ben was elated when James told him Carter was restarting the nuke project and immediately offered his support and use of the resources under his control.

This was the phase that could not start quickly enough for Carter. By the time they were meeting with Sean Walker again, Carter was about ready to gather a private army of mercenaries and invade a country. The only thing that held him back was he didn't know which country.

James and Irene could understand Carter's urgency. The stress of uncertainty and lack of information was taking its toll on them too; God only knew how Carter was managing to cope with it.

"Jim, Irene, I've done a lot of thinking since I heard that my family is alive," he paused before continuing, his voice strengthening, "I am determined, I'm going to be involved in the mission to extract them…"

The two of them were not entirely surprised by Carter's announcement. "Carter," James spoke softly, "I don't know, I mean I can grasp your feelings about that but…"

"No buts Jim; no buts," Carter interjected. "I *am* going on that mission. I'm not asking yours or Irene's permission; I'm informing you just so you make sure you include me in the planning. When my family needed me the most in Jerusalem, I wasn't there for them. That's not going to happen again; never again. And that's the end of it."

Carter's determined expression told James to tread carefully. Carter was a patient and good-natured person, but James had seen men like him pushed over the edge a few times during his lifetime. He hesitated; *drive that kind of man too hard, and you could end up with serious trouble on your hands James ole boy.*

James had his hands up. "Noted. It's not going to be easy, but ..."

Carter's eyes were fiery. "I told you, no buts. Make it happen; no excuses. I'm going in with the extraction team; I don't care who or what they are."

James shrugged. "We will have to work out how that would be possible Carter. If it's a covert operation, which I anticipate it will be, you don't have the training and skills for it. You could become a serious liability to them, maybe even get yourself killed or jeopardize the entire rescue."

Irene's eyes were as wide as two saucers. She had never seen Carter like this. Granted she hadn't known him as well or as long as James had, but she was a pretty good judge of character. Carter's behavior didn't fit her psychological profile of him. However, she had to admit that if it were her family they were talking about, she would probably turn into a ferocious bear mother attacking anything that was threatening her cubs.

"That problem is easily solved, Jim," Carter countered. "When we meet with Sean later today, support my request to make some of his resources available to train me."

James nodded slowly.

"I'll pay for it," Carter said. "We do it on Freydis and wherever it's necessary. It will be a contract between Executive Advantage and me, and have nothing to do with A-Echelon. All I need from the two of you is to support my request to Sean."

James and Irene glanced at each other and finally nodded in silence.

"Good. Thanks for that," Carter said and paused as he let out a sigh of relief. "I'm sorry about that…"

Irene touched his arm. "Nothing to be sorry about

Carter. We understand and we support you, unconditionally."

"Carter, I'm past my use-by-date," James chuckled. "I thought I'd seen my last mission years ago; now I'll have to get back into shape again."

"You're not going anywhere," Carter and Irene said at the same time.

"You don't expect me to sit around this office while Carter is out there having all the fun kicking those terrorists' asses! That isn't going to happen," James was serious. "Nope, no way is that going to happen," he continued shaking his head.

Irene rolled her eyes and sighed. The two men reminded her of her two teenage boys in an argument. "Boys, boys! Listen to me. You can't both be out of the house! Who's going to take care of mommy and the house?"

James smiled. "Mommy is a big girl and capable of taking care of the house on her own. If my little brother goes, then I go. I'll have to be there to make sure he's okay and doesn't do something stupid. And to use his words, I'm not asking for permission; I'm informing you."

"Well, that's settled then," Carter said with a grin. "We both go. Can we please go and see Sean now?"

However, there was something Irene felt was important to say. "Carter, please allow me to give you an uninvited piece of my mind."

Carter nodded.

She continued, "There is every reason to believe that the attack in Jerusalem was aimed at you and your family. And it is probably correct that if you and Mackenzie didn't work for us, none of that would have happened…"

Carter was glowering at her. "What are you trying to say?" he snapped.

Irene remained calm and held her hand up, "You and I, all of us, have to accept those as the facts. However, there is one positive thing among those horrible facts, and I'm afraid you are missing it." Carter opened his mouth to speak, but she stopped him. "Hear me out, please. The fact that you got out of it alive and that you were not abducted is the positive. If it were not for that, the case would have been closed, and we would all have tried to move on. You being alive and with us is what's going to help us rescue them."

Irene's words gave Carter reason to pause. He had a look of humiliation on his face when he spoke again. "Irene, Jim, I'm sorry. Please accept my apology. Of course, you're right about that. I will remember it. It's just so damn difficult…" His voice was shaking.

Irene put her hand on his arm again and smiled. "It's all good Carter. Let's go and talk to Sean now."

Two hours later they'd returned to the EA safe house in Herndon to meet with Sean.

James, Irene, and Carter briefed Sean in detail about Carter and Mackenzie's involvement with A-Echelon and the projects they were working on. They covered the events of the past few months including the Jerusalem tragedy, the evidence about the abductions, the suspected mole, and the disappearance of the Sirralnnudam. As before, Sean listened intently, interrupting them only to get clarification when necessary.

"So Sean, as you can see, we find ourselves in the

predicament that we can't even conduct our own investigation into any of this," James said with a sigh. "Because of our internal security issues, we will have to outsource the whole thing to you. Irene and I will be your only contact with A-Echelon and no one can know that you're working for us."

"Understood," Sean nodded. "I'll need a day to think this through and assign the best resource lead to the operation. Is that okay with you?"

"Yes," James answered. "As you can understand we are raring to get going on this, Carter more so than anyone else. Just tell us what you need from us."

"That's understandable," Sean replied. "From this moment on it is EA's number one priority."

James leaned back in his chair. "Okay, now the next request," he grinned at the look of surprise from Sean. "Professor Indiana Jones here," he jerked his thumb in the direction of Carter, "says he's going with us on the rescue mission…"

Sean's eyes squinted, and a frown creased his brows as his gaze darted between James and Carter. He held his hand up. "Jim what are you talking about? And who is 'us'?"

"Well, I suspect once we find out where Mackenzie and Liam are kept we will have to launch a hostage rescue mission," James said. "Carter and I are going with you or whoever is going…"

"Ah…hang on…wait…mhh…" Sean stuttered trying to get his thoughts in order. He saw the determination on Carter and James' faces. "Guys, hang on; not only is that not a good idea, but it could also be a problem…"

"No," Carter interjected. "There is *not* going to be a

problem. That is a condition of this agreement, and it's not negotiable. It's part of the deal, or there's no deal."

James nodded. He shrugged as he looked at Sean as if to say, *there's nothing I can do about it, it's part of the deal.* "Carter wants to make a contract directly with EA to train him and prepare him for such a mission."

Sean had a lot of misgivings about this all of a sudden. He knew James Rhodes by reputation as he was still held in very high regard among the ranks of the CIA operatives. He didn't know anything about Carter Devereux. The man made a good first impression on him during the first meeting, and nothing had happened since to diminish that impression. But a good impression was not a good enough reason to take him along on a life-threatening hostage rescue operation.

He kept his composure. He needed to think about this and speak in private with James before he made any commitments. "I'll be straight with you Carter; I have serious concerns about the whole idea. However, let me think about it, and we'll discuss it tomorrow when we meet again."

Carter was not entirely happy to leave without a commitment but decided that he would be better off letting Sean think about it and, he was sure, have a quiet word with James later.

Sean contacted James that night, after their meeting, to get background information about Carter.

James shared the results of Carter's psychiatric evaluation during his induction at A-Echelon and the results of his tests and training, including the comments of his instructors. Reluctantly, James also had to admit that in all his years in the CIA and A-Echelon, Carter was still the only recruit who managed to kick his ass in that first day's sparring session. A grueling session that was intended to quickly identify and weed out anyone who didn't have what it would take.

"So, Jim, listening to you, I get the impression Carter has the ability to have passed any of the Special Forces selection courses?"

"Without a doubt, Sean," James replied without hesitation. "He is a man with willpower, motivation, determination, and a robust body. If you can give him the training, he will not be a burden on any team, quite the contrary, I'm sure he would be an asset."

"Okay, Jim I feel a lot better about him," Sean replied. "Now there's only you, we have to talk about." Sean smiled on the other end, but lucky for him James couldn't see it.

"Now, listen to me, Sean Walker," James said. "I've been hunting bad guys since you were still a sparkle in your daddy's eyes, so there's nothing to discuss. If there is a rescue operation, as we think there will be, I *am* going with you, or whoever is going. Period. End of discussion."

"Okay pops," Sean laughed. "I was just yanking your chain. I knew you wouldn't want to sit out. See you tomorrow."

Little snot nose brat, James mumbled when he put the phone down. *Pops! Can you believe it!* But then he paused, Sean was right; he was getting a bit long in the tooth for this type of stuff. But there was no way he was going to send Carter into harm's way without him being there.

Let's hope and pray there will be an easier, less dangerous, solution.

Chapter Twenty-Nine

THE BRIEFING

As promised, Sean was ready for them the next day. They met at a different safe house, this time in Arlington, Virginia about six miles from Capitol Hill.

Sean introduced them to Dylan Mulligan, his 2IC – Second in Command -whom he'd assigned to Carter's case, and who would be in charge of finding Mackenzie and Liam. It would also be up to him to see that Carter was fully trained and prepared to be part of an extraction team if it became necessary in the future. Sean gave them a brief background sketch about Dylan. They were like the Biblical David and Jonathan. Dylan was Sean's 2IC in SEAL Team Six. They were old school and college buddies. They'd joined the military together, went through the SEAL selection process and training together, and had fought side by side in many battles. The two of them left the military at the same time to setup Executive Advantage.

What Sean didn't tell them, which James, Irene, and Carter would only find out later, was that Dylan was one of the best snipers in the military, probably in the world, but that would have been difficult to ascertain. Officially he had 135 kills accredited to him in conflicts around the globe when he left the military. Unofficially that number would have been closer to 250. Dylan was not the type of man who made notches in his rifle butt to keep track, and he would never talk about it. But one thing was sure; there were many men and women alive today because of Dylan's extraordinary skills with a rifle.

Dylan was a brilliant operator with unmatched skills and ability to rapidly summarize a situation and take action. Sean had the knack to plan a mission, prepare for it and execute it with deadly efficiency. Between the two of them, they were a formidable team.

The meeting went late into the night as Sean and Dylan went through every bit of information in detail; every bit was analyzed and questioned to the nth degree. To Carter, initially, it was a mind-numbing experience, but as the meeting progressed he was filled with a feeling of veneration for these two men. Their meticulous demand for detail spoke of experience and skill that instilled an enormous measure of confidence in him. It was the first time in the days since James told him that Mackenzie and Liam were alive that he felt tranquility slowly start to wash over him.

They were having yet another coffee; Carter had stopped counting after his fourth while Sean did a recap of the decisions.

Because the only person who could lead them to Carter's family was the mole in A-Echelon, their strategy was for Carter to start the nuke project again. Selected pieces of information out of Carter's research would be 'fed' to the A-Echelon servers where Rick Winslow's hidden tracking software would lie waiting to detect and follow the path of the data when accessed by anyone.

Rick would gain access to the A-Echelon servers under the pretense of a network and server audit by a team of CIA IT specialists, which James would request. It was standard operating procedure for government organizations, especially those that were handling classified data, to conduct regular security audits on their networks and servers. James would just be doing his job by requesting such an inspection.

They would establish two streams of communications; 'apparently concealed' and 'definitely concealed.' In their 'apparently concealed' communications they would keep up the appearance of secrecy but drop in tidbits of information for the mole to keep him or her, or them, interested. Their 'definitely concealed' communications were to be held absolutely one hundred percent secret. No one must ever know they had another communications channel. Those phones and tablets provided by Rick were never to be used in public, never. No one must see or hear them use those; ever. The success or failure of their strategy depended on that.

In regards to the original ancient nuke project, nothing of the magnitude or urgency of Carter's initial brief had changed; the threat to national and global security remained as dangerous as before. Therefore, those nukes had to be found before a terrorist group discovered them. James had Ben Friedman's promise of cooperation from the Mossad, and they would use that.

Carter would lead a team of archeologists, which would include a few undercover EA operators for security, to the City of Lights in Egypt to continue the search for that hitherto elusive library. Another team of experts, which would also include undercover EA operators, would be sent to Professor Chandra Pillay's dig in North India to conduct an extensive underground survey.

As for Mackenzie's respirocyte project, it was decided to keep that on hold for now. They were speculating as to why the terrorists were holding Mackenzie and Liam and had not used them to make a ransom demand. It could've been that they were using Liam as leverage to force Mackenzie to work for them, or it could just be that they were waiting for the right time to make such a ransom demand. Neither A-Echelon nor Executive Advantage had anyone with the expertise to head up the respirocyte project. And because of the security concerns, it was not advisable to bring such a person on board at this stage.

Rick Winslow would configure Carter's satellite link on Freydis to conform to his encrypted secure communications methods.

Sean would provide Carter with a list of special equipment that would be required for his training, which he had to purchase and take with him when he returned to Freydis.

Sean and Dylan would work out a training plan and roster for Carter. His bodyguards, while he was on Freydis, would consist of a team of two former Special Forces operators who would also take responsibility for his training. The bodyguards would be rotated on a regular basis.

Carter would divide his time between his research and training.

"I'm only going to say this once, Carter," Sean said looking him directly in the eye. "You have just entered Special Forces training. You will not be shown any mercy, nor will your trainers cut you any slack. This is a serious mission, and I won't endanger the lives of my team or your wife and child just to take you along. I've agreed to let you train, but if you can't cut the mustard and be a true asset to the team, you're not going. Understand?"

Carter was furious and started to argue with him, but

then realized a soldier wouldn't argue with his commander. *I will be an asset; I won't let my family down.* Carter straightened to what he hoped resembled an 'attention' stance. "Understood, Sir. I'll be ready."

Sean suppressed a smile; he had seen the fury flash in Carter's eyes and also the decision to become a soldier. "See that you are," was all he said before he turned away. *He's off to a good start.*

Chapter Thirty

NOTHING CAN BE TRACKED BACK TO US

Nate Gordon relaxed in the back of the limousine while returning to the CRS office after his trip to Georgetown where he'd had a meeting with his most valuable contact in DC, in fact, not just in DC; the man was his most valuable contact, period. The man had his finger on the pulse of the entire political system of the United States. There was not a single government department that he couldn't get access to with the tip of a hat. He had or could easily get, if required, access to every single government project in progress, in planning, and even if it was still only in concept. Besides his immense political clout, the man was rich beyond measure. He came from a wealthy family who had wide-ranging business interests, which included pharmaceutical, medical, and real estate.

Gordon liked this man. They shared a lot of common traits. Both of them had business minds, but neither of them relied solely on brains for their success although they both had plenty of those. To be successful, they both believed you needed a little bit of luck, a lot of insight, unrivaled powers of persuasion, and, most crucial, ethical flexibility. Ethical flexibility meant simply that you could ignore your reservations when extraordinary strategies were required. In other words, if you wanted something, you took it.

There were only two people who knew about the relationship between Gordon and his top contact, and that was Gordon and his top contact. This man was the silent partner in CRS, and only Gordon knew who he was. The other CRS board members never asked; all they knew was that this silent partner was responsible for more than half of the company's revenue. That was good enough for them; they didn't have to know who he was, and they were happy to refer to him only as NTC – Nate's Top Contact.

Gordon was in an excellent mood when he walked into Dwayne Miller's office and closed the door.

"Morning, Nate," Miller smiled when he saw Gordon. "Good to see you. Come on in and have a seat. What can I get you to drink? Coffee? Tea?"

Gordon looked at his watch. "It's past 11:00 I'll have a Scotch on the rocks. I'm in a celebratory mood."

"That sounds good," Miller laughed as he turned to the liquor cabinet and prepared the drinks. "Can you tell me more?"

Gordon thought about it for a moment. NTC had just given him a heads-up about a new Alzheimer drug that was about to be submitted to the FDA for evaluation and approval. Until now, the pharmaceutical company involved in the development had been able to keep it secret. Lab tests and animal trials were extremely promising. The next phase was human trials, and if they were successful, it could very well be the end of Alzheimer disease. *CRS has a number of clients in the pharmaceutical industry that would pay handsome amounts to get their hands on the technical details of a drug like this.*

Miller stopped and looked at Gordon, who hadn't answered him. "Nate?"

Gordon came out of his reverie. "Oh, sorry. I was deep in thought there for a moment. No problem, I can tell you."

Miller's smile grew bigger as he listened to Gordon. His eyes were flashing dollar signs, and his mind was already calculating bonuses.

"Thanks for that Nate. I will get a team onto it right away. Just out of curiosity. Was this a tip from NTC?"

Gordon nodded and took a sip of his scotch.

They both smiled, and Gordon asked Miller to give him a status report on the Devereux projects.

"Well, as far as Carter Devereux is concerned, the project is in full swing. We have deployed a surveillance team to track and follow him. I'm receiving reports every other day from the team."

Gordon nodded. "Sounds good. What have you learned so far?"

"He's been in DC for the past two weeks, and it looks like A-Echelon has assigned bodyguards to him now. Two of them around him at all times from what we can see."

"Bodyguards?" Gordon frowned. He didn't like the sound of that at all. "Do you think they know he's under surveillance?"

"No, I don't think so. He's been under guard since Jerusalem according to my information. Our surveillance is non-intrusive, we've got tabs on his phones and Internet activities, and the team is making sure they keep distance between themselves and him, rotating observers frequently, you know, the usual stuff."

"Then why has he sprouted bodyguards? I don't like it; something's up."

"Well, given that he's been investigating ancient nuclear weapons and that he was placed under guard right after the attack in Jerusalem, I'd say that someone is paranoid that maybe he was the target of an assassination attempt by that bomb blast and is taking precautions," Miller suggested.

"Hmm," Gordon mused. "Well, I still don't like it, but I suppose that is a possibility. Keep an eye on things and proceed carefully."

"I'll do that, but I'm pretty sure no one in his circle knows he's being watched."

"Alright, so where is he now and what's he doing?"

"He went back to his ranch in Canada two days ago, accompanied by two bodyguards of course. It's a bit more challenging to follow and observe him there."

"Why is that?"

"Well, the place is more than 50,000 acres, and there are no access roads. He gets in and out of there by plane. It's too much of a risk to send people onto the property, at least not for long periods of time. So our only means of surveillance out there is to make use of drones."

"Aren't those things easy to spot?" Gordon looked a bit worried.

"We're not using commercial drones," Miller smiled smugly. "We've got a few military drones. Those babies operate above 2,000 feet and are controlled from about 30 miles away."

Gordon nodded. "We should be okay with that then. Now, what about that book we are looking for?"

Miller shook his head. "I'm afraid all our searches came up empty. If there is anyone out there that knows anything about the book, they are definitely not talking about it on the Internet. I guess we will have to launch that international search as suggested by El Fadl."

Gordon shrugged. "Yeah, that's unfortunate. But I suppose we don't have much of a choice then. Just make sure that nothing can be tracked back to us."

"Understood. Give me a few days to see what I can do and I'll let you know."

They took the last swirls of their Scotch, Gordon got up to leave, and they said their goodbyes.

Chapter Thirty-One

FOUR DAYS OF HELL

On Carter's return to Freydis, he was accompanied by Roy Taylor, originally from Saskatchewan, and Andre Levesque a French-speaking native of Quebec, who grew up in Quebec City. They were both former JTF2 - Joint Task Force 2 operators, who had worked closely with USA Special Forces in Iraq and Afghanistan. JTF2 was one of three units in the Canadian Special Operations Forces Command consisting of CSOR - Canadian Special Operations Regiment, the Canadian Joint Incident Response Unit and 427 Special Operations Aviation Squadron.

Carter took an instant liking to the two younger men. On the trip back there was a lot of time to talk and Carter discovered that Andre had a love interest back in Quebec City, and that was part of the reason why he was so excited with the assignment at Freydis, he was closer to her. The two of them were planning to get married the next year. Roy, on the other hand, had sort of permanently moved to DC, not that he wasn't loyal to his country of birth, his decision to make the move had to do with a beautiful dark haired woman, to whom he was married and who was a lecturer at Georgetown University. They had no children yet. His explanation, "we're still practicing," made Carter smile.

All this talk about family and girlfriend soon had Carter's mind returning to a time that seemed like only yesterday, when he and Mackenzie met and started dating. He had his own wonderful memories of special moments, collected over the years, carefully wrapped up and stored in a very secret part of his brain, from where it was possible to recall them when things got tough. The difference was, Carter thought, being ten years older than the two young men beside him, he had more of those memories stored than they had even had the opportunity to experience yet. He hoped, over the years ahead, that their minds would be filled with experiences just as delightful as his.

Later on, their conversation turned to Freydis and the next two weeks during which time they would all have much to do. Carter had to get the nuke research going again, and there were two expeditions to plan; one to the City of Lights and one to North India.

They were planning to start their days at six am with a five-mile run which would, over time, build up to ten miles, followed by an hour of hand-to-hand combat training, then breakfast. After that another five hours of training covering various Special Forces skills such as the use of hand weapons, field craft, urban warfare, small tactics, observation, and survival. Carter had made arrangements with Bly to cook dinner for them every night. He couldn't give her too many specifics over the phone. He would explain all of it when he was back.

Carter was not a novice when it came to firearms, in fact, he was not a bad shot at all. His grandpa, Will, taught him how to shoot, hunt and handle guns from a very young age, but what he was about to experience was in an entirely different league.

They were not planning on letting him use live ammunition for months. There was a lot of dry shooting (without ammunition) training Carter had to go through before he would fire a single live round. It was going to require hundreds of hours of practicing stances, aiming and learning the art of pulling a trigger. Then he would be ready to fire a shot with a laser gun. He had to become equally skilled with either hand and be able to achieve a hundred percent hit rate with the left and right hand, and even while holding a gun in each hand.

It was going to take at least 100 hours of practice before Carter would be given a gun that fired a laser beam, mimicking a real shot. Another 200 hours with the laser guns would bring him to the point where he would be ready to fire a live round. They were planning to use handguns with silencers when they reached that point. Carter's weapons training would take up two to three hours every day. Andre and Roy explained to him that by the time he fired his first live round, he would have squeezed a trigger around half a million times.

The huge expanse of Freydis provided the ideal space for them to train without any fear that they would be seen or heard. Carter had no illusions that these young men were going to give him a hard time, but he was ready for that. That's what he asked for and what he paid them to do. They were planning to build various obstacle courses and silhouette shooting ranges to mimic real life situations as best they could. The airplane hangar, sheds, and other buildings around the homestead would be used for close quarter combat techniques.

The Wolves of Freydis

When they landed at Freydis Ahote, Bly and Jeha were there to pick them up with the electric carts and help them move their luggage to the cabin. Jeha couldn't get enough of Carter's attention and immediately made friends with the two new guys as well. Providentially, Will had built a large cabin with four bedrooms when he started out on Freydis. Maybe he was expecting Carter to fill them all up with great grandchildren one day. Roy and Andre each had their own room.

When they were unpacked, Carter and Jeha went over to visit Ahote and Bly, and fill them in on the events of the past two weeks in DC, the plans they had made, and the new arrangements. He also told them that Roy and Andre did not have all of the information; all they knew was that they were here for his protection and training.

As far as Roy and Andre were concerned, Carter's family was killed in a bomb explosion in Jerusalem. They had no idea about Carter's research projects. The reason he required the training was that he had to be prepared to work in dangerous places on high risk, secret projects around the world.

Carter didn't share any of the sensitive information or the strategy they had in mind with Ahote and Bly either. However, he had to give them the real reason for why he wanted to undergo the training.

Ahote laughed when Carter told them. "So now you're going to turn into Rambo!"

"Maybe not quite as vicious as that, although I wouldn't say no if I could have his capabilities," Carter chuckled. "But seriously Ahote, it is vital for me to be there when Mackenzie and Liam are rescued. If it is going to be a covert operation, then I don't want to be in anybody's way."

Bly shook her head. "Carter, the past few months were

bad enough – let's hope and pray that a peaceful solution will present itself so that no one else will be killed or injured."

Bly was happy to help with the dinners and to have the two young men around. They reminded her of her own children who were about the same age as Roy and Andre. They made a good first impression on her.

Ahote was keen to help Carter to gain better bushcraft and survival skills.

Six o'clock the next morning found the three men outside ready for their run. Carter still had some discomfort from his injuries, but he didn't say a word when the pain started eating at him after a mile. He gritted his teeth and continued. He was totally out of shape after the months of inactivity in the hospital, and many weeks afterward with casts on his arm and leg. At the three-mile mark, he was in severe pain but forced himself to keep going another mile and then he walked the last mile back home.

Roy and Andre didn't say anything. They knew about his injuries; they were impressed that he didn't start walking after a mile. They waited for him on the lawn in front of the cabin and started his first hand-to-hand combat lesson. They were skilled in Krav Maga, Taekwondo and Brazilian Jujitsu techniques. Although Carter's existing tai chi skills had equipped him to give a good account of himself in hand-to-hand combat, he quickly realized that krav maga and taekwondo were aggressive forms of self-defense. The tai chi philosophy was never to initiate violence, the krav maga and taekwondo philosophies were the opposite; engage and destroy the enemy as quickly as possible.

When they took a break for breakfast, Carter felt like he was about ready to collapse. But that's just what his body felt. His mind told him he was okay.

They took their mugs of coffee and went outside to the porch. "I don't know about you guys," He smiled, "but I must have had quite a few hundred gallons of coffee in my life, and yet this coffee is the best one ever."

"It's strange how one can appreciate simple things, which we usually take for granted when you have to do without it for a while," Andre said in perfect English with a hint of a French accent.

"Let me tell you Carter, the best drink I ever had in my entire life was a glass of cold water, and that was in the middle of winter." Roy laughed.

They finished their breakfast and went over to the big shed where Carter got his first lesson in the use of handguns. Crawling, rolling and jumping, running and crouching while practicing to draw and point the gun at targets around the shed. No finger on the trigger, just drawing and pointing.

By 1:00 pm, seven hours after they went for the run, they were done for the day and Carter plonked down on the shed floor with his back against the wall; he was exhausted and in pain. Andre and Roy walked up and held their hands out to pull him up.

"Come on old timer," Roy teased. "Let's go home and give you something to eat. You did well today."

Andre chimed in. "Yeah, the next three or four days are going to be hell, but your body will get used to it. To be honest, neither of us thought you would make it to the three-hour mark."

Carter grinned. "In that case, I'm looking forward to the days after the next three or four then."

They all showered and had lunch after which Carter planned to get on with his research work while Roy and Andre reconnoitered a two-mile area around the homestead. They took pictures and drew maps of the area; they had to know where every tree, bush, and rock was. Then they went about deploying a whole range of solar powered electronic surveillance gadgets, which included laser trip wires, cameras, and microphones - all wirelessly connected to two computer screens inside the cabin. By the time they were finished, the Freydis homestead was a fortress. No one would get within two miles of the place without them knowing. That was if they could get past the wolves in the first place.

Carter and Ahote still had to introduce them to the wolves of Freydis.

Once alone in his study, ready to settle down, Carter suddenly felt lost. He was in severe pain after the morning's workout and thankful for his foresight to renew some of his prescriptions for pain relief the doctors had given him to take if necessary.

A glass of water and two painkillers are the first order of the afternoon and then he thought, *on with work.*

He soon discovered it was not going to be that easy. It would have been such a relief to sink down into his thoughts of the City of Lights. He still believed that it contained what he needed to lead him to a better understanding of the ancient nukes and also, he hoped, to finding out more about who else was interested in the subject and if they were the ones holding Mackie and Liam. It seemed so easy, and yet it was just not possible. His tired brain reverted to his first emotions when he learned they were still alive.

He went to lie down on his bed, hoping to sleep for a

while, but it didn't work. Nevertheless, he stayed lying down in the hope his physical pain would diminish.

It was just such an enormous seesaw of emotions. The belief he had lost them both and wishing he was also dead and that terrible knowledge, dragging on week after week as he slowly, sometimes against his will, recovered. Then the relief and yet fear that came when James learned they were indeed alive.

If they were alive, where were they and who had them? Were they being taken care of or were they neglected, forgotten in some prison somewhere starving and ill. He had no way of knowing, and it was eating at his soul.

How in the hell can I get away from these thoughts long enough to make the break I need to get to the research that must be done?

He got up and had another cup of coffee, followed by another, and after four hours, he took two more painkillers. Slowly the pain receded and with it the sharp mental agony and pictures he had of his loved ones.

With a small amount of relief, knowing full well it was the Codeine that was giving him the break, he finally got his head down over the research that needed to be done before they could return to the City of Lights.

Two hours later he surfaced from his research. He was tired, but the pain had eased considerably, and he was able to accept the fact that, in a few hours' time, he would be taking on another grueling day with his tormentors.

Dinner with Bly and Ahote gave a welcome break for all three men. Roy and Andre made a big hit with Bly, keeping her laughing at some of their stories about their days in Special Forces and all the awful things that happened, and the torture they went through.

Carter was amused at the humorous spin they put on the things they experienced, and thoroughly enjoyed hearing of their training days and the errors they'd made; it made him feel he was doing okay after all.

Ahote sat there grinning broadly; he could so easily relate to these two, it reminded him of the rigorous training for undersea work he'd gone through as a young man.

Roy highlighted the pain and agony of the long runs and the heavy loads they were expected to carry over miles and miles of rugged terrain, which, in his opinion, was up higher mountains and down deeper valleys more rugged than anything around Freydis. Andre complained of the awful food that was supposed to sustain them, and then asked for a second helping of everything.

They asked about the City of Lights and the city in the caves of Cusco. Ahote and Bly enjoyed Carter's re-telling of the story as if they were hearing it for the first time.

All in all, it was a happy meal, a healing meal, and one that sent Carter to bed with a more cheerful and relaxed feeling than he'd had in a long time; confident he would get his family back.

It was the next day in the afternoon, after Carter had a bit of rest from another gruelling seven hours of running, hand-to-hand combat, and weapons training, that Ahote said it was time the men were introduced to the wolves.

"No one is altogether safe if we don't introduce them. Not to say they would harm anyone, but we'd certainly be told if there were strangers on the land."

"Are they domesticated?" Andre asked.

"No, not at all, their contact with us is purely their own idea. If Carter isn't around, they vanish. Unless there is a good reason, we don't see them until Carter returns. Although you can be assured they have watched everything you have done since you arrived."

The Wolves of Freydis

"Everything?" the two men exchanged glances thinking of the surveillance equipment they had set up.

Carter grinned, "Don't worry, they won't touch anything, just go over everything to check you both out."

"It sounds as if they are part of the old legends of wolves who take care of humans." Ray commented, "Does anyone remember Mowgli in India being raised by wolves? And that's not just a story, it has actually happened many times." Ray continued, "The First Nation peoples' beliefs are that there are wolves who are special. Usually, they pass unnoticed by us, but if someone needs them they suddenly appear, then just as suddenly vanish again."

Ahote, a Hopi Indian knew and understood that well.

"That sounds like Keeva and Loki," Carter joined in, "not that anyone was in dire need when they first turned up, which was before I met Mackenzie, but once we were married they adopted her and things have been strange ever since," Carter added.

"Strange?" Andre asked.

Carter went on to tell them of the experiences they'd had since with the wolves of Freydis and how special they had become to the people here.

"That's eerie isn't it. You have to wonder how it happens, that they knew when no one else did." Ray commented

"Yes," Andre joined in, "and yet there's no denying that it is becoming increasingly clear that animals do know and sense far more than we are aware of, maybe it's just us that are slow." He grinned quietly to himself knowing he was right.

They had walked a short distance from the homestead when movement under the trees exposed Keeva and Loki watching them.

Carter stopped them, "Hang on while I go and get them to come in."

They watched as Carter walked a little further and raised his hand at which both wolves moved forward to greet him then followed him back to the three men who were watching.

"Put your hands out like this." Carter put his hand out and they copied him.

"Loki, Keeva here is Ray, and indicated Ray's hand, each wolf sniffed the hand and then licked it. Carter then went on to introduce Andre and the wolves repeated their scrutiny and acceptance.

They allowed both men to pat them before once again vanishing back into the woods.

"Well, I'll be!" Ray smiled, "I've never experienced the like, what a beautiful thing to happen."

Andre was grinning, "That's the best thing I've ever known."

Chapter Thirty-Two

THREE MEETINGS

James Rhodes was a little nervous as he prepared for his meeting with the President, and Irene picked up on it. Hunter Patrick had always taken care of these types of meetings only calling James in occasionally, as needed. Hunter was good at managing upwards; James didn't think he had the same skills. Irene helped him to prepare, and like a mother figure, although she was easily ten years younger than James, did manage to calm him down and boost his self-confidence.

The meeting was in the Oval Office, attended by the President, Vice President, Director of the CIA, two members of the National Security Council, and the Secretary of Defense.

The first few minutes were spent congratulating James on his permanent appointment as Director of A-Echelon and then a discussion of the tragedy of the Jerusalem bomb explosion. Everyone in the room except James believed that Mackenzie and Liam were killed in that explosion along with 23 others, and James had no intention of sharing his knowledge with any of them. The attendees were all glad to hear about Carter's recovery and grateful that he was prepared to come back and continue his work on the ancient nukes.

James gave them an overview of all the A-Echelon projects and answered their questions. The Ancient Nuke Project was discussed in more detail than any of the others and the Vice President wanted to know what the plans were for the continuation of Mackenzie's respirocyte project.

James explained that they were in the process of finding someone with the right skills and who would be able to pass through the stringent security clearance process.

At the end of the meeting, the President suggested that James bring Carter around for a quick get together the next time he was in DC.

James was relieved when the meeting was over, the presentation went well, but the idea of hiding information from the President and the rest of the people in the group distressed him. Nevertheless, he had no choice; the security leak could be anyone inside A-Echelon or anyone outside who knew what was going on. He had to keep the information contained within the small group, which consisted of himself, Irene, Carter, Sean, and Dylan. Those were the only people who would have the whole picture until the problem was resolved.

Irene was waiting for him when he returned from the White House.

"How did the meeting go, Jim?"

"Thanks to your motherly oversight and reassurances during the preparation, it went very well," James grinned. "The only awkward part was where I deliberately had to lie to them. I just hope that my withholding information from them doesn't come back to bite me in the ass later."

"I can understand those feelings, Jim, but I don't think we have many other options at this point. Maybe you could share it with the Director of the CIA. We both know him, have worked with him, and we trust him. But that wouldn't serve any purpose other than to make you feel better, and that's just a 'maybe' it would help you feel better."

"Yeah, you're right. Unless I have a good reason to go and talk to him we should keep it to ourselves and deal with the fallout if it happens."

About 6,700 miles to the east of Washington DC, in Riyadh, Saudi Arabia, it was 9:00 pm when the deputy director of the General Intelligence Presidency of Saudi Arabia, Ibrahimi El Fadl was shown into Xavier Algosaibi's study.

The two men greeted each other and talked a bit about their families, their health and the politics of the day before they got to the reason for El Fadl's visit.

"Mr. Algosaibi, I'm here to give you an update on the two projects at the Institute of Scientific Research and Development – ISRD – which you have placed under my oversight."

Algosaibi took a sip of his coffee and waved for El Fadl to continue.

"The first good news is that we have just received word from Mr. Nate Gordon of the CRS that A-Echelon has started work on the Ancient Nuclear Research Project again."

That brought a big smile to Algosaibi's face. El Fadl knew it was the right tactic to soften the old man's mood by leading with the good news first.

"Professor Devereux has recovered from his wounds and has apparently agreed to continue the research. He was in Washington DC the last two weeks and is now back at his ranch in Canada."

"It sounds as if CRS is doing a good job of following and studying him," Algosaibi smiled.

"Indeed sir. I'm impressed with how much information they have been able to collect in such a short time. They also know that Devereux is now under 24/7 protection by a contingent of bodyguards."

"Mhh, I can't say I blame him." Algosaibi pouted as he remembered that Carter Devereux could have been in their custody now were it not for Youssef Bin Bandar's screw-up of the Jerusalem operation.

"I'd say it would take maybe another six to eight months before we have received enough information from CRS to enable us to start planning a mission for the abduction of Professor Devereux."

"Why so long?" Algosaibi asked as he leaned forward. "I would have hoped we could do it in a matter of weeks, not months."

"Sir, it's become more complicated now that he has the bodyguards looking after him. Also, when he is on that ranch, it's not easy. It's an enormous place; more than 50,000 acres and it's very isolated with no access roads. Devereux uses an airplane to fly in and out. On the one hand, that might be the ideal place to abduct him, but on the other, it's going to take very careful planning. While CRS is collecting all the information about him, they must take extreme care that their observers are not discovered. So at the moment, they do all their observations with high altitude military class drones, which they control from 30 miles away."

Algosaibi had his hands in a steeple under his chin, deep in thought. After a long silence, he said. "I want to speed this up. Let CRS know the contract price, for this half of the two-fold contract, has been doubled. They will be paid $50 million if they can deliver the information which would lead us to Devereux's capture in 60 days."

El Fadl wanted to argue about the wisdom of that but decided that not only was it not his place to argue for CSR but that it would also be better not to oppose the old man. "Yes, sir. I'll get the message through to Mr. Gordon right away."

Next, they talked about the respirocyte project, and El Fadl explained that Mackenzie was now leading the research and although that meant the project team had to go back to the drawing board. Daiyan Nasser, the Director of the ISRD, felt that they were now heading in the right direction. Progress was slow but promising. The major stumbling block for them remained the fact that they had lost the Sirralnnudam.

Algosaibi clenched his fist, *another one of Bin Bandar's stupid screw-ups,* he thought. "What progress has CRS made with that?"

"Unfortunately, not much, sir." El Fadl was a bit nervous, but he knew it was better to give Algosaibi the truth rather than a rose-colored version of it. "CRS is now looking at alternative methods to try and find a copy."

Algosaibi thanked him for his time, got up and accompanied him to the door where they said their goodbyes.

Nate Gordon's smile looked as if it was stretching from ear to ear when he read the decoded message from Ibrahimi El

Fadl. *$50 million if you can help us capture Professor Devereux within 60 days.*

He threw the message on Dwayne Millers desk puffing his chest out with self-satisfaction and sat down.

"Holy shit!" Miller exclaimed. "$50 million! Man, we have to do this."

Gordon smiled and nodded, "Yep, we have to. Can you throw more resources at this?"

"You can bet your ass on that. I'll pull them off other projects."

Chapter Thirty-Three

ARCHEOLOGICAL SPECIAL OPS TRAINING

Andre's predictions about the four days of hell were spot on. Not counting the recent injuries, he had sustained in the bomb explosion; Carter could not recall any time in his life when his body had felt as battered as it did for the first few days of training. The morning of the second day, his muscles were so stiff and sore that he could barely get up and get dressed; and he had a hard time bending down to tie his shoelaces. It was the images of Mackenzie and Liam that got him moving and kept him moving every inch of the way. They did a few stretches and warm up exercises and then tackled the five-mile run. After a mile, Carter felt like walking but convinced himself nothing had changed from the day before it was still the same body and the track was the same. *If I could do four miles yesterday, I can do four miles today*. And he did.

The third day was the worst of them all. By the fourth day, he thought he felt slightly better than the day before, but he wasn't entirely sure. On day five he managed to run four and a half miles before he started walking. It was also the first day he was able to put in five solid hours of good research after the training.

He would have smiled if he could have heard Andre and Roy talking about him when he was out of earshot.

"You know Roy; I didn't think Carter was going to get up for the run on the second day, but here he is; it's day five, and he's still going."

Roy nodded. "Yeah I'm not sure how old he is, but my guess is he must be pushing forty. He's still recovering from severe injuries, but I've not heard a single groan escape his lips. I can see he's in pain not only physically, but mentally as well."

"He certainly is one tough cookie; that's for sure." Andre said. "With the right training, he would be an asset on any Special Ops mission."

Roy agreed and started laughing. "We'll have to be aware that before too long the old man is going to kick dust in our eyes Andre, and not just on the run, but in the hand-to-hand combat training as well. He almost punched my lights out with one of his punches in that sparring session this morning."

Carter, in the meantime, had been studying all the collected information on the City of Lights, some of it provided by the current expedition leader Daan Hannah, a professor at Alexandria International University and father of Sameha Hannah. She had been the cartographer and photographer who was part of Carter's team when they did the first site survey on behalf of the Egyptian government.

James and Irene had given Carter the go ahead to start the preparations for the next trip to the City of Lights, and he was now working on that. Roy and Andre would be part of the group; in fact, they begged to be part of it when they first heard about Carter's plans to revisit the place.

The Wolves of Freydis

Dylan Mulligan, Sean's Second in Command (2IC) at Executive Advantage was in charge of the Devereux mission. When he spoke with Carter earlier on the secure phone, he told him that he was planning to visit Freydis in about ten days' time. He wouldn't give him the exact date or time, explaining that for security reasons no one should know when the visit would take place. The reason for his visit was to see how Carter's training was progressing and to bring in two new bodyguards to relieve Andre and Roy.

With Dylan's visit in mind, Carter rounded Roy and Andre up for a talk and to advise them of their CO's upcoming visit. Just when he was about to start, Ahote turned up, and Carter invited him to join them for coffee.

He winked at Ahote, who immediately caught onto the fact that Carter was up to something. "Okay guys, I just got off the phone with your CO, Dylan Mulligan and he has approved your request to join me on the expedition to the City of Lights."

Roy and Andre high-fived. "Great Carter. Thanks for arranging that."

"No problem," He smiled. "That was easy. Now we have to talk about your training."

"Training? What training?" They looked perplexed.

"You two thought I'm the only one that needs training to go on a dig? No, no, no, this is a dangerous place we're going to. You both will need archeological special ops training."

Ahote had to turn his head away as he struggled to contain his laughter.

"Archeological special ops training?" Andre looked incredulously at Carter. "What the hell does that mean? How to use a brush or something?"

Carter managed to maintain his composure although he

was about to explode in laughter. "To use the brushes on an archeological dig requires specific techniques and is a very advanced skill, I'm not sure we'll have enough time to teach you that. No, we'll have to start with the basics first. It's called how to dig."

Roy started smiling, but he wasn't sure. Was Carter joking or not?

"Dig? You're joking!" Roy paused, looking at the frown on Carters face and then asked nervously, "right?"

"Do you want to go on this dig or not?" Carter said in his best mock anger voice. "You can't just go shoveling gleefully away on an archeological dig; in your carelessness, you might damage something valuable or even destroy an ancient artifact. You have to know what you're doing and what digging tool and technique to use in every situation."

"Ok, man. I'm sorry," Roy said humbly. "I'm willing to learn; I didn't mean to sound . . . I mean, I don't want to be careless. Show me what to do and I'll be very careful."

Carter had nearly bitten through the side of his cheek to keep from laughing, but managed a stern, "Right then. So let's begin the first lesson right away. As I've said, we don't have much time to get you up to skill. I want you two to go over to the shed and bring back all the shovels you can find in there. We have some serious digging to do."

Roy shook his head and started to get up. He looked at Andre, but he had totally blank expression on his face. No guidance there. He looked at Carter, but his face was deadpan. He didn't know what to think.

"Okay, Andre let's get going."

Ahote had cleared his throat loudly and disappeared into the kitchen to get the coffee machine going. When Andre and Roy had vanished around the corner on the way to the shed, he could hold it in no longer and crumpled over with laughter.

A few minutes later Roy and Andre returned, each carrying an armload of spades. On the way to the shed, they had discussed this weird turn of events but agreed Carter looked serious, and they also decided they would do whatever it took to get on the team that was going to the City of Lights; even if it meant acquiring some special digging skills.

Carter took them about twenty yards away from the house in an open area, visible from the front porch where Ahote was sitting struggling not to burst into laughter again.

Carter started to explain why each shovel was shaped differently and what the purpose of each was and how it should be used. But that was as far as he got before he started laughing. He laughed so much he had to sit down.

That's when Roy and Andre realized they had just been taken for a long ride. They both leaped forward and pinned him to the ground. Roy shouting, "You're a Professor you're supposed to be an honest and trustworthy man!"

A fierce wrestling match ensued; Carter had to give up in the end. The two guys together were way too strong for him. He had to tap out and apologize when Andre finally managed to get Carter's arm in a very painful grip behind his back.

Back on the porch, each with a mug of coffee in hand Carter explained that it would be necessary, for security reasons for both of them to have fake archeological profiles. They would need to have at least a basic understanding of the site and as much archeological knowledge as they could learn between now and their arrival at the site to keep up the deception. No one on the dig must know that they were Special Forces operators.

The two of them were eager to learn more about the City of Lights, and anything Carter had for them to study, and so archeological studies became a part of their daily routine until their departure to Egypt.

The details of the planned expedition to the City of Lights, date of departure, arrival, and duration of stay were all tightly guarded amongst their group of five. The four expedition members who would accompany Carter would be placed on notice to keep themselves ready to leave on very short notice. Professor Daan Hannah, in charge of the dig, would not be notified either. The arrival of Carter and his team in the City of Lights was going to be unexpected.

Irene was in charge of making all the necessary administrative arrangements, which included setting up profiles for the men who would be going with Carter to make sure their profiles would withstand any background scrutiny. A part of Irene's tasks was also to discreetly secure the items on the list of equipment that Carter provided.

Three weeks after Carter returned to Freydis accompanied by Andre and Roy, he got a call from Dylan Mulligan, telling him he was about half an hour out from Freydis. Executive Advantage owned a twin-engine, four-seater Beech Baron 58. Dylan, being a qualified and experienced pilot, had no need for a pilot, so he was arriving with only the two new bodyguards, Kevin Cooke and John Arevalo plus a surprise for Carter, thus keeping the numbers of people knowing where he was down to a minimum.

Kevin Cooke, nicknamed KC because of his initials, was a 31-year-old former Delta Force operator, about five eleven, blond hair, blue eyes and called Denver, Colorado home.

John Arevalo was a 32-year-old former Navy SEAL

from Fort Myers, Florida. He stood about five nine and had dark hair and dark brown eyes.

The fourth person who got out of the plane, Irene O'Connell, was a big surprise to Carter. He was elated to see her but then immediately started worrying about sleeping arrangements until he realized that Bly might welcome female companionship in the all-male world. And that's precisely what happened. Shortly after Irene had put her luggage down, Bly arrived and solved Carter's problem.

For the next three days, Dylan reviewed Carter's training progress and the security measures implemented by Roy and Andre.

Carter's aches and pains of the first week were gone, and he was able to run the five miles with a lot more ease by now. He still wasn't quite able to keep up with the younger, and much more physically fit, Andre and Roy, but was making real progress. Carter was ready to increase the distance to six miles the following week

His hand-to-hand combat training was progressing very well, which Dylan experienced firsthand in two sparring sessions with Carter. After the second session, he told John and Kevin that Carter was ready to start training in the use of knives, sticks, and other weapons.

Dylan was impressed – it was evident Carter was a quick study and not only that, what impressed him most was the sheer determination and positive attitude about his training radiating from Carter. He gave everything his best, and he never complained. In private conversations with Andre and Roy, they could not stop talking about Carter's dedication and astonishing progress.

Another pleasing aspect for Dylan was when he observed Carter's shooting skills during the firearms training session.

Carter was two to three weeks ahead of schedule on all the training goals that Sean and Dylan had set for him in the beginning. Dylan sat down with Carter, Kevin, and John and revised the training plan and goals for the next four weeks. Due to Carter's rapid progress, Dylan introduced survival training two weeks ahead of schedule.

In the afternoons, after Carter's seven-hour training sessions, Carter, Dylan, and Irene worked on Carter's project, planning for the trip to the City of Lights and other matters. On both of the days while they were there they would break early and go for a long walk to the various lookout points around the homestead. Irene and Dylan both were instantly in love with the flawless beauty of Freydis.

Andre and Roy did a handover to Kevin and John bringing them up to speed with what they were doing around Freydis, showing them the exact locations of the surveillance and security equipment and the archeological information that they had to assimilate before they departed for the City of Lights. They also told them about the unusual meeting with the wolves.

In the mornings, while Carter and the boys were in training, Bly and Irene spent time together. Bly could not have hoped to have better female company than the easy going, no pretenses, Irene O'Connell. Irene wanted to know everything about life on Freydis; wanted to see all the domesticated and as many of the wild animals as she could in the short time available. She wanted Bly to tell her in detail about the wolves of Freydis and their behavior. They were both a bit sad when Irene had to leave and exchanged contact details. Bly insisted that Irene come and visit her again soon. Irene didn't require any persuasion to accept Bly's offer; the two of them got along like a house on fire.

Carter, Kevin, and John would return to DC in three to four weeks to make the final preparations before their departure for the City of Lights.

Chapter Thirty-Four

COME HAVE A LOOK AT THIS

Keeva was restless; Loki watched her pace back and forth in front of the cave entrance stopping to pant before she moved on.

He was disturbed, he sensed the time for the pups had arrived, Keeva smelled different, and she was irritable with him. He'd decided to lie quietly and wait to see what she might need.

With no pack to guide her, Keeva felt alone; she had Loki, but he was annoying her. The cave had been chosen some weeks ago, and she'd dug and formed a birthing pit with all the care and concentration her genes directed. It was waiting for her now, but as yet she wasn't ready to enter while leaving Loki outside and alone while she labored alone inside.

Mackenzie turned over in her sleep and was suddenly awake; something was amiss, but what? She waited, lying quietly in the dark. Then cramps rippled through her, only mild ones. *That's odd, why now? Okay, I'm nearing the end of my second trimester, and I remember having Braxton Hicks, those 'practice' cramps early on when I was expecting Liam.* Mackie said to herself, *but these don't feel real.*

What on earth do I mean by that? She ran her hands over her swelling belly waiting for them to begin again. There they were, just mild and with no sense of movement under her hands. She hesitated to call Seema; she didn't feel the need for anyone yet. She'd wait and see.

Later having returned to sleep, she felt a cold, wet nose pushing against her cheek. In her dream, she woke to find Loki standing beside her bed nudging at her. *Loki?* She whispered, very aware she didn't want to wake Liam, who had formed a habit of sleeping light so he could hear her. She put out her hand and ruffled his fur, *what is it?* The cramps fluttered over her tummy once more, and she began to understand what was going on, *it's not me, it's Keeva!*

In her dream, she sat up and looked deep into Loki's eyes. *Keeva's having her babies, is that it Loki?* He moved closer. *You're feeling confused and don't know what to do.* She ran her hand over his head and around his ears. *She's on her own in the cave, and there's no one else to help her, and you're worried she won't want you near her.*

He licked her hand. *Loki, go to her, she needs to have you close; you're all she has at this time, go now.* She watched him as he faded from view and then she lay down again.

Quietly she waited, knowing the cramps were fading as each pup was born. She slept and by morning, she knew all was well on Freydis once more.

Later in the morning, she shared her news with Liam.

For Loki, the reassurances he received from Mackie were all he needed. Rising from where he'd been lying quietly, dreaming his contact with Mackenzie and with his tail down in a humble attitude, he quietly joined Keeva in the cave.

She was panting, one pup was born, and she was getting ready to give birth to the second. Loki stretched out his nose and tentatively touched the newborn, expecting Keeva to snap at him, but instead she relaxed and closed her eyes waiting for the next contraction. He licked the pup, tasting its newborn taste on his tongue, knowing Keeva had cleaned it. He began cleaning it again, gently massaging it with his tongue as his tail wagged slowly back and forth in the dust of the cave floor.

When the second one was born, he waited and watched patiently, while Keeva cleaned it and ate the placenta, which was nutritious food for her at this time. When she was done and had lain down once more before labor began again, he gently nudged the first pup towards her underbelly and began to lick and massage the second one.

Loki was in heaven as he'd never been before. The pups were sheer joy and magic. He was unaware just how many young wolves were welcomed into a wolf pack; all he knew was how he rejoiced in these new lives.

He settled quietly and waited as the last of the four was born and all were nursing. He watched Keeva put her head down to sleep and when he was sure all was safe, he too put his head between his paws and dozed.

It was a week later that Carter saddled his horse and took off for a well-earned break, telling the guys he needed some time on his own, something they both understood.

He'd planned to take a trail that went over the mountain and down into a quiet valley away from his usual haunts, a valley he'd not seen for several years. As he headed in that direction, Loki suddenly appeared and yipped at him, then ran across in front of the horse and back again causing Carter to stop his horse in its tracks.

Carter had not seen the wolves for well over three weeks and had wondered about Keeva and her litter. Realizing something was odd, he turned the horse to follow Loki and took the trail to the cave. As they drew closer Loki ran ahead, looking back to make sure Carter was following; he frowned to himself, it wasn't like Loki to behave this way, was something wrong with Keeva? Dread filled him; he should have come out this way sooner.

Suddenly it felt like it was still a very long way to go, but in fact, five minutes later he was able to tie up the reins, let his horse go, and follow Loki to the cave mouth.

Loki entered the cave, then reappeared wagging his tail as if to say, *come have a look at this.*

"Loki, are you trying to tell me you've become a father? Is that it?" he bent and patted Loki's side causing thumping noises as his hand pushed the air out of Loki's thick coat, an action Loki seemed to like. Loki licked the hand and then retreated to the cave once again, then reappeared and waited.

"Am I allowed to go in and see? Is that it?"

Carter was well aware that this was hallowed ground at present, and maybe Keeva would not be pleased to see him. He hesitated but once again Loki invited him in, so he proceeded with caution.

As his eyes grew accustomed to the dim light, he could see Keeva lying stretched out on the ground and then he saw the pups.

He went down on his knees, "Oh Keeva, you clever lass; you smart, clever lass." He whispered.

Her tail moved, wagging slowly. Carefully he sat down

near her and patted her head; she licked his hand. Loki crouched next to him staring at him and then at the pups.

"Four pups. Oh, my word. Oh just wait until Mackie sees these, she'll be over the moon; indeed, she will. As for Liam, well what can I say? You know how he feels about small animals." He reached out a hand and tentatively ran his fingers over the tiny bodies, then just sat back and smiled.

Keeva stood and stretched, resting her chin on Carter's shoulder before she stepped forward, picked up one of the pups and put it in his hands. Tears started in Carter's eyes; this was more special than he could ever share with anyone. He turned the tiny pup over, and he cupped it in his large hands and noted it was a little girl.

"Keeva, you have a daughter." He paused, "May I name her?" Keeva licked his cheek, "May I call her Winona for first born?" He held her to his cheek feeling the soft fur. "May I see the others?"

Keeva pushed his hand away, and he accepted her law, replacing Winona among her siblings.

"Oh, how often do you guys give me something more to hang on to, to believe in, to know one day Mackie and Liam will be back here with me. If I didn't know any different, I would say you are miracle workers. As it is, you might not yet be that, but by God, you come pretty damned close."

Carter spent the rest of the afternoon in and near the cave. He and Loki went down to the river where he shed his clothes and swam before racing up and down the banks as he used to when he was first getting his strength back after recovering from his injuries. Loki watched him and seemed to be mildly amused – that is if wolves could be mildly amused.

Later they returned to the cave to find Keeva had left

the pups for a little while and was watching them from a vantage point above the cave entrance. She joined Carter as he sat on a log and watched the beginning shades of an evening sky before he bade them goodnight and returned to the homestead, his heart full of peace.

Somehow, once again, the wolves had imparted some internal knowledge that told him Mackenzie and Liam were okay.

Chapter Thirty-Five

THERE WAS NO LIFEBOAT

Mathias Fisher was a retired police officer from the German Federal Police, Bundespolizei. He retired at age 65, and at 68 was still in good physical and mental condition when he started his own private investigating business to supplement his pension. Between his experience and the contacts, he'd developed over the years, his business quickly built up, producing an income that allowed him and his wife to take six-week holidays in exotic locations around the world twice a year and still have money left to add to his savings.

Today Mathias was traveling alone on business for a rather unusual request. He boarded the train in Berlin and spent the hour and a half trip to Brunswick pondering the request and watching the landscape pass by the window. It was a rather pleasant way to pass the time.

A collector of rare books in California had contacted him for assistance in locating a unique book titled The Sirralnnudam. The client hadn't been able to give him much information, other than that the book was discovered by a German archeologist, Karsten Rischmüller, about 50 years ago at a dig site, Çatalhöyük, not far from Konya, Turkey. Rischmüller apparently gave the book to the Mesrop Mashtots Institute of Ancient Manuscripts in Yerevan, Armenia. The book had been lost, and Mathias was hired to find it. It wasn't the easiest commission he'd ever accepted, but it was certainly going to be the most lucrative if he was successful.

Mathias was under very strict orders from his client to veil his investigation in complete secrecy. At no point was Mathias to reveal his own or his client's identity to anyone. Mathias was almost 100% sure that his client was not who he said he was, but he couldn't see anything illegal in his client's request; collectors of rare artifacts seldom wanted their identities known. Moreover, the contract price offered by his client was enough encouragement to keep Mathias as tightlipped as required.

With his contacts in the police and a bit of research, it took him less than a day to track down the retired Doctor Karsten Rischmüller at an address in Brunswick.

He'd phoned the number one of his contacts had given him and spoke to Mitzi Scheider, Rischmüller's daughter, introducing himself as Jurgen Ruschin, a freelance archeology journalist, and blogger from Düsseldorf. Mitzi was very kind and helpful, explaining that although her dad was 85 and suffering from Parkinson's disease, he still had bright moments especially if he could talk about his favorite subject – Turkish history and archeology.

For Mathias, finding Rischmüller and managing to arrange a meeting was an excellent start in his quest to find the book and earn the $35,000 on offer from his client.

Upon arrival at the residence, Mathias rang the bell, and the door was opened by a woman with silver-gray hair who looked to be in her early fifties. Mathias guessed, correctly, that she was Mitzi Scheider. He introduced himself, and she invited him inside taking him through to the lounge. "Please make yourself comfortable," she said indicating where he could sit. "I will get my father in a minute. I told him about your visit, and he is quite excited to talk to you. What can I get you to drink Herr Ruschin? Coffee, tea?"

Mathias told her that a cup of coffee was just what he needed after the early morning train ride.

She left to fetch her father and then vanished again to return with a tray set for coffee. "My father won't have coffee Herr Ruschin, so do help yourself.

Karsten Rischmüller was in a wheelchair; it was clear the Parkinson's was in an advanced stage. Mathias stood and went over to gently shake the old man's hand "Thank you for seeing me Doctor Rischmüller, I am honored you agreed to meet.

There was a spark in the old man's eyes when Mathias explained the reason for his visit

The first part of the conversation proceeded well; Mathias could follow most of what Karsten was saying but after half an hour the quality of his voice and the audibility started to drop off. Mitzi joined them, sitting beside her father and repeating some of the questions and answers. This helped immensely, but she finally suggested they take a short break so she could give her father some tea while Mathias read some of her father's field journals.

Mathias made notes as they were talking, and two hours later he and Mitzi agreed that it was time for Karsten to get some rest.

"Do feel free to stay Herr Ruschin and continue to read my father's journals, I will be getting some lunch in a little while, you are very welcome to join me.

Mathias accepted with pleasure; there was so much here he still wanted to read; Karsten's journal entries talked about the discovery of the Sirralnnudam, and there were also a few black and white photos of the book.

Close to twenty pages of neatly handwritten notes explained what the Sirralnnudam was. Karsten was able to read proto-Arabic, the language in which the book was written, and had even included a few translated paragraphs from the first pages of the book, which he'd translated into German.

According to Karsten's notes, no one could say how old the Sirralnnudam was and who the original author or authors were. At some stage, it had been kept in the legendary Library of Alexandria somewhere between 300 B.C. and the time before the library was destroyed by Julius Caesar's legions in 48 B.C.

Some scholars believed that it was one of the many thousands of books placed in the library by general Ptolemy I Soter, Alexander the Great's successor, and the person who built the Library of Alexandria.

Karsten's notes also included a brief summary of the contents of the book. The exciting news was Karsten's remark that one of his co-explorers at the time had a theory that there was possibly a second copy of the Sirralnnudam. This he believed, had also existed in the Library of Alexandria and both copies had somehow survived the fire in 48 B.C. that destroyed the Library. Karsten had made note of this but didn't go into any details except to say that he was of the opinion that if it did exist, the second copy was probably somewhere in private hands.

When Mitzi returned after making sure her father was comfortable she agreed Mathias could take photos of the pages and images in the journal. This occupied his time until Mitzi announced lunch.

It was a pleasant interlude in which he learned more about Karsten Rischmüller and the work he'd done in his hay-day. "It's a subject dear to his heart, Herr Ruschin and I know just how much he has appreciated your visit today. Not a lot happens in his life anymore that has real value, but today was, for him, special."

"It has been that for me as well, a very special day, and I want to thank you for your hospitality."

When lunch was over, and Mathias had gathered his notes and camera, she saw him to the door and bid him good-bye.

When Matthias got back at his apartment in Berlin, he logged onto the dead letter email account, which his client provided, and left a message in the drafts folder explaining that he had found Rischmüller and met with him. He gave a summary of the meeting and what he had in his possession. Informing his client that as soon as the first payment was in his account the documents would be uploaded to client's secure cloud account, he signed off

Three hours later Mathias got confirmation that the $5,000 had been paid into his international Credit Card account. He copied the information to the cloud account and left a message for the client in the draft folder of the dead letter email box.

Mathias was a happy man; it was the easiest $5,000 he had ever earned in his PI business. The next thing on the agenda was planning what to do next to locate that second book. Retrieving a beer from the fridge, he decided it would be worth the trouble to return to Karsten Rischmüller's house early in the morning in the hope of catching him at a time when his mind was still bright enough to give out more information about the potential second copy.

He called to confirm this was acceptable with Mitzi

Mathias' client used compression and encryption software to secure the information and dropped it off at a dead letter box in Los Angeles. He didn't know who the recipient was and into whose hands the information on the flash drive would eventually end up.

It took another two days before Dwayne Miller the CEO of CRS had the decrypted information from the flash drive in his hands. Initially, the information he was reading caused a bit of excitement but disappointment set in quickly as he read to the end of the report.

They certainly knew a lot more about the Sirralnnudam than they did before, but there was nothing that could help them find it - if it still existed. Dwayne decided that the next step would be to seek out and persuade a reputable archeologist to publish an article in various archeological journals and magazines regarding the book and see if something emerged from the woodwork.

A week later Matthias went back to Brunswick but left disappointed an hour later. Rischmüller remembered the speculations of his colleague but admitted he'd not paid much attention to his theories at the time, as he believed that the man's ideas were a bit flimsy and unfounded. Matthias suggested he would like to speak with the colleague, but was disappointed when Rischmüller told him that unfortunately, it wouldn't be possible as the man had passed away a few years ago.

Mathias kept his client up to date with his progress on the case. Not that there was much progress to report; he had hit a dead end by the time he finished his last meeting with Karsten Rischmüller.

The business relationship came to an abrupt and tragic end when both Mathias Fisher and his wife drowned one night after jumping overboard to escape a fire on board their yacht while vacationing in the Bahamas. Investigator's indicated that a leaking gas stove caused the fire, but were at a loss to explain why there was no lifeboat on board.

Chapter Thirty-Six

STEP UP THE SURVEILLANCE

At the end of the seventh week of Carter's training, he, Kevin and John flew out to Quebec City from where they caught a commercial flight to DC. Of the three, only Carter knew they were due to depart for Egypt within the next two weeks. Kevin and John, like Roy and Andre before them, were nice, level-headed guys; Carter liked them, as did Ahote, Bly, and Jeha. The wolves of Freydis had also accepted them.

Kevin and John turned out to be tough taskmasters when it came down to Carter's training. They were every bit as tough, if not more so, than their predecessors, Andre, and Roy. Carter was now up to a seven-mile run every morning, half of which he and his trainers did while shouldering a backpack stuffed with 20-pound sandbags.

Carter's body had substituted twenty pounds of fat for twenty pounds of muscle and the strength training, which included hundreds of sit-ups, push-ups, and chin-ups on a cross bar every day, was showing on his shoulders, arms, and stomach.

He had progressed to laser-gun shooting and was able to hit the target with his left hand 75% of the time, and 90% with his right. Every three days they would do a 3-hour hike of 15 miles carrying a 40-pound backpack and rifle. On these hikes, Carter had to keep a lookout for hidden silhouettes and shoot them with the laser. With a gun in each hand, he could hit two different targets in less than a second more than 80% of the times.

In the hand-to-hand combat sessions, he could take on either of them and beat them; it wouldn't be long before he'd be able to take on both of them at the same time with a better than 50% chance of beating them.

They had started his close quarter combat training the week before, showing him how to work with a team of operators to clear a house, room by room and to know the positions and tasks of everyone in the team.

In the evenings after dinner, training continued with memory improvement and observation exercises. They showed Carter a video or a picture, and he would recount what he saw. Sometimes they put various items on a tray, let him look at it for three seconds, then covered it with a cloth and required him to tell them what he saw and the position of each item.

Because of his eidetic memory, Carter excelled at this. Within a week, he was able to recite what he saw with one hundred percent accuracy almost every time. Carter's memory skills had Kevin and John shaking their heads in wonder. This was the type of challenge that most people improved with over time but never mastered; very few people ever got full marks. Carter was reaching those extraordinary levels after the first week.

The plan was for Carter's training to continue while he was in DC; Irene and Dylan had pulled a few strings with some of their CIA contacts who would allow Carter to fire his first live rounds at their secret training facility on a farm in Virginia.

Since the Saudi client had upped the contract price on Carter's head, Dwayne Miller had stepped up the surveillance efforts. He instructed a team to move closer and obtain better information about Carter's plans and movements. Two drones had been deployed over Freydis. It raised both Miller's and Gordon's eyebrows when they learned that Carter was going through some type of special training. Why? Was it part of a plan? Was it just to prepare himself better for his future work on the nuclear research project? They had to find out.

When Miller received word that Carter and his bodyguards had left Freydis, he instructed the drone team to visit the Freydis homestead and collect more information.

A surveillance team was placed on alert to be on the lookout for Carter in DC.

The next day they reported spotting Carter as he entered the Smithsonian. They immediately activated their IMSI – International Mobile Subscriber Identity – equipment, which would lock onto a mobile signal and siphon data from it. It would not only collect data from the device, but it would also track location and movements.

Back in DC, Roy and Andre took over Carter's protection and training again for the duration of his time there giving John and Kevin a break.

The first morning when Carter arrived at A-Echelon's offices, he and Irene met with James and gave him an update on their progress and plan to return to Egypt and the City of Lights.

"Carter, didn't you forget something?" James had a little smile playing on his face.

"What?"

"You made me a promise that I could accompany you on the next trip to the City of Lights. Didn't you?"

Carter smiled. "Yeah Jim, now I remember, but I also distinctly remember that we agreed you'd be the cook."

"Jim, you're not seriously considering going out there?" Irene looked a bit worried. She wasn't always sure when Carter and James were just having fun and when they were being serious.

James and Carter shared a quick look and continued the wile. "Of course, I'm serious; a promise is a promise, and I'm going."

"Jim! You are not going to drop this place in my lap while you go and play desert rat."

"Well Irene we need a cook, and if Jim can't go then, you'll have to go." Carter joined in.

Irene stood and took a step back. She looked at them in turn and said. "If you fancy suffering from food poisoning I'll go and cook for you. But Jim is staying here, or I go and book myself into the hospital right now for a major operation or something."

Carter and James shook their heads and held their hands up in surrender. None of Irene's options sounded good.

"Okay Irene, in that case, we will both stay." James laughed.

When the meeting with James was over, Carter

suggested that he and Irene go and get a coffee on the outside before they returned to her office to continue with their preparation work.

Irene had taken a seat, and Carter was standing at the counter, waiting to order their coffees, when his cell phone started buzzing. He took his phone out of his pocket and looked at the message. It was from Roy. He and Andre were in different locations outside keeping a watch.

How much longer are you going to be???

Carter was half-surprised when he read the message, but then the three question marks struck him. It was their code for *you are being watched; don't say anything.* He quickly hit reply and responded *about 20 minutes*!! He was careful to include the two exclamation marks which meant to divide the value of the number in half twice; 20 became 10 and 10 became five, meaning he would be out in five minutes.

Ordering the coffee to take away he paid for it picked up the two cups and, walking over to Irene smiled as he said, "Here's yours, let's go."

She looked at him inquisitively, then seeing the slight movement of his head and eyes; indicating that they should leave, she got the message; smiling she took the cup and joined him as they walked outside.

Back in the safety of her office, Roy and Andre described what they'd seen.

"Shortly after you two entered the coffee shop a van pulled up and parked across the road from you," Roy told them. "It looked like a plumber's van with all the canisters, pipes, and things on the roof and sides; it also had a plumber's signage on it. What caught my attention was that no one got out of the van and the windows were tinted so I couldn't see what was going on inside. I told Andre via the throat mic to have a closer look. He was nearby on the same side of the street as the van."

Andre nodded. "I was looking through the shop window at a woman who entered the shop shortly after you did. She was hanging around until Irene took a seat and then she took a seat, two tables away from Irene."

"The woman with the turquoise scarf?" Irene asked.

"Yes, that's the one." Andre nodded. "Can't say for sure if she had anything to do with this, but she certainly drew my attention for one reason or another."

Andre continued. "That's when I got Roy's message to try and check out the van without raising any suspicion, so I walked past it. When I got closer, I saw the wires leading out of the canisters on the roof into the cabin. They hadn't bothered obscuring those lines, and I've seen that setup before. Those PVC canisters are used to hide parabolic antennae and other surveillance equipment. I'd bet my bottom dollar if I opened the back door of that van we would have seen people with headphones sitting in front of panels with sophisticated listening equipment."

A lengthy and uneasy silence settled over the four of them as they absorbed the information.

"Do you think they know you spotted them?" Carter asked.

"Difficult to say. They didn't do anything to give that impression." Andre replied. "But I assume they probably know Roy and I are your bodyguards. We have never tried to hide that from anyone. That's part of body guarding – to be a visible deterrent."

When Andre and Roy left, Carter turned to Irene. "Do you think the mole has poked its head out of the hole?"

Irene shrugged. "It's possible. However, first we don't know if that van had surveillance equipment on it. If it had, we can't be sure you and I were their targets. If we were the targets, you could be certain, even if we grab them and hold their feet to the fire, they wouldn't know who they're working for. But it's definitely going to be worth putting a few of our own people onto them to see where it leads us."

"I've got an idea," Carter said. "If these people are so keen to hear what we say to each other let's feed them a bit of information and blow a bit of smoke up their skirts."

"Exactly what I was going to suggest," Irene smiled. "Let's talk to Sean and Dylan and see what they think."

The day before, Lex and Jason were watching the video feed coming from the two drones over Freydis, 25 miles away, and saw Carter and his two bodyguards pack their luggage into the Piper Seminole and take off.

Judging by the luggage, it looked as if the three men were going to be away from Freydis for a while. They let their manager know and waited for further instructions. They were hoping for a break from the monotonous routine. Sitting in a log hut in the middle of the wilderness with no Internet or cell phone connection was driving them bonkers. They were not allowed to use the satellite connection to the Internet for any purpose other than sending the data feeds back to the offices in Montreal.

During the daytime, they, at least, had something to do when they were controlling the drones and watching the video feeds coming in. At night, there was nothing to do. They'd read all the books and watched all the videos, which they'd brought with them, at least three times. Although both of them had military training, neither one of them were the outdoor, nature-loving, type and they were bored stiff.

When they saw Carter and his companions leaving, they thought maybe their manager would let them go back to Montreal and wait there until Carter returned. They were both thoroughly pissed-off when they were told to stay put and wait for instructions.

A few hours later, they received their instructions. They were to go and check out the Freydis homestead, break into the place if they could, and collect as much information as possible. That would have been all okay with them – it sounded like a bit of an adventure – but that was only until they were told that they had to cover the 25 miles from their location to Freydis and back on foot.

"A 50-mile round trip on foot!" Lex shouted after the call with the manager ended. "What the hell does he think we are? Pack mules or mountain goats or something? Is he fuckin' crazy?"

"Maybe he is," Jason shrugged, "but the problem is if we don't do it he might just leave us in this godforsaken place forever. So I suggest the quicker we get it done, the quicker we can go back to our girls in Montreal."

"50 fuckin' miles!" Lex shouted again. "It's going to take days to do it."

"Well, then we better get going," Jason grinned.

Sean and Dylan had questioned Andre and Roy in detail about the morning's encounter and agreed that the safest assumption to make was that the van was equipped for surveillance purposes and that Carter and Irene were the targets.

They suggested that the best approach would be not to let their observers know they had been discovered and to act normally. Carter and Irene would go back to the same coffee shop the next morning and every day after that. Apart from Roy and Andre, who would be there and make their presence known, three more people would be assigned who would try and get a better look at the van or any similar vehicle. They'd take pictures of it and try to get close enough to stick a small tracking device on it. They'd also take photos of all the people in and around the shop.

If the vehicle was there the next day, they would have their confirmation and would follow it. They were not going to jump them too quickly; they wanted to observe them for a while to see what they could learn.

"So, Carter for the next few days you and Irene go back to that coffee shop, but instead of ordering takeaway you sit at a table next to the window facing the street, and you talk shop." Sean smiled. "That is when we're going to blow some smoke up their skirts as Carter suggested."

"We're going to let them know Carter is on his way to the City of Lights and that he and his team are planning to leave in two weeks."

Carter and Irene nodded their understanding.

"However, in the meantime, I suggest we fast track your departure Carter and get your ready to leave in three days' time. Do you think that can be done?"

Carter looked at Irene. She nodded and replied, "Yes, we have all the equipment ready, the men are on standby prepared to go with an hour's notice. The only reason we were planning to go in two weeks was to give Kevin and John a bit of time to be with their girlfriends and to put Carter through more training."

"I spoke to Kevin and John, and they were both happy

with Carter's progress and current skills," Dylan said. "He's not nearly ready for a hostage rescue mission, but that's not what he is going to be doing out there in the Egyptian desert. So I'm comfortable with him going there with the four bodyguards."

"I will just double check with our Egyptian contacts that Daan Hannah is onsite and has no plans to leave soon," Irene said. "Then I'll arrange with our private charter company to have a Gulfstream jet ready to fly the five of you out in three days. I already have everyone's passport and will make the necessary arrangements for border control to stamp their departure but make sure it is not entered into any records."

They spent another hour discussing the details and finalizing the plans before Carter and Irene returned to the A-Echelon offices.

The next morning shortly after Carter and Irene took their seats in the coffee shop Carter got a text message from Roy. *Just got good news. Jane is pregnant!*

That was the signal; the van has arrived again.

Carter replied. *Well-done! Great news!* The code that he understood and they were proceeding as planned.

He and Irene had to suppress the urge to stare out the window to try and see the van. They spoke about family, weather and politics and then turned the conversation to their preplanned agenda.

"I heard this morning that you're going back to Egypt soon," Irene said.

"Yep, things are finally coming together for a return trip."

"When do you leave?"

"Not soon enough for me," Carter laughed. "The week after next."

"I'm excited for you, Carter. You must be thrilled to be going back to the City of Lights again."

"Yes, very excited. It's an intriguing place, Irene, but difficult to describe it to anyone. You have to experience it. The wondrous thing is when those lights come on at night. It feels like you are in another world."

She laughed, and they continued the conversation for another ten minutes, and then left when they had finished their coffee.

Later that afternoon Sean told them that they had tracked the van; it belonged to AMZ Security, a company located on the outskirts of DC. Rick Winslow, their IT guru, was already on the job, hacking into their servers and scanning their personnel records and financial data.

Lex and Jason unenthusiastically stuffed their backpacks with food and water bottles and set course for Freydis just before sunrise the next morning. There would be no weapons or special clothes, and no camouflage. Their cover was that they were hikers, and if they were discovered on Freydis, they'd say they were lost and looking for shelter and directions to get back to civilization.

They were hoping to reach the Freydis homestead that same night, but they had misjudged the terrain, the distance, and their state of fitness.

Instead, they were forced to spend a nearly sleepless night under a rock overhang, on the hard ground. The following morning just before midday they reached a summit from where they could see the Freydis homestead still about two miles away. Lying low for the rest of the day, they waited until it was dark to approach the buildings unnoticed.

Loki and Keeva were on the hunt; the pups were now old enough to be demanding solid food and had ravenous appetites. They faced into the soft, almost undetectable, breeze from the east, picking up scents from a variety of small creatures that had come out to forage. The pickings were good, and they could afford to be choosy.

Behind them, their four pups were safely asleep in the cave.

Lex and Jason arrived at the homestead, feeling their way around in the dim light of their small flashlights.

Lex clumsily bumped into an empty four-gallon gas can knocking it over and causing a thunderous crash when the can hit the concrete.

Both men froze in their tracks, switched off their flashlights, and waited.

About three miles away Loki stopped and lifted his nose into the breeze; his ears were raised. Keeva heard it as well, there was little they would miss when it came to sounds or smells over the vast Freydis property, their senses were sharp and honed to perfection.

Loki turned aside and moved quickly, dropping into a full lope in the direction of the sound, Keeva settled into the easy, mile-eating gait beside him.

Nothing stirred, and the men began to relax.

"Be careful, you clumsy twit," Jason whispered as he switched his flashlight back on and started moving towards the house again.

They reached the house and started circling it searching

for a window they could break that would allow them easy access in and out.

A mile away Loki stopped, his nose lifted, as did Keeva - an unfamiliar scent reached them. Humans, but not the humans he and Keeva knew and protected. He snorted to clear his nostrils then tore out at full speed with Keeva close behind.

After a few minutes, Lex and Jason found an ideal window on the porch for the break-in. Jason went back to look for something he could use to break the glass. There were no burglar guards on any of the windows and as far as they could see, no alarm system. He found a spade in the shed and returned to the porch.

He was halfway up the stairs when he heard quiet snarling and spun around.

To his horror, in the moonlight he saw two wolves, their lips drawn back exposing their fangs. They were large and threatening, and their growls, a rattling sound deep in their throats, terrified him.

They were moving very slowly towards him, their eyes glowing green-gold in the flashlight.

He started yelling. "Oh God, Lex, *RUN! WOLVES!* They're going to attack us!"

Jason tripped on the top step and fell backward onto the porch floor but jumped up like a rubber ball. He had the spade in his hand but had dropped his flashlight on the ground. He could see the wolves still moving slowly towards him and hear their deep threatening snarls.

His terror grew; he started screaming and lifted the shovel above his head ready to strike if the wolves attacked. He didn't know where Lex was. Maybe if Lex would come and stand next to him, they could scare the animals away.

He yelled, "Lex come here. Fuck man, come now! Immediately!"

Lex had seen the wolves and was scared frozen. When Jason started screaming at him, he'd heard him, but couldn't move. He felt his bladder empty into his pants, and still he stood motionless in a puddle of his own urine.

Jeha, who was at Ahote and Bly's house, heard the commotion and went berserk. Ahote got up from the lounge chair and walked outside. He heard the clamor coming from the direction of Carter's place. Running back into the house, he told Bly to lock the doors. He put his shoes on grabbed the flashlight and his rifle and raced up the road towards Carter's cabin. Jeha was hard on his heels and barking furiously.

Jason kept on screaming at Lex while he took small steps backward, but for every step he took, the two wolves took one forward.

When he was next to Lex, he gave him a fleeting glance and screamed. "You piece of shit, you pissed yourself instead of helping me. Well, the moment I've passed you those wolves are going to have your ass, and I'm gone."

Lex didn't need any other motivation; he started moving back with Jason. They were heading for the rails furthest away from the wolves, that were now, both on the porch.

They were planning to jump over the rails and run for their lives, but just as they felt the rails against their backs, they heard a dog barking and saw the reflection of a flashlight through the trees to their left. Jason dropped the spade, turned his back to the wolves, grabbed the rails, and threw himself over.

Lex took a second or two longer; he had the upper part of his body over the rails when he felt the teeth of a wolf sink into his ass. He kicked and screamed, fell to the ground landing on his knees, jumped up and started running with burning pain in his buttocks. Behind him, the two wolves cleared the rails and gave chase.

Ahote and Jeha arrived on the porch in time to see Loki and Keeva racing down the paddocks. Far off he could hear screaming.

Half an hour later, on the still, silent air of Freydis, he heard howling and knew the two wolves were letting their prey go and would be returning home.

Ahote sat on the top step waiting, feeling sure they would come to him. Jeha had stopped barking and settled in to wait beside Ahote, leaning slightly against his leg.

They arrived quietly and greeted him.

"Loki, Keeva, what in the world is going on over here?" Ahote tutted to the animals. "Did we have intruders? Is that right? You found them and have given them such a fright they will never return, eh?" He chuckled quietly, as he pictured the scene that must have played out on the porch where a spade had been dropped. "Well done!"

Loki moved forward slowly, with a wagging tail. Ahote held his hand out, and Loki came closer so that Ahote could touch him. "Clever boy, clever boy," Ahote whispered as he scratched Loki's ears and head.

Soon Keeva joined and allowed Ahote to scratch her ears and head as well. "You're an ingenious pair. Thank you."

About ten minutes later the two wolves left and disappeared into the night.

Ahote took the flashlight and walked around the house and outbuildings making sure the intruders didn't break in. He found their backpacks outside the shed and took them with him.

There was not much more he could do in the dark. He

was pretty sure the intruders were still running and would not return to Freydis of their own free will ever again.

He returned the next morning for a better inspection. In the daylight, he saw the blood on the rail and a ripped piece of bloodied denim. Picking up the tracks of the intruders, he followed them for about half a mile, finding drops of dried blood on the twigs and grass as he went. He went back home, saddled his horse, took his rifle and picked up the trail again.

He followed their spoor for about fifteen miles, right to the border of Freydis before turning back toward home. They were about nine to ten hours ahead of him and by now were probably back in their vehicle and out of the area.

He would phone the police, but it would probably be late afternoon before they arrived.

He could call Carter, but there was not much he would be able to do, and there was no need to upset him about this yet. Loki and Keeva had frustrated any attempt by the trespassers to break into the house – if that's what they had in mind. He was also very sure that none of them would be thinking of coming back, at least not without guns and not as long as they knew the place was guarded by wolves.

There was nothing in the backpacks to give Ahote any clue to the identity of the intruders.

Neither Ahote nor the snoopers knew that when they arrived at the homestead, they had set off the motion sensors activating the night vision cameras. On the computers inside the house were a few very clear images of their faces.

Chapter Thirty-Seven

THE CLEANUP WAS COMPLETE

The five men were told by the pilot of the Gulfstream jet to take their seats and fasten their seatbelts for the takeoff. The four former Special Forces operators, Kevin, John, Roy, and Andre, were impressed with the luxurious surroundings inside of the aircraft. They were used to jumping out of military planes with a parachute or fast-roping out of helicopters; those aircraft were practical and sturdy but not built for comfort.

Dylan, their CO for this mission and 2IC of Executive Advantage, had personally collected them from their homes and apartments and drove them out to the high-security area of the Joint Base Andrews in Prince George's County, Maryland. It was an area reserved for aircraft used in top-secret operations by the CIA and Special Forces.

None of them expected that the departure to the City of Lights was going to happen so quickly. When Dylan picked them up, they only had time to say goodbye to wives and girlfriends, collect their pre-packed bags and get in the van. Once inside, Dylan required everyone to remove the sim cards and batteries from their cellphones and pack them away in their bags.

They were not allowed to take any weapons with them; they would be supplied with those by a CIA contact in Cairo before they boarded a helicopter to the City of Lights. These they would keep concealed at all times unless needed.

Carter and Rick Winslow arrived just as Dylan and his team gathered in the hangar where the Gulfstream was waiting for all of them. Their equipment was checked, and Rick gave them an hour-long demonstration of the communications, surveillance and counter surveillance equipment they would be taking with them.

It was a ten-hour flight, and after the initial excitement was over, they all settled down, some to sleep, others opted to watch movies.

Carter reclined his seat and closed his eyes. As calming classical music filled his ears through the headphones, his mind wandered to Mackenzie and Liam. *Where are they? How are they doing? Are they ok? When will this end? When will I see them again? Who are the people that have been following me? So many questions and not even a hint of an answer to any of them.* He sighed. A few minutes later, he fell into a dreamless sleep.

Carter and his team were in a helicopter, about an hour away from the City of Lights when, back home, Dwayne Miller got a report from Montreal. He felt the anger rising within him; the men failed to get into Devereux's house. Wolves had attacked the two idiots, and one of them was badly bitten on his ass and had to be taken to the hospital for treatment.

What a bunch of incompetent hoodlums! They will not get another assignment from CRS.

If Miller thought that was the tally of the day's bad news, he was in for another nasty surprise. Carter Devereux and Irene O'Connell did not go for their coffee break this morning. That was not out of the ordinary – they could have been caught up in something else, but he became more and more irritated as he continued reading.

The surveillance team had finally checked Devereux's hotel; he'd apparently not left, but neither was he in his room. They saw him entering the place the night before but hadn't seen him leave. They'd checked with their contacts at Border Control to find out if he had returned to his ranch in Canada but was informed that according to their records Devereux had not left the USA.

What the hell? Where did he go? He couldn't have disappeared without a trace; the surveillance team had lost him. Another bunch of nincompoops.

Miller was getting worried. Today was not a good day; things were not going as he would have expected.

Late that afternoon he felt the roil of apprehension in his stomach, and a prickle began between his shoulder blades when he got an encoded message from CRS' Egyptian contacts wanting to know why he hadn't informed them about Professor Devereux's change in travel plans. Apparently, Devereux and four companions had arrived earlier in the day, went through customs, and were transported to the City of Lights by helicopter.

"How the hell did that happen?" Miller screamed.

"Mr. Miller, what's wrong?" His secretary stood in the door of his office with big eyes.

"Shit, shit, shit…" Miller had his face in his hands. "Don't even ask."

"Anything I can do to help sir?"

He shook his head. "No, Tracey thanks. It's okay. I'll sort it out."

She left.

Miller knew that Carter and his friends had somehow found out about the surveillance. Everything all of a sudden made sense. The daily coffee sessions, all the talk about going to Egypt, it was just too easy. He should have known that. Disappearing out of the hotel under the noses of the three observers; it suddenly fell into place as a feeling of nausea threatened to overpower him.

That meant the surveillance team would have been tracked; the hunters had become the hunted. It would just be a matter of time before the thumbscrews were put onto AMZ Security and they spilled the beans.

Fuck this is messy.

"Three things to do now," he mumbled to himself. "Get ahold of Nate Gordon, stop the surveillance team immediately, and wipe out all tracks leading back to CRS."

He called Gordon's number and made another mental note while the phone was ringing. *Tell the Egyptians to lie low; no surveillance of Devereux and his team as they were probably outfitted with the best-of-the-best counter surveillance equipment the CIA have.*

Gordon was in Miller's office in less than an hour. For the next three hours, they put out fires. The accountant assured them that there was no financial traceability they had to worry about. CRS' books would stand up to the closest scrutiny; there was nothing illegal or untoward in the company's records. One weight dropped off their shoulders.

There remained one more significant problem, and that was the Director of AMZ Security. He was the only one who knew who their client was, making him a single point of failure.

After a bit of back and forth, considering various options, Gordon shrugged. "He is an old man, almost seventy. He has had many good innings."

"Nate, you know this means we can kiss that extra $25 million goodbye?" Miller noted.

Gordon had his eyebrows raised. "And our alternative is?"

Miller nodded. He knew what had to be done.

By 10:00 am the next day Miller let out what felt like the first breath in 24 hours.

The team of observers had been called off and reassigned. If any of them was picked up for questioning all they could say was that they had instructions to follow Professor Carter Devereux and report to Mr. Schwall, one of AMZ Security's directors, but unfortunately, Mr. Schwall had tragically and very suddenly died of a massive heart attack early this morning.

The tracks ended there. They'd acted just in time.

The cleanup was complete.

Chapter Thirty-Eight

SHUT UP UNTIL YOU HAVE PROOF

When Carter and his men landed in Cairo, he contacted Daan Hannah the expedition leader of the dig at the City of Lights. Daan was a professor of archeology at the prestigious Alexandria International University and father of Sameha Hannah, the cartographer, and photographer who was part of Carter's team when they did the initial survey of the City of Lights on behalf of the Egyptian government.

Professor Hannah was pleasantly surprised to hear from Carter again and more than happy to accommodate him and his men even on such short notice. "The desert is big Carter; there is always place for more here." He laughed.

He knew that a visit from Carter meant more funds and more underground surveys. Ever since Carter had discovered that underground burial chamber, during his last visit, Hannah had the burning desire to open it up and get the full picture of what was going on in there.

By the time the helicopter arrived with Carter and his four assistants, their sleeping quarters were ready. Hannah and his daughter Sameha welcomed them at the helipad and escorted them to their tents.

Daan and Sameha could only speak broken English; Carter was fluent in Arabic, so the conversation was conducted in Arabic with Carter acting as an interpreter when necessary. Daan and Sameha had heard about Carter's loss and sympathized with him. After they'd unpacked and had their first cup of strong Arabica coffee, Carter's men, none of whom could speak Arabic took a walk around the camp to familiarize themselves with their surroundings.

Carter told Daan and Sameha he intended to stay for two weeks, during which time he wanted to open up the underground burial chamber and complete the underground survey with the sophisticated GPR (Ground Penetrating Radar) equipment he had brought with him. That was music to Daan's ears – he immediately offered the help of his crew.

A few hours and a few more cups of Arabica later, Carter was able to take his men on a tour of the ancient city where giants lived until 50,000 years ago. Although none of the four men with Carter were history or archeology scholars they were blown away by what they saw. They were literally slack-jawed as they walked around the place with Carter as their tour guide.

They took pictures nonstop. Andre summarized their thoughts when he said, "Carter this is the most amazing thing I've ever seen in my life, I've got no idea how to describe the feelings I have right now to my family and friends. They'll probably think I've lost my mind."

Carter laughed. "Well, you've got the pictures to prove that you're not telling them a fairy tale." Carter looked at the position of the sun. He smiled. The boys were in for another surprise in about two hours or so when the sun set and the lights came on.

When darkness fell, right on cue, the four men were like children walking in the streets around their neighborhoods at Christmas time fascinated by the lights. Even Carter, who had seen it many times before, still felt the excitement as he looked around him at the mysterious marvel.

Roy, Andre, Kevin, and John had completed their security assessment of the environment, deployed Rick's surveillance detection, and countermeasure gadgets before they went on the guided tour with Carter. They gave him a brief overview of their assessment and told him that there were currently, no active surveillance efforts deployed against them. However, that status could change very quickly, and they should all remain vigilant.

They would continue with some of Carter's training while they were there, including a ten-mile run, without backpacks, every morning, and evening. Hand-to-hand combat training and target shooting with the laser guns would take place out of sight of the archeological team in one of the big tents that Daan's crew had set up for them. Those activities would be kept to early mornings before the desert sun became too hot.

The first two days after their arrival Carter showed his team how to use the GPR equipment and put them to work to survey the area he had mapped out for them. He and Daan and a few of his crew returned to the burial chamber to determine the best way to enter the place without causing unnecessary damage to the door.

They opened the hole in the wall that they'd previously made for the robot and deployed the robot again, this time, for the sole purpose of studying the door mechanism.

Carter had thought a lot about the door since the last

visit and had considered the idea that the door operated with some sort of electromagnetic mechanism. His efforts were rewarded with the discovery of an electromagnetic field by the EMF meter attached to the robot arm. He made a scaled drawing of the door, mapped the source of the electromagnetic field on it, and then used one of the GRP devices to scan the door from the outside trying to find the locking mechanism. A few hours later, he had it all figured out.

The only challenge now was to find out how to activate the locking mechanism, which would have been located on the outside of the chamber. However, there was nothing on the outside, which looked like a switch. Did some type of remote control device open the door? Alternatively, were they missing the switch, not recognizing it?

Carter walked away from the chamber door to a large rock about ten yards away and sat down on it facing the door. If he were a smoker, this would have been the time when he would have lit a cigarette or pipe. Instead, he took a few long sips from his water bottle while he stared at the door. The answer was somewhere on the outside. *What am I missing? Electromagnetic fields, a lock mechanism clearly visible on the GPR images...*

When he swallowed the third sip of water from the bottle, he had an idea. He got up and told Daan that he would be back in a few minutes. He walked over to where his four men were busy working with the more powerful GRP scanners and asked them to bring the two scanners over to the chamber door.

When they arrived, he told them what he had in mind. They had to try to lift the scanners up and run them across the rock face of the door and to the sides. He knew the scanners were sending out intense electromagnetic pulses and hoped that those would find and trigger the locking mechanism. It was a very long shot but worth a try.

Roy and Kevin were working on the right side of the door when Carter heard something and swung around to where the noise was coming. It had sounded as if there was some movement but then it stopped.

"Okay, guys we got it!" He shouted. "Move your machine back and forth slowly in the area where you are now."

A few minutes later, they found the spot again, and Carter's eye caught the slight movement. He took three steps back held his arms out, open palms towards the door and in a loud deep voice said, "Open Sesame."

Daan smiled but the four Special Forces men looked at him with a mix of suspicion and disbelief. Suddenly the door lifted about a quarter of an inch; then the whole slab started moving backward then slowly slid to the left, revealing a ten by fifteen feet entry.

The six men gawked at the opening with incredulity and back at Carter with open mouths.

"Open fuckin' Sesame. And it opens a 50,000-year-old electromagnetic door. Nobody is going to believe me," Roy muttered. "They will be wondering what I've been smoking lately."

Carter managed to keep his look serious. "You have to know how to say it."

"Shit, this is sensational," One of them whispered.

Despite Daan's lack of command of the English language, he knew what was going on and started laughing. They all realized Carter had just pulled another fast one on them and started laughing, although a bit nervously.

These four guys were hardened combat soldiers and had experienced the scariest of situations imaginable, but they were still human. What set them apart from most other people was their ability to manage and overcome fear, not to ignore it. However, what they had been witnessing now was weird, not frightening, but certainly eerie. Nothing like they'd ever experienced before.

Carter was still chuckling when he retrieved a flashlight from his backpack and slowly walked through the entrance stopping after about two yards to let the light play on the walls. He had seen this on the video feed from the robot before, but that was not comparable to the thrill he experienced when looking at the real thing.

He stood there, for what felt like a long time, trying to comprehend what he was looking at, the necropolis of the giants. He was the first human in 50,000 years to set foot in this place.

For a fleeting moment, he was startled when lights suddenly went on, illuminating the entire place as far as he could see with light as bright as the daylight outside. It was like entering a room with motion detectors in a modern day building where the lights went on when someone entered, only these lights were much brighter than anything he'd ever experienced.

He took a few steps towards the wall in front of him; his eyes fixed on the engravings, which he had seen on the robot's video feed months ago. Then he remembered his colleagues on the outside and turned back to the entry.

"What are you guys going to do? Are you going to stand out there all day wondering what it looks like in here? Bring those GPR devices inside and come and have a look for yourself."

They grabbed their backpacks and equipment and followed Daan.

"The first rule of archeology," Carter said when they were all inside. "Don't touch anything."

They nodded.

"What's the second?" John grinned.

"Shut up until you have proof," Carter replied tersely, to the amusement of all.

They all went quiet and started looking around.

Carter went back to the engravings and studied them carefully. He was happy to confirm what had been concluded before; those engravings were not pictures, they were words, letters from an unknown alphabet. The first written words found in the City of Lights. *What language was this?*

Carter stood back again and turned his head at various angles. Daan stood next to him the same questions must have been going through his mind. Carter started walking along the wall, remembering what it felt like when he saw what he was looking at now, a few months ago on a video feed. That same feeling returned – it was beyond anything he could ever have imagined in his wildest dreams.

The paved walkway spiraled down deep into the earth; high stone walls faced with white marble rising twenty feet up on both sides. In the walls on each side, the cavities marked the catacombs of the distant past, the tombs of the people who had lived here long ago and walked the roads of this glorious ancient, city.

Carter's head was spinning as he again realized the enormity of the discovery.

He stopped at one of the tombs, shone the flashlight into it and looked at the mummified body; robes were still draped around the body of a person who would have been at least fourteen feet tall - a giant. He continued and inspected a few more tombs before he stood back.

Daan, who had been following him quietly, broke the silence. "There are engravings above each tomb," he pointed to the wall above the cavity they were looking at.

Carter took a step back and looked at the engravings. "Nothing new under the sun," he murmured.

"What did you say?" Daan wanted to know.

"I said there is nothing new under the sun." Daan, who was Coptic Christian, smiled when he heard Carter quoting from the Bible and nodded his head.

"We are doing the same thing today," Carter said. Daan was looking at him inquisitively. "We put inscriptions on tombstones, the name of the person, date of birth, and date of death. I believe that is what we're seeing here."

Daan nodded in agreement. "Now the most intriguing question is; how many were the years of their lives?"

"Well, Daan," Carter smiled. "The oldest man I have heard of was Methuselah, 963 years old. So let's play it safe and say anything from 40 to 963 years."

Daan enjoyed Carter's humor. "The problem we have here is that all we see are names and dates, it won't help us much to translate this language."

Carter nodded. "We have to keep searching for that library Daan; that's why I'm here. We have to find it."

Carter said he wanted to go back to the entrance and look around there a bit more, Daan was more intrigued by the how deep down the structure went and what else there was to see on the lower levels.

As Daan started walking down the ramp, Carter returned to the entry, to study the door mechanism closer. He was also intrigued by the first four or so yards of the wall by the entry that had no tombs in it.

He crawled around on his hands and knees inspecting each part of the door and was not entirely surprised when he realized the doors were not sliding on rollers or bearings but on what he thought could only have been electromagnetic levitation technology. This ancient technology was very similar to what modern day engineers are using with high-speed trains where the train is suspended on a magnetic cushion above a magnetized track.

After a while, he stood and looked at the distance between the door opening and the first tomb. *Why didn't they use that space on the walls to fit in more tombs?* Something stirred in his subconscious mind but hadn't quite reached conscious thought. He knew the feeling very well, and the only way to force it to the surface was to keep on throwing questions at it.

Then he saw it. It was there right in front of him. He spun around and looked at the wall behind him and saw the same thing. A door, so well-constructed in the same material as the wall, so precisely fitting in and blending with the wall, it was near impossible to see. He looked around; everyone else had gone down the ramp; he was on his own.

He went right up to the door, looked at it up close, and then retrieved a pair of German made binocular loupes from his backpack, placed it on his head and studied the markings. He did the same on the opposite wall and found it to be identical. Then he took pictures and video footage, adjusting the focus of the camera lenses for close-up photos. He wanted to study this in privacy later; he was not ready to talk about it yet.

When Carter stepped back, he knew he had found two more doors leading, he could only venture a guess as to where, and reminded himself of the second rule of archeology; shut up until you have proof.

Chapter Thirty-Nine

I'M COMING TO THE END I FEAR

Mackenzie lay in her narrow bed in the dark, tears rolling down her cheeks as she tried not to make a sound that would wake Liam. The gray stone walls of her narrow room were encroaching on her mind, squeezing the very life out of her.

Her daily life underground was dragging her down and down, the gloomy little kitchen, where each morning she made her and Liam's breakfast, was gritty and grimy. The room where she and Liu eked out their lives in front of endless, incomprehensible texts was stultifying and the Three Stooges an endless ugly view of men she wished would drop dead.

Her situation was hopeless, and she knew it. For months now she had tried to keep up the pretense that once the work was complete, she would be allowed to leave with Liam and go home. But as the months passed and the baby inside her grew and developed she became more and more morbid.

There's no way they are going to let me go; they'll kill me the moment my usefulness is over, and God knows what they will do with Liam. She shuddered as she thought of the baby inside her and its dependence on her, *if I lose my life the baby dies too, that is, unless they wait until it's born and, if it's a boy, farm it out to a good family and raise it as one of their own.*

She sat up and turned her pillow over, seeking a cold side; the baby kicked, and she put her hand on her tummy to calm it down. *There's no fooling you, is there, my love? You're too close to me.*

For days now she'd realized her mind was seeking escape, any escape, and with that idea, thoughts of what chemicals she might find in the laboratory that she could take to terminate her life. *Liam would be safer if I weren't here, he's a boy, they'd hand him over to a good Muslim family, and he'd be okay. I'm the problem in his life.*

If only Carter would come, she'd waited and waited in hope believing he knew she was alive. But as time dragged on she began to fear he had no idea, had probably even held a memorial for them both, and was now getting on with his life, maybe he'd even marry again one day.

She sat up, *I mustn't think this way, it's dangerous, what would Liam do if he heard my thoughts? He'd be terrified.*

By morning, Mackenzie had managed a couple of hours' sleep, but she was exhausted and not just from lack of sleep, but from the lack of just about everything that was good for her and her growing child. No sun, no wind, no cool breezes, no quiet private moments with Carter. The food was plain, bland, and thoroughly dull. She'd grown used to shoveling it in and not thinking about it, but how she longed for an orange or an apple, banana, anything fresh out of an orchard or a garden. She missed the smell of roses and lavender, the hum of bees, and the call of birds. She even missed the traffic in the city - the honking of car horns that she never heard anymore because she'd grown so used to them when she lived in Boston. She wanted proper clothes, not these dreadful black sacks, and to have her hair trimmed and washed in warm water with real shampoo and conditioner. How she longed to manicure her nails and use polish, even just the clear stuff to give them shine.

Casting these longings to one side, she dressed and help Liam into his clothes, then made breakfast. Another day of Naan bread and oatmeal porridge with maybe a sprinkling of brown sugar and nutmeg; it was all right for sometimes, but not every day.

Liam tried so hard to pretend he still enjoyed it, but like her, he was slowly losing the battle. He had dark circles under his eyes and was listless. The excitement about the baby had long vanished even when she let him feel it moving. He made an effort one day and asked her "What do you think you'll call it Mom?"

"Well," she answered, "I thought if it's a boy I'll call it after your grandfather Steven, my father and maybe give it 'Carter' for its second name, what do you think?"

"Steven Carter Devereux, that's not bad. What about a girl?"

"After my Mother, I think, her names are Mary Elizabeth. I don't really like Elizabeth very much, but if I shortened it to Beth, then she'd have her grandmother's name but shortened. So, like you are William after your Great Grandfather, but we call you Liam, we could call her Beth, which is the short form of Elizabeth if you follow me." She suddenly drifted off, her eyes becoming vacant.

"Mom, are you all right?" Liam was shaking her.

"Mmm? Um, yes darling, I'm fine, just so tired, and I must get back to the Three Stooges and see what they're up to today."

"Are they treating you alright?"

"Yes, I don't think they'd dare not to for fear Nasser would be very angry with them." She gave him a wan smile.

The three men approached her later that morning while she and Liu were working side-by-side trying to decipher more of the texts. The two of them had given up trying to speak to each other long ago; it was too dangerous, and there was very little to say anymore.

The men told her they felt they had reached a stage where it was necessary to take their research out of the test tubes and begin again on animals and humans.

Mackenzie lifted her head from the text she was working on and stared darkly at them through the niqab. She slowly rose from her chair; they may not have been able to see her eyes too clearly, but as she stood up to her full height, there was no mistaking the rage emanating from her.

"If you *ever* suggest such indescribable and filthy experimentation again, I will report you to Nasser. You already know he has banned such disgusting research, and you well know what he would do if you approached him with this request." She continued to stare down at them, "You would not only be out of a job but very likely executed." They were not very tall and certainly not imposing. Finally, they slunk away, and she gratefully sat down again.

She held her hands in her lap waiting for them and her legs to stop shaking.

"Mackie, are you okay?" Liu whispered.

"I don't know how much longer I can hold out Liu, I'm coming to the end, I fear."

The Wolves of Freydis

The wolves were agitated. All day they lingered near the cave and their pups that came out to play when the sun was high.

They hunted nearby, eating rabbit then disgorging it to fill the pups' tummies; it was a full-time job.

They'd checked the environment again but knew there were no threats. All nearby creatures were aware of the Freydis wolves; the big ones respected them, and the small ones feared them.

There was nothing to disturb their wellbeing, yet still they paced back and forth, back and forth panting until finally as if of one mind, they turned and loped towards Ahote and Bly's homestead.

Bly was out settling the chickens into their yard for the night, feeding and watering them when she looked up and saw Loki and Keeva standing some distance away waiting patiently for her. They were familiar with her evening routines and knew she'd be nearby.

"What on earth do you two want?" she asked as she walked towards them. "I didn't expect to see you again until Carter comes back." She stopped and stared at them; their ears were back, their tails down.

She sighed, "Okay, so what's wrong. It's obviously not good." She went over and fondled their thick fur, scratching behind their ears. Each of them rubbed against her, looking up into her eyes, as no wolf would normally do. "So, I take it something has gone wrong somewhere, and you need to pass it on." She sighed again, "Oh hell; I know what you're going to do now; you've given me the message so you'll soon walk away from me and go back to your cave and your babies, and leave me with the worry."

That was exactly what they did moments later, turning and loping off into the trees, vanishing from sight.

"Thanks, guys," Bly had her hands on her hips watching them go. "Hmm... I don't think I will share this visit with Ahote; he'll only fuss and not sleep. Whoever it is, and I fear it's probably Mackie, Liam, or oh hell, maybe even Ahote. I'm sure I'll know soon enough; or perhaps not."

As she turned away, she muttered: "May as well call me Chief Worry Wolf, yeah, that's me."

She sat on the porch until Ahote arrived home; "Well, it's not him, that's a relief." With that, she stood and went inside to start dinner.

Chapter Forty

AN ETHICAL DILEMMA

By the fourth day on the site, the number of participants in Carter and his four companions' early morning and late afternoon runs had increased to ten people with the inclusion of some running enthusiasts amongst Daan's crew and a few of the soldiers from the camp.

One of the enthusiasts was Khalid Abbasi, from Daan's crew and a marathon fanatic who was preparing to run the Cairo marathon later in the year. He told Carter that he had been participating in marathons and even a few ultra-marathons all over the Middle East, including the Dead Sea Marathon, the Mobility Jeddah Marathon in Saudi Arabia and once the 220-kilometer Marathon des Sables in the Moroccan Sahara. However, he just shook his head when he told Carter that it was madness; he would never do that again. Running 220 kilometers through the Sahara Desert while carrying your water and food with you in a backpack had nothing to do with fun; it was torture.

Khalid told Carter that he had a lot of pictures and videos on his tablet about some of the marathons, that he had participated in and would show it to him if he were interested. Carter told him he would indeed like to see them.

The other parts of Carter's training were kept private and out of the public eye. These sessions were held in the big tent that Daan's crew had erected for him and his men shortly after their arrival.

After they had managed to open the door to the ancient cemetery, Daan and some of his crew had diverted their attention there to conduct an initial survey and mapping of the place before they would allow anthropologists to visit.

Carter had joined them, but not for the same purposes as they had. He had studied the pictures and videos of the two hidden doors and managed to conduct GPR scans while no one was watching him.

The scans confirmed his initial assessment, those were definitely doors, and there were large open areas behind both of them. However, the GPR could not penetrate deep enough to tell him how big they were. It wasn't long before he confirmed that the doors operated with electromagnetic mechanisms, the same as the first one.

Carter had a constant, almost electric sensation that a treasure trove of information was awaiting him behind those doors. Once he collected all the information it was time to once again demand 'Open Sesame.'

However, he hesitated, he brooded on it for quite a few days. Since he discovered those doors, he had been fighting a battle with his conscience. On the one hand, as a revered archeologist, he was obliged to share his findings with Daan, the expedition leader; after all, Carter and his men were there at the invitation of Daan, who trusted Carter and his men. On the other hand, there was the reality of the threat to the world from ancient technology that could cause unimaginable death and destruction. Information about that technology could be behind those doors, and if that were the case, it was his duty to ensure it would not land in anyone else's hands.

Should he tell Daan about his discovery? Or should he wait until he had a chance to see what was in the chambers behind the doors? *Shut up until you have proof.*

If he discovered anything of significance there, should he hand it over to Daan or should he keep it and study it first? *Shut up until you have proof.*

Another issue he had was that his own team was not aware of the real purpose of his search. They had no idea about the ancient nukes, nor were they aware of the fact that Mackenzie and Liam were alive. As far as they were concerned, Carter's family died in a bomb explosion in Jerusalem several months ago, and they were with him to protect him while he was doing his job as an archeologist in a foreign country.

Carefully weighing up the various options and consequences, he decided the safe option was to keep the status quo. That meant; find out what was going on behind those doors first, and then make the next decision.

He called his team together, and after Andre had assured him that the counter surveillance equipment would block out their communications to outsiders, he continued.

"Now guys, I know what I'm about to tell you might sound strange, even unethical but hear me out first. It's also vital that what I'm about to tell you stays between us; hell, it's not just vital, it's crucial."

They all nodded their agreement. The four of them had spent enough time in the world of clandestine operations; they knew how important it was to keep your mouth shut if you wanted to stay alive.

"Good," Carter continued. "I found two concealed doors just inside the burial chamber. As far as I know, no one else has spotted them." Carter pulled up the videos, pictures, and GPR images, and showed them.

They all had a good look at it, and Andre said, "So let me guess. You'd like to go and have a look behind those doors without anyone else knowing?"

Carter nodded. "Yes, and that's the part that's probably a bit unethical."

"Why?" John asked.

"Well, we're here as Daan's guests. Moreover, we're here to participate in *his* expedition and it goes without saying that whatever we discover must be handed to him. We have no rights to it."

"So why don't you want to do that then?" Andre asked.

Carter was expecting this line of questioning, and he had already decided that the best way to handle it was to be honest with them. "Okay guys, I've got a bit of a dilemma. I want very much to tell you the whole story; but I'm bound by an oath of secrecy, so, unfortunately, I'm unable to share it with you."

"In other words, 'yours is not to reason why, yours is but to do or die,'" Kevin smiled as he quoted the old military jingle.

Carter could see a bit of disappointment on their faces, but they were used to the 'need-to-know' principle. He smiled wryly, "Yes, something like that. But let me give you some background information which might clarify things a bit."

They all looked at him in anticipation.

"Look around you," Carter said. "We have a city here; the last inhabitants left this place about 50,000 years ago. We don't have any idea how long they lived here before that. There is no record of the existence of this place anywhere in any written history. Until that desert storm removed the sand and revealed it, it simply didn't exist. Giants occupied the place, as you have already seen. However, up until this discovery very few people believed that giants had ever walked the earth. It was believed they only appeared in fairy tales."

Carter could see that his words were sinking in with them.

"These giants understood and harnessed the power of electricity in ways we don't even understand; you've seen it working here. Humans have been studying electricity for millennia, but it was only in the late 1800's that we learned how to use electricity for our own purposes. The giants preceded us by more than 50,000 years, not only that, but they were using technology so advanced our scientists have yet to figure out how it worked."

Carter had stopped talking and was looking at them to see if he had said enough or if he should continue. It was difficult to judge by their facial expressions; therefore, he left them with one more thought.

"The Giants were much more advanced in certain aspects of technology than we are today, that much we know. However, we have only discovered their electricity and electromagnetism. The question is; what else did they know that we haven't uncovered yet? What we don't know is what's dangerous."

"Don't worry Carter," Roy smiled, "we've got it. You don't have to explain anything else."

"Okay, with that out of the way, what's your plan?" John asked.

"We have to sneak into that place at night and have a look. I suggest one of you come with me and the other three, stand guard, ready to create a diversion if anyone approaches and to alert us on the inside."

"Right," Kevin said, "the four of us will check everything out tomorrow during the day, plan it, and if everything seems to be good we can move in late tomorrow night. At least, we know that Daan's people are usually all asleep by 11:00 pm."

It was shortly after 1:00 am the next day when Carter and Kevin arrived at the burial chambers, opened the main door, entered, and swiped the GRP on the inside wall to close it behind them.

On the outside Roy, Andre and John were positioned in various places from where they would be able to observe anyone approaching and create a diversion if necessary. They had small, handheld two-way radios which they used to keep in contact with each other, as well as with Carter and Kevin on the inside. Kevin had a signal booster that he placed just inside the main door to improve the signal strength of the little radios.

As expected, the first door opened soon after Kevin started probing the area on the wall, pointed out by Carter. It was the area where his earlier scanning with the EMF meter showed the most electromagnetic activity.

When the first door slid backward and then sideways, Carter walked forward into the chamber and stopped. Seconds later the brilliant bright lights went on, as he expected and he took a deep breath. Kevin stood next to him in silence; he had stopped breathing and was standing in awe at what he was seeing.

Carter turned to him, "Breathe, Kevin, I need you here," He chuckled.

The air was fresh and cool, almost cold. There wasn't a single speck of dust anywhere as far as their eyes could see;

it felt as if the place had been fitted with air-conditioning. If Carter expected to enter into a spacious place, he would have been disappointed, but over the years he'd learned to have no expectations; but to search and explore, and enjoy the surprises when they came.

At first glance, seeing this room wasn't a breathtaking moment for him. It was a small room, about ten by ten feet square with beautiful marble walls, but no engravings anywhere. In the center was a granite table with a rectangular marble box on top. The box appeared to be about one-foot-wide, three feet long, and two feet deep. It had, what looked like a solid marble lid covering it. The minimalism of the room and its contents stood in sharp contrast to everything else in the City of Lights. It was almost an anticlimax.

That feeling lasted only until he and Kevin carefully lifted the lid. The first surprise was its weight. It looked like it was solid marble but it couldn't be. It was as light as a feather; any one of them could have lifted it with a pinky. Staring into the box, Carter was now the one gasping for air.

"What is this?"

Kevin was already looking at him for an answer. "Breathe, Carter," he whispered, and then shook his head, "No idea."

The box was about one-third full, with three neatly stacked bundles of flimsy, metallic looking sheets. Carter donned a pair of cotton gloves and slowly and carefully retrieved one of the sheets; it was thinner than paper. When he held it up, he thought it looked and felt like a sheet of cellophane, yet it had an unmistakable metallurgical aspect to it; nothing like he had ever seen before.

"What do you think?" Kevin asked.

Carter was startled out of his reverie. "The Chronicles of the dead." He murmured.

"What?"

"I think these sheets hold information about the people who have been buried here."

"But there's no writing on it."

Holding the sheet up again, Carter pointed with his finger to the rows and rows of tiny dots, about the size of a pinhead covering the entire sheet. "The writing is inside those little dots."

"How the hell…?"

"Nanotechnology," Carter smiled. "In 2007 scientists used nanotechnology to print the entire Old Testament of the Bible onto a silicon chip which was less than 1/1000th of an inch, in other words in a space that was much smaller than a pinhead. They used a focused ion beam (FIB) generator to shoot ions onto a gold surface covering a base layer of silicon. The actual 'writing' of the full text took just 90 minutes."

"From 50,000 years ago?" Kevin shook his head. "Nanotechnology? Wha … how… nah… just forget it, don't even try to explain. I've just gone crazy, much easier to deal with a mind that has gone around the bend than this."

Carter laughed. "Okay, let's go and have a look at the other room."

They left and walked across a passage, and seconds later, stood in a room identical to first. The only difference was the table in this room held three boxes the same size as the one in the first room, and these boxes were all filled to the brim with the same type of sheets.

"So if the previous box contained the chronicles of the dead, what is this?" Kevin asked. "But remember I've lost my mind already so you can tell me anything, I can't get more disturbed than I already am."

Carter chuckled, "Maybe it's the library of the giants."

"Oh ok... if you say so," was all that Kevin could muster.

"Alright, Kevin; the moment of truth has arrived," Carter uttered in an almost formal tone. "I have to get these boxes out of here and then find a way of smuggling them back to the States. We have to decipher the language and discover what is written on those sheets."

Kevin nodded.

"Now I am not asking you to appease my conscience," Carter was uneasy but he felt what he had to say was important. "I'm admitting to you now that what I'm doing is wrong. If I'm caught, I will take the rap for it, you have my word that I'll never mention you or any of your teammates."

Kevin looked at him a bit stunned. "Carter, we already sorted that shit out the other night. This is in the interest of National... wait maybe even in the interest of humanity. Stop talking and let's get these boxes out of here ASAP. And don't forget, I'm crazy, there's nothing I could say that anyone would believe."

On the one hand, Carter was relieved that Kevin had made it easy for him. On the other hand, his sense of right and wrong was not just accusing him, it was screaming at him. Then, on the other hand... there was no other hand... he *had* to do it; there was just too much at stake. If he had to choose between unethical behavior and saving millions of people's lives he chose the latter. If he had to choose between unethical behavior and the lives of his wife and son, he would again, choose the latter.

Kevin called Roy, who was closest to the main entry, on

the radio and asked that the three of them come and help them. Twenty minutes later, they were back in their tents. They'd sealed the three boxes with duct tape, wrapped them in blankets, dug holes in the sand under the tent floor, placed the boxes inside, and covered them with the floor canvas. They now had to figure out a way to smuggle everything out when they returned to America in three days' time.

Of course, Carter had to explain to the rest of the team what he and Kevin had found. He showed them one of the sheets and watched three more incredulous faces when he told them what he thought they could be, and about his idea that it was accomplished with nanotechnology. After listening to Carter and Kevin's comments the three of them joined Kevin's corner. They thought it was a better idea to surrender to lunacy than to try and explain all of this.

Carter came up with the idea the next day that they should remove the sheets from the boxes, pack and wrap each of the bundles individually, put them in different containers, and return the empty faux marble boxes to the hidden rooms. That way, if anyone discovered the concealed doors, they would find the empty boxes and conclude that the Giants had probably removed the contents when they left 50,000 years ago.

The bundles were removed and packed according to plan, and they returned the empty faux marble boxes to their tables the next night.

The empty cartons that contained the rations they brought in when they arrived at the site were perfect to pack and transport the stash of ancient sheets out of the City of Lights.

Carter had to use all his willpower not to grab one of those sheets and study it more closely under a microscope, but the risk was just too high, he had to wait until they got back home. Sitting in an Egyptian jail for artifact theft was not a pleasant thought to him or anyone on his team.

The day before their departure, after the 'desert-rat race' as his team had dubbed the early morning runs, Khalid Abbasi, the marathon fanatic told Carter he would come over later in the day to show him the pictures and videos about the marathons he had participated in.

It was shortly after lunch when Khalid turned up with his tablet PC and sat down to show him as promised. Carter found it intriguing to see the places where people were prepared to go and run to experience the joy of torturing their bodies.

The last video clip Khalid had was of his participation in the annual family fun run in Riyadh. It was not so much the environment and his participation that had Khalid excited about this particular race; it was the performance of the winner that year.

"Look at that," he said. "That's the ten-kilometer mark and that man is already eight minutes ahead of his closest rival. A pace of two minutes per kilometer."

Carter made a few quick calculations in his head. "He can't maintain that pace. No human can."

Khalid shook his head; he wanted the end to be a surprise. "There is the 21-kilometer mark, he covered it in exactly 42 minutes; the second man was already 21 minutes behind him at this point."

Carter's mind was working overtime. *Something's wrong; the video's a fake or that man had been drugged.*

"There," Khalid pointed his finger at the screen, "he's three kilometers from the finish line, and he is still going at two minutes per kilometer."

"It's humanly impossible," Carter whispered. "I don't think even with drugs it's possible."

Khalid was on his feet when he said very excitedly, "There is the finish line. That man broke the world record by 40 minutes! He maintained a pace of two minutes per kilometer for the entire race. Can you believe it?"

"No, I can't believe it. It's just not possible," Carter replied. "You're sure this video isn't faked, Khalid? I mean… hell man, no human can do that."

"Well, I was there in that race; I didn't see him, but there was a lot of talk about his man."

"What's his name? Why hasn't the world heard of him again?"

Khalid shrugged. "Nobody knows his name. Nobody had seen him before in any race, and nobody has seen him since that race. He has been nicknamed the ghost-runner of Riyadh. There are many rumors and conspiracy theories, but I have no idea what to believe and what not to."

"What a weird story," Carter said slowly. "What are the rumors you've heard?"

"Drugs, he was not human, a cyborg or robot, some new technology, that sort of thing."

"Do you mind if I take a copy of that video?" Carter asked. "It's intriguing. I would like to look at it again."

"No problem."

Carter handed him a flash drive, and he copied the video onto it.

Khalid left shortly afterward. Carter just could not put the video out of his mind. If that video was real, something was out of place with that runner. He didn't know to what extent drugs could boost performance, but he was almost sure no drug could achieve what that runner had done. If that 'man' were a robot, it could explain everything; but then he thought that fact would have been made public. Breaking the marathon world record by forty minutes should have been world headline news. Yet very few people knew about it.

His thoughts were interrupted when Daan turned up so that they could study the final GPR images and Carter could hand it all over to him. Daan was grateful for the financial assistance, which Carter had organized and very pleased with the opening of the burial chamber. As a token of his appreciation, Daan's team had prepared a traditional Arabian dinner for Carter and his men.

The next morning, shortly after sunrise, the helicopter arrived, and they all had to say their goodbyes.

Chapter Forty-One

HE TRIED TO SLEEP BUT HE COULDN'T

Carter and his men were a little nervous going through Egyptian customs but in the end, it was a non-event, and they all sighed with relief and clapped their hands in applause when the Gulfstream jet cleared the runway and lifted its nose into the air.

At about the time that Carter and his men had settled in and started relaxing for the ten-hour flight back to DC, Harry Auden walked into James Rhodes' office. Harry was a short, skinny, man in his mid-sixties, with silver hair and gold-framed glasses, and a linguistic genius. He was A-Echelon's ancient language specialist. Irene once told Mackenzie, "I sometimes get the impression that Harry Auden can speak all languages ever known to man."

He had accompanied Mackenzie on the trip to the Mesrop Mashtots Institute of Ancient Manuscripts in Yerevan, Armenia where they studied the Books of the Elders of Medicine, which eventually led them to the Sirralnnudam. It was also one of the very rare occasions where Harry had been unable to translate an ancient text.

Part of Harry's job at A-Echelon was to keep his eye on archeological publications from across the globe and keep his superiors up to date with the latest finds, speculations, and theories.

While he was paging through one of the publications, his attention was drawn to an article by a Greek professor of archeology titled 'The Sirralnnudam – The Tragic Loss of Another Irreplaceable Artifact'.

The article explained how German archeologist, Karsten Rischmüller, on a dig site at Çatalhöyük, Turkey about 50 years ago, discovered the book and gave a brief history of it. At some stage, it was kept in the legendary Library of Alexandria somewhere between 300 B.C. and the time the library was destroyed by Julius Caesar's legions in 48 B.C. It was believed that Ptolemy I Soter, the successor of Alexander the Great, placed it in the Library of Alexandria.

The article stated that Rischmüller had given the book to the Mesrop Mashtots Institute of Ancient Manuscripts but that it had recently been stolen from the establishment and authorities had been unable to find the culprit. The article ended by mentioning that there was some speculation that a second copy of the book could have survived and was in the hands of an unknown private collector. The professor left his contact details at the end of the article in the hope that, slim as it might be, he would hear from anyone who might have knowledge of the second copy.

Harry placed the article on James's desk and turned the magazine so that James could read it. "That's the book we spoke about a few months ago."

James leaned forward and read it. "Yes, that's the one," he nodded slowly. A few thoughts crossed his mind, none of which he could discuss with Harry. "Thanks, Harry, I appreciate it. Can you ask my secretary to make a photocopy for me?"

"Sure, no problem. Have a good one." Harry left.

James sat back in his chair and interlaced his fingers behind his head. *Someone is looking for that book. Is it really just that Greek Professor with a sense of loss? Or is there more to it? Someone behind him maybe? I'll have to let Carter and Irene know and see what they think of it.*

Carter flipped through the news channels trying to find a station where he could get a quick update on what was going on in the world. He hadn't seen the news for the past two weeks and was feeling a little deprived. Suddenly his eye caught something about the Vice President, and he stopped on that channel to listen.

The Vice President was about to announce his intention to run for president in the next election, eighteen months away. Carter didn't care much for politics; he found it mostly boring and, generally speaking, frustrating to deal with politicians. They were not his favorite breed of the human species.

Nevertheless, because he'd once met Vice President George Robertson in person, he listened for a few minutes. The man was a born talker; he had the talent. Some people had a knack for numbers; others were born athletes who could break a defensive line and bring crowds to their feet. Robertson was an orator who could bring crowds to their feet.

"Why are we here today? Why aren't we out fishing and camping? It's a public holiday. Why aren't we at home having a beer while watching the Yankees?"

The crowd was quiet, waiting for him. He had their attention.

"I say it's for the love for our country; isn't it? America is hurting, it's on a very slippery slope, and we can't sit by and watch it go down the drain any longer."

The crowd roared with applause.

"We want our country back! We want it restored to its former glory. The American dream, that's what we want back."

He had to stop as the noise from the crowd erupted and overpowered his voice on the amplified speakers throughout the stadium.

"Our country is approaching a crossroads in history. America is facing a crisis worse than any previously known in our nation's history. And do you know why? I'll tell you why."

He held two fingers in the air.

"Failed policies and incompetent leadership."

Carter was wondering what the President would think about that statement. Politics was a dog eat dog environment, and if you didn't know it when you entered the political arena, you were in for a rude awakening.

"We've become a country of stress and anxiety instead of a country of hope and prosperity. Unemployment has reached a new record high. We are drowning in red ink; our national debt is growing at almost $3 million a minute, more than $4 billion a day. My fellow Americans, we have to stop this insanity. We have to take our country back."

The crowd was on its feet.

"Your votes are going to make or break this country. Think on that."

Carter mumbled, "don't we always hear that?"

"You can feel it in the air and on the airwaves! This time, it's serious! It's more far-reaching than at any other time in our history!"

Carter had lost interest; he'd had heard all of this

before. Every election cycle sounded the same; the only things that changed were the faces and the voices saying it. *Same tune, different station*, he thought with a disgusted shake of his head.

Robertson turned his attention to the evangelicals. He needed their attention and their votes to propel him into power.

"Those who call themselves Christians, who avoid politics, I say to you this not an option anymore. We are all needed; needed I say, to participate in the electoral process. When Jesus said, 'render unto Caesar what is Caesars' this is what he meant.

The 60 million U.S. evangelicals are the people who can turn this country away from disaster. The future is in our hands. If every evangelical of voting age would take the responsibility to cast a ballot in each of our local, state, and federal elections, the United States will be a better place. 60 million Jesus-loving, God-fearing men and women are called upon to step boldly into the voting booths this election season and elect a Christian president."

Carter turned the TV off; he was a Christian, but this was playing religion for political ends. Robertson would not get his vote. He placed headphones over his ears, found his favorite classical music, reclined his seat and closed his eyes.

His mind returned to his family, as it always did every free moment he was awake. *Where are my Mackie and my Liam?*

That must have been the thought that triggered his knee-jerk reaction when he shouted "Respirocytes!"

Everyone in the cabin jumped and stared at him. He realized he couldn't say anything more about it, and he waved his hand saying sheepishly, "Sorry, bad dream." He tried to smile as he settled back into his seat.

The ghost-runner of Riyadh had been injected with respirocytes!

That was the only way the man could have run like that for that distance. He found his tablet and replayed the video

Khalid had given him, stopping and rewinding it as he went along. He wasn't sure what he was trying to find; maybe he just wanted to feed his brain more information and images so that it could work out the answer.

Hours later he was still thinking and conjecturing; *that marathon was in Riyadh. Was that runner from Saudi Arabia? Who were the people who manufactured the respirocytes? Where were they? Where were their labs?*

Are Mackie and Liam somewhere in Saudi Arabia?

Who is doing respirocyte research in Saudi Arabia?

Who is doing human trials?

Questions, questions, and more questions hammered his brain until he had a headache. He had to wait until they landed in DC when he could talk to James and Irene.

He tried to sleep, but couldn't.

Chapter Forty-Two

THE DEBRIEFING

Carter stared out the window as the Gulfstream taxied into the hangar and the doors closed behind them. He saw James, Irene, Sean, and Dylan on the ground, waiting for them. None of them had any idea of the artifacts Carter had on board.

After they had disembarked, greeted each other, and exchanged the how-are-you's and other pleasantries, Carter pulled James, Irene, Sean, and Dylan to one side and told them about the contents of the cartons. They needed a quick decision about where the boxes could be kept safely, and they all immediately agreed that definitely would not be at A-Echelon.

Instead, it was decided that Sean and Dylan would take the containers with the artifacts into safe keeping. They would store them at one of the CIA's training facilities in Virginia where only they had access.

Carter also informed them that he had to divulge some information to the men who accompanied him and requested that Sean and Dylan reiterate the requirement for secrecy with their men.

When everything was unpacked from the plane, they proceeded in separate vehicles to one of Executive Advantage's safe houses for the debriefing.

Roy, Andre, Kevin, and John stayed only for the first part of the debriefing and left to go and enjoy a few days of R-and-R before they returned to duty. Two of them would return to Freydis with Carter.

When they left, Carter gave Sean and Dylan a glowing report about the four men who accompanied him.

The discussion then turned to the artifacts and how to go about deciphering them. As this was outside their area of expertise, everyone was looking at Carter for guidance.

"I need to look at the sheets first before we decide how to proceed, and for that I'll need an electron microscope and a quiet, secure place," Carter said.

"I'll see what I can arrange with DARPA," Irene replied.

"If the sheets contain text, then we might be able to copy the contents onto an electronic storage device and work from there. I would prefer that those sheets are handled as little as possible. Besides, I don't want anyone else to see them."

They all agreed.

"Once we have copied the data from the sheets to another medium the real fun starts when we have to decipher it," Carter smiled. He was excited to get to that part.

Next, Dylan and Sean told Carter about their investigation into the organization that had been watching him before he left for Egypt. The organization involved was AMZ Security. EA had conducted a few discreet inquiries, and spoken to some of the people who were on the team watching him. They didn't know anything other than that they were following the instructions from one of their bosses, Mr. Schwall, who was one of the directors of AMZ. Mr. Schwall, however, died of a heart attack before EA's investigators could talk to him. None of the other managers or supervisors at AMZ had any idea about this operation.

Rick Winslow's digging in the company files and financial records produced nothing, confirming that no one else knew about the operation. There was nothing left they could act on.

"AMZ would not have acted on their own initiative; they would have been doing the job for someone else. That someone else made sure nothing could lead back to him or her," Dylan concluded.

Carter nodded. "It's a strange feeling to know you are being followed; sort of a constant itch between your shoulder blades."

All of them knew the feeling very well. It was Carter's humorous but very accurate description that gave reason to chuckle.

"Fact is, Carter, we now have confirmation that you are being watched," Sean said. "Although that's what we wanted, to lure them out and feed them false information, we also must tread very carefully."

"So now that they have been exposed do you think they will back off?" Carter asked.

"I doubt that," Sean replied. "All they'll do is be more careful and sophisticated; with what is at stake here, you can be sure they won't back off."

Dylan got up and started the coffee machine while they kept talking. When he had served everyone their coffee, Carter took his tablet out and switched it on.

"I've got something I want to show you. It kept me awake the whole trip back here."

Turning the screen so that they could all see it, he started the video of the Riyadh Marathon he'd copied from Khalid Abbasi, giving them a running commentary just as Khalid had done for him. When the video ended, he looked at them. They were shaking their heads in mistrust.

"Not possible," Dylan and Sean said as if on cue.

"That's hogwash, Carter," Dylan said. "There is no way on God's green earth that any human could do that."

"As you know, I've got a Ph.D. in Human Biology," Irene responded. "Admittedly, I haven't done much in that field since I've moved over from DARPA to A-Echelon, but one thing I'm pretty sure of is that no human can do what you have shown us on that video," she was shaking her head. "I'll check it with the DARPA scientists just to make sure, but I'm positive they will confirm what I've said."

Carter chose not to tell them what he was thinking just yet; he didn't want to influence their thinking.

"Okay, let's assume for a moment that what we have seen there is real. In other words, it was not a scammer out there who concocted the video and published it on YouTube. Then we are left with a few other options …"

"Like what?" James interjected.

"It could have been a robot, cyborg, alien or something like that," Carter grinned, as he knew James was going to throw a fit.

"Bovine droppings!" James exclaimed. "Why have robots run in a marathon? There aren't any robots that can run like that."

Carter cracked up laughing, "Relax, Jim; I was just having you on," Carter held his hands up. "I haven't had a laugh at your expense for two weeks; I couldn't wait to get one in as soon as possible."

"It's so good to have my two teenage boys back home again," Irene snickered.

"Okay, but seriously," Carter brought them back on topic. "What about drugs Irene? Can drugs make a man perform like that?"

"Drugs can certainly enhance an athletes' performance, which is one of the main reasons why they are banned in competition, but they certainly couldn't give a man the capability to run a 42-kilometer marathon at a pace of two minutes per kilometer. No way. Well, at least not any of the drugs I'm aware of."

"So there is a slim possibility that there could be some sort of a super drug out there that we are not aware of yet that could produce those results?" Carter asked.

Irene shrugged. "I can't rule that possibility out, but I really doubt it. You see the thing with drugs is that it wouldn't make you perform better than your body is capable of. For example, if your body has the strength to lift 200 pounds, drugs can't enable you to lift 400 pounds. The only way you could lift 400 pounds is if you have some sort of mechanical, computerized exoskeleton – the stuff you see in Sci-fi movies and which DARPA has been building and experimenting with for many years."

"Mhh, I see," Carter murmured. "We haven't seen anything of that kind on that runner."

James noticed Carter's body language and questions and decided Carter had something in mind but didn't want to talk about it yet. *What is he thinking?*

"Resi pi thingamabobs!" James' shout startled everyone.

They were all staring at James and didn't notice the grin on Carter's face. "What was that?" Sean asked.

"Yes, man those funny-name thingamajigs Mackenzie was working on. She told me they could make humans stay under water for four hours with one breath and run at full speed for 30 minutes and that sort of stuff."

"Respirocytes!" Irene laughed for a few seconds and suddenly stopped. "Wait a minute. Hang on there for a moment." She took a deep breath, "That is definitely another possibility."

Sean stopped them. "Okay, I know Mrs. Devereux has done research on respirocytes, but I'm afraid you will have to explain a bit more about it to Dylan and me before we continue."

Dylan nodded.

Irene spent the next few minutes explaining what respirocytes were and how they could enhance human performance to incredible levels. "However, as far as I know, and last time I checked with DARPA, it is still very much a theoretical concept. There are a few biotech companies doing research in this space, but thus far there have been no promising results. Forget about pumping it into humans."

James pushed back in his chair and looked at Carter. "You have something in mind, I can see that. What is it?"

"Jim, I don't have to tell you or anyone else here that it is impossible for me to remain objective in my opinions as long as my family is held captive somewhere. Maybe I'm chasing shadows…" Carter had to clear his throat to get rid of the quivering, "but I have been wondering: What if that man was injected with respirocytes? That is one plausible explanation for what we saw on that video. If so: Who did it? Where are the labs where they would have created the respirocytes? That race was in Saudi Arabia: Is that where the lab could be?"

Jim nodded slowly and proceeded to say carefully,

"Carter, those are all valid questions, but it's only relevant if it could be proven that the runner had been injected with that stuff. And the problem is, I can't see any way for us to establish that."

"I understand that Jim. I'm just wondering if it would be worthwhile trying to find out if there are any labs in Saudi Arabia. That someone is, maybe, conducting research in this field?"

"It's certainly worth turning every stone we can. Irene and I will put our heads together and come up with a way to go about answering those questions without raising any suspicions."

"DARPA might be a good place to start," Irene agreed. "They told Mackenzie and me that although they are not doing any research about respirocytes themselves, they had been following all research about it for years. It's something in which they are very interested."

"Let us know if you need anyone on the ground in Saudi Arabia," Sean said. We have a few good contacts in Oman, former Desert Phantoms."

Carter raised his brows curiously.

Sean explained, "The Desert Phantoms are the Omani Special Forces. There is nobody on earth that knows the desert better than they do. They are the hardest men I've ever encountered. They train British and American Special Forces teams in desert warfare and survival, and we have often embedded some of them who were on special operations in those parts of the world. If there is something out there in Saudi Arabia to be found they *will* find it."

Carter looked at James and Irene. "If our other methods don't produce results we'll certainly come knocking on your door, Sean."

For the moment, there was nothing more to discuss. Carter's two new bodyguards were introduced and left with him, James, and Irene.

The next morning Irene took Carter over to the DARPA offices and introduced him to the two medical nanotech scientists who had met Mackenzie before, Dr. Cate Nelson and Dr. Scott Watson.

Irene explained to them that she and Carter were working on a project but that she could not divulge too much information about it. The two scientists had no problem with that; they had been working in a highly confidential environment for many years.

She asked them about the capabilities of performance enhancing drugs and got confirmation that her ideas were correct. No drug can boost performance to beyond the physical capacity of the person. They were also sure that there was no secret drug available, which could do it. Otherwise, they would have heard about it from the CIA and other intelligence agencies.

They could not recall off the top of their heads any research facilities in the Middle East working on respirocytes. However, they would double check and were happy to supply a copy of their list of known labs to Irene later in the day.

The last request Irene had for them was to provide Carter with a secure room and an electron microscope. They were happy to help with that, and let her know that the room and microscope would be ready for Carter's use the next day.

James had asked them to drop by his office when they were finished with the DARPA meeting. They gave James a quick overview of how the meeting went and then James showed them the copy of the article Harry had found in the archeology periodical and pushed it across his desk so that they could read it.

"What do you think?" He asked when Irene and Carter looked up after reading the item.

"Well, like I told you yesterday, it's impossible for me to be objective," Carter started. "But my first reaction is; someone is looking for that book."

James nodded and looked at Irene.

"What Carter said," she responded, "someone is looking for the book, and somehow I get the feeling Professor Anatolio Kakos… yeah, no, I don't know. Let's stick with that for now. Professor Kakos is looking for the Sirralnnudam."

"Okay, I happen to agree with you; and I have that same uneasy feeling about the Professor, but can't lay my finger on it. I'll get Ben Friedman to put a few tabs on him."

The entire time in James' office Carter had a mysterious feeling that he couldn't shake off. He knew Mackenzie was one of the last people who held the Sirralnnudam in her hands. The book had literally gone down into the drains of Yerevan, months ago. All of the sudden, Professor Anatolio Kakos is looking for that book.

"Jim, do you think we could get a copy of the records of the Mesrop Mashtots Institute of Ancient Manuscripts to see who else has checked that book out over the years?"

"That shouldn't be too much of a problem. Irene? You've got the contacts there."

"I'll check it out," She replied. "You're starting to think like a real investigator Carter. That's good," she laughed.

"One more thing," Carter said. "Would it do any harm if I have a good look through Mackenzie's research?"

Irene smiled as she looked at James. They had been

talking about it before, hoping that they would be able to get Carter to do exactly that, but they hadn't wanted to put any additional emotional stress on him, so they had delayed the request. "No Carter, no problem at all. In fact, it's a little earlier than we anticipated, but Jim and I were planning on asking you if you felt up to doing that.

"Good that's settled then. Now I have to get into those ancient sheets and see what we can learn from our gigantic ancestors," Carter said referring to the giants as he stood.

The next morning Carter and Irene went to the DARPA offices and on arrival were escorted by Dr. Cate Nelson to the secure room equipped with the scanning electron microscope as requested.

Carter was worried that the microscope, which used a beam of accelerated electrons as a source of illumination, could damage the ancient datasheets. However, due to the requirement for absolute secrecy, he could not call in any outside expertise to help him analyze the sheets to determine a nondestructive analysis method. He was on his own and had to take the risk. After discussing the matter with Irene, they agreed that it would be best to use one of the sheets from the box that Carter believed contained the names of the dead. They reasoned that if one of those sheets were damaged, it would not be as big a loss as library information would be if that is what was on the other sheets.

Irene was holding her breath as she watched how carefully Carter retrieved one of the sheets from the container and put it in place.

"Carter, this whole thing of ancient nanotechnology is

really mindboggling. It feels surreal to think that we might be looking at 50,000-year-old technology which could be more advanced than our own."

Carter grinned. "Yeah, it's hard getting used to it."

"So do you want to venture any guesses as to how they could have done it? That's of course if it was nanotechnology they used."

"Well, nanotechnology is not really my bailiwick, so all I have to go on is how Israeli scientists have done it with the Old Testament."

"How did *they* do it?"

"My understanding is that they printed the 'Nano Bible' as they call it, which is the Hebrew Bible, on a gold-plated silicon chip one-hundredth of an inch square; that's about the size of a pinhead. The text consists of a little over 1.2 million letters. Apparently, they used a focused ion beam, which dislodged gold atoms from the plating and created the letters, very similar to the way inscriptions were carved in stone."

"Amazing! So how would one be able to read that Nano Bible then?"

"You'd need a microscope capable of 10,000 times magnification or higher, which only electron microscopes can do. With electron microscopes, you can get up to 10 million times magnification, whereas most light microscopes are limited to between 100 and 1,000 magnifications."

The first images appeared on the screen, and they both leaned in closer to look. "There you go!" Carter whispered breathlessly, as they stared at the screen. Carter let out a sigh of relief. "It worked; no damage to the plate."

Irene had stopped breathing as her eyes darted across the rows of mysterious characters. Her hands were shaking when she touched Carter's hand. "Can you read it?" Her voice was almost inaudible and filled with hope.

Carter heard her, but nothing registered. His mind was digging into the deep storage vectors of his mind, trying to find the connection between what he was staring at and what was stored in his brain. Something on the screen almost wanted to look familiar.

"Carter?" She whispered again.

"Mhh…?"

"Can you read it?"

He was shaking his head. "All I can say for now is," he pointed to the screen, "it certainly looks like letters of an alphabet, forming words, with spaces between them. I've seen something… similar," He brushed his hand through his hair, "it reminds me of some ancient Semitic scripts I've seen."

She moved back in her chair, closed her eyes, took a deep breath, and relaxed. "What is the origin of the Semitic languages?"

"Well, the name Semitic refers to Shem, one of the three sons of Noah in the Book of Genesis. Semitic languages were widely used in 3,000 to 2,000 BC in Mesopotamia, which covered the Akkadian, Babylonian, and Assyrian civilizations. There are more than 330 million people today that speak one form or another of a Semitic langue, such as Arabic, Hebrew, and a few others."

"Interesting. Do you think there is a chance that the root of the Semitic languages could be antediluvian?"

"Yes, I definitely think so. Why? What are you thinking?"

"If I still remember some of my Sunday school classes correctly, somewhere in Genesis, if I'm not mistaken there is a verse that talks about 'giants in the earth' or something to that effect."

Carter smiled. "Genesis 6 verse 4 *'There were giants in the earth in those days; and also after that, when the sons of God came in unto the daughters of men, and they bare children to them, the same became mighty men which were of old, men of renown.'"*

"Have you memorized the Bible?" Irene asked in disbelief, looking at Carter as if she expected the answer to be 'yes.'

"No, not all of it," Carter said casually, "but I'm getting there." When he saw the look on Irene's face, he held his hand up, "I'm just pulling your leg, Irene. I do remember a few verses, Genesis 6 verse 4 just happens to be one of them because of the research we've been doing."

I wonder how many is a few?

"You and Jim are going to drive me crazy one day." She laughed. "I never know when the two of you are serious or just fooling around. Okay, where were we? Oh yeah, before the flood. I was wondering if the language on those sheets could be the precursor to the Semitic languages."

Carter nodded. "Yes, I agree with you, but only as long as you don't tell any of my archeological colleagues that I said so."

"I promise," Irene giggled. It was heartwarming to see how the zest for life had returned to Carter since he learned that Mackenzie and Liam were alive.

"All right. I'm relieved we achieved what we came here to do," Carter said. "We know we can read the data on those sheets without damaging them, and we know we can copy the data over to an electronic mass storage device. I would like to spend a bit more time to try and analyze the language before we call in the help of linguists."

"Do you want to copy some of the data over now before we go?"

"No, I don't want to spend any more time here. I'm going to buy one of those electron microscopes for myself and take it to Freydis," Carter replied.

"But those things are expensive!"

"It's safer that way. Besides, I frequently find myself in need of, and wishing I had, one and this is a good enough reason for me to get own."

Chapter Forty-Three

MR. GREED WON THE BATTLE

Carter was excited to get back to Freydis. He always enjoyed visiting Washington; he'd made good friends there with James and Irene. But his heart was always on Freydis, that's where he grew up, that's where his beloved grandfather lived and was buried, it's where his friends Ahote and Bly lived. It was the place he and Mackenzie and Liam were devoted to, the place that gave him so many wonderful memories. The old saying was true – home is where the heart is.

After Carter had completed the initial work on the ancient data sheets from the City of Lights, he collected the data received from the research team in Northern India involving the GPR surveys from Professor Pillay's dig. He then took a quick one-day trip to Boston to visit his in-laws Steven and Mary Anderson.

It was good to see them again, but it was also tough for Carter to hide from them the fact that Mackenzie and Liam were still alive. He could see their suffering and pain. At one stage, a burning desire to ease their misery and tell them almost overcame him. He loved them, and it was hurting him to see their grief. Only the thought of Mackenzie's and Liam's safety stopped him.

When they said goodbye late that afternoon, Carter invited them to come and visit him on Freydis for a while as soon as they could fit a few weeks' holiday into their schedule. His invite seemed to cheer them up. It would give them a badly needed break and finally get the chance to see the place that Mackenzie and Liam could never stop talking about every time they returned from Freydis.

Andre and Roy returned to Freydis with Carter and on the way, they lightheartedly warned him that he had a lot of catching up to do. Carter responded that they also might need a bit action, saying that he was of the opinion they were getting fat. This lead to more threats from them, ignoring them with just a reminder that whatever torment they wanted to inflict, would be revenged during the hand-to-hand combat sessions if he felt they were too hard on him.

Half an hour out from Freydis, Carter called Ahote to let them know they would be landing soon. Ahote had been expecting them back for a few days, but he knew he couldn't ask about that on the phone or email.

Ahote and Bly were at the hangar with the electric carts, waiting for them when they landed. Jeha was with them but waited until Carter placed his feet on the ground before she leaped from of the cart and rushed towards him, squeaking and barking with excitement until Carter picked her up and held her in his arms where she immediately started licking his hands and face. It looked as if the little dog was about to jump out of its skin with excitement.

Bly was almost as excited as Jeha to welcome her boys back home.

Ahote helped them unload their luggage. He noted that there was a lot more of it than when they left a few weeks ago. He asked about it, and Carter told him it was a few 'odds and ends' he needed for his research. Ahote just smiled at that – he knew better than to ask more questions. Carter would tell him when he thought it was necessary to know.

When all their stuff was safely stacked in the cabin, they sat around the kitchen table. Each had a mug of coffee and a fat slice of Bly's chocolate cake which she'd baked the day before hoping Carter and his guards would return in time to have some of it before Ahote made it all disappear.

Ahote then related the events of the attempted break-in to them.

Carter tried to hide his alarm as best he could while Ahote told them what happened.

"I don't think there is anything to worry about," Ahote said. "The police came out and looked around, took the backpacks with them but I haven't heard from them again. Doubt if we ever will. Loki and Keeva scared the living daylights out them." He chuckled, "I'm not sure which of the wolves it was, but one of them got a good piece out of one of the thugs. I followed their trail up to the border and let me tell you, they were running all the way. Nah, they won't get close to this place again."

"Oh well let's hope Loki and Keeva have scared them and anyone else with silly ideas away for good," Carter tried to make light of it. He didn't want to scare Bly and Ahote by telling them he had been followed and watched while in DC and that this incident was probably related to that.

Instead, he bent down, picked Jeha up from the floor and scratched her ears. "I hear you have been a very bright and brave girl while I've been away."

They visited a while longer, but as soon as Bly and Ahote had left, Roy and Andre jumped up and went through the security camera feeds that were stored on the two computers. They quickly found the images of the culprits and immediately sent them via the encrypted link to Rick Winslow, who would use the CIA's facial recognition system to try and identify the two.

The rest of the afternoon, they unpacked their stuff and helped Carter set up the electron microscope that he'd purchased.

Later, while they were walking over to Bly and Ahote's place for dinner, Carter saw Loki and Keeva waiting for them next to the path.

Carter approached them first and scratched their backs; murmuring to them, he thanked them for chasing away the intruders. After a while, he got up, and the two moved over to Andre and Roy, sniffed them and wagged their tails, then turned, and disappeared into the trees.

"'The wolves of Freydis' welcoming committee," Andre laughed. "It's just the most amazing thing ever."

The next morning Carter, Roy, and Andre were back into their routine: running, sparring, shooting, and close quarter combat training. It was nearing the time when they would start to introduce bushcraft, stalking, and survival skills.

Carter had decided to divide his days into three parts; the first part was for training, the afternoons were for research on the ancient nukes and in the evenings after dinner, he would take up the respirocyte research.

Shortly after Carter, Roy and Andre cleared customs at Quebec City on their way to Freydis; Dwayne Miller was notified by his contact with border control. He instructed his new subcontractor in Toronto to get his men out there and deploy the drones over Freydis. He also gave the subcontractor very strict orders about security, secrecy, and traceability. He demanded that the best men be put on the job. He didn't want any excuses, no comebacks, no trails, and no loose ends. There must be absolutely nothing that could lead investigators back to CRS.

The near disaster caused by the carelessness of AMZ Security, when Carter's bodyguards detected their men in the white van outside the coffee shop, didn't go over well with Nate Gordon. He was especially angry after he had to contact Ibrahimi El Fadl in Saudi Arabia and explain to him that not only had the whole surveillance operation in DC been compromised but that they had also allowed Carter to slip out to Egypt from under their noses. That had wasted a golden opportunity to capture him while he was in Egypt.

"Telling El Fadl about it the first time was the easy part," Gordon told Miller. "The embarrassing and most annoying part came a few days later when I had to listen to that camel jockey ranting for almost 30 minutes while passing on the threats and disappointment of his boss. I don't even have a bloody clue who the asshole is. Never met him, don't know his name but I have to say yes sir, no sir, I'm sorry sir to this high and mighty ghost's fuckin minion."

"I'm sorry about that Nate."

"Don't be sorry Miller, be careful!"

Miller had never seen Gordon like this. He could only imagine how annoying that telephone call must have been.

"I didn't even tell them about the cluster-fuck on

Devereux's ranch. Can you imagine what El Fadl's mighty boss's message would have been if he heard that you sent two guys there but wolves bit one of them in the ass, and they had to run away and be evacuated by a helicopter!"

"I'll fix it, Nate. I'll get another company to do the job this time. It won't happen again."

"You better make sure they don't fuck it up like those other monkeys. You were lucky once, and now that Devereux and his buddies know someone is watching his ass, it won't be so easy to wipe your tracks out again. They will be all over you like a fuckin' bad rash. You are the one who will be thrown under the bus, whose ass will be in jail when this thing goes tits up."

Miller just nodded.

"Next time you fuck up Miller, don't even call me. Just disappear! Jump out the window, throw yourself off a bridge, I don't care, just *don't* call me!" Gordon shouted and stormed out of Miller's office.

Dwayne Miller sat back and wondered. *Is it time to resign? Get out while I can.*

But it was not easy to say goodbye to a quarter of a million-dollar salary, plus $150,000 in tax-free fringe benefits. Neither would it be easy to walk away from the $1.5 million performance bonus which he had received each year for the past three years, this year it was going to be more than $2 million.

Mr. Greed won the battle.

Chapter Forty-Four

WHAT HAVE YOU DONE MACKIE?

The evening had arrived after a long day of running and workouts as well as working on the ancient data sheets from the City of Lights. Carter now set himself to the task of going carefully through all Mackenzie's analysis in the hope he would find something, anything that would lead him closer to her.

Sitting at his desk after dinner, Carter brought up Mackenzie's research papers on her computer. Andre and Roy were watching television in the other room, unwinding for the day and preparing to get a good night's sleep.

A slight breeze from the window moved the golden key ring that he'd hung from his desk lamp, causing it to glint and catch his eye. This was the key ring he'd had specially made for their 6th wedding anniversary. Not only did it hold keys, but hidden inside was a small camera and a flash drive. It had intrigued Mackenzie, delighting her immensely.

Putting the computer lid down and contemplating the

key ring he realized it had come to the point where he was strong enough, and ready, to look at the photos on the drive.

It was the thought of seeing those photographs that had kept him from looking at the small gold item months ago when he believed they were dead. He knew one day he'd look, but at the time, he was faced with a dread of seeing those much-loved faces shining out at him and knowing they were gone; that had proved too hard to do.

Now, of course, it was the opposite. Knowing the photos were there, and that Mackenzie and Liam were alive somewhere in the world, made him not want to see them as he remembered them, when for all he knew, they were starving and ill in some god-forsaken prison, forgotten and lost forever.

He took the small item into his hand and held it for a while; it grew warm and seemed to beckon him. Finally, taking a deep breath, he slotted it into the USB port on his computer and downloaded everything. When the transfer was complete, he saw dozens of pictures, including ones of him laughing with Liam or hugging Mackie as she took 'selfies' of them together. There were pictures of the places they'd been and seen in Jerusalem before the explosion. These were just a little close to the bone, and he found it hard to look at them.

Shutting the computer lid, he moved away from the desk toward the window and stared out into the night. Looking up at the stars, he tried to imagine where his family was; *can they see the stars? Does Mackie look at the moon and wonder how I am? Does she even know I'm looking for her? Probably not, how could she possibly know. Does she even know there was an explosion? Is there any hope for her and Liam at all?* His skin crawled with stark terror at the thought of her and his son in such dire circumstances and not even being sure if they were alive.

His emotions see-sawed between desolation and violent fury.

"Hang in there my darlings, I will find you, I promise. I won't stop until I do," he whispered. As he spoke those words, his thoughts left his heart with such urgency he could only hope they reached her. Surely there were ways people could reach each other if they loved strongly enough.

He went back and sat down, once more opening the computer and staring at the photos, drinking them in as he realized these were how they looked before they were lost to him, smiling, healthy and alive – so alive.

Okay, Carter, come on, get a grip and move forward, what else is here? He moved the pictures along the screen peering at each of them, taking in every little detail. He hadn't seen his loved ones for many months, and this was something so precious that he lingered over each and every photo.

Finally, coming to the end of the photos he saw there was more; a letter apparently written by Mackenzie to herself.

Wednesday
> *I must calm down.*
> *I have to do it.*
> *It is important; I can't stop now.*
> *I'm so afraid of being caught.*

Thursday
> *I had to do it; it was too valuable to leave it behind.*
> *I know how wrong it is but the whole of humanity needs this and, despite all the moral issues, I know I've done the right thing – haven't I?*
> *What would Carter say about what I've done?*

Carter stopped and read it again, thinking.

What have you done Mackie?

What is it that's troubling you so much my dear?

You are echoing the same doubts I had when I lifted those records from the City of Lights.

I had to do it despite it being morally wrong. Too much hangs on them not getting into the wrong hands. I had to do it.

Now, what did you do Mackie?

What he saw next made him sit bolt upright and yell with shock. Trying to muffle the sound by slapping his hand over his mouth as he remembered this was not to be talked of, this was so secret it was buried almost so deep underground no one could ever reach it – figuratively speaking, but at that moment, Andre and Roy appeared at his door, guns drawn.

"Carter! What? What happened?" Roy demanded as he took in that there was no one else in the room.

Andre stood and observed him quietly once he saw there was no visible threat.

"Sorry guys," Carter hid his shaking hands, "Sorry, I just came across something in the files that startled me, a real 'Eureka' moment. All is well I promise," he grinned at them and they slowly relaxed and returned to their television muttering things about people yelling wolf and spoiling a man's movie... "Idiot," Andre was heard to mumble, "Carter wouldn't call wolf, he'd have to call tiger or panther."

Carter chuckled and shook his head; it was their wacky sense of humor that got him every time.

Calming down, he looked at what he'd uncovered. What followed was very clearly page after photographed page of the Sirralnnudam. Beautifully colored plates one after the other of an incomprehensible language to Mackenzie, which she knew was vital to her research and to humanity.

He ached to phone James immediately but thought better of it. Andre and Roy were still up and moving around, it was not a good idea, no matter how important it was to let James know. It had already waited for months; another few hours wouldn't make any difference. It was something Irene, Dylan, and Sean had to hear, and it wouldn't take long for Sean to arrange transport first thing in the morning to fly them up to Freydis.

Nevertheless, he knew he was in for a sleepless night. How could he sleep with such an incredible discovery in his hands? He looked at the photos of Mackenzie and Liam again.

Mackie you have given us the key! Just hang in there; I will be with you and Liam soon. Just hang in for a little while longer. Will you?

With this, they could make up a copy of the original manuscript and use it as bait for the Greek Professor.

His mind was flying, but it flew on wings of silver in a blue sky above the clouds. This would lead him to Mackie and Liam; he just knew it would. Soon the borers would come out of the teak, and he would be waiting for them.

It was four o'clock the next morning, Andre and Roy were still sleeping soundly, and with no fear of waking them, he closed the door of the study and rang James; gleefully getting him out of bed.

"What in hell are you doing ringing me at this unearthly hour, Carter? I'm human; I need my sleep you know. It'd better be good."

Carter laughed.

"Why the hell are you so cheerful?" James snarled. "Is this another joke on me then?"

"No James, it isn't; I promise. I've found a treasure you will not believe until I can show you. You need to gather Dylan, Irene, and Sean and get up here ASAP."

"What on earth can you have found that would cause this much elation this early in the morning?"

"I'm glad this is a secure line because otherwise your reaction would wake the whole world."

"Get on with it then," James' tolerance had been stretched as far as Carter dared.

"I have a copy of the Sirralnnudam!"

"You WHAT?" James was suddenly alive and breathing.

"You heard me. I have a copy of the Sirralnnudam!"

"You can't…"

"I can."

"No shit, how?"

"Mackenzie had it on the key ring I gave her. The one you had in your hands in Jerusalem. She was not comfortable leaving the only copy of the book behind when she came home from Yerevan, so she photographed it, from beginning to end, each and every page, both sides, as well as the front and back – in color. We have the whole manuscript, James."

"Oh my God, I can't believe it. That conniving little red-hair fox! That cunning little fox! Oh my, that wicked little fox. Oh, the darling girl. I am going to make sure she gets a medal for this." Carter could hear James was in tears, which made him wipe a few of his own from his cheeks.

"We'll be there Carter, get that coffee machine going. Sean can hire a plane and fly us out; we'll be bringing Dylan too; they both need to know what's going on; we won't be long."

Carter could hear Andre and Roy muddling around in the kitchen making coffee, so he hung up and made his way out to greet the new day. It was the brightest, most beautiful day he'd seen in a very long time.

Carter warned the men they were expecting visitors; he didn't need them suddenly going on high alert when the plane flew overhead.

Right at midday, they arrived to be greeted by everyone including Bly and Ahote. It felt like Family Day on Ye Olde Farm, and Bly, alerted to expect visitors, had surpassed herself making a lunch that would ground them all for the afternoon.

Later, Ahote and Bly returned to their homestead taking Roy and Andre with them. They invited the young men to stay for dinner while those at Freydis would be having the leftovers from lunch which Bly had left in the fridge for them.

Irene promised Bly she'd be over the next morning for a good long chat.

As they departed, Roy and Andre told Carter in no uncertain terms that he would pay dearly for this break in his routine fitness regimen. Once the house was clear, the remaining five went into the study where Sean and Dylan were brought up to date on Mackenzie's work and the lost Sirralnnudam.

Finally, they settled down to look at the manuscript for themselves and to marvel at Mackenzie's courage in taking such a risk.

"She must have been pretty convinced it was in danger, in fact, she must have felt they were in danger as well. It's not something she would have done lightly," Irene observed.

"Yeah and how right she was about that," James whispered. "Clever girl…"

"I'm sure she didn't do it lightly, and I'm also sure she feared my anger when she would have to tell me what she'd done," Carter said. "It's only because I've had to do the same thing myself, bringing the City of Lights' records out of Egypt, that I understand the moral dilemma she was in and how awful it feels to betray the very roots of one's belief."

Irene leaned forward, "Carter, there is something that both you and Mackenzie know, but you have let guilt overwhelm you. Both of you are carrying colossal loads of responsibility for the human race. Neither of you would ever have expected to be in such a position as this when you made the decision that you'd never become corrupt. I will make this clear, you are not and never have been, either of you, corrupt in any way. You had no choice; you didn't destroy artifacts; you did not do what you did to benefit from it. You were doing it for all people who want to remain free, for the world."

James gave Irene a long appreciative look, "Bravo Irene, I couldn't have said it better myself. Carter what we have to do now is sort through this and make sure we protect your and Mackenzie's reputations. None of this will ever leave Freydis, and when it's over, and all is safe, we will never refer to it again."

Carter sat listening, taking it all in. He'd not asked for or expected exoneration for his and Mackenzie's actions. A load slipped off his shoulders, never to return. When he had Mackenzie back in his arms, he would tell her the same thing.

Oh, I'm going to hug and kiss the breath out of that red hair angel when I see her again.

Silence settled for a while and then Dylan suggested coffee, so they drifted out to the kitchen where they made themselves comfortable at the table with mugs of strong coffee and large chunks of Bly's carrot-cake.

"So, where do we go from here?" Dylan asked.

"Well, first and foremost I'm going to bring my friend Ben Friedman from Mossad in on this." James stated. "But where to from here?"

"I've been thinking about that all night long," Carter started, and everyone joined in "Oh poor baby missed his sleep, Diddums!" which ended up in raucous laughter all round.

"As I was saying," Carter continued, "I've been thinking about that. We know someone is searching for a reputed second copy of the Sirralnnudam, and I believe we are just the people to supply it. It will be a replica like no other and impossible to fault in any way. All we need is someone who knows how to choose the right medium – and how to age it, and then we can transpose the photographs onto it."

"Yes, we must have an expert for that," Dylan said, "I think I can supply one; I'll need a day or so, but it's doable."

"Right, great!" James said, and then we approach that Greek professor with our second copy of the manuscript and watch what emerges from the depths of the murky lagoon."

Chapter Forty-Five

TIME TO TALK TO HIS FRIEND

Dwayne Miller was still licking his wounds and sulking about the dressing down he'd received from Nate Gordon. He was again contemplating his options when his thoughts were interrupted by a sound from his laptop alerting him to the arrival of an encrypted message in his secured email inbox.

Four additional people had just landed on Devereux's farm in a six-seater twin-engine Piper Seneca III. Video footage and images of the people's faces were attached. Miller grinned. This Toronto outfit was professional. *They won't stuff up like those clowns from Montreal.*

When he looked at the attachments, he immediately recognized James Rhodes and Irene O'Connell but not the other two. Studying them carefully on the video, he could quickly spot by their behavior that they were military or ex-military. Being in the company of Rhodes and O'Connell meant they were part of one of the alphabet soup of intelligence agencies or on contract to A-Echelon.

The only person who could put names and positions to

those faces would be Nate Gordon's secret contact aka NTC – Nate's Top Contact. As much as Miller hated the idea of contacting Gordon so soon after their unpleasant encounter, he had no choice.

He encrypted the message and attachments again and forwarded it to Gordon. Then Miller called him on the encrypted phone and asked him to check his email to see if he could help identify the strangers in those images.

The next morning when he checked his secure emails, he was surprised to find a reply from Nate Gordon.

Those two guys with Rhodes and O'Connell are Sean Walker and Dylan Mulligan, former Navy SEALs commander and 2IC of SEAL Team Six respectively, and now CEO and 2IC of Executive Advantage. They were the CIA's blue-eyed boys whenever there was a situation where security and intelligence agencies found themselves with an intractable problem that had to be dealt with where commercial, diplomatic, and political solutions were not an option.

Executive Advantage consists of a core group of about ten people, highly skilled specialists in the various disciplines of modern day warfare and intelligence operations. They also have access to a large number of subcontractors with a variety of skills and expertise, which they call on from time to time as the circumstances dictate.

"Something important has happened on Devereux's farm," he said to himself.

Dwayne Miller was a good CEO, a man who knew how to manage and motivate people, not always in the most ethical, politically correct way, but he got results, and that's why he got the job at CRS. That's why CRS was making obscene amounts of money.

However, Dwayne Miller also had enough brains and

experience to recognize trouble when he saw it. And he knew he was looking at it now.

Sean Walker and Dylan Mulligan, former commander and 2IC of SEAL Team Six; CEO and 2IC of Executive Advantage.

A cold shiver descended slowly down his spine. *This is not good. Not good at all.*

He took a piece of paper and a pen out of his drawer and spent the next three hours creating a balance sheet of his financial position.

Xavier Algosaibi had a sense of impatience, and it annoyed him; it was a trait that was not part of his makeup. He was a man who could always wait patiently for the right moment, to speak and to act. That's what made him successful. Maybe it was because he was getting older and he so desperately wanted to see his dreams, his mission, and his destiny fulfilled in his lifetime.

Maybe his impatience was because of the failure of his lieutenants to produce results. Failure to capture Carter Devereux, messing up a simple operation and almost killing the man he so desperately needed. Missing a golden opportunity to capture Devereux when he was less than a 1,000 miles away. Spending millions of dollars on the respirocyte project to create a super-soldier just to learn it was all in vain and having to start again. Letting the Sirralnnudam, the one book that possibly held the key to the respirocyte breakthrough, wash down the storm water drains of Yerevan.

Maybe his impatience had something to do with the fact that Hassan Al-Suleiman, the self-anointed Sultan of Syria, and his True Sons of the Prophet's armies were marching across Syria and almost half of Iraq already. Accolades and reverences were raining down on Al-Suleiman. Peace and prosperity followed in his wake; he was a hero. Hassan's brigade of spies and propagandists had opened up a new front in southern Egypt, their eyes fixed on Cairo in the north. Al-Suleiman was scratching in places where Algosaibi was not itching.

The time for the Foundation of the Real Princes of Saud to stand up and make themselves known was rapidly approaching, and there was nothing he could do to slow it down, to wait for the right moment. He and his fellow members of the Foundation of the Real Princes of Saud had set the wheels in motion, and they couldn't be stopped. It irritated him that it felt as if things were spinning out of his control, seeming to charge toward him like a wounded bull. And he had no nuclear weapon; neither did he have his super soldiers.

He was not desperate; Algosaibi was not one who acted in desperation. It was time for him to get in touch with his primary contact in America. Years ago, when he was the deputy director of the General Intelligence Presidency of Saudi Arabia, Algosaibi had befriended a young American politician. That friendship had proven to be advantageous for both men.

It was during those years the two of them discovered they both had ambitions. Ideas and dreams about a world where America would be allowed to be America and Islam would be permitted to be Islam.

Over the years, it was that man who helped Algosaibi create his empire, providing him with exclusive distributorships for pharmaceutical products, and telecommunications technology contracts throughout the entire Middle East. The exchange of valuable insider information between them at the right time to win lucrative contracts and obtain the right strategic positions had made both of them very wealthy.

Between them, they had created Competitive Response Solutions. So discreet were they in their actions that not even the shareholders and directors of CRS knew what was going on. Nate Gordon was the only other man on the planet who knew, this man was the silent partner in CRS. NTC – Nate's Top Contact.

It was NTC who provided the information that led them to the Sirralnnudam; it was his information which gave them Dr. Mackenzie Devereux and almost Professor Carter Devereux. Unfortunately, it was the idiocy of Algosaibi's trusted right-hand man, Youssef Bin Bandar, who failed to deliver.

What was starting to worry Algosaibi was that he had always been able to rely on CRS to do a perfect job with every assignment he channeled to them, but they had blemished their impeccable record in the past few weeks with a few stupid blunders.

It was time to talk to his friend.

Chapter Forty-Six

SHAKE TREES AND RATTLE CAGES

It was Sean's first time on Freydis, and his reaction to the place was the same as everyone before him; he was immediately in love with it. He wanted to go for a walk and if it was possible, to see it from the air. Carter suggested they make the aerial trip the next morning; Irene, James, and Dylan would join them.

For the rest of the day of their arrival, after the scrumptious lunch provided by Bly, and late into the night, they worked on the plan. Sean suggested, and they all agreed, it was time to cast their net wide.

James would have Ben Friedman get his Mossad agents onto Professor Anatolio Kakos' case, put surveillance on him and tabs on his phones. He requested they learn everything there was to know about the man; who his friends, family, and associates were, and any other contacts he might have, however obscure. They needed to try to get access to his computers, email, and financial records, and to find out if he wrote that article in the archeological magazine because he loved rare books, or had he been instructed or paid to write it? If it were one of the latter, there could be a record of it somewhere.

The list of medical and pharmaceutical labs that Irene got from DARPA had to be checked out. Maybe that was another job for Ben Friedman to take on.

Apart from the constant fear of terrorist attacks and nuclear annihilation by Iran, Pakistan or other Muslim states with a nuclear arsenal, Israel's intelligence community was also very aware of the real threat of chemical and biological weapons in the hands of their enemies.

Those weapons were much easier and cheaper to produce and hide than nuclear weapons. Mossad would almost certainly have far more detailed information about medical and pharmaceutical labs around the Middle East.

Now that Carter was back from Egypt, it was the right time to start dropping fake information about the nuclear project onto the A-Echelon data server. He would make up information that would look significant, important, and top-secret. It would be presented as the results of his latest research coming from the City of Lights and Professor Pillay's dig site in Northern India.

The information would slowly grow and become more and more intense as he seemed to get ever closer to the unearthing of the ancient nuclear weapons.

In the meantime, Rick Winslow's tracking software would keep a watchful electronic eye on who was accessing that information and where it is sent.

It was almost 10:00 pm when they were ready to go to bed. Carter walked Irene over to Bly's house.

The next morning shortly after breakfast, Sean took off on a scenic aerial view of Freydis with Carter, James, Irene, and Dylan onboard the Piper Seneca, which had enough seats for the five of them.

Sean took the plane up to about 3,000 feet. Carter sat beside him as co-pilot, and they all had headsets on listening to Carter's running commentary.

Suddenly Carter stopped talking; he squinted and looked again, no his eyes were not playing tricks on him. It was unmistakable.

He whispered as if someone else would hear him. "Sean, can you see over here, about four o'clock, that's a drone, is it not?"

Sean banked the plane slightly to have a look. "Well, well, well, what have we here? Dylan, can you see it?"

"Yep got it," Dylan replied.

James and Irene were in the seats on the left side of the plane and couldn't see what Dylan was looking at. As the plane leveled out again, Irene looked out the window on her side and said, "I'm not sure if I'm looking at the same drone as you boys but there is one down here on the left at seven o'clock."

Sean and James saw it at almost the same time. "That's another one," Sean said as he adjusted the nose of the plane to a slightly downward pitch.

"What the hell..." Carter exclaimed watching the drone below him. "Won't they be able to spot you coming in?" Carter asked.

"They might have radar that could detect us, but the rest of their equipment will have been purposed to look down to the ground, not up. I'm not going to hang around them; I'm going to stay on course but just drop down a few hundred feet and slow down a bit so we can get a better look."

"Who the hell would be operating drones out here?" James mumbled.

"I don't want to borrow trouble, James," Dylan said, "but I think we've just discovered that Ahote's lost backpackers who had that encounter with the wolves were drone operators."

A few minutes later Sean said, "Predator surveillance drones. US military issue, live-feed video and infrared cameras, heat sensors, and radar."

"Are you serious?" Irene and James asked almost in unison. "Military drones over Freydis?" Irene continued.

"Dylan?" Sean asked.

"I'm afraid so," Dylan replied. "Those are Predators. Sean and I have seen them thousands of times, no doubt about it, those are Predators. We've used them over and over again in our missions in the sandpit." 'Sandpit' was the soldiers' slang for the deserts of the Middle East.

"Look at that." Sean pointed to the drone on his left. "They have picked us up on their radar and are changing direction, trying to get away from us."

"Let's chase the..." Carter started. "No, maybe not."

"You're starting to think like a real spook, Carter." James chuckled.

"Okay, military drones," Carter started again. "Does that mean the US military wants to know what I'm doing here? I suppose no one but the military is allowed to own those types of drones."

"One would think so, Carter," Sean laughed. "But if I tell you what sort of military equipment has landed in civilian hands, either through crooked quartermasters or stolen by unscrupulous people, you won't sleep."

Carter turned back to look at Dylan, who nodded in confirmation, then at James and Irene making the same gestures.

"Let me see if I have the full picture," Carter said as he stared out the cockpit window in front of him. "Two days after I left for DC last time two people try to break into my house. Arriving in DC, I discovered AMZ Security deployed a surveillance team to watch and follow me and listen to my conversations. Now I'm back here for two days, and we find military drones snooping around."

"Yep, that's about this size of it, Carter," Dylan replied. "You're definitely a man of interest to someone."

"Looks like our mole has his head out of the hole," Carter grinned.

"Sean, I think it's time to shake some trees and rattle a few cages. We need to smuggle some drone counter surveillance equipment in and track the operator's base down. Then send a two-man reconnaissance team after them."

"Great minds think alike," Sean grinned. "You okay with that James, Irene?"

"Of course, go for it," James replied.

"Carter, have you got satellite images and topographical maps of Freydis and surroundings," Dylan inquired.

"Yes, I've got all of it in my study at home."

Chapter Forty-Seven

LET'S GO TO WORK

When they got back to Washington, after spending two days on Freydis, there was a lot to do. The discovery of the Sirralnnudam and the drones over Freydis provided big excitement and motivation for all of them. They knew it was now just a matter of time, patience, and careful maneuvering before they would know where Mackenzie and Liam were.

James and Irene scheduled a meeting with Ben Friedman to brief him on the situation and request his assistance while Sean and Dylan got busy working out a plan to track down the base of operation of the drones over Freydis, and briefing a reconnaissance team. Dylan reached out to his contact that was an expert in the preservation and restoration of old and rare books and asked him to make a convincing copy of the Sirralnnudam.

There might never be a need to use the contrived version of the Sirralnnudam, but they wanted it ready 'just in case'. It was all dependent on who Professor Anatolio Kakos really was, a genuine rare-book enthusiast, or a proxy for someone else. It was entirely possible that he didn't even want the book and that he just had an honest interest in knowing if another one of the books existed. Whatever the situation was, they were not going to take any chances; the book had to be ready before they could approach the Greek professor.

On Freydis, things were no less hectic. Carter continued his training and worked on building a portfolio of fake information about ancient nuclear weapons on the A-Echelon servers. He scanned the ancient data sheets from the City of Lights and copied the contents over to a mass storage device, and he was reading the Sirralnnudam, which was written in a language he could read, although not fluently. With great concentration and effort, he was slowly making sense of it.

Although he was very busy, Carter had a constant awareness of the drones overhead, watching him and everyone else on Freydis. In his mind, those drones hung around like the smoke from a wildfire. The constant itch between his shoulder blades, to which he'd referred before, was beginning to feel more like the sharp end of a dagger.

Carter had a three-week deadline, set by James, to load a sizeable chunk of fake information onto the A-Echelon servers. James explained that he had another meeting scheduled with the President in four weeks, and he needed the data to create his presentation.

Carter, James, Irene, Sean, and Dylan had a long and intense thinking session before they made the decision to withhold information from the President and the rest of the members who would be attending the meeting. None of them wanted to risk giving anyone else the information they had when there was so much at stake. Nevertheless, they had no illusions about the consequences for them if their trickery was discovered.

However, Carter assured them he would fall on his sword to save them. He could afford it and besides that; the way he intended to go about it, James, Irene, Sean, and Dylan would be able to claim that they acted on Carter's information.

"Plausible deniability," Carter told them. "The 'get-out-of-jail-free' card carried by all politicians and senior government officials in their inside pocket at all times."

Andre and Roy offered to help if Carter was willing to show them how to operate the electron microscope and safely handle the sheets. In the evenings when Carter was busy reading and translating the Sirralnnudam, they were busy scanning and copying.

James got in touch with Ben Friedman and explained to him that there were urgent matters to discuss, which had to be done face-to-face. They agreed to meet at Caesar's Palace in three days; anyone listening to that conversation would immediately have made arrangements to get observers out to Las Vegas. They would have been very disappointed to know that the Caesar's Palace the two of them were referring to was not located at 3570 S Las Vegas Blvd, Las Vegas, Nevada, but was a Mossad safe house located in Hamburg, Germany.

James handed the reigns of A-Echelon over to Irene two days later and made his way to Hamburg on a private charter, traveling as 'Daniel Smyth,' an international business consultant from New York.

"No need to haul a planeload of electronic equipment over the border into Canada," Rick Winslow told Sean and Dylan when he heard what they wanted.

"What do you suggest then?" Dylan queried.

"I'll get a bit of time on one of Langley's spy satellites the next time it travels over that part of the world."

"How long is that going to take?" Sean wanted to know.

"The SSO's – sun-synchronous orbit aka heliosynchronous orbit satellites, which Langley uses, complete 12 round trips a day. I can get you a trace on those drones in less than an hour once I've locked onto them." He grinned at the surprise on their faces.

"Shit and we almost invaded Canada!" Sean laughed, shaking his head.

"That sounds all good and dandy, but will anyone know you have used the satellites?" Dylan asked.

"I work for them, remember?" Rick laughed. "It's my job. I have to check that those satellites remain in good working order, that no one hacks into them, and I have to test them regularly."

"What else can you get while you're at it?" Dylan continued.

"Tell me what you want. I can probably hack into the data feed, which the drone beams back to the control center. Maybe I can do the same for the feed from the control center to wherever the collected data is being sent, the location of the control center and that sort of stuff."

"We want all of that and might be back for more. But those will give us a good start," Sean replied. "What do you reckon Dylan?"

"Yeah, that's a good start. Thanks, Rick. Let us know when you've got it."

James Rhodes arrived in Hamburg, Germany early in the morning and cleared customs without any problems as Daniel Smyth. He kept an eye open for any signs of a tail while the taxi transferred him to the luxurious Louis C Jacob Hotel where his room was reserved.

After he had checked in and unpacked his luggage, he took a shower, put on some casual clothes, had breakfast and a few cups of good strong coffee in one of the restaurants in the hotel, and then hailed a taxi to take him on a sightseeing tour of Hamburg. He got off at various sites to look at the historic buildings and features, used different taxis and even public transport on some occasions. After more than four hours of sightseeing, it was time to meet with Ben Friedman, and he was sure that he had not picked up a tail since his arrival in Germany. He was less than a quarter mile away from the safe house, code named 'Caesar's Palace', by him and Ben years ago.

He and Ben shook hands and hugged; they were always glad to see each other.

Ben offered him coffee and a seat.

"Jim, my friend," Ben started, "your good condition leaves me with no doubts that Carolyn is still taking very good care of you," Ben laughed. "One day I have to meet this wonderful woman of yours. Any woman who could keep a man like you in such good shape at your age must be worth meeting."

"Yeah, Ben," James grinned. "I'm not sure I want her ever to meet you. She has lived a very sheltered life up to now, and I don't want to ruin that by letting her meet someone like you."

Ben chuckled. "Jim, you haven't lost your diplomatic

touch!" Ben sipped his coffee before enquiring, "Before we get too serious, what is the grassroots political climate over in America? Who is going to be the next president?"

"The election is still more than sixteen months away. At this stage, all the candidates can still afford to be vague. You know, making all those old patriotic rumblings – we want our country back – promising to turn the country around – create jobs – get China off our backs – sort out the immigration and health care problems on the first day in office, nothing specific and nothing of substance."

Ben nodded. "You know the Israelis are always interested in who will be the next American president. The person occupying the Oval Office determines, to a large degree, how we shape our foreign policies and how secure we feel."

"Well, if the election was held today," James replied, "that's if the polls are to be trusted, Vice President George Robertson would be the next occupant of the Oval Office, by a landslide."

"Mhh, can't say that we'd be very enthusiastic about that," Ben commented.

James didn't like the Vice President either, but he wanted to know what Ben's reasons were. "Why is that?"

"It's as you said before," Ben replied, "telling the voters what they want to hear but leaving out the specifics. We are a bit concerned that, in all his years as ambassador in various Middle East countries, he has not made one single statement about the Middle East and what his vision is for the region."

"Yeah, that's true, but as you know, America's Middle Eastern policy has become a big-ticket item in our politics, it's on a par with illegal immigration and the economy. At this stage, none of the candidates wants to be tied to a policy that might have to change overnight. You know how volatile politics in the Middle East are."

"That's understandable, Jim, but one would have at least expected Robertson to have said something, even if it was vague. Nevertheless, that's not my primary concern. What bothers me, and many of my colleagues is that Robertson is badmouthing the sitting President for his own gain. That is something we have never seen before, a Vice President demeaning his own boss. Always before, even if your President and Vice-President didn't see I eye to eye on matters, their differences were always kept in-house, and a united front was portrayed to the public."

James nodded. There were many rumors and hushed conversations floating around in the hallways of Capitol Hill about the disdain the President and his Veep had for each other.

Ben continued. "And last, but not least, is the fact that the man all of a sudden came out of the closet, declaring himself an evangelical Christian while the Mossad's profile of him says he is an atheist."

James was not surprised to hear about the Mossad having a file on the Veep. In fact, he was sure they would have a file on most of America's senior politicians and government officials. "I agree it's worrying to see him so openly courting the evangelical vote, portraying himself as one of them, and unscrupulously misleading people."

"Ah, well, Jim, you and I won't be able to swing the outcome of an election, that's for sure," Ben chortled. "Let's get to our business."

"The election is, thankfully, still a long way off, things might change," James said.

He then continued and brought Ben up to date with all that happened since the last time they had contact, filling him in on the details of Carter's trip to Egypt and the discovery of the surveillance operations against Carter.

"Someone is undoubtedly fascinated by this friend of yours, Jim. And I guess you don't need more than two brain cells to figure out that the people who are interested in him now are the same as those who were interested in him before the bomb explosion?"

"Yep, that's our assumption."

"What about the nukes, Jim? They're causing me nightmares."

James explained that Carter had discovered some information in the City of Lights, which he was working on 'as we speak,' that might contain information about the nukes. He also discussed his belief that the people who were holding Mackenzie and Liam were very likely the same individuals who were after the nukes.

"We've had a few significant breakthroughs lately," James explained. "Please bear with me so that I can give you the full story."

Ben nodded for him to continue and James told him about the marathon video, which Carter saw in Egypt and how it led to their suspicions that it was a respirocyte human trial they were witnessing. He showed Ben the video.

Ben had a few questions and then asked James to continue.

He told Ben about the Sirralnnudam article in the archeological magazine and wound up with Carters discovery of the copy Mackenzie had made of the document.

"Shit Jim! That's great news," Ben grinned. "All of a sudden, a dark situation has been flooded with rays of sunshine."

"That's exactly how it feels Ben, like rays of sunshine."

James took a sip of his coffee, "Okay, so there are two things we need your help with."

Ben put his cup down and said, "Ready, willing and able Jim. Bring it on."

James took out the list of medical and pharmaceutical labs that DARPA provided to Irene and handed it to Ben. "I know the Mossad will have a much better list than this one. I'm pretty sure you've got better insight or rather I should say, much better inside information about the labs of the Middle East than we have." James looked at Ben with raised eyebrows.

Ben nodded with a faint smile on his face. "Yes, for obvious reasons we do keep a close watch on all of them, known and unknown, above and below ground."

"Well, our theory is that Mackenzie and Liam are being held at one of these labs. As someone with a doctorate in human molecular biology, Mackenzie would be a valuable asset to them. And with her son in their custody, they would have absolute control over her to ensure her cooperation."

"I'll start shaking those trees as soon as I'm back in Israel," Ben agreed.

"We used the same analogy the other day; shaking trees and rattling cages," James laughed.

"Okay, the cage we would like to rattle is the one in which Professor Anatolio Kakos lives. He's the guy who wrote the article about the loss of the Sirralnnudam in the Journal of Archeological Science," James pulled out the copy and handed it to Ben. "There's the article, Kakos' photo, and his email address is at the bottom of the article."

"No problem. I've got a few good agents in those parts of the world. We'll put the tabs on him right away," Ben responded.

"We want *everything* on this guy, Ben. From the day he

was born; his friends, family, and associates, financial records, habits, everything. I don't have any evidence, but my instincts are screaming at me that this guy is just a proxy for someone else."

"You know my opinion about instincts, Jim," Ben smiled. "They are the result of the cooperation between my emotions and my brain. I never ignore them."

Chapter Forty-Eight

ON OUR RADAR

The first few days after Carter started working on the false information about the ancient nukes, he found it especially difficult. His whole life he had been hunting and reporting the truth.

It was not always easy; Carter more often than not had to listen to and endure the ridicule of his colleagues in the archeological community. However, he had always been able to rise above that pettiness and had proved them wrong on quite a few occasions.

He and his grandfather Will had many discussions about the fact that certain archeological specifics were just too inconvenient for some to admit. Deliberately hiding the truth was at best very difficult for him.

Nevertheless, despite the many ethical arguments raging in his mind, while he was creating this whole farce on the A-Echelon servers, he only had to look at Mackenzie and Liam's pictures, which he had set as the default background on his computer screen, to convince him that the end justified the means.

He checked with Rick Winslow to be sure that everything was in place and then started loading the false information on a daily basis.

GPR 3-D Images of the sites in North India and Egypt were uploaded, accompanied by his interpretation of the images. He also created and uploaded a report about the discovery of the burial site of the giants and included detailed information about the mysterious lights and a hitherto unidentified source of electricity in the city of the giants.

He added lots of speculation and several theories about the technological capabilities of the ancients, including the giants, and even quoted some of Mackenzie's discoveries to prove his point.

They didn't expect the mole to set off Rick's traps on the servers in the first few days after Carter started loading information but they certainly started raising their eyebrows after two weeks of no nibbles or bites. James and Irene were wondering if the mole might somehow have become aware of their plans. Maybe the mole got scared after the botched surveillance operation on Carter. However, they decided that Carter should keep on doing what he was doing, loading new information onto the servers on a regular basis. If he were to discontinue those activities, it would immediately raise red flags with the mole if he or she looked at the data on the servers again.

A few days before James' meeting with the President, a delegate of wealthy and influential businessmen from the Kingdom of Saudi Arabia visited the United States. They were on a commercial foray to meet with American business leaders who would be interested in their money. These people had money to burn, and they wanted to invest in American companies.

A banquet in their honor was hosted by The Department of Commerce, and Xavier Algosaibi's trusted friend was the guest speaker at the event.

The two men were elated to see each other in person after so many years. Communicating via encrypted phones and emails just didn't match a face-to-face conversation.

"It's been such a long time my friend, far too long," Algosaibi smiled when they shook hands.

"Yes, you can say that again," his friend replied.

"You look good my friend; I can see that time has been kind to you," Algosaibi laughed.

"And to you Xavier. Your wife must be looking after you very well," the man smiled.

Algosaibi chuckled. "I know you are a very busy man, but would you have a few minutes later so we can have a quick private discussion," Algosaibi whispered.

"Xavier, I'm so sorry; I would have liked nothing more than to have a few minutes in private with you. There are so many things we need to catch up on, but I have been summoned by the President immediately after my speech. I won't even be able to stay till the end of the dinner."

Algosaibi smiled. "Not to worry my friend, I know all about it. I sometimes get that type of summons from the King. Well, then I guess we won't see each other again before I leave."

"My sincere apologies Xavier; I wish it could be different."

Algosaibi stepped forward and extended his hand, leaned forward and whispered to his friend while shaking his hand. "Read the letter on there; it's become critical that we step things up. Time is running out."

When Algosaibi walked away, his friend said, "Excuse me" placed his hand in his pocket, took out his handkerchief, and sneezed. In the process, he had dropped the flash drive he had just received from Algosaibi in the same pocket.

Rick Winslow lived up to his reputation as the best of the best computer Special Forces gurus in the CIA. Within a few hours of getting access to the SSO's - sun-synchronous orbit – spy satellite, he had data streaming into his computer from the drones hovering over Freydis. Not only that, but he had also hacked into the drones' control center and was copying the data sent from there to the head office in Toronto.

In the process, he pinpointed the location of the control center 25.34 miles west of Freydis and had the exact street address of the base in Toronto.

Sean and Dylan were quietly impressed when Rick showed them what he had. "Good work, Rick. I don't know how you do it; you always make these things look so easy."

"It's not that difficult," Rick snickered. "Not much different from kicking a door down and shooting a few bad guys. Once you know where to look and which buttons to press its easy sailing."

"Yeah right, I hear you," Dylan grinned while he plotted the GPS coordinates on the topographical maps Carter provided.

They asked Rick to maintain the surveillance and data collection until they told him to discontinue.

After Rick had left, they called in two of their operators and briefed them on the mission. The two men would cross the border into Canada at Niagara Falls, go to Toronto, check out the head office of the surveillance company, and plant bugs and deploy other observation equipment.

Once the first part of their mission was completed, they would make their way east to Quebec and launch the second part of the mission. There the objective was to get as close as possible to the drone control center, deploy more surveillance equipment and get out undetected.

Their cover story was that they were American students, backpacking in those parts. Therefore, they would take no military equipment with them.

Sean and Dylan's strategy was to collect as much information as possible without being discovered.

When Carter heard about the mission, he was very keen to be part of it. "I have all these newly acquired skills – stalking, observation, you name it, and I don't get to use them," he complained.

"You'll have to wait your turn Carter," Dylan chuckled. "Just relax, let our guys take care of it this time. You've got more important things to do for now. Besides, if your face disappears from Freydis all of sudden, you might just scare the drone operators away. We don't want that. We want them to think you're oblivious to what they are doing."

The day of James's monthly meeting with the President arrived quicker than he wanted. He had to give him an update on the A-Echelon projects, and Carter helped him to prepare for the meeting.

They held the meeting in the Situation Room at the

White House. In attendance were the President, Vice President, Director of the CIA, one member of the National Security Council, and the Secretary of Defense.

During the first part of the meeting, James gave them an overview of A-Echelon projects and answered questions. As in the past, the Ancient Nuke Project was discussed in more detail than any of the others.

"As you are aware, Mr. President," James explained, "Professor Devereux has recently been to Egypt to visit the City of Lights, and I have a few pictures and video clips from that trip to show you." The President waved for him to continue and he showed them some of the photos and videos of the City as well as the burial chamber and the 3-D renderings created from the GPR scans.

After they had a look at the visuals, James continued. "During his visit they discovered an underground burial chamber and for the first time since the inauguration of that dig, they found inscriptions of what he believes to be the language of the giants. Until his most recent visit, that was one of the mysteries; there was no evidence of a written language.

"Professor Devereux always maintained that any civilization as advanced as theirs appeared to be must have had a written language."

The President was about to speak when the Vice President interjected. "What bearing does the discovery of their language have on the nuclear threat we're facing?"

James caught a fleeting squint of annoyance in the Presidents eyes. *So the rumors are true, they don't like each other.*

James looked at the President to see if it was okay for him to continue and answer the Veep's question. The President gave a slight nod. "In the City of Lights, advanced technology has been discovered; in fact, it is so advanced our scientists have been unable to explain it. The wireless transfer of electricity is an example of one of them, the source of the energy another."

"Yeah, yeah, yeah, I get that," The Vice President said impatiently. "What I'm asking is; what has that got to do with the ancient nukes?"

Before James could reply, the President answered for him. He was very calm and collected, but James could see it was because he had made an effort to control his irritation. "I imagine if the Giants were so far advanced in electro technology that they might also have known a thing or two about nuclear technology which we don't." He lifted his eyebrows inquisitively at James.

"Yes, sir," James nodded. "That's precisely the reason Professor Devereux is so frantically trying to find the library of that city. He believes that somewhere they would have a library of some sort. In the meantime, he has already started working on the translation of those inscriptions.

"Has he had any luck with that yet?" The President asked.

"No, sir he says the script looks like it could belong to a proto-Semitic language but so far he's been unable to make any breakthrough. He'll probably have to call in outside linguistic experts soon."

"Is there anything else there that makes him think the answer could be in that place and not somewhere else?" The Director of the CIA asked.

"Yes sir, the relative proximity of the City of Lights to the places where ancient nuclear explosions supposedly took place. The city is not too far from the Saad Plateau in Libya where signs of a nuclear blast have been found; it's also not too far from similar explosion sites in Syria, India, and

Pakistan. The anomaly is that it seems the City of Lights existed during the times when those explosions took place, but there is no sign that they ever suffered the same fate."

James had to fight the urge to crack up with laughter after giving them that preposterous rambling which Carter had prepared for him in anticipation of such a question.

"Maybe the Giants were the ones who attacked everyone else," The Secretary of Defense noted. "Could they have been the ones who owned those weapons?"

"That's entirely possible sir. That's why Professor Devereux is so keen to find more of their written records," James replied. He knew if he had to give one more of these ramblings that Carter prepared, he was going to embarrass himself by laughing, and that would also be the end of his career.

"Do you have more detailed information available that we can look at?" The Vice President asked.

"Yes, sir, we've got a lot more technical and detailed information stored on the A-Echelon servers. Do you want me to put that on a mass storage device and bring it to you?" James replied.

"Thanks. That would be good," The Veep replied.

The meeting ended with the Vice President wanting to know what progress had been made toward the continuation of Mackenzie's respirocyte project and getting a replacement for her.

James managed to remain vague without raising suspicion, by telling them that they were looking at a few options now and that he was confident he would be able to give them more details at the next meeting. He again explained that it was hard to find a person with the right skill sets who would also be able to pass through the rigorous security clearance process.

Nate Gordon had just come out of another stealth meeting with his top contact, NTC, as the man was referred to in CRS. He was on his way to the CRS headquarters to convey a few messages to the CEO, Dwayne Miller. The relationship between them had been strained since their last conversation when he had lambasted Miller because of the screw-ups on the Devereux Project. Miller was a good CEO and manager, he produced results, but recently had become complacent, and that almost dumped CRS into big trouble.

Gordon shrugged. *I don't care about his moping. Cowboys don't cry. This is serious business and serious money.*

"Good morning, Dwayne," Gordon had a big smile on his face as he walked into Miller's office.

"Good morning, sir," Miller replied and stood, very formal, almost stiff-necked.

"Ah, come-on Dwayne what's with the sir thing today? Don't tell me you're still sulking after our last meeting."

Miller grinned half embarrassed. "Please have a seat. What can I get you to drink?"

Gordon asked for coffee, and as soon as Miller's secretary had served them and closed the office door, Gordon looked at his watch and said, "I've got 10 minutes, so I'll be succinct."

Miller nodded, pulled his writing pad towards him, and looked at Gordon to let him know he was ready.

"Okay, I just had a meeting with NTC, and there are a few crucial things we need to talk about. NTC has recently been in contact with his primary contact in Saudi Arabia. Now I don't know who that is, but I'll let you in on a dirty little secret if you don't already know about it. NTC and his Saudi Arabian contact are the people who founded CRS.

They are the ones who put up the money and got us our first clients."

Miller shook his head. "I had no idea."

"Well, now you do," Gordon grinned. "We are doing a lot of work for those two ghosts; in fact, they are responsible for close to 60% of this company's income. I don't know, and I'm sure you're completely unaware when CRS does work for them. They are involved in more industries and ventures than you can shake a stick at. They do their business through subsidiaries, front organizations, third parties, proxies you name it. There is no way anyone will ever be able to unravel their business dealings."

Miller just nodded. He was only going to talk when it was necessary.

Gordon looked at his watch again. "So the long and the short of it is this; NTC has been put under pressure by his friend to step up the Devereux Project. He wants to see things happening faster. He also wanted me to pass on his friend's disappointment about the recent mishaps."

Miller cringed inwardly and nodded again.

"I won't go there again," Gordon waved his hand, "as far as I'm concerned I have passed that message on before, so no need to repeat it."

"Thanks," Miller whispered.

"What they want is Professor Devereux," Gordon continued. "You'll have to call in your experts on these types of matters and produce a detailed plan for the abduction of Devereux and provide them with the information within the next six weeks."

Miller opened his mouth to say something then closed it and sat back in his chair. *Stepping things up last time is what got us into trouble.*

Gordon saw Miller was ill at ease. "You don't look

comfortable with that request Dwayne; what's bothering you?"

"It might be a bit tight to pull it off in six weeks. However, I'll ..."

Gordon interjected. "Wait, sorry. I didn't mean they want to complete the operation in six weeks' time, only that they want a detailed plan in six weeks."

"Oh okay, I understand," Miller breathed a sigh of relief. "I'll get to work on it immediately and will keep you posted."

"There's just one more thing to be aware of, Dwayne; NTC says his friend told him he is going to pull all the Saudi Arabia contracts if we fail again." Gordon got up, thanked Dwayne for the coffee, and left.

Miller dropped his head into his hands, elbows on his desk. *Swell.* Over the past few weeks, he'd spent many hours pondering his resignation from CRS. Getting a doctor's certificate confirming a fake health issue that prevented him from continuing his work might do it. If the doctor booked him into a private clinic and while there, he handed in his resignation he could relax. He had enough money to retire, not quite as comfortably as he would have liked, but there was enough.

There was only one thing that prevented him from doing it. He was sure that neither Nate Gordon nor any of the other four directors would accept his resignation.

His CEO role at CRS was a tacit until-death-do-us-part job.

After the meeting with James in Hamburg, Ben Friedman had briefed his operatives in Greece to put the tabs on

Professor Anatolio Kakos. It took them a few days to set things up, but then the information started filtering through to Ben.

He kept James up to date with their progress. After two weeks of observations, which included not only following Kakos, but also getting access to all his electronic records, computers, emails, and phones, a picture of the real man emerged.

Professor Anatolio Kakos was not only an academic interested in rare books; his primary interest was rare artifacts, and he didn't mind crossing ethical divides to get his hands on them. He had a solid network of legal and illegal artifact dealers who were happy to pay good money for genuine items.

Carter, James, and Irene had gathered to discuss Ben's first report.

"Look at this," James said. He was pointing at the financial section of the report. "He has offshore accounts in the Bahamas, how convenient."

"I wouldn't be surprised if we find a bank account or two in Switzerland as well," Irene commented. "On the other hand, he probably knows that Switzerland is the first place people will look if they investigate him. The Bahamas have tight banking secrecy due to their privacy laws which makes it an excellent alternative to Switzerland."

"Well, looking at the financial transactions going through his Bahama accounts over the past year, he has been doing well for himself," James noted. "It's very clear that his full-time job at the University is not nearly as lucrative as his part-time job."

They were looking at his contacts and associates when Carter said.

"Hang on, here's a name I've seen before; Mark Miller.

He's the guy who had a little side business dealing in stolen artifacts at the Cusco dig. Jacob caught him red-handed, and he was fired. In fact, he was arrested and as far as I know he is in jail."

"Well, looking at the last date he and Kakos were talking to each other, Miller is either dealing out of a prison cell with a telephone and internet connection, or he is not in jail anymore," James grinned.

"Yes, look at this," Irene said. "The contact dates coincide with the time when that article about the Sirralnnudam was published, a few weeks before and a week or so after."

"Let's see if any financial transactions were going on at the same time," Carter said. "Here you go; $5,000 was deposited into his Bahama account three days after the date of this article. It came from a Swiss account."

"Mark Miller has just appeared on our radar," James said.

Irene nodded. "I'll brief Sean and Dylan."

Xavier Algosaibi smiled from ear to ear when he saw the title of the unencrypted folder on his computer. *It was a good thing I went to Washington. I haven't lost my powers of persuasion yet.*

Professor Devereux's latest reports had him excited. Although there was no direct evidence of an ancient nuke, Devereux's arguments about the advanced technological state of the civilization of the Giants held a lot of promise. In the end, they might not have had a nuclear weapon, but they might have had something similar, maybe even more powerful.

How will we ever know unless Professor Devereux returns to the site and finds it?

The Institute of Scientific Research and Development, six miles south of Mecca, was less than 500 miles from the City of Lights. A Special Forces team from Hassan Al-Suleiman's army would be able to get in and out of the City of Lights before the Egyptians could blink an eye.

I'll ask my friend to hasten Professor Devereux's return to Egypt.

Chapter Forty-Nine

THE BOOK IS READY

Dylan was overseeing the Canadian operation to collect information about the drones that were spying on the occupants of Freydis.

The two operators were doing an excellent job. They'd completed the first part of the mission in Toronto, collecting all the information about CanSec, the company who owned the drones and whose operators were controlling them as they soared over Freydis. They'd also obtained the detailed floor plans of the headquarters, took hundreds of photos of the employees, their vehicles, and carefully noted their office routine and security measures.

During the second part of the mission, they had relocated to Quebec, and set themselves up a few miles away from the farmhouse where the drone operators controlled the drones on their flights over Freydis, 25 miles away.

The two men were constantly in contact with Dylan. They were able to establish the drone operators' routine and reported the two men as indolent, slack individuals who were undoubtedly bored out of their brains. They also didn't have the slightest clue that the roles had changed somewhat, and they had now become the watched.

Dylan's men were able to get inside the farmhouse one night and planted a few microphones around.

When Carter, Roy, and Andre returned to DC, the drone operators suspended their observation activities and returned to Toronto for a bit of R&R. Dylan's men used the opportunity to bug the farmhouse appropriately and then returned to DC.

Ben Friedman had a report about the Middle Eastern laboratories ready for James and called him to advise him to expect the report. He requested that James call him back after he had read it so they could decide on the appropriate action.

When Rick told him the information had arrived and had been decrypted, James and Irene met with Sean and Dylan at a safe house to discuss the contents.

"So we have five labs of interest," James said after they'd all read the report. "The labs in Syria and Iraq which they were interested in before have all been destroyed, no activities going on there anymore.

"You have to admire those Mossad guys," Sean smiled, "they are good. Recruiting insiders onsite at all those labs across the Middle East couldn't have been an easy task.

"When it comes to intelligence gathering, we can learn a lot from them," James replied. "They are unrivaled; I suppose you have to be when you live in the midst of almost 300 million people who want to obliterate your country."

Sean nodded. "That's for sure. You must be doing something right to survive overwhelming odds like that for so long."

Looking at the five labs he discussed in his report," Dylan said, "it seems as if we can put the two in Iran and the one in Riyadh on the back burner for now. From his report, I'm satisfied that they know what is going on in those labs, and their intel suggests there is nothing untoward. However, the information about the remaining two, that lab in Jordan and that one there in the Southwest of Saudi Arabia near Mecca seem to be a bit flimsy. What do you reckon?" Dylan looked at James, Irene, and Sean in turn.

James nodded. "Yes, I agree. I'm a little bit surprised that the lab in Jordan is on their watch list. Israel and Jordan signed a peace agreement in 1994 and since then they have always maintained good relations. On the other hand, the Jordanian population is mostly Palestinian, and they despise Israel.

"Israel's relationship with Saudi Arabia has been very different from their relations with Jordan. As a result of Saudi Arabia's refusal to recognize the State of Israel's right to exist within its current borders, the diametrically opposing views have assured that there are no diplomatic relations between them.

"The only alliance between them is covert, behind-the-scenes diplomatic and intelligence cooperation, and that is only because of their mutual fear of the expansion of regional influence by Iran. Although they try to keep it secret, we know that the Saudis have promised to provide Israel with an air corridor and air bases for rescue helicopters, tanker aircraft and drones in the event Israel decides to bomb Iran's nuclear plants."

"Politics sometimes make for strange bedfellows don't

they," Sean chuckled. "The enemy of my enemy is my friend I guess."

"Sean, didn't you mention a while ago that you have a few Desert Phantoms on standby?" James asked. "I think we need to get them to go and check out that lab close to Mecca and see if Ben can get some of his contacts to get more information about the one in Jordan. I think he would prefer to stay out of Saudi Arabia if at all possible."

Sean nodded. "Yes, they're ready. They are in Muscat, the capital of Oman. From there to Mecca is a three-hour flight. If you would, get as much information as possible that is available about this place, including satellite images et cetera, from Ben, while Dylan and I see what we can collect from CIA sources, then we'll brief the Phantoms."

Dylan's contact called him to come over and inspect the faux ancient copy of the Sirralnnudam, which he had painstakingly been creating over the past five weeks. Dylan was impressed; he had no expertise in ancient relics, he could only make a visual comparison between the pictures that Mackenzie had taken of the original book, and the one he was looking at now. He had a keen eye for detail, but he could not spot any inconsistencies. Every bit of detail he could see on the pictures was present in the real book; he was more than happy to pay the artisan.

With the book and the detailed information about Professor Anatolio Kakos in hand, they were ready to proceed.

James looked at Irene and tried to suppress a smile. "Irene, I've been thinking how we should go about setting this all up."

She nodded, "Tell us about it."

"We should get an old lady to email Kakos and tell him she's got the Sirralnnudam. She inherited a whole library of rare books from her grandfather, and it was one of them."

"Okay, so far so good," she replied. "Who is the old lady?"

Carter, who was watching James' face, saw what was coming, stifled a snicker and glanced at Sean and Dylan, who were already hiding their faces behind their coffee mugs. Their twinkling eyes gave them away.

James went quiet and stared at Irene. She looked at him, waiting for an answer but as he didn't offer one, she looked at the other three who were also staring at her and then it dawned on her. "James Rhodes! Didn't your mother ever teach you not to-? Are you serious?" She looked at each of them in turn, trying to find support; maybe even a little sympathy, but she would've found a lot more empathy in the face of the Sphinx.

She tried again; opening her mouth to protest, only to close it again without uttering a word. They all started laughing. Fortunately, Irene was a good sport and joined them in the fun, explaining in between their bouts of laughter how many different forms of pain she intended to inflict on the four of them.

Once the fun was over, and Irene had forced four half-hearted apologies out of them, they discussed the details. Despite the initial shock to her and the subsequent humor, Irene agreed to be the front person in the sting operation. After all, she had been an experienced CIA field operative, and although she'd never had to present herself as an old woman with a walking stick, bad hearing, and bad eyesight, she was capable of playing the role.

Professor Kakos could feel the surge of excitement when he saw the email heading – *Copy of the Sirralnnudam* – among the other emails in his inbox.

When he wrote the article and received $5,000 for his effort, he was almost sure he'd never hear another word about it. Now he was looking at a potential $25,000 payday. All he had to do was persuade this widow to let him make a copy of the book. He didn't have any idea why an artifact dealer would want to pay so much for a copy, but for $25,000 he was more than happy to get it, ask no questions, and keep his mouth shut. If only all of his assignments were so easy.

The only inconvenience would be that he had to fly to Washington DC to meet with Margaret O'Connell, an octogenarian widow whose physician wouldn't allow her to travel to Greece.

However, Professor Kakos had been in the artifacts business long enough, and had burned his fingers enough times to know how this game was played. Before he would even consider booking flights anywhere, he wanted proof. Therefore, he asked Margaret O'Connell to send him a few pictures; he wished to see the cover, the table of contents, a few pages, and the back cover. The more pictures she could send him the better.

The email conversations back and forth with Margaret, and of course in secret to his client, to get Professor Kakos to the point where he was convinced that she indeed was in possession of the Sirralnnudam, took more than two weeks. The final evidence that swayed him to book his flights was the picture of Margaret holding the book in her hand next to that day's edition of the Washington Times, the date on the newspaper and the headline news of the day, clearly visible.

He would meet Margaret for lunch in three days' time at an elegant little French restaurant on Wisconsin Ave in Tenleytown, Washington, DC.

On the one hand, he was a bit worried that Margaret didn't want to set a price for a copy of the book. She just kept insisting that he 'first have a look at it and make sure it is indeed the book you want, and then we can talk price.' On the other hand, he appreciated the fact that she was not much interested in the money; maybe there was an opportunity for him to make a bit more out of the deal. How would his client ever know what price he'd agreed to with her?

Once Ben Friedman's operatives got access to Professor Kakos' computers, his life and actions became an open book to them as they tracked every one of his communications and activities. They had a copy of his email contacts, his phone contacts, and email archives, everything he ever did on his computer since the day he bought it.

They saw Margaret O'Connell's email arriving and 'followed' him around on his computer as he logged into one of his many Gmail accounts and left an email message in the drafts folder for his client. It was an old trick, used by spies and terrorists. At one point, quite a few years ago, it was a fairly secure method of hiding messages, but it didn't last long. The Mossad, CIA, and other intelligence agencies knew about the practice and figured out how to overcome it. With access to Kakos' computer, it was a no-brainer; they didn't even need special software or favors from Internet Service Providers or the NSA.

They waited for Kakos' client to visit the email account, and when he did about 18 hours later, they scanned the IP address of his computer and passed it on to Rick Winslow. It took Rick less than 30 minutes to track the man down where he lived in New York and provide his details to Sean and Dylan. It was Mark Miller, the person who was supposed to be in jail for illegally selling artifacts from the Cusco dig in Peru.

However, this situation was different from what Miller did in Cusco; this time there was nothing illegal about Miller's or for that matter, Kakos' actions, to get a copy of the Sirralnnudam.

With Rick's help, tabs were placed on Mark Miller, and by the time Professor Kakos was en route to DC, Sean and Dylan knew everything there was to know about him; right down to his shoe size. They knew he was divorced, living in a studio apartment in Manhattan, and that he had one brother older than he was, Dwayne Miller, who was the CEO of Competitive Response Solutions in DC.

James read the information about Mark Miller and sat back. *Competitive response; competitive intelligence gathering; competitive analysis; all catch phrases for industrial espionage.* He called Irene and asked her and Carter to join him in his office.

"Have a look at this; all the information about your lunch date's client." He chuckled and looked at Irene.

"Jim, my children have a saying; *'you're cruisin' for a bruisin'*," Irene said pretending anger. "Doubling my age – you could have been a gentleman and added only 20 years or so but no, you had to rub it in and double it."

Carter put his hand over his mouth to stop himself from exploding into laughter.

"Okay, I didn't call you two in here to discuss Irene's age," James changed the topic. "Have a look at this guy's brother, Dwayne Miller, CEO of Competitive Response Solutions in DC."

"What about him?" Carter asked.

"CRS is in the industrial spy business; I know they have all these fancy names for them these days: competitive intelligence gathering, competitive analysis et cetera. Whatever you want to call it, it's industrial espionage. Granted, some of it is above board and legal, but much of it is not."

Carter and Irene nodded in harmony. "You think this is another tree that needs shaking?" Irene asked.

"Yes, definitely; I'd like to know the whole family," James grinned. "No harm in too much information."

The King Abdulaziz International Airport located in Jeddah was about 60 miles from the city center of Mecca. It was the busiest airport in Saudi Arabia; 15 million Muslim pilgrims on their way to Mecca would pass through this airport every year. The airport was built to handle 47 planes simultaneously, and capable of processing up to 3,800 pilgrims per hour during the Hajj season.

In such a crowded environment, the two former Desert Phantoms, Abbadi Haijar, and Rayan Qureshi had no problem blending in and getting through customs without raising any suspicions as to the purpose of their visit.

They did not travel together, but arrived in Jeddah on different days and stayed in separate locations in Mecca. They would contact each other, in secret, only if circumstances demanded.

Abbadi's assignment was to get all the environmental information about the Institute of Scientific Research and Development (ISRD), which included the exact location, surroundings, access roads, layout, entries and exits, floor plans, building security, and routines.

Rayan was to concentrate on the people working at the Institute. His objective was to gather information about the employees, their personal lives, and work routines. He was tasked with finding one or more employees whom he could persuade to cooperate with him and tell him what was going on inside the building. Of course, the jackpot would be confirmation that the American woman and her son were there.

Chapter Fifty

CLOSED THEIR EYES AND RELAXED

Mackenzie woke suddenly in the middle of the night; her back was aching. It wasn't long before she felt the contractions begin. It was time to let Seema know so she could contact Dr. Gabor, her obstetrician.

"Liam," she called quietly, "Liam, can you wake up love?"

"Mom? Are you okay?" he appeared at the door, sleepy-eyed but mentally alert.

"I think your little sister has decided it's time to arrive."

"Mom… what? Ah, my little sister!" His eyes popped wide open.

Mackenzie smiled and nodded. "Yes, your sister is about to be born. Could you please go and get Seema; ask her to come over immediately?"

"Yes, Mom. Are you okay?"

"Yes, my dear, there is nothing to worry about."

Liam sprinted down the corridor to Seema's quarters.

She appeared next to Mackenzie in minutes.

"Would you contact Doctor Gabor to come, please? I'm in labor."

Liam was holding Mackenzie's hand, and he looked worried.

Seema looked at him and smiled; she liked the boy who was always so respectful and friendly. "Liam, will you please stay and take care of your mother? I'll go and call the doctor. Don't worry; your mom is going to be okay."

Liam nodded and gently stroked Mackenzie's hair.

"Thank you, Liam. I love you, you know that don't you," Mackenzie said.

He nodded slowly. "I love you too, Mom. Is it going to hurt?" He asked.

"No, my dear; it won't, not one bit," Mackenzie smiled to reassure him.

He relaxed and smiled back. Seema arrived shortly after and announced that Doctor Gabor was on her way.

Mackenzie rested, closing her eyes. She was in distress, not because she was in labor, but because she was, in a way, alone. Where was Carter when she needed him? She needed him so desperately right now.

All the time the baby had been growing, she hoped and prayed for him to appear magically and get them out of this hellhole. She had tried so hard to remain positive while she and Liam learned Arabic, went to work and school, and existed without ever seeing the sun or feeling a fresh breeze on her face.

She wanted someone of her own ilk with her, someone whom she'd known outside this building. Mackenzie looked at Seema and insisted that she wake Nasser and ask him to allow her friend Liu to be with her for support. At first, Seema was hesitant, but she could understand how Mackenzie felt.

Mackenzie reasoned with Seema, telling her that as she and Doctor Gabor would be in attendance, it wouldn't be as if they could talk about anything other than the pending birth.

Seema finally nodded in agreement and went to bargain with Nasser on Mackenzie's behalf. She promised him she would be there the whole time and that nothing would pass between the two women that he would have to worry about.

When Seema came back, she told Mackenzie that Nasser had agreed; Liu was allowed to be with her and would arrive shortly.

Thankfully, Mackenzie's good behavior and professionalism in her work had won Nasser over at least to a point where he believed Mackenzie would be better off to have her friend with her at a time like this. It was not lost on him how much the working conditions had affected both women, and they had, in some small way, earned his respect that they didn't complain but got on with what they had to do.

Mackenzie spoke very gently to Liam and explained to him that he couldn't stay, that he should go with Seema, who would take him to the quarters of one of the families on the same floor.

Liam was reluctant to leave her alone, but when Liu arrived, he was okay. He gave Mackenzie a big hug and said. "Don't take too long Mom. I can't wait to see my little sister," he smiled, took Seema's hand and left.

Mackenzie watched him go, and the tears began to flow.

Liu just shook her head. "What a lovely little boy he is Mackenzie. You can be so proud of him."

"Oh Liu, I just want Carter here so badly," she sobbed. "I miss him so much."

"Mackie, I know dear, I do know," she took Mackenzie's

hand, "but right now you have a baby waiting to be born. One day I'm sure you will see Carter holding her in his arms; so now let's try and do our best to help the little one into the world."

Mackenzie cast her eyes around her cell, taking in the gray cement walls, the iron single bed, simple bedside table, and wardrobe. "There's no color here, nothing bright and welcoming; it's all so drab."

"I think we can be sure the little one won't mind at all, just to be held in your arms will be enough."

Mackenzie sighed; slowly she dropped into sleep as the time crawled by, waking when the contractions demanded her attention but waking less every time as she sunk into deeper sleep. This concerned Doctor Gabor but, in fact, Mackenzie was not sleeping she was only escaping to her own comfort place where she knew her wolves were waiting for her

Soon she found Keeva beside her and could feel the wolf's warm breath on her face, and her hands dug deep into Keeva's fur. "Keeva? You know don't you? You know I'm having a baby. I'm having his baby, and he isn't here. Keeva nudged her and lay down beside her; she curled up alongside the wolf's body.

It proved to be a quick and easy birth with Mackenzie only opening her eyes as the baby came into the world.

"Keeva?" She stirred and realized she was back in the cell and Liu was crying and saying, "Mackie, you have a little girl, a daughter, she's beautiful."

She smiled, "where's Liam? He must be told; he must come and meet her. Liu, can you get him please?"

"Just let the Doctor finish tidying up and we'll put you in a fresh nightdress. Liam's been prowling around outside like a caged tiger."

Liu was smiling. Mackenzie looked at her, "Liu, why have I not realized before what a good friend you are to me? Why have I not told you?"

"You didn't have to Mackie; you are the same for me, a dear and steadfast friend." She bent and kissed Mackie's cheek as Dr. Gabor, holding the baby wrapped in a shawl came to hand her to Mackenzie.

"She is perfect Mackenzie, a truly beautiful child," Doctor Gabor smiled.

"Thank you Ameera; I am so grateful you were here for me."

"I am blessed with being able to help a new child into the world."

Eventually, everyone left, and Liam was allowed to come in and see his sister and hold her. "Oh Mum, she's beautiful," he laughed out loud, "Oh look at her hair, it's red like yours." He giggled, "And see the little hands and feet; they are so small!" He was beaming.

Mackenzie looked with tenderness at the little bundle in her arms and said, "Beth, this here is your brother Liam. Welcome into the family. We have been waiting for you."

Two heads bent over the child as she slept, the brightest little light in that dreary cell.

In their cave, 5,800 miles to the west, the wolves of Freydis closed their eyes and relaxed.

Chapter Fifty-One

THE LUNCH DATE

Professor Kakos checked into his hotel, took a shower, had something to eat, and then got a taxi to drop him off at a coffee shop in Alexandria, Virginia where he would meet a representative of his client. Although he and Mark Miller had business dealings in the past, he'd never met the man in person. It didn't really matter to Kakos; Miller had been an excellent client who always paid on time and never squabbled about his fees.

The man he met at the coffee shop introduced himself as Michael but didn't give a last name. Kakos didn't mind, in the shadow world of artifact dealing, the less people knew about you, the better.

After they had ordered their coffees, Michael looked at Kakos and said, "Professor, this is a crucial project for Mr. Miller. I'm here to make sure you understand the importance of this deal, and also how Mr. Miller wants to handle it."

Kakos nodded. "Please continue."

For the next 10 minutes, Michael explained what was

expected of the Professor. He was to wear a wire to the meeting with Margaret O'Connell, and there would be three men outside the restaurant who would be listening to their conversation; they were also there to protect him in case something went wrong.

Kakos' ears pitched when he heard that. "Wait a minute. What's going on here? Why do I have to wear a wire and have people to protect me? This is an entirely legal, above board transaction. This is making me very nervous."

"I told you this is critical for Mr. Miller; these measures are just to make sure nothing goes wrong," Michael smirked. "You may be unaware of it, but other people also want that book. The protection is for your sake."

Kakos was alarmed, something was amiss, and it unnerved him. "Well, you can pass the message on to Mr. Miller that I'm not happy with this, not happy at all."

"Does that mean you are pulling out?"

Kakos was looking at Michael when he asked the question, and something in his facial expression gave him pause before he answered. "No, I will do it," he hesitated, "but I want to make sure Mr. Miller knows I'm not happy. I don't like to conduct business in this manner."

"I'll pass the message on," Michael grinned.

After Michael had left, Kakos looked around, waved at the server and ordered another coffee. When the coffee arrived, he took a sip and stared out the window.

Kakos: *"Maybe I should just go back home now."*

Mr. Greed: *"Just drop $25,000 on the table and walk away?"*

Kakos: *"Yes ... something is wrong here."*

Mr. Greed: *"Are you crazy? You're not doing anything illegal. This would be the easiest money you've ever made. What can go wrong?"*

The venue they picked was convenient for two reasons; one they could choose a place where the observers could hide securely, and two; the owner was an old schoolmate and friend of Irene's, which gave them the opportunity to prepare the venue in advance.

Irene sipped her coffee while a competent young makeup artist spent more than an hour applying some sort of rubber cement stuff that made her look 40 years older. The woman used shading to deepen her eyes, powder to lighten her skin, fitted a slightly purpled and graying wig over her hair, outfitted her with bifocal glasses, hearing aids in both ears, and hooked the microphone to her bra. When she had finished, she stepped back to gauge her handiwork and smiled, "Grandma Margaret."

Irene grimaced, got up, and walked out of the room. Carter, James, Sean, and Dylan were waiting for her. She dropped her glasses onto the tip of her nose, pointed the walking stick at them while she stared at them over the rim of her glasses, and said, "Not a single word from any one of you; not even a squeak."

The three men immediately repressed their smiles. Like a real gentleman, Carter bowed slightly, stepped forward, held out his right arm for her, and led her to the waiting taxi outside.

As soon as Irene's taxi left, Carter, James, Sean, and Dylan got into an SUV and made their way to their observation post in a building across the street from the French restaurant on Wisconsin Ave. Rick Winslow was waiting for them; he had already positioned all the surveillance equipment, and a drone was circling a thousand feet overhead. On the table, he had set up a few monitors giving them a full view of the inside and outside of the restaurant. There were three EA operatives in strategic positions, one inside, and two outside, from where they would be able to get to Irene quickly if necessary.

Ten minutes before the appointed time, Professor Kakos arrived in a taxi and got out. His arrival was followed by the arrival of three more vehicles, parking at different locations on the street not too far from the restaurant.

Sean smiled, "Snoop convention in Tenleytown, Washington."

When Irene arrived a few minutes later, it was show time.

As soon as Irene and Kakos had introduced themselves to each other and were seated, Rick, who had already scanned and hijacked the radiofrequency that Kakos' followers were using, jammed their signal. Any doubts that those three men were tailing Kakos were erased as Sean and the rest of the team saw on the screens how the three of them were grappling with their earphones and other electronic equipment to revive the signals.

If it were not for the soundproofing of the room from where James and the rest were watching and listening, anyone on the street would have heard the riotous laughter. Irene was a natural.

"Professor Crackross you said?"

"No ma'am Kakos – K-A-K-O-S," he spelled it out for her.

"What a strange name, son. Where did you say you're from again?"

"Greece ma'am; I live in Greece." The expressions on his face made it clear that he was having his doubts about the woman across the table from him.

Irene saw that and decided not to overplay her hand.

"Oh yes," She said. "Sorry at my age the old mind is not so agile anymore."

Kakos nodded and waved his hand. "Not to worry Mrs. O'Connell, I understand."

"Now why did you-" She paused for a short while and started, "Oh yes, you're the gentleman who is interested in that book, what's that name- The Squirrels Dam? hmm… Why do you suppose squirrels would build a dam?"

"The Searle-in-dum," Kakos pronounced carefully.

"Oh yes, yes that's the one."

"I'm very interested in that book Mrs. O'Connell-"

"It's not for sale," she interjected. "I am not selling that book." She sounded almost aggressive.

Kakos held his hand up. "No, Mrs. O'Connell, I don't want to buy the original. I'm only interested in a copy, as I've said in my emails to you."

"Oh yes, now I remember."

Their lunch order arrived, and they started eating.

After taking a few bites, Irene said, "So, where were we? Greece was it?"

"I said I don't want to buy the book -"

"Of course you won't; it's not for sale!"

"I'm only interested in a copy."

She paused, "Yes, that's right. You're the one who wants a copy of it." Slowly she nodded, "I have inquired about the cost of making a copy. It's not going to be cheap you know."

"How much will it cost?"

"I showed the book to a person who specializes in the restoration of old books, and he said that it is in a very fragile state and has to be handled with great care." She elaborated until she saw the frustration forming on his face. "It will cost about $10,000."

Kakos feigned surprise.

The Wolves of Freydis

Irene continued. "The man told me he would have to use special equipment."

"Did he say how long it will take him to make a copy?"

She didn't answer him immediately; she returned to her food and took a few more bites, avoiding his gaze.

"Mrs. O'Connell?"

She looked at him inquiringly.

"How long will it take him take to make the copy?"

"Of what?"

"The book Mrs. O'Connell."

James and the rest were doubling up with laughter in the room across the street.

"Oh yes, the book. So what did you wish to know about it?"

"How long before I can get a copy?"

"Two or three days."

"Good. Can you ask your expert to make the copy?"

"Wait a minute mister ... what's your name again."

"Kakos ma'am," He sighed.

"Aren't you forgetting something Mr. Craxros?" She stared at him.

Kakos looked perplexed. What did he forget? "The money! I'm so sorry Mrs. O'Connell," he smiled. "The price is not a problem; I'll pay it."

Irene put a wicked little smile on her face and leaned forward. She cooed, "As they say in the movies, half now and half when I deliver."

Carter had to sit down as he doubled up with laughter. "Irene has been in our company for too long Jim! She has caught on to our monkeyshines. We better be on the lookout from now on."

Kakos opened his mouth to object, then closed it and nodded.

Irene scratched around in her handbag, got out a small old fashioned ring-binder paper notepad, then spent another two minutes trying to find a pen. She then gave it all to Kakos.

"Write this down," she said. "This is my bank account number," she read it to him from a card she held in her shaking hands. "My bank manager will let me know when the money comes in. Then I will get the copy made."

"Thank you, Mrs. O'Connell," Kakos smiled as he was pleased to see Mrs. O'Connell's mind seemed to be functioning a lot better since they started talking about the money. "I will also email you as soon as I've deposited the money. Then we can arrange to meet again."

Irene nodded. "Thank you."

Kakos wasn't sure what to say or do next. He folded the napkin, placed it on the table, and said, "Mrs. O'Connell, will you please excuse me? I have to go and arrange to get the money transferred to you. May I call a cab for you?"

Irene looked up at him smiled and said, "No it's okay. I'm going to have another coffee. Have a good day Doctor Cracks."

She could swear she heard someone laughing.

Kakos left; he was thrilled with the prospect of getting a copy of the Sirralnnudam and the paycheck if he delivered the copy to his client. The operative phrase here was – *if he delivered the copy to his client* – Mrs. O'Connell's absentmindedness was a bit of a worry.

When the Greek Professor walked out of the restaurant, he was under the impression his followers had taped the conversation. His cell phone started ringing shortly after he got into the taxi; it was Michael who wanted to meet immediately. He gave Kakos the address of a coffee shop and told him to be there in 20 minutes. Kakos redirected the taxi.

At the coffee shop, Michael explained the technical mishap to Kakos and asked him to repeat the conversation he had with Mrs. O'Connell.

Irene had another coffee while she waited for the message from James that all was clear. When his voice came over her earphones, she nodded slightly at her old school friend. Slipping through a side door in the corridor, she found a storage room where she got rid of her outfit, makeup, and wig, then combing out her own glossy hair she exited the restaurant through a back door where an SUV with tinted windows was waiting to take her to the safe house.

When she walked into the room where James, Carter, Sean, and Dylan were waiting for her, they all got up and applauded her loudly.

"Irene, please let me send this video clip to Hollywood. You will have a movie contract in your hand by the end of the week," James laughed.

Irene joined in the mirth that followed. The pressure was off. Now all they had to do was follow the money trail to the big fish.

Rick Winslow's spider web was ready, waiting to track and report the source of the money when it was paid into the bank account of Mrs. Margaret O'Connell, Irene's mother.

After Kakos and Michael had left the coffee shop, things started to happen quickly. Michael had passed the price and Mrs. O'Connell's bank details on to Mark Miller, who immediately contacted his brother, Dwayne Miller. Rick's tracking software followed the trail.

Twenty-four hours later, Mrs. Margaret O'Connell got a

call from her bank to inform her that the $5,000 she had been expecting was in her account; a little while later she also got an email from Professor Kakos to confirm the deposit.

Sean and the team were ready. They had all the confirmation they needed.

Chapter Fifty-Two

THE FIRST LINKS IN THE CHAIN

In the weeks leading up to Irene's lunch date with Professor Kakos, Sean and the rest of the executive team of the Devereux operation, James, Irene, Dylan and Carter created a plan of action. As the information started to come in, they fine-tuned the plan. When Rick's report unveiled the chain of connections from Kakos up to Dwayne Miller, they went into action with a multipronged attack.

Carter, Kevin, and Joe Costa, took a commercial flight from DC to Quebec City. Joe was one of the two-man team who reconnoitered the drone operator's hideout a few weeks before. Roy and Andre, both Canadian citizens, were already in Canada, for a week, visiting family. They would meet Carter and the other two at the private airfield outside Quebec City and accompany them to Freydis.

Carter and his four companions' arrival on Freydis was timed for shortly after nightfall. When they arrived, Kevin and Joe remained in the plane and only got out after the plane was inside the hangar and the doors had been closed.

Not even Ahote and Bly knew the two of them were there; Carter would brief them the next day about the plan and what was expected of them.

If the drones were overhead, they wouldn't detect that Carter all of a sudden had four, instead of the usual two, bodyguards.

Later that night when Carter, Roy, and Andre were in the house and their drone detection equipment indicated the sky was clear, Kevin and Joe left the cover of the hangar and set out on foot toward the farmhouse where the drone operators were based. They intended to cover as much of the 25 miles to the farmhouse as possible while it was dark, hide during the day, and hit them the next night.

In the meantime, four additional three-man teams were dispatched; one in Toronto, two in DC, and one in New York. They would locate their targets, keep close to them, and wait for Sean to give them the go ahead.

It was 7:45 pm the next night when Kevin and Joe stood outside the farmhouse where the two drone operators were based. The drones had been retrieved at 5:00 pm and placed in the shed. The two men were having their second beer in front of the TV, watching a movie, when Kevin, with a black balaclava over his face, appeared in the doorway of the living room pointing a 9mm VP9 Heckler and Koch pistol at them. He took one step into the room and moved to his right to allow Joe to enter; he was also wearing a black balaclava over his face and had a 9mm Sig Sauer semiautomatic pistol in his hand.

Laurel and Hardy, as Joe had dubbed them while he and Kevin were observing them earlier, went slack-jawed and froze in place at the sight of Joe and Kevin, the whites of their startled eyes clearly visible emphasizing the terror on their faces.

"Good evening gentlemen," Kevin said. "Just sit right where you are, and don't move." He nodded to Joe to turn the TV off.

Laurel and Hardy were speechless and ashen.

Joe deadened the TV; turned and grabbed Laurel by the collar, pulled him up from the couch, and pushed him towards one of the chairs. He searched him, relieving him of his cellphone, forced him to sit, then took cable ties out of his pocket and tied his arms and legs to the chair. He repeated the procedure with Hardy, putting him in the chair next to his friend.

Joe didn't say a word; the muzzle of the VP9 spoke the universal and wordless language understood by everyone on the planet, including Laurel and Hardy.

"Excellent," Kevin said. "You guys have really been very cooperative so far. Keep it up, and this will be over soon."

Laurel and Hardy nodded slowly. It seemed as if they were still afraid of their own voices.

"Apologies for dropping in on you like this. Unfortunately, we're in a bit of a hurry, so we won't be watching the movie with you. We just want to ask a few questions, shoot you and be on our way." Kevin smiled under the balaclava, but his voice sounded deadly.

"No! Please; what do you want? Food? Money? Just say it. Please don't shoot us!" Laurel cried.

"Information."

Tears were running down Hardy's cheeks as he opened his mouth but no sound came out, he closed it.

"What do you want to know?" Laurel's voice trembled. "I'll tell you everything you want to know. Just please, don't shoot us."

Kevin looked at Joe. "What do you think? They're asking so nicely. Maybe we just shoot them in the knee?"

Joe shook his head and pointed his gun at Laurel.

Hardy had closed his eyes, waiting for the shot. Laurel was trembling and stuttering, making inaudible noises.

Kevin held his hand up to Joe. "Okay wait; let's just hear what they have to say first. If they lie to me, you can shoot them. If they give me the right answers, maybe we can reconsider shooting them. What do you reckon?"

Joe shrugged his shoulders and lowered the gun.

"Let's start with the easy stuff." Kevin said. "Who do you work for?"

"CanSec in Toronto," Laurel whispered.

"Who is your boss?"

"Stephen Byrne, he's the owner of CanSec."

"You're doing great," Kevin said. "Two more questions. Is Stephen Byrne the man that you send your daily reports to?"

Laurel nodded, "Yes."

"Is anyone else getting your reports?"

Laurel shook his head, "No, only Stephen."

Kevin looked at Joe. "I think he did pretty well there. Do you figure that was good enough for a pardon?"

Joe nodded.

"Okay then, keep an eye on them for a minute please," Kevin said. "I need to make a quick phone call; but don't shoot them. Okay?"

Joe nodded again but raised his gun when Kevin walked away.

Laurel and Hardy both started squeaking. Their eyes were closed.

Kevin went outside the house, and when he was out of earshot, he pulled his secure satellite phone out and called Sean Walker.

Sean, Dylan, Irene, James, and Rick Winslow were in an

operations room at one of the CIA's secret training facilities in Virginia, waiting for the call. The room was furnished with satellite communications equipment, computers, wall-mounted flat screen TVs, and tracking equipment. They had a visual and audio connection with every one of the four teams.

When Sean answered, Kevin said. "Canuck one complete. It's their number one." The conversation between Sean and Kevin was short and cryptic.

"Thanks. Enjoy the holiday," Sean replied and disconnected. Number one meant the man the Toronto team had to get was Stephen Byrne, the sole proprietor of CanSec.

Although they suspected that CanSec was doing the surveillance job on Carter under contract for Dwayne Miller of CRS, they needed the confirmation. Dwayne Miller was the biggest fish in the pond at that stage of the operation, but they were also convinced that he was just another link in the chain.

Sean turned to the people in the room and said. "That was Kevin. Our man at Cansec is Stephen Byrne, as we suspected. I'm giving orders for the Toronto team to move in. Any objections?"

"Bring it on," James replied on behalf of them all as he felt the adrenaline rushing through his body.

Sean contacted Chris Jones, the leader of the Toronto team, and gave him Stephen Byrne's name and the go-ahead.

Kevin and Joe went through the farmhouse, pulled all the hard drives out of the computers, collected all the surveillance and other electronic equipment, pushed the drones out of the shed onto the landing strip then rigged it all with C4 explosives and a timer.

They tied and gagged Laurel and Hardy and pushed

them into the back seat of their double cab truck, set the timer on the explosives for one hour and drove off in the direction of Freydis. They would be able to get to within twelve miles of the Freydis homestead with the truck, hide the truck amongst the trees and cover the rest of distance on foot.

Stephen Byrne was the sole proprietor of CanSec, a small but successful security company based in Toronto. The information in his personal file, which Chris Jones studied, said Byrne was about five ten, in his mid-forties, and as a former ice hockey player, in good physical shape. He had divorced about a year ago and lived in a studio apartment not too far from the CanSec offices.

Byrne worked hard, putting in long hours and on weekdays usually worked until 9 pm. The floorplans of the offices showed a reception area, four offices, and small meeting room. Byrne's office was at the end of the hallway behind the reception area.

The reconnaissance team visiting the CanSec offices a few weeks ago had collected all electronic data including Wi-Fi router settings, network administrator password, and the access codes for the office security system.

Chris Jones, David Beckett, and Budd Clarence drove around the block, noted the parked vehicles, office lights, and people on the streets. Once they were sure, they hadn't been followed, and that Byrne was the only person in the CanSec offices, Budd Clarence was dropped off at the entry to a dark, side alley.

Budd walked to the end of the cul-de-sac, looked

around to make sure no one was watching and jumped over the low brick wall. The back of the CanSec building was about five paces away, through the window, he saw Stephen Byrne sitting at his desk, and his back was to him.

Budd hunkered and moved to the right of the building where he could hide in the shadows behind the rubbish bins. He pulled his tablet out, scanned for the Wi-Fi signal and connected to the CanSec network. Budd shook his head; the security system was archaic, at least 15 years old. *I thought a security company would have the latest and greatest in security equipment, but I could be wrong.*

Within three minutes, he had control of the office security system and whispered into his throat mic, "Ready to go."

Chris and David had parked their old Toyota Camry about hundred yards down the street from the CanSec offices, waiting for Budd's signal. "Thanks, on our way." Chris replied.

Chris and David carefully opened the front door and entered, closed the door without making a sound, pulled their silenced Sig Sauer P220 pistols out, lowered the balaclavas over their faces and sneaked down the hallway towards Stephen Byrne's office and the sound of jazz music.

Byrne was glaring at the document on his computer screen and was startled out of his reverie when he saw movement. His eyes flared as his brain registered the masked man with a pistol pointed at him. A low deep grunt escaped from his throat. His right hand went to the top drawer of his desk.

"That would be a very stupid move Mr. Byrne," The masked man said, "put both your hands on the desk, and don't move them."

Byrne half obeyed the order, his eyes kept on darting around, it was obvious to Chris that the man was planning to resist. He took a few steps into the office, closer to Byrne, without dropping his aim or eye contact.

When David's masked face appeared to Chris' left side, Byrne threw him a quick glance, must have seen the second pistol pointed at him and sighed. It looked as if Byrne realized he was outnumbered and outgunned.

"What do you want? I don't keep money on the premises." His voice was surprisingly calm for someone who had just received a nasty shock and was staring at the business end of two silenced Sig Sauer P220 pistols. It was a situation, which would have scared most human beings shitless.

Without taking his eyes off Byrne, Chris said to David, "Close the blinds and clean out his desk drawers; I got the impression he's got some hardware in the top right-hand drawer."

David found Byrne's loaded .38 revolver in the drawer, as Chris had suspected. He cleared out the rest of the drawers, picked Byrne's cellphone up from the desk, removed the battery and shoved the phone into his pocket.

"Tie him up," Chris said.

David retrieved a few cable ties from his pocket and moved towards Byrne. Chris kept his gun trained on Byrne and studied his face closely for any signs of sudden action. Before David could be warned, Byrne suddenly propelled himself out of his chair towards him trying to bowl him over.

Unfortunately for Byrne, David was alert. He saw the move, stepped to the left, his right hand shot out, and hit Byrne in the throat with a controlled blow. Byrne fell to the ground clutching his throat, making gurgling sounds as he tried to suck in air through his dented airway.

"Byrne, don't be stupid," David said calmly. "We don't want to hurt you; we just want to ask you a few questions. However, don't confuse my kindness for weakness; I don't have any scruples about hurting you either."

"What the fuck do you want?" Byrne croaked as he got back into his chair still struggling to breathe. He didn't move while David tied his arms and legs to the chair.

"You have two boys with drones posted out in the sticks north of Quebec City, to spy on Professor Carter Devereux. Right?" Chris said.

"Don't know what you're talking about," Byrne denied.

"Byrne, don't test my patience," Chris said pushing his left hand into his jacket pocket he pulled out a Taser X26.

Byrne's eyes expanded slightly; he knew how painful a shot from one of those could be; he issued them to all his guards. A few years ago, after a few drinks too many, he felt brave enough to accept the dare and allowed one his men to shoot him with a Taser. A very stupid decision; when he came to his senses he was sober, the bravado was gone, and he had the terrible memory of the most excruciating pain he had ever experienced; breaking his leg during an ice hockey match in his young days didn't even come close.

He tried to hide his fear.

Chris saw the twitch in his eyes, raised his left arm, and pointed the Taser at Byrne. "One more time. Those two boys out there are yours?"

Byrne nodded.

"Good. Now we're getting somewhere. Who is your client?"

"Can't tell you; that's privileged," Byrne snarled for a split second but then his face froze mid-snarl as he realized he had just exhausted the patience of the man holding the Taser.

Byrne's body stiffened as the shot hit him and his muscles cramped; the spasms tipped him and the chair over, hitting the floor like a bag of potatoes off the back of a truck. David held a rag over Byrne's mouth to stifle his screams.

A few minutes later, David pulled Byrne and the chair upright and whispered in his ear, "My friend is in a real shitty mood tonight. Even I'm a bit scared of him. I haven't ever seen him like this - ever. It must be the fact that he found his girlfriend in bed with another man earlier tonight. Unless you want 50,000 volts running through your body for the rest of the night, I suggest you tell him what he wants to know."

Byrne considered the old good-cop-bad-cop trick for a moment, but decided there was no way he was prepared to take another hit. This was much worse than that time when he took a Taser hit when he was drunk, now there was nothing that numbed the pain.

Chris looked at Byrne and said, "Who is your client?"

"Competitive Response Solutions," Byrne mumbled.

"Who is your contact there?"

Byrne's eyes darted around the room. "Mhh I…"

Chris raised the Taser.

"Miller! His name is Dwayne Miller. He's the CEO of CRS," Byrne blurted eagerly.

Chris spoke into his throat mic to Budd. "Got that?"

"All of it," Budd responded.

"Good, pass the message on."

Budd called Sean on the secure satellite phone, "Canuck two done. It's Delta Mike."

"Thanks, see you later," Sean responded and ended the call. He turned to James, Irene, Dylan, and Rick and said.

"Dwayne Miller has his fingers in both pies. I'm kicking off the next stage. Any objections?"

James held his finger up, looked at the rest of the team and they responded in chorus, "Bring it on!"

The remaining three teams on standby got their marching orders from Sean and Dylan and swung into action.

In Toronto, Budd brought their car to the front door, and Chris and David, who had Stephen Byrne gagged and tied up, shoved him into the trunk of the Camry, and drove off to a farmhouse twenty miles outside the city.

The teams that had to snatch Mark Miller and Professor Kakos had an easy task. It was not necessary for them to extract any information from their captives; they only had to be captured and moved to secure locations where they would be kept under guard to prevent them from raising the alarm to Dwayne Miller or anyone else.

Within an hour of receiving their go-ahead instructions, they had the two men in their custody and out of the way.

Kakos was paralyzed with shock when the two masked men entered his hotel room. His heart skipped several beats, he should never have let Mr. Greed persuade him to stay in DC; he should have put his ass on the first plane back to Greece days ago. Although confident he'd done nothing illegal, it was too late to change his mind; he would have to face the music. He knew that he didn't necessarily have to do anything illegal to piss certain people off, the only question was; *who did I piss off?*

Mark Miller had been out with a few friends, prematurely celebrating the discovery of the Sirralnnudam, and the $120,000 his brother was about to pay into his account. After his friends had driven him back to his apartment about 11:00 pm, Miller continued the drinking spree - solo. When the EA team picked him up about 12:30 am, he had just set a new personal record level of inebriation. It would take almost twenty-four hours before he recollected his wits and realized he was not in his own apartment.

Chapter Fifty-Three

THE SECOND LINK IN THE CHAIN

So far everything had worked out precisely as planned; they had double confirmation of Dwayne Miller's complicity in the Devereux matter and had five people in custody. Despite their success, they were all painfully aware that everything they had done thus far had been entirely outside the law. American citizens had entered Canada, kidnapped three Canadian citizens, and were holding them captive. They had captured both a citizen of Greece and the United States on American soil and were holding them captive as well. None of their prisoners had committed a crime, the captors had no legal authority to arrest or hold anyone in either Canada or the USA, and kidnapping, anywhere in the world, was a serious crime.

Their only way out of the dire situation was to make sure their captives would never recognize them and to get irrefutable proof that would link their prisoners to the serious crimes they all believed were committed by Dwayne Miller and CRS. It was a big gamble with potential international repercussions; they had thought about it long and hard before deciding they had no choice. It had to be done.

When Sean got the call from Chris Jones out of Toronto, Dylan had grabbed his bag of weapons and tools, hid it in the cavity behind the back seat of his car, and drove back to Washington to meet with the team who would bring Dwayne Miller in for questioning.

Miller was married to his second wife, a fashion designer, who was currently away from home, in Los Angeles on a two-week business trip.

Dylan had about an hour's drive to get to the gym where Miller worked out five days a week. He showed up punctually every day at 5:30 am and spent an hour on various exercises before starting his day at the CRS headquarters. Miller was about six two, no more than 200 pounds and in much better shape than ninety-nine percent of other men at the age of fifty-four.

On the way, Dylan was mulling over all the information they now had. Ben Friedman's agents had infiltrated the forensic lab in Amman, the capital of Jordan. He'd already supplied them with floor plans, the number of workers, security arrangements, street maps, access to the computer systems and all other pertinent information.

The two former Desert Phantoms, Abbadi Haijar, and Rayan Qureshi, who were gathering information about the lab on the Southside of Mecca, in the Jabal Thawr Mountains, also had some success. The lab was called the Institute of Scientific Research and Development – ISRD. The Director of the facility was one Daiyan Nasser. It was a private organization, owned by a group of wealthy Saudi Arabian business people.

Rick Winslow's dexterity with anything computer related provided detailed personal information along with a lot of interesting background data about the ISRD investors.

Abbadi and Rayan had learned about a section below the Institute that consisted of six subterranean levels. The surprising fact was that, as far as they could establish, no one in the above ground facility knew that anything was going on below their feet.

The two Phantoms found the concealed entry to the underground section and had been monitoring it intently, noting who was coming and going. After a few days of observation and head counting they suggested that there could not be more than 30 people working below ground.

Rayan had made contact with some of the construction workers on a site, a block away from the Institute and got the name of the architect and construction company who developed the ISRD a few years ago.

Once the two Phantoms had the name and details of the company, it was as easy as taking candy from a baby for them to get into the company's offices late one night, and acquire the architectural drawings.

Dylan arrived at the gym shortly before 5 am and was met by John Arevalo. There were already a few fitness fanatic cars in the parking lot, so he drove the car as far as possible away from the main entrance to the building

The other two members of the team, Bill, and Sam were busy following Miller from his home en route to the gym

All four men maintained contact through their earpieces, so Dylan and John were alert when Miller arrived in the carpark. They saw the lights, identified Miller's $50,000 red BMW X4 M40i, and the license plates before Dylan started the engine of the Ford Focus and waited for Miller to select his parking spot. When Miller turned into the space, Dylan put the Ford into drive and slowly approached Miller's car, heading for the empty parking space on the driver's side of Miller's car. Miller was going to make it easy.

He pulled up next to Miller and switched the engine off. John got out and walked to the back of the Ford as if he was going to get something out of the trunk. Dylan waited until Miller got out of his BMW and had closed his door. When Miller started moving to the back door to get his gear, Dylan opened the driver's door of the Ford and got out leaving his door open, thus blocking Miller's path.

"Good morning," Dylan said. "Nothing like an early morning workout." Miller looked towards him, nodded, and mumbled something.

Dylan's friendly greeting was enough distraction to allow John to move out from behind the Ford, take two steps, insert the needle into Miller's neck and depressed the plunger. Miller spun around, opened his mouth, and collapsed backward into Dylan's arms before the sound could reach his lips.

John grabbed the keys out of Miller's hand. Dylan tied Millers hands and feet with duct tape, pushed a clean piece of cloth into his mouth, and secured it with duct tape.

Three minutes after Dylan greeted Miller, he pulled out of the parking space in the Ford Focus with Miller in the trunk.

As Dylan was leaving, John phoned Sean and gave him a cryptic update before returning Miller's luxurious BMW to his house, where he parked it in the garage and then caught a bus to his next destination.

After Sean had shared the message with the rest of the people in the operations room, Irene called Carter and told him he could return to DC.

Before they ended the call, Carter said, "Irene, I saw the four wolf pups this morning. It was wonderful."

"I would love to see them, Carter!" She beamed.

When the call ended, Irene told the rest of them that Kevin and Joe had arrived at Freydis with the two former drone operators and that Carter was on his way to DC.

Dwayne Miller woke up with the mother of all headaches and through dazed eyes, looked up from the cold concrete floor where he lay. It was a small room with white walls, no windows, a small table, two chairs, and a single light high up on the ceiling. A steel door guarded the only entrance. He was utterly confused; however, as his memory slowly returned he recalled the carpark in front of the gym, two men, one saying something, then a sharp pain in the neck.

The steel door swung open, and a man who appeared to be in his mid-fifties walked into the room. He was about six-one, had dark hair that was graying at the temples, tan skin, not an ounce of fat on his body and lively dark brown eyes. Miller recognized him – it was James Rhodes the Director of A-Echelon and it scared him.

The man looked at Miller and said. "Get up and sit your ass down in that chair." The man pointed to the chair closest to Miller.

Miller reluctantly did as he was told.

"My name is James Rhodes. I work for the CIA, and I have a few questions for you."

Miller held his hand up. "I know who you are and you can hold your horses' right there mister. Who the hell do you think you are? I'm not about to answer any questions; I demand that you let me go immediately. I'm going to sue your ass, seven ways from Sunday."

James leaned a bit forward and looked Miller straight in the eyes. It was the first eye contact Miller made with James and shivers started running down his spine as James held his gaze and spoke softly and measuredly.

"Miller, I'll explain the rules to you once, and once only. Now, look up to that corner above the door. See that camera there?"

Miller nodded.

"On the other end of that camera is a computer screen, and in front of that screen at this very moment is one lean, mean, angry bastard of a man whom I had a hard time convincing not to walk in here and shoot you. That was the first rule; you talk to me, or you find out what it feels like to be shot. The second rule; there will be no lawyer or telephone call because this is not a police station. This is jungle justice. The third rule; I ask the questions; you give the answers. And, if you lie to me, think about rule one."

James took a deep breath. "I know everything about you Miller, so I know you can read, write, and speak English; and that there is nothing wrong with your hearing. So I'm not going to ask if you understand the rules."

Miller's throat had gone dry, and he struggled to swallow. James' eyes were shooting fire, and it gave him the creeps. He nodded.

"Okay. I'm going to sketch the scenario for you, and then I'm going to go out and have coffee to give you the opportunity to think about things. When I get back, you and I are going to have a chat like old friends. No secrets."

Miller didn't reply; he just stared down at the table.

"Here's the scenario. CRS landed on the radar of the CIA and FBI a few months ago. We've been digging around in your networks and communications for a couple of months and discovered a few very nasty projects you have been working on. Words like espionage, treason, and murder come to mind; you know, the kind of stuff that would guarantee you a seat in the electric chair."

Miller shut his eyes. He tried to swallow, but he couldn't. His hands were shaking, and he placed them on his lap so that James couldn't see them.

"Miller, listen carefully. I'm offering you one chance to get out of this alive. When I get back from my coffee break, you start talking and tell me everything. You do that and I might be able to cut you a deal; you know what the alternative is."

James got up and left the room.

Miller was pale; sweat pearled on his upper lip and forehead. He sighed and leaned back in the chair for a moment then leaned forward again, putting his elbows on the table and dropping his face into his hands. His whole world imploded.

When James walked into the observation room where Irene, Dylan, and Sean were waiting for him, Irene said, "Excellent work, Jim. I think you got through to him; he's going to talk without any further persuasion." She pointed at the computer screen showing Miller sitting with his face in his hands.

Sean laughed, "Jim, who is this lean, mean, angry bastard of man you were talking about?"

James grinned and said, "We can flip a coin between you and Dylan."

Irene handed James a mug of strong black coffee, and they stared at Miller on the screen.

"The son of a bitch," James muttered. "I see Mackie, Liam, 23 dead people and scores more wounded in front of me; I feel like choking the living shit out of him, not talking to him."

Irene slowly nodded, "Those are only the ones we know about, Jim."

James finished his coffee and got up.

Miller looked up when James walked back into the room. He had made up his mind. He looked at James and pointed to the camera and asked, "I take it everything I'm going to say will be recorded?"

James nodded.

James looked at his watch and said, "It's almost 9:00 am. I'm going to call your office, and you'll tell Tracey, your secretary, you've come down with a nasty bug, and the doctor has ordered you to stay flat on your back at home for a few days."

"Thanks, that's what I want, I need time to explain it all to you."

James dialed the CRS office and when Tracey answered he handed the phone to Miller. He was brief; he didn't have to fake a sick sounding voice. He ended the call and handed the phone back to James.

"You can start, I'm all ears," James said.

Dwayne Miller started talking. It was as if he was unloading a burden. He had to get it all out, almost seven years of it. For the next three hours, he explained how Competitive Response Solutions was founded, how they started off as an organization that specialized in legal industrial competitive information gathering and analysis, and how they started branching out into illegal activities and arrived at their current position. He gave details of their projects and clients.

James interrupted him now and then to ask questions

The Wolves of Freydis

for clarification but otherwise allowed him to talk unhindered most of the time.

In the observation room, Sean shook his head, "All these years we fought the bad guys thousands of miles away and ignored the enemy within."

Dylan nodded, "Why is it that I have this nauseating feeling that this guy has only revealed the tip of the iceberg?"

Irene swung her swivel chair to face Dylan and Sean, "This guy is as close to the bottom of the chain as you can get. I'm too petrified to even think what we're going to find at the top."

When Miller finished his narrative, James started questioning him in detail about the Devereux case.

Who is the CRS person who deals with the Saudi's?

"Nate Gordon."

James had heard the name on the Hill but had never met the man.

"Who are his contacts in Saudi?"

"His primary contact was Youssef Bin-Bandar, but he died of a heart attack and has been replaced by Ibrahimi El Fadl…"

James felt the shock waves reverberating through his body, "Youssef Bin-Bandar and Ibrahimi El Fadl the former and current deputy director of the General Intelligence Presidency of Saudi Arabia?"

Miller nodded slowly.

James was struggling to repress his shock but somehow managed to keep his expression impassive.

In the observation room, Irene felt a cold quiver crawling down her spine. Sean cursed.

James asked the question on everyone's mind, "Does that mean the King and the House of Saud are in on this?"

"No. They have no idea about Youssef Bin-Bandar's and Ibrahimi El Fadl's dual loyalties."

"So who is this other person those two have been working for?"

"No one in CRS knows. Nate has a contact in the government, someone high up, and that person knows who those two men have been working for. Not even Nate knows."

"Who is Nate's contact in government?"

Miller shrugged. "That's another secret that no one in CRS knows. We call him NTC, Nate's Top Contact, and honest to God I don't have any idea who that is. I have never tried to find out; all I know is that NTC is responsible for more than 50% of our income, including the contracts from Saudi Arabia and other Middle Eastern countries."

"Any guesses?"

Miller shook his head. "No idea, but whoever it is, he has clout in DC. It could be the Chief of Staff, the Secretary of State, the Secretary of Defense, Director of the CIA, NSA, FBI I just don't know, and Nate would never share that information with me."

Sean looked at Dylan, and his lips formed the words, *Nate Gordon*.

Dylan nodded. "Irene, can you tell James to take five? We need to have a quick chat."

Irene spoke into the mic connected to James' earpiece.

James stopped Miller, asked him if he wanted something to drink, got up, and left the room.

When he arrived in the observation room, Sean said, "Dylan and I think we need to pick Nate Gordon up immediately. What do you say?"

"I thought you already had him here," James grinned. "Get that bastard's ass in here as quickly as possible."

Sean and Dylan made a few calls. Compliments of Rick Winslow, they already had detailed information on all the CRS directors and senior staff. It took Rick less than three minutes to locate Nate Gordon's position; he was at home.

Dylan had a plan. "James I think the easiest and quickest way to do this is to get Miller to phone Gordon and ask him to come over to his house. Tell him he's sick but there is some urgent matter to discuss. I will go out there, pick up two of our operators on the way, and wait for Gordon at Miller's house."

The four of them carefully stepped through Dylan's plan a few times and gave him the nod. It was not the ideal plan, but they were running against the clock.

When Dylan headed for the door, Irene stopped him and smiled, "Please be careful Dylan."

Dylan waved his hand, smiled, and disappeared down the hallway.

James returned to the interrogation room with two Styrofoam cups filled with black coffee. He sat down and pushed one of the cups over to Miller.

"Now let's get back to Nate Gordon."

Irene's voice came over his earpiece, "Carter is here." James nodded his head slightly in acknowledgment.

Miller took a sip of the coffee, cleared his throat, and waited for James to ask his question.

"What other Saudi contacts does Gordon have?"

"There is only one other man I'm aware of, his name is Dr. Daiyan Nasser; he is the Director of a research institute, but I don't know where the institute is."

James nodded. *I might have an idea where that Institute is. But I think Nate Gordon will be able to confirm it.*

"Good let's talk about the Sirralnnudam."

Miller nodded.

"CRS was involved in that botched up operation in Armenia where they lost the book. Is that right?"

"We were involved to the extent that we provided Dr. Mackenzie Devereux's travel arrangements and research to Nate, who passed it on to NTC. I have no idea who NTC would have given that information to, nor how the operation was executed."

"You hired your brother, who hired a Greek Professor, Anatolio Kakos to publish an article in an archeological magazine in an attempt to get a copy of the book."

Miller nodded, "Yes."

"Who wants that book so desperately?"

"Ibrahimi El Fadl contacted Nate and asked him to try and get the book."

"How much?"

"$25 million."

James had a hard time trying not to explode. "They are desperate to get that book."

Miller didn't reply.

"What was your involvement in the bomb explosion in Jerusalem?"

Miller started shaking irrepressibly and buried his face in his hands. "Oh my God! It was never meant to be like that!" He began sobbing.

James looked at him, his gaze filled with revulsion. "Miller, save your regrets for later. What was CRS' role in that?"

"Same as before; we provided NTC with all the information via Nate."

"How and where exactly did you get that information?"

"NTC got it and gave it to Nate."

James loathed his next question, but he knew Carter was

watching and listening, and he would want to know. "Are Dr. Devereux and her son still alive?"

Carter had stopped breathing. Irene could feel his hope.

Miller looked up at James with tear-filled eyes and nodded. "Yes, they are," He sighed.

Carter fell to his knees; he looked up and breathed, "Thank you, God."

Irene put her hand on his shoulder and whispered, "I'm so grateful, Carter."

Sean got up and slapped him on the back, "We are going to get them out, Carter. I promise you; we are going to get them out."

James continued the questioning for another hour before Irene told him it was time for Miller to call Gordon.

James pulled Miller's cellphone out and told him what he had to do.

Miller followed his instructions to a T. It was clear that Miller's reflection on his personal work history, spanning the past seven years as CEO of CRS, had given him enough to be very anxious. He feigned his urgent need to see Nate Gordon so well that the latter dropped everything he was working on and hurried over to Miller's house.

When James got back to the observation room, he shook Carter's hand. "Mackie and Liam are alive son, and we're going to get them out."

Irene asked James to take a seat. "Jim, I now know why the mole we thought operated inside A-Echelon never triggered Rick Winslow's traps. There is no mole inside A-Echelon."

James stared at her. "How did you get to that?"

"If the mole operated from inside A-Echelon, he or she would have triggered Ricks traps. The mole is one of the people who have access to the information which you and

Hunter presented at the monthly meeting with the President."

"So you're saying, in effect, Hunter and I have been carrying the information to the mole all this time?"

Irene slowly nodded.

"Oh-my-God! What a glorious cluster-fu…" He stopped and shook his head in disbelief. "A traitor in the highest halls of power in the country."

Chapter Fifty-Four

THE THIRD LINK IN THE CHAIN

On the way to Miller's house Dylan stopped at Executive Advantage's offices to meet with and brief Rachel, one of their female operators as well as John and Sam, who were part of the team that helped capture Miller earlier.

When everyone was in place at Miller's house as planned, Dylan notified Sean. A few minutes later, Sean called back and told him that Gordon was on his way. Rick had a GPS track on him and kept them posted as Gordon approached the house.

Gordon had his hand out to ring the bell when the door opened suddenly revealing a stunning, six-foot-tall, blonde woman, in her thirties. She wore a very short skirt, exposing bare legs that went on forever, and she smiled at him.

"Hi! You must be Mr. Gordon. I'm Lucinda, Dwayne's half-sister. Please come in, he's waiting for you," She turned around and took a few steps away.

Despite Nate Gordon's fifty-seven years and the inevitable decline in libido that comes with age, he felt a rush of testosterone when he looked at Lucinda's legs as she walked away. His brain and senses had moved south as he started to follow the woman to wherever she was taking him. His eyes were 100% focused on those legs and hips, and he didn't see the man behind him. He felt a sharp sting on his neck, which shocked him out of his erotic fantasy, and gave him just enough time to grab at his neck before everything went dark around him.

Gordon squinted at the bright light and closed his eyes again. A throbbing headache made him feel nauseous; he became aware of the cold concrete floor beneath him, and he tried to look again. He was in a small room, with white walls, no windows, a small table, two chairs, and a single light high up on the ceiling. A steel door guarded the only entrance. *What? Where am I? How* - His memory came back. *Miller's house, the blonde girl, stinging pain in the neck, darkness.*

The steel door swung open, and he looked at a man he had seen before but could not remember from where or what his name was. The man walked up to him, pulled him up off the floor, pushed him into one of the chairs and took the seat on the opposite side of the table.

James Rhodes! Director of A-Echelon; I saw his face on photos.

"My name is James Rhodes; I work for the CIA."

"Don't try and bullshit me. I know who you are, and you don't work for the CIA; you're the director of A-Echelon," Gordon growled.

"Good. No further introductions necessary then," James replied impassively. "There are a few questions I'm going to ask you and I trust you will answer them quickly, as I'm in a bit of a hurry."

"Listen, Rhodes, go fuck yourself!" Gordon yelled. "You don't have a clue what you've gotten yourself into. You are going to be very, very sorry about this very soon."

"Really? Why is that?" James laughed.

Gordon glowered at him. "Do you have any idea who I am and who my friends are?"

James kept his smile. "No, clearly I don't. Those were exactly what I was going to ask you about. Do you care to tell me then?"

"What?"

"Who you and your friends are."

Gordon grinned, "You'll find out soon enough asshole. I'm not telling you anything."

James nodded slowly while he kept his gaze on Gordon. "I see. Well, that's exactly what Dwayne Miller said earlier when I spoke to him. He didn't want to tell me anything either. I sketched a scenario for him, gave him a few minutes to think about it, and when I came back, he was very keen to talk to me. He told me everything about CRS, the projects, your involvement, he even told me about your dealings with certain influential Saudi's - names, titles, the work you are doing for them, you know, that sort of thing."

The sudden twitching of Gordon's lower lip was not lost on James.

"You see Gordon, the way I understand the laws of our country; you are looking at treason, espionage, murder, and a whole truckload of other criminal charges. Now I won't tell you how much jail time you are facing, that's irrelevant because you are looking at the death penalty."

Gordon stared at James in defiance. He had his lips pressed together and it was evident he was not going to say another word.

"Gordon, I will extend you the same latitude as Miller. I'm going to grab myself a coffee and give you a few minutes to think carefully about your future," James stood and walked out.

"Jim, this one is going to be a hard nut to crack," Sean said when James walked into the observation room.

Carter was sitting quietly in a recliner chair in the corner of the room, staring at nothing. He didn't know what to feel; he was filled with joy after finally getting confirmation that Mackenzie and Liam were still alive. However, the hate he felt towards Nate Gordon was threatening to overpower him as he looked at the image of the man responsible for the abduction of his family and killing and maiming many others. Gordon probably knew where his family was but was refusing to cooperate. At times, Carter felt he could take Sean or Dylan's gun and go down to the interrogation room for a one-on-one chat with that psychopath.

James finished his coffee and returned to the interrogation room.

"Okay, Gordon. I hope you have reconsidered?"

"Listen, Rhodes, I'm getting fed-up with this shit of yours. I told you I've got nothing to say to you," Gordon snarled. "Do whatever you want to do, but just remember what I stated in the beginning; you have no idea what a tornado of shit you have gotten yourself into."

James was contemplating his options. Waterboarding, sleep deprivation, physical pain, all of those would work; no human being had ever not talked. Everyone cracks eventually; some just take longer than others, but the end result is always the same.

Although James was highly motivated to apply those methods, he also knew the shortcomings of those procedures. Most important was the fact that it was a time-consuming process and time was a luxury they didn't have. Not with seven people in their custody in Canada, New York, DC and Virginia. It was only going to be a matter of twenty-four hours or less before the family and friends of the captives would become worried, and the police would be out looking for them.

Gordon had to talk, and it had to happen quickly.

Rick walked into the observation room and handed Gordon's cell phone to Sean. "I've removed the password and copied everything off his phone. There are a few video and audio files which I think you might find enlightening."

"I'll look at it later; in the meantime, just give me the highlights," Sean replied.

"Well, it seems Gordon has a habit of recording some conversations on his phone. I guess it's some sort of insurance policy for him if things went tits up in the future. I suspect he copies and stores the information on a computer somewhere which is why the current recordings go back only two months. I'll -"

Sean held his hand up. "Okay, skip the details for now, what's on those recordings you have listened to?"

"Business conversations. I did voice matches. Of the six conversations stored on the phone, I could discern three different people, other than Gordon. All of them were business dealings. Three of the calls contain discussions about Carter's case. I -"

"Put that thing on speaker, get the volume up and play it," Irene interrupted.

Rick started fiddling with the phone, and Irene told James in his earpiece to take a break and come up to the observation room.

By the time James arrived Rick was ready and he pushed the play button.

The room went quiet as they all listened.

For many months, they had been hunting information about the location of Mackenzie and Liam. Events of the past few weeks had brought them closer to the answer. But for the past twenty-four hours, the information had been snowballing at a rapid pace, and they all sensed the periphery of the breakthrough they so desperately wanted; Carter, of course, was more anxious than anyone else.

Nevertheless, when they set out in pursuit of the information they wanted, there was nothing that could prepare them for what they would uncover along the way. Dwayne Miller's revelations that started pouring at 8:30 that morning almost knocked them off their feet. They had no idea what they were about to hear when Miller had changed his mind and started speaking.

Now, after listening to ninety minutes of the most damning of evidence they could ever have imagined, they looked at each other utterly thunderstruck. The absolute corruption and delinquency extending right up into the highest strata of the political hierarchy in America was redoubtable, nauseating, and shattering.

James spoke softly, "I think we have heard the voice of the mysterious NTC."

"Rick, please tell me you are already running your voice recognition algorithms on all those voices?" Dylan asked.

"Already in progress boss," Rick smiled, "but be aware it can take weeks, if we are very lucky, maybe four or five days."

"Mhh, not what I was hoping for; I had something like a couple of hours in mind," Dylan mumbled.

Sean Walker's face was pale with rage. When he spoke his voice was hoarse. "Okay, listen to me. I'm not asking you; I'm telling you. All of you, except Dylan, get out of this room. Now. Go and wait in the games room down the road."

"What the hell…?" James started.

"No arguments, Jim. Take everyone and leave. I'll call for you when I need you."

James suddenly realized what was going to happen. He quickly glanced at Carter, Irene, and Rick and saw they didn't know what was going on. That was good. He was not going to tell them. The less they saw and knew of what was about to happen the better.

"Come on," James said and spread his arms as if he wanted to herd them all through the door.

Outside Carter looked at James, "What just happened in there, Jim?"

"We got sent out of the room," James replied without meeting Carter's gaze.

"Why? For what purpose? We need to kick Gordon's…" Carter stopped as the realization dawned on him.

James nodded. "You don't want to know."

Irene just shook her head, remained quiet, and kept on walking. She also knew.

Sean opened the door to the interrogation room, pulled the .45 Glock 21 out his shoulder holster, and closed the door behind him.

"Now looky here!" Gordon grinned smugly relaxing arrogantly back in his chair. "Who do we have here? Let me guess. Sean Walker, CEO of Executive Advantage. I take it you are going to play the role of the bad cop."

Sean didn't say a word. He walked up to Gordon and shot him in the left knee.

Gordon tumbled to the ground and two seconds later, when the pain had registered in his brain, a scream exploded from his throat.

"Are you fuckin crazy!? Shiiiiiit!" Gordon was curled into a bundle on the floor, both hands squeezing his knee while the blood started seeping through his fingers. The inestimable pain radiating from his knee was threatening to plunge him into unconsciousness. "Fuck you to hell!"

Sean stood silently, the gun trained on Gordon, waiting for him to reach a point where he would pay attention.

Gordon stopped swearing for a moment and glimpsed at Sean.

"Who is NTC?"

"Fuck..." Gordon swallowed the rest of the sentence when he saw Sean pointing the gun at his right knee.

"Sean, please stop it," Gordon begged. "Give me some morphine; I'll tell you everything."

"You can tell me everything later. Last chance. Who is NTC?"

"George Robertson... the Vice President," He stuttered.

Sean felt how the hair on the back of his neck rose. He didn't show any emotion, he just nodded and started for the door.

"Wait! Hang on; you can't leave me like this. I'm in pain... I'm -"

Sean stopped and slowly turned around. "Gordon, sooner or later in life, we all sit down to a banquet of consequences. This is yours." He walked out and closed the door amid Gordon's shocked curses and wailing.

Back in the observation room, Dylan stared at Sean when he entered. "The Vice President? How the - what else - I mean - Sean, you and I have seen and done some pretty nasty shit... but -"

Sean nodded slowly. "Dylan Buddy, this is the grandmaster of all fuckups. The Veep is untouchable; we won't get within two miles of him. And even if we could get to him, what are we going to do? I can't just shoot him in the knee or the head can I?"

Dylan stared at the floor. "Okay here's what I suggest we

do right now. Get Rick to hack into Gordon's computers and if he can't get in, we send a team to go and collect the damn machines. We send a team to the CRS offices tonight and clear everything out before the sun comes up. It's 10:00 pm we have to get moving."

Sean nodded. "I'll call James and the rest to come back so we can share the delightful news."

When they'd all returned, James eyed the computer screen, and he sighed. Gordon was still alive although squirming on the cold and bloodied concrete floor of the interrogation room. He could see Gordon's mouth moving but couldn't hear anything; Sean or Dylan must have muted the sound.

"Sit down," Sean said. "Believe me; you will want to be seated when you hear this."

They all took their seats, their eyes moving between Sean and the computer screen showing the writhing Gordon on the concrete.

Sean cleared his throat. "Nate Gordon's top contact aka NTC is George Robertson our Vice President."

A long, stunned, silence stretched out across the room.

Irene opened her mouth, her lips formed words, but no sound came out; she closed it.

Carter stood, took two paces, turned back and dropped back in his chair.

Rick was vehemently trying to clean his glasses.

James was the first one to speak. "This is going to bring the President down. My God, it will bring the government down. It's like Mount Everest; it makes its own weather."

Carter found his voice, "I don't know much about politics, never cared much for it. But if I understand it correctly, the Vice President is the second most powerful man in the country. He is only one heartbeat away from the being President," Carter paused for breath. "This man, our Vice President, has been selling top secret information to the Saudi's and God knows who else, he's our honorable Vice President, yet he's responsible for the killing and wounding of scores of people and the abduction of my wife and six-year-old son. And," he paused, "let me guess; he is untouchable." He was shaking with fury.

"That's about the size of it, Carter," Dylan nodded.

Irene looked up and said, "Remember Carter, Judas betrayed Jesus with a kiss."

"Yes and Judas committed suicide afterward. I have my doubts that we would get so lucky with this bastard," Carter replied. "Dylan, just give me a sniper rifle; I'll go and take care of this little problem right now."

James held his hand up. "Carter, believe me, your suggestion is very appealing to me, but we need to finish Gordon's interrogation first. While I'm busy with that, Rick needs to do a voice match on those recordings. We must be beyond sure that the voice we heard indeed belongs to the Vice President."

"Dylan also suggested we raid Gordon's and CRS' computers tonight and retrieve every scrap of information we can get out hands on," Sean said.

James and Irene nodded their agreement.

"Okay Carter and everyone else, before we scatter, just spare me one more minute for a short lecture on the Constitution," James said.

They all stopped and looked at him.

"The Veep is not entirely beyond reproach. It's true the President can't fire him. To throw him out requires a majority vote of the House and a two-thirds majority vote in the Senate; in other words, a shambolic affair. On the other hand, the President can send the vice president home;

sort of place him under house arrest, although he would remain the Vice President of the United States."

"Sounds pretty befuddling to me," Carter mumbled.

"Of course, house arrest is the immediate step the President can take. There is nothing that would prevent his impeachment in the longer term."

"Let's hope he takes the hint from Judas," Carter grumbled. "I volunteer to send him a clearly marked copy of the Bible as a hint."

James and Irene gathered a few medical necessities and went down to the interrogation room. Irene bandaged Gordon's knee with a sterile dressing and gave him a shot of morphine. The morphine was just enough to numb the pain but not his senses. There was still a lot to discuss.

Gordon had plenty of time to rethink his position and enough pain to motivate him to be very keen to share everything he knew with James. By 4:00 am, about an hour before Dylan and Rick returned, James and Gordon's friendly chat had just ended.

While Gordon was talking, James had been carefully comparing his version with that of Miller's. James threw in a few curveballs just to make sure, but Gordon came through with flying colors every time; he and Miller were telling the same story.

Gordon was able to elaborate on a few facts which Miller didn't know, reconfirmed that Mackenzie and Liam were still alive but didn't know where they were kept or who the Vice President's primary contact in Saudi Arabia was.

Gordon's contact list on his phone was a goldmine of information; more than half of his contacts were politicians.

Gordon gave James the details and the nature of the involvement of every person on his contact list. Of course, not everyone on that list was corrupt; after all, not all of CRS' business activities were outside the legal boundaries.

Irene came back to the room when James indicated he was done, checked the dressings and gave him another shot of morphine which knocked him out shortly after.

Rick reported that he was able to hack into all of Gordon's computers and copy all data without having to send an ops team in to physically retrieve the equipment. While he was downloading the data from Gordon's computers, one of his team members was able to match the Vice President's voice to the voice on Gordon's cellphone. Rick also found all of the earlier recordings of Gordon's business meetings, which had been stored on his computers.

Dylan had taken a five-man team to the CRS office, and they extracted all the hard drives from the server and computers and had stacked them on the table in the observation room.

Carter, James, Irene, and Sean had time to discuss and agree on their next move.

Chapter Fifty-Five

HOW DID IT COME TO THIS?

They were bone tired; for the past 48 hours they had been functioning on very little sleep, fueling their bodies with caffeine, a few sandwiches, and adrenaline. But they all knew sleep was a luxury which they could not afford for at least another 12 hours. By their calculations, they had three hours before the CRS staff would arrive at their offices and raise the alarm. The worry was that the news might reach the Vice President. By now their captives' families would be putting pressure on the police to find their relatives, and the CanSec staff had no doubt, already raised the alarm when their boss, Stephen Byrne didn't turn up for work the day before. According to Rick, Miller's and Gordon's wives had been phoning every few hours, leaving text and voice messages when the men's cellphones kept going directly to voicemail. Their messages had started off on a good note but had grown in intensity until finally turning into extreme distress.

When the phone on William (Bill) Griffin's bedside table started ringing at 5:00 am he sighed. He was the Director of the CIA, and if that phone rang, it was urgent. If it rang that time of the day, there was a serious crisis. He was about to find out just how severe the crisis was.

"Bill, it's James Rhodes. Sorry to wake you up, but we have a crisis that can't wait. Can we meet at the farm as soon as humanly possible?"

"That serious, huh?" Bill was already out of bed and on the way to the bathroom. His wife of 45 years knew the drill and was already taking his clothes out and laying them on the bed.

"Yes, I'm afraid so," James replied.

"I'll be there in about 40 minutes. Get the coffee machine going. Oh, and make it extra strong I suspect I'm going to need it."

"You're right about that one Bill, this is the mother of all -" James ended his sentence abruptly.

It was precisely 5:43 am when Bill Griffin stood in the door of the operations room on the farm, the CIA's top-secret training facility in Virginia. The moment he entered his eyes scanned the room; he'd already met all of them. Carter once, and the rest of them were either working for him or had worked for him before. His gaze returned to Carter. *Ancient nuclear weapons – indeed, the mother of all -*

Everyone in the room stood and shook hands with the Director. When they sat down, James handed him a mug of coffee and started.

"Bill, I'm going to keep this as succinct as possible; I think after you've heard what I have to say you'll want to talk to the President."

Bill shook his head, "that bad?" *Bringing bad news to the President; what a wonderful way to start the day.*

When James completed the 15-minute narrative

covering the events of the last 48 hours, the Director glanced at everyone in the room and back to James.

"Good God, Jim! The Vice President!" Slowly he shook his head as if he refused to accept what he heard. "Do you know what's at stake here? Shit man, are you categorically resolutely sure about this?"

James nodded, pointed to the screen on the wall, and waved at Rick Winslow, "Listen to this."

Rick had prepared a few clips of the recordings extracted from Nate Gordon's computers and cellphone, as well as the records of the interrogations. He pushed the play button on his tablet and turned the sound up.

Bill didn't require any electronic equipment to identify the Vice President's voice. He spoke to the man almost on a daily basis, if not in person then on the phone. He would recognize that voice anywhere.

Rick had prepared about 30 minutes of audio and video clips, but the Director stopped him after 10 minutes, "You can stop it there. I'm calling Sam to tell him we're on our way over."

Sam's full name was Samuel Houston Grant, he and Bill had been friends since college. Bill was one of a very few people who called him Sam; everyone else called him Mr. President. As a result of their friendship, Bill was one of the very few people who could meet with the President in his private residence at the White House and based on his position as Director of CIA, he could call the President directly.

And that is what he was doing at that very moment.

"Sam, it's Bill. I know you're an early riser so I won't apologize for waking you up."

"Yes, I'm awake, Sam; have been for an hour already. What's up? I'm sure you haven't called to check on my sleeping habits. Something's wrong; I can hear it in your voice."

"Serious trouble Sam; very serious. You're going to hate this. I suggest you clear your schedule for the day, and I'm not sure, but you may want to extend that for the next few days after you're heard me out."

"When can I expect you?" The President asked with alarm in his voice.

"I'm arranging for a helicopter. I'm bringing James Rhodes, Carter Devereux, and Sean Walker with me; we'll be there in about 45 minutes," Bill replied.

"Okay, I'll get my schedule cleared before you get here," the President said and leaned back in his chair. His mind started racing. *Carter Devereux? The man whose family was killed in that terrorist attack in Jerusalem. The man who is doing research on the existence of ancient nukes. Sean Walker? Executive Advantage, they are only called in when things are about to spin out of control. Does that mean we have a nuclear crisis on our hands?*

The head of the Secret Services got a phone call from the President telling him to expect the Director of the CIA and three others. He advised his agents on-duty of the imminent visit and ordered them to escort the men to the Private Residence immediately upon their arrival.

The President rose when the door to his private study opened and the agent told him that his guests had arrived. "Show them in please."

They all shook hands and the President asked them to take seats. Bill looked at his old friend; the man was under incredible pressure just doing his job. When the President took office more than seven years ago, he'd had shiny dark hair with just a few gray hairs visible on close inspection. Now it would require close examination to find the dark hair, and his best friend was about to make sure those would vanish too.

Bill cleared his throat and gave the President the condensed version that James gave him earlier.

Samuel Houston Grant was a strong man; his first names testified to his descent from a long line of brave and illustrious men. He was a Texan, and Texans loved to quote John Gunther: *If a man's from Texas, he'll tell you. If he's not, why embarrass him by asking?*

Bill looked at the President. Usually, the man was a force of nature. He had weathered many storms and disasters in his life, the worst of them over the past seven years as the Commander in Chief. Now, though, his friend was in shock.

The President's hand was shaking as he tried to pick up the cup of coffee. He hesitated for fear of spilling it and instead brought both hands to his face, pressing his fingers to his forehead as he frowned. "George Robertson -" He breathed softly. "The Vice President of the United States of America; a traitor to his own people."

The four men staring at him felt his shock and grief.

"Sam, we'll have to move on this immediately," Bill said.

The President nodded and stood. He moved over and stopped behind his desk from where he looked at them; it was as if the word PAIN had been etched on his face in big letters.

"Carter, I am so sorry - that - that a member of my administration has caused..." He stopped and bowed his head in shame for a few seconds.

"Mr. President, please, there's no need - you didn't -"

The President waved his hand cutting Carter off while he shook his head. "It's my administration, Carter; the buck stops with me. I'm going to right this wrong to you and your family. By God, if it's the last thing I do in this office so be it. This is going to end today - even if I have to shoot the bastard myself."

He moved around the desk. "Bill, I place you in charge of this operation. I want Carter's wife and child back, alive, on American soil in 72 hours, if not earlier. If you need weapons, soldiers, warships, planes, bombers, nukes, you just say so. You understand me, Bill? Seventy-two hours, not one minute more -"

Bill interrupted him. "Sam we don't even know where they are."

"George Robertson knows, and believe you me; he is going to tell us. In fact, I suspect he will *want* to tell us."

Bill nodded silently. Sean and James felt the adrenaline pump starting up, Carter stared around the room; this was a situation he had never experienced, but he felt the intense excitement that electrified the men grab hold of him - 72 hours!

The President picked up the phone on his desk and pushed a button. "Dan," he was talking to the Chief of Staff, "please get ahold of the Secretary of State and the Secretary of Defense. Contact the Chairman of the Joint Chiefs of Staff, the Attorney General, the Secretary of Homeland Security, and the Director of the FBI, and tell them to meet me in the Situation Room in one hour. I also want you to join us."

"I take it you want us to join you as well?" Bill inquired when the President put the phone down.

"Yes, we're all going," The President replied. "Now excuse me for just another minute."

Bill and the rest stood to leave the room, thinking the President wanted them to wait outside.

"Where are you going? Sit. I want you all to hear this," he grinned.

The President picked the phone up again and pushed a button. "Please get the Vice President on the line for me right away," he said.

A minute later the phone rang, and the President answered, "George, sorry to trouble you so early, but something serious has come up. I need you to get back to DC immediately." The Vice President was in a hotel in Raleigh, North Carolina, on the campaign trail.

"Yes, George it's that serious," The President rolled his eyes. "Yes George, you could be back in Raleigh in time for your speech tonight," The President didn't voice what he really wanted to say. *That's if you still think you can be president of this country after I've had a chat with you.*

While they waited for the Chief of Staff to contact everyone summoned by the President, Bill and James continued to fill the President in on more details and played a few of the audio clips for him.

By the time everyone had gathered, and the secret service agents held the door open for the President and his entourage to enter the Situation Room, the President was still shaking a little, but not from shock anymore – it was from anger.

Everyone stood when the President arrived. He nodded for them to sit down, but he remained on his feet. He introduced James, Carter, and Sean as employees of the CIA to everyone who hadn't met them before.

After the introductions, the President got right to the point. It took him 20 minutes to lay it all out for them. He deliberately left out any mention of A-Echelon and Executive Advantage and their activities.

A profound silence followed when he came to the end.

The Attorney General had the first question, "Do we have any concrete evidence other than what these gentlemen told you?" She pointed at James, Carter, and Sean.

The President nodded at James, who opened his tablet, and started playing the sound bites.

They all listened for about five minutes before the Attorney General waved her hand and said, "That's good enough for me, sir. What do you want me to do?"

The President raised his finger slightly, "I'll tell you shortly, let's just hear if there are any other questions." He looked around the room with raised eyebrows.

"We're going in to get Dr. Devereux and her son out." That was a statement of fact, not a question, from the Chairman of the Joint Chiefs of Staff.

"Yes. And not next week or next month either. I want their feet back on American soil in 72 hours. This might very well be my last act as President, and I don't care. This atrocity happened on my watch, I'm ashamed, and I am going to rectify it."

The Chairman smiled; that's what he liked about this President. He was a man who never wavered once he had decided to take action. He never acted in haste, but once he made up his mind, he would see it through.

"No more questions?"

Everyone shook their heads. There was not much more to say, but a lot to do.

"Good. Bill Griffin is in charge of this operation. He has only one person to answer to, and that's me. Every one of you will work with him and give him what he wants when he wants it. Is that clear?" The President waited for everyone to signal their understanding and acceptance.

"Kate," he looked at the Attorney General, "you've got two hours to get ahold of an expert on the Constitution and advise me what steps I can take against the Vice President. I already know I can't fire him without the appropriate votes from Congress and the Senate, I also know I can send him home. But none of those are good enough to keep him isolated and incommunicado. We have to come up with something to keep him from contacting anyone. And if you can't arrive at a legal way to do it let me know. I - never mind. Just let me know."

The Attorney General nodded.

"Next I want you to work with the Director of the FBI. Get ahold of a judge and get a warrant to search the houses of Dwayne Miller and Nate Gordon as well as the CRS offices. Take everyone you find on those premises into custody and hold them for questioning."

Kate and the Director of the FBI nodded.

"Okay, you two are excused. Get busy and keep Bill and me posted."

When they had left, the President looked at the Secretary of Homeland Security, "I want you to change the Vice President's protection detail. Select men and women who have never worked for him before. Do I need to explain more, or do you understand what I have in mind?"

"It's crystal clear sir, no further explanation required," the Secretary grinned.

"Good. Thank you. I suggest you go and work out the new protection detail while we carry on with the meeting."

When the Secretary of Homeland Security had left, the President turned to the Marine Corps General and Chairman of the Joint Chiefs of Staff, John Crawford. "John, as soon as the Vice President tells us what we want to know, I want you to take these four men," he pointed to Bill,

James, Carter, and Sean, "and come up with a plan to extract Dr. Devereux and her son from wherever they are being held. I suggest you start thinking about who else you might need for the planning."

"Yes, sir," General Crawford replied.

Next the President turned to the Secretary of State, Joshua Bartlet. "Josh, based on the information we currently have, I'm speculating that Dr. Devereux and her son are held in Saudi Arabia. We already know that Ibrahimi El Fadl, the deputy director of the General Intelligence Presidency of Saudi Arabia is involved in this; what we don't know is who else in their government is involved. My suggestion is you start working on scenarios because there sure as hell are going to be political repercussions to deal with when this is all over."

"Yes sir, I'll get on it right away," Joshua Bartlet answered.

"The challenge for you, Josh, is that you can't talk to the Saudi's under any circumstances; none of them. For now, you treat them all as if they are suspects."

Bartlet nodded, "Understood sir, I agree." He got up and left.

Those remaining in the room with the President and his Chief of Staff were Bill, General John Crawford, Carter, James, and Sean.

The President was looking grim as was everyone else. "How did it come to this?" The President asked to no one in particular. "How did the Vice President, and if the polls are to be believed, and may God forbid, the next President of the United Sates, become so utterly corrupt and evil? And right under my nose. How did he slip through the security network? How did -" The President fell into his chair for the first time since he walked into the Situation Room.

Placing his elbows on the table, he dropped his face into his hands and mumbled a few inaudible words before looking up again.

"Sam, how do you want to handle the situation when the Vice President arrives? Do you want to have a one-on-one with him or…"

"No Bill," The President interjected, "if you leave me alone with him for longer than a minute, I'll be the first President in history to be guilty of murder. No; I'm going to bring him in here, and we are going to talk to him."

Bill nodded. "I suggest we get ourselves something to eat and drink, stretch our legs, and then discuss our strategy."

"Good idea, let's do that," The President agreed.

By the time the Vice President's plane touched down in DC, the Attorney General and the Director of the FBI were back in the Situation Room.

The Director of the FBI gave the President an update; they had obtained the warrant from the judge, sent out SWAT teams to the houses of Dwayne Miller and Nate Gordon as well as the CRS offices. Everyone found on the premises were in custody and being questioned. All files and computer equipment were confiscated, all phone lines were blocked and cellphones seized

The Attorney General was next. "Sir, I'm afraid there's not much that you can do. There are no loopholes we can exploit. All you can do is, as you have said; send him home, and in this case, home means California. But he remains the Vice President until Congress and the Senate vote to remove him. As you know, we can impeach him etcetera, but I know that's not what's required now."

"Thank you, Kate. I was ever hopeful there would be some obscure rule somewhere I could use," The President said. "Just one more question. Is there anything in the rules that prevents the Secretary of Homeland Security from assigning a new secret service protection detail to the Vice President?"

"No sir," Kate smiled as she realized what the President had in mind. "The protection of the President and Vice President is the responsibility of the Secret Service, which is part of Homeland Security. Therefore, the Secretary of Homeland Security has sole responsibility and authority."

"Thank you, Kate. I would like you and the Director of the FBI to stay for the meeting with the Vice President."

They nodded, "Yes, sir."

The President leaned over to the Chief of Staff. "Can you contact the Secretary of Homeland Security and make the necessary arrangements?"

"Sure," Dan nodded and left.

Chapter Fifty-Six

THE FINAL LINK IN THE CHAIN

The Vice President's motorcade roared to a halt, and he watched the Secret Service jumping into action. His limousine door opened, and he stepped out smiling broadly. He was taller than all of his agents except for one, and he made a mental note to have the tall agent removed from his detail.

The Vice President was his usual aloof self when he and his Secret Service protection detail walked into the White House. He didn't pay much attention to anyone or anything around him. His mind was focused on the election and the polls which showed he had a very comfortable 25% lead over his nearest rival.

Just a few more months and I will be known as Mr. President around here, he thought smugly to himself. He was escorted to the Situation Room and when he entered and saw the people already gathered there he was a bit confused. *This is a strange collection of people.* He knew all the senior officials; he just didn't know what business they had in a meeting about national security, which is what he expected the meeting to be about. He paused again when he recognized Carter,

James, and Sean Walker and for a second thought about their presence.

"Have a seat, George," The President said curtly pointing to the vacant chair next to Sean.

The fact that the President didn't welcome him was lost on the Vice President, whose mind was still in campaign mode. He sat, placing his briefcase on the floor next to him, and then looked at the President.

"George, there is no easy way to say this. I will try and keep it as brief and as civilized as possible," The President started.

The Vice President detected the distress in the President's voice and sat up.

"What's up?" he asked feigning concern.

"Early this morning these four men," the President pointed to Bill, James, Carter, and Sean, "turned up on my doorstep and shared some very upsetting information with me. They told me that you have been leaking top secret information to the Saudis."

"And you believed them?" Robertson snapped.

"George, my suggestion is that you say as little as humanly possible. I don't know why I'm even giving you good advice. So please remain quiet and listen carefully."

Robertson didn't reply; he pressed his lips together and stared at the table.

"I've been listening to a few short audio clips of your meetings with Nate Gordon, one of the directors of Competitive Response Solutions. I'm told there are many more audio clips that I haven't heard yet, all with your voice on them George.

I have also been given a verbal summary of Gordon's testimony as well as the testimony of Dwayne Miller, the CEO of Competitive Response Solutions.

George, the evidence against you is not only overwhelming; it is damning.

Robertson was shocked at the amount of information that had been discovered, but he wasn't going to let that stop him. *I've got to get out of here and do some heavy damage control, quickly.*

"Stop! I don't have to listen to this madness! You may think you have something on me, but you don't know jack shit about anything. Even if you think you've got proof, there's next to nothing you can do about it. I'd think very carefully if I were you, Sam before you go any further."

"Shut up, George, and listen!"

"Have you lost your mind? I'm the Vice President; I don't even work for you. You can't order me to do a damn thing. You can't touch me, and you know it. If I am accused of something Sam, you know what you have to do." He grabbed his briefcase and got up. "Excuse me; I'm out of here."

When Robertson turned toward the door, he found Sean standing in front of him; he had just enough time to catch a glimpse of Sean's eyes before he felt the fingers of Sean's right hand tightening around his throat.

Sean leaned close to him and whispered very softly, "Sit down asshole, the President of the United Sates is talking to you. And please don't interrupt him again, it's very rude."

The look in Sean's eyes and the inability to breath had a very persuasive effect on Robertson and he sunk back into his chair.

"I'm glad you've decided to stay George," The President continued as if nothing had happened. "As I was saying, the evidence against you is damning, it's atrocious, to say the least. You are responsible for the killing of 23 people, the wounding of 60 more, and the abduction of Dr. Devereux and her six-year-old son. And that, George, is only what we have discovered the last 48 hours. I'm sure we will find a great deal more."

"You can't tie any of that to me."

"On the contrary, we already have. You, Mr. Vice President of the United States, have blood on your hands; the blood of innocent people."

"Fuck you, Samuel Grant! I…"

Sean grabbed Robertson's wrist and gave it a sharp, painful, twist and leaned closer to him whispering, "I told you to mind your manners. I suggest you now shut the fuck up, or I will break your wrist to start with."

Robertson glared at Sean but went quiet again.

The President continued, "George, I can keep on going but I guess this will all come out during your treason and murder trial, so I'm not going to waste any more time on it. I have a few questions for you, and then we will discuss your political future."

Robertson didn't reply.

"First question; who are your contacts in Saudi Arabia?"

"Go fuck yourself," Robertson replied.

A snap was heard in the room, followed by a yell of anguish, "You Son of a Bitch! I'll have you up on assault charges."

"I did warn you, asshole," Sean said, "next time I suggest you listen."

"Second question; where are Dr. Devereux and her son being held?"

Robertson looked defiantly at The President, tightened his jaw, and shook his head. "You have no idea who you are dealing with," he said through clenched teeth.

Sean got up and swung Robertson's chair so that he

faced him and leaned toward him. "No; it is *you* that has no idea who you are dealing with," he said menacingly.

Robertson tried to take a swing at Sean, but he saw it coming a mile away, swiped the striking arm away and hit Robertson in the solar plexus. The next thing Robertson knew he found himself lying on the ground clutching his stomach and dry retching.

Everyone in the situation room froze, and then looked to The President. He sat motionless, staring at the table in front of him as if nothing was happening. The rest of the people looked at each other, shrugged, and followed the President's cue; they stared at the table in front of them in silent agreement - let Sean handle the situation as he saw fit.

"Where are they, George?" The President asked again when Robertson stopped groaning.

"Didn't you hear about the bombing in Jerusalem? They're dead."

That was too much for Carter. There was a blur of motion as Carter jumped up and moved around the table toward Robertson. "Where are they?" he yelled.

James sprang after Carter, grabbing hold of his arm to intervene before he got his hands on the man responsible for the devastating events in his recent life.

"Easy, Carter," Sean said as he and James pulled him back from the man writhing on the floor.

Carter's eyes were wild. "He knows where they are. I'll beat it out of him even if I have to kill him in the process," he said struggling to get at the Veep. "I'll kill him," he hissed.

"Attention, soldier," Sean commanded. Carter stopped struggling and looked at him, then nodded his head as he relaxed, indicating he had himself under control again.

Turning back to Robertson, Sean pulled him off the

floor and twisted his left arm behind his back. "Where are Mackenzie and Liam?"

Robertson shook his head.

Sean jerked Robertson's arm up toward the back of his head in a quick move, and a sickening, dull, snap was heard as the shoulder dislocated.

Robertson screamed, "Mecca! They're in Mecca! Oh my God! Stop! Please Stop!"

As soon as Sean released his arm Robertson sank to the floor writhing again, swearing into the carpet, but this time, it wasn't directed at anyone, it was from pain.

Once Robertson had settled down, Sean helped him off the floor and pushed him into his seat. "Start talking. Be clear. Don't hold anything back. Or I will do the same to your other arm and then your knees."

Robertson's mind searched briefly for a way out, an escape, anything, but there was nothing; all that remained was the tornado of fear and pain raging in the deserted hallways of his mind. He hung his head in defeat and sighed as he felt his future slip out of his hands, never to be regained. "What do you want to know?" the broken man asked softly.

"Who are your contacts in Saudi Arabia?" The President asked again, "and where exactly are Dr. Devereux and her son?"

Robertson looked up at the ceiling and started talking, his voice trembling and croaky. "The top person and most important contact is Xavier Algosaibi," He breathed. "Dr. Devereux and her son are being held at the Institute of Scientific Research and Development, located about six miles south of Mecca, in the Jabal Thawr Mountains."

"Who else in my administration is involved in this cabal of yours?"

"No one else in your administration is involved. I'm the only one."

The President swallowed, took a deep breath, and asked, "Why George?"

Robertson slowly shook his head. "You will never understand, Sam. You've never lived in the Middle East as I did. You don't understand them the way I do. You and everyone else - ah, just forget about it - it doesn't matter anymore – "

The President nodded. "I'm not sure I want to know. Now listen carefully. Here is how we're going to untangle this mess. You are going to have an incapacitating stroke in the next hour; you will be placed in intensive care at a secured facility, and your campaign will be suspended immediately. Once Dr. Devereux and her son are safely back in America, your condition will improve slightly, and you will resign immediately. Any questions?"

"What happens after that?"

"I have no idea George," The President shrugged. "I suggest you get yourself a good lawyer, one way or another you'll make history, but I'm sure it's not going to be something to be proud of."

Chapter Fifty-Seven

TELL ME THAT! WHERE IS HE?

Mackenzie turned over in her narrow bunk and pulled the blanket over her head.

Not another day. Please God, not another day; I've had enough.

She curled tighter and tried to go back to sleep, but she knew that once she was awake it wouldn't happen. It was only sheer exhaustion that allowed her some respite nowadays.

Her breasts were overflowing with milk and in minutes, she would have to get up to change and feed Beth.

Do you know God; if it weren't for my children I'd have joined You months ago? I don't know how to go on; only they are keeping me alive now. Carter doesn't know we are alive; I know he doesn't, God; if he did he'd be here by now.

She turned over and pulled the blanket tighter trying to shut out her awareness of the impending day. *How is it that I was blessed with a brain and the ability to use it, just to end up in this dump of a place working for the enemy?*

Suddenly, tears rolled onto her pillow; it was a common happening lately. *God, are you really there? Sometimes I wonder if you are. Maybe this truly is a God forsaken place.* She turned over again and sat up, giving up the fight for further sleep. *It never happens anyway; I can only sleep when I'm too tired to keep my eyes open.*

She sighed, as Seema appeared in the doorway, the doorway that could not be locked for privacy. There was nowhere she could find to be truly alone, not ever. "Oh for God's sake, go away and leave me alone," she muttered quietly.

Beth made a small sound, and it was with relief that Mackenzie was able to turn to her instead of having to face Seema. Even Seema, who had really tried to relieve Mackenzie's plight, was not welcome today. Mackenzie wanted to be alone to do nothing; she wanted just to sit, stare into space, and be.

That'll never happen again. She thought to herself as she lifted the baby, changed her, and then opened the front of her nightgown to feed her.

Liam appeared in the doorway from his small cubicle next door; he was sleepy and pale, her heart reached out to him. *Poor little boy, where's his father, God? Tell me that! Where is he? Liam needs him; I'm not enough on my own, and how often do we get to spend time together anymore anyway?*

Beth nuzzled her, and the tiny starfish hands reached out to pummel at her breast; her heart melted with the love she felt for the little girl. *Look at her God; she's beautiful, how can You allow us to be trapped here forever? She needs the sun too."* Grief swept over her, almost overwhelming her, grief at all she'd lost; the grief that she'd never be able to give the children what they both so desperately needed, sunshine, fresh air and a proper home – Freydis.

"Mom?"

"Hmm?"

"Can I stay with you and Beth today?"

She looked at him and pulled him close with her free arm, snuggling him beside her on the bed, "Are you not well darling?"

"Oh I'm well; I just want to be with you and Beth."

She nodded, "I know the feeling. Many times I just want to be with you two; just us, maybe sitting on a beach somewhere looking at the water. Do you remember that day we all went to the beach?"

He nodded, "and we swam in the ocean, and found shells." He smiled at the recollection.

She looked at his face and sent up a prayer. *Please, God, can we swim in the ocean again? Just once more before something awful happens, and I never see them again.*

She checked her tears; Liam had seen too many of them. They had cried together often. "We'll do it again one day, I'm sure."

How I wish I believed that, I don't anymore. One day Liam will go to a family to be raised as a good Muslim, and Beth will be taken from me. When that day dawns I will die; I won't continue to live. I will find a way to go to sleep forever.

Once Beth was sated, Mackenzie began to prepare for the inevitable day ahead of her. The effort it took was exhausting. Just having a shower plunged her into fresh despair. *I want to stand in the pouring rain, not his dribble of misery.* Dressing all in black, hiding her face, walking along the gray corridors to the laboratory, and facing the Three Stooges yet again was mind-deadening. *Once the children don't need me anymore, I'm out of here. I won't die here at their hands; I'll do it myself. It's no good waiting for Carter; he's never going to come.* A cold wave of anger swept over her; she felt rejected by him, discarded and of no significance in his life. *Surely if Loki and*

Keeva know I'm here, he'd have some inkling I was alive she reasoned.

Settling down at her workstation, she saw Liu arrive minutes later. She and Liu were keeping each other sane, each of them knowing they shared this awful life together. She smiled up at her. Even though she knew Liu couldn't see her smile, and she couldn't see Liu's, she knew she returned it.

Just recently Nasser had agreed to let the baby stay with her through the day instead of leaving her in someone else's care. Beth needed feeding, and as Mackenzie was breastfeeding, it required her to leave her work and make her way back to another part of the compound to attend to Beth. In the end, between Mackie's distress over the baby being with someone else, and the time she had to take away from her work to go the baby, feed it, and return, he agreed it was better for the child to be with her so she could feed her as she worked.

He'd even arranged for a screen to be brought so she could feed Beth in privacy, away from the Three Stooges.

Work was slow, each section of the books they were transcribing was carefully studied and if something seemed possibly related to respirocytes it had to be tried and tested by the Stooges before it could be discarded as useless for their project.

Sometimes there was hope, and even the Stooges became excited. Those were the times that for a short while Mackenzie became inspired again, but then failure once more plunged her back into depression and despair.

Liu still occasionally set up messages to chat with her using the language they were becoming so familiar with. Those times went a long way to cheer them both, as they would seek out happy memories in their lives and put words up on the screen to recall them.

Sometimes Liu started it, other times Mackenzie did. Words like 'rose' or 'wind' would elicit a response from the other who would write, 'red and perfumed', or 'wild and wet.' It worked for a time, and they kept it going to save their sanity.

Once, Mackenzie asked Liu in their message chat, "What do you think will happen to us?"

"We will succeed in this and become famous," Liu had replied.

The idea was so ludicrous Mackenzie almost burst out with a hoot of laughter, but quickly quenched it.

Now Liu's answer had changed, "I wish I knew Mackie, I can't think anymore."

At the end of another long, drawn out, exhausting day of failure, with Nasser becoming increasingly desperate for success, the two women were returned to their rooms, not allowed to see each other again until the next day. There were no evenings of gentle talk and peaceful relaxation, just another night of tossing and turning and dreading the future; a future which Mackie was trying hard to accept would be without Carter, without Freydis, without her wolves, without everything she'd ever loved.

Only the children kept her alive and trying.

Chapter Fifty-Eight

THE WOLVES OF FREYDIS

Shortly after the Vice President was wheeled out of the White House strapped to a gurney, with an oxygen mask over his face and an IV drip attached to the back of his hand, preparations for the extraction of Mackenzie and Liam got underway. There was one immediate hurdle; Carter's and James' insistence on being part of the mission.

Understandably Director Bill Griffin and General John Crawford, Chairman of the Joint Chiefs of Staff, had serious misgivings about including the two men. None of their arguments and threats could persuade Carter and James to change their minds. And the fact that Sean backed the two of them, because he made the promise long ago, left Bill and the General with no choice but to escalate the matter to the President.

The President called them all in with the intention of putting a swift end to the standoff by reading them the riot act. However, he soon found out that not even the President of the United Sates could talk Carter and James out of it.

Sean still backed them and finally swayed the President

when he said, "Sir I have no hesitation about taking them along. These two can take care of themselves and then some."

The President threw his hands up in surrender. "Okay you can go, one condition, though; I want your word that you won't do anything stupid like getting yourself killed." And with that, the matter was settled, and they started the preparations for Operation Freydis; the name proposed by the President.

Sean contacted Dylan, requesting he join them and bring with him all the information collected by Abbadi Haijar and Rayan Qureshi, the former Desert Phantoms. James had a quick catch-up briefing with Irene to relay the outcome of the meeting with Vice President and to hand the reigns of A-Echelon over to her while he was busy with the mission.

Bill made arrangements for a few spy satellites, already conducting surveillance in the region, to focus their attention on the Institute of Scientific Research and Development.

They considered the option of covertly inserting the extraction team into one of the five US airbases in Saudi Arabia and launching the operation from there. However, they quickly abandoned the idea because of the distance from the airbases to Mecca.

After a few more hours of deliberation, they settled on a plan to insert the extraction team from one of the Navy's amphibious ships that were part of the fleet of warships in the Gulf of Aden and the Red Sea. General Crawford immediately ordered one of the dock landing ships, carrying a contingent of US Marines, to set course for a point south of Jeddah, about 60 miles from the location of the Institute of Scientific Research and Development.

The ship was equipped with a flight deck from where an MV-22 Osprey could be launched. The Osprey was a hybrid between a helicopter and a high-speed turboprop aircraft. It was capable of carrying 24 combat soldiers with their equipment in addition to the four crew members. The Osprey was a versatile piece of war equipment capable of vertical takeoff and landing (VTOL), and short takeoff and landing (STOL) like a helicopter and could reach flight speeds in excess of 300 miles per hour.

That was the easy part of the planning.

The devil was in the detail, and they didn't have enough of that. Abbadi and Rayan's reconnaissance efforts certainly provided valuable information, but there was still so much more they needed before they would be able to plan the finer details of the operation.

Sean and Dylan were the experts on these types of missions, and once they started listing the gaps, everyone realized that the 72-hour deadline imposed by the President was not realistic.

"Sam, there are no promises in battle," Bill said to the President, "when men are engaged in mortal combat with bullets flying around, bad shit is inevitably going to happen. All I want to do is to prevent stupid shit from happening at the same time."

The President, Bill, James, and General Crawford were all old enough to remember the disastrous Operation Eagle Claw, ordered by President Jimmy Carter in 1980. It was an attempt to end the Iran hostage crisis by rescuing 52 embassy staff held prisoner at the United States Embassy in Tehran. The mission ended in failure on April 24, 1980; nine people were dead, eight American service members and one Iranian civilian. A helicopter and other expensive military equipment had been lost. The President was humiliated in the ensuing public debacle, and America lost prestige worldwide.

The President demonstrated his leadership prowess and wisdom by moderating his 72-hour demand. "I agree Bill; that's why I put you in charge. When you tell me we are ready, then I'll accept we are ready. Just please, see that you don't take a moment longer than absolutely necessary."

"Thanks, Sam. It will take the pressure off us and allow us to avoid making asinine mistakes in our rush to meet a deadline."

Once the battleship was in place off the coast from Jeddah, spy drones fitted with infrared cameras, thermal vision, and Ground Penetrating Radar would be launched to gather the much-needed Intel.

The floor plans provided by Abbadi and Rayan had to be verified and updated where changes had been made to the structure since its construction seven years ago. The drones and spy satellites would help to identify the living quarters, workspaces, and the number of people on the inside at various times of the day.

The two-man Dessert Phantom team was reinforced by two locals who were undercover Mossad agents to help them map out the facility's power supply, security system, and routine.

On the second day after the planning started, Sean and Dylan had selected two six-man teams from their special operators and started preparations. Sean would lead one team, which would include Carter, and Dylan would lead the other that would include James. A scale model of the ISRD was constructed, and the teams got busy practicing the drills.

As information became available, the plans were fine-tuned. The approach, the landing, the attack, extraction of the hostages, assembly points, fallback positions, the evacuation, and what-if scenarios were stepped through and practiced incessantly. To the surprise of the seasoned Special Forces operatives, the two "old-timers" as they wittily called James and Carter, matched them in endurance and ability every step of the way.

Carter was the king of hand-to-hand combat; the youngsters loathed a sparring session with him.

Seven days after Bill Griffin led Carter, James, and Sean into the President's private study and gave him the shocking news, the Wolves of Freydis, as James had baptized the group, had all the information they needed. Sean and Dylan invited Bill and the General for an inspection and assessment of the teams, and to get the nod from them.

On the night of the eighth day, Carter stood in the hangar from where they would depart on their mission, waiting for the President to arrive. He looked at the men around him and a lump rose in his throat when he remembered his grandfather Will's words from years ago. *"You take a bunch of guys from all over the country with diverse socio-economic backgrounds, toss them together in the same bunkhouse, let them suffer together, and out comes a fighting force which will crawl through the depths of hell for each other."*

President Grant arrived. He didn't make a speech; it wasn't necessary to convince or motivate anyone. Instead, he started at the left end of the line of men, stopped and shook hands with every man, calling each one by his first name and making a short conversation with him. Bill had provided him with their photos and names, and he had memorized it.

Carter was the last man in the line; James was second to last.

When the President got to them, he took a step back,

looked them up and down, and then threw a quick glance at Bill, who was standing next to him. "The two old-timers I presume?" The President chuckled, stepped forward, shook their hands, and gave them each a hug.

He walked back to the middle of the line and moved a few steps back so that he could see them all. He thought of Winston Churchill's words; *'We sleep soundly in our beds because rough men stand ready in the night to visit violence on those who would do us harm.'*

I am proud to know these men that Winston Churchill spoke of. "May God bless you and protect you." The President saluted the men and walked away.

Nothing more had to be said.

Chapter Fifty-Nine

POINT AND FIRE

Receiving 15 million visitors a year required unusual security measures for a city the size of Mecca. During the Hajj, the annual Islamic pilgrimage to Mecca, an obligatory duty to be fulfilled at least once in a lifetime by all adult Muslims who were physically and financially capable of doing so, security personnel would increase to more than 100,000. Even in the quiet times, Mecca had 14,000 operational police officers and more than 10,000 security cameras.

Ten-foot-high fences topped with rolls of concertina razor wire surrounded the compound where the ISRD was located. Four guards were stationed outside, two in a guardhouse at the main entrance, while the other two patrolled the perimeter. The entrance to the main building was also secured with guards, and more were stationed on each of the six floors above them.

The concealed entry to the underground section of the complex was located about 300 yards away in a parking garage. People who worked below ground had to use a special swipe card to access a hidden lift that would drop them many feet below street level.

When they reached the basement, and before they could enter the passage leading to the ISRD underground facility, it was necessary for them to go through a high-level security check. This included a full body scan for metal detection, as well as a scan of any peripherals such as briefcases, handbags, shoes etcetera.

They then had to present their ID cards, and enter their names and signatures into the security logbook, before the guards would let them through. There were no guards on the underground levels.

There was a surfeit of surveillance cameras in operation on the outside of the building as well as every floor above and below ground.

Another challenge they had was that one of Saudi Arabia's largest naval bases, the King Faisal Naval Base, was at Jeddah right on the doorstep of where they were going to execute their mission.

General Crawford had always maintained good relations with his counterpart, the Chief of Staff of the Royal Saudi Armed Forces, Lt. General Omar ibn Saleh El-Hashem. And that was who he called to inform about the intention of the US Naval Forces in the Gulf of Aden and the Red Sea to conduct various training exercises over the course of the next two weeks. That meant the Saudis could expect to see a lot of warships maneuvering and aircraft flying around, but there would be nothing for them to be alarmed about. As in the USA where the President was the Commander-in-Chief of the armed forces, in Saudi Arabia, it was King Al Saud, who was the Commander-in-Chief of the armed forces.

The Secretary of State, Joshua Bartlet, had decided to

go on an unscheduled and unpublished surprise visit to a few of the most strategic US Military Bases in the Middle East. His last visit would be to the Riyadh Air Force Base in the Saudi capital; one of the most important American Military bases due to its proximity to the Middle Eastern hotspots of conflict.

The final constraint was of an international relationship nature. All the information they had pointed to the fact that the King of Saudi Arabia and his government were not part of the conspiracy. The facility the extraction team was planning to invade was no doubt going to be staffed by many innocent people who would have no idea who they were working for, much less about the evil plans they had unsuspectingly been contributing to. For those reasons, the extraction teams were under strict orders to use minimum force and to kill only when their lives were in danger. In other words, they could not ride into town with guns blazing.

The less damage to life and limb they caused during the execution of the mission, the better the President's chances were of maintaining good relations with the Saudis.

For a few of the men, including Carter, James and the two computer sages, the ride in the MV-22 Osprey was a first. Carter and James found it spine-tingling. Rick and his friend hated it. Rick was heard mumbling something to the effect that, *"A plane makes sense because it adheres to the laws of physics, but a helicopter doesn't make any sense whatsoever, it just beats the laws of physics into submission. And this $71 million flying sarcophagus is an attempt at combining those two things."*

Despite Rick's misgivings, shortly after midnight, the 14

members of the Wolves of Freydis and their equipment were delivered safely onto the deck of the US Navy's amphibious ship about 15 miles off the coast of Jeddah.

Carter stood next to his equipment, staring towards the east; he didn't notice James and Sean standing next to him when he said, "Mackie, Liam, we're here, less than 70 miles away from you; just hang in there for another 24 hours. I promise I'm coming to get you."

Sean put his hand on Carter's shoulder and said, "She can count on it, Carter."

The men packed their equipment in their quarters and joined the commanding officer in the mess for something to eat and drink. About an hour later, the commander introduced Sean, Dylan, James, Carter and Rick to the intelligence officer on board and left. The rest of the Wolves went to their bunks to sleep.

The six of them looked at the latest intel gathered by the drones and the forward team, consisting of the two Dessert Phantoms and two CIA assets. Their preferred plan was for Rick and Samantha to hack into the ISRD's computer network and electronic security system and take control of it. Once that was accomplished, they would eliminate the guards and evacuate Mackenzie and Liam.

If Rick failed to break into their computer and security systems, they would have to land the team a few miles away from the Institute and approach in vehicles. Doing it that way meant they would have very little opportunity to get into the place by stealth and almost certainly meant they were going to be engaged in a heavy firefight.

There were 14 armed guards; not an insurmountable number for 12 Special Forces operators with the element of surprise on their side.

Rick and Samantha had 18 hours to break into the

Institute's electronic systems. If that proved to be impossible, Plan B would kick into operation.

The drones were recalled to the ship, where Rick and Samantha upgraded the onboard firmware, and software then re-launched them.

When the drones were returned to their surveillance positions over the Institute three hours later, they started collecting and sending information about the Wi-Fi routers. It took Rick and Samantha less than an hour from the time they received the first data from the drones to break into the Institute's computer network. From then on it was as Rick loved to say, "Once you know where to look and which buttons to press its smooth sailing."

By 7:00 am the next morning Rick was smiling from ear to ear when he joined Sean, Dylan, Carter and James at the breakfast table, and told them Plan A was on. He and Samantha had collected every bit of information they needed, wiped out their electronic tracks, and were ready to go into the system again that night.

They had a little less than 17 hours to H-hour, the military terminology for the time of day at which a significant event such as an attack, landing, or any other military operation is scheduled to begin.

H-hour was 00:05 when a white twin-cab Toyota Hilux pulled up and parked on the side of the road near the main entrance to the ISRD. Two men, Abbadi Haijar, and Rayan Qureshi, dressed in the uniforms of SASS – Saudi Arabia Security Solutions, the security company contracted by ISRD, got out and approached their two 'colleagues' on duty in the guardhouse.

SASS was a big company with well over 300 staff working in different locations and shifts around Mecca, and they didn't all knew each other. To the two men in the guardhouse, seeing uniforms identical to their own was enough; they didn't suspect anything.

The two visitors introduced themselves and explained that they got lost on the way to a site that they had to attend because of an alarm that went off.

Abbadi got the attention of the two men when he pulled out his cellphone, displaying a map, and asked them to show him on the map where they were now and where they should go.

Rayan took a step back so that the two could stand beside Abbadi. With their backs turned to him and their attention on Abbadi's cellphone screen they didn't see Rayan pulling the two hypodermics from his jacket pocket. They almost didn't feel the slight sting when the needles entered into the muscle at the base of their necks.

While, Rayan pulled the unconscious guards into the bathroom at the back of the room, tied, and gagged them, Abbadi went outside and called the two roaming guards to come to guardhouse saying there was an urgent message for them from headquarters.

70 miles away on the warship, the Wolves of Freydis were all strapped into their seats inside the two Sikorsky MH-60 Seahawk helicopters, ready for takeoff the moment they got word from Abbadi and Rayan.

Rick and Samantha would remain on the ship from where they would conduct the electronic invasion of ISRD. For the Seahawks, it was a 25-minute flight from the ship to their destination.

The extraction team would have 20 minutes from the time they landed to eliminate the remaining guards, extract the hostages and be airborne again; any longer than that would place them at risk of having to deal with Saudi reinforcements and their police.

In Washington, DC, 6,600 miles away, the President, Gen Crawford, the Chief of Staff, Bill Griffin, and Irene O'Connell were watching from a small conference room adjoining the main conference room referred to as the Situation Room. They had direct audio and visual connections with the two team leaders, Sean, and Dylan, through a live feed from a drone flying overhead.

The men in the Seahawks were all quiet; the noise from the engines and rotors made it nearly impossible to carry on a conversation anyway. Sean looked around, assessing each of his men, noting their alert high tensile awareness.

Henry Louis "H. L." Mencken, a German-American journalist, satirist, cultural critic and scholar of American English once said, *"What men will fight for seems to be worth looking into."*

Through the ages military commanders had sought to understand man's psychology in battle and how to stimulate combat motivation. The ability of a group of combatants to recognize and defy danger, group bonding in times of anxiety, the focus to achieve a single objective, selfless dedication, the ability to overcome the innate survival instinct and willingness to die for others, were important survival traits and basic human nature.

Carter was seated next to Sean. It wasn't hard for Sean, a veteran warrior, to know exactly how he was feeling. After so many years and so many missions, he still felt as if it were the first time, and that was good; a complacent soldier was a dead soldier.

He noticed the telltale signs of anxiety on Carter's face, leaned over and said, "make sure you stay close to me, exactly as we have done during training and everything is going to be okay."

Carter gave him a nervous smile and a thumb up.

If asked, Carter would have been hard put to describe his feelings. Certainly he was tense about the mission - his first mission, but it was far more than that. It was Mackie and Liam, the thought of seeing them again after so long. He was excited, but what if she wasn't there after all? There was a dreadful mix of anticipation and terror. How would he feel, how would he cope if it turned out they'd made a mistake? What if she were somewhere else instead? After all, they had not been able to confirm she was there; they were relying on the word of a crooked Vice President; was he lying?

It was 00:09 when Rayan's voice came over loud and clear in Sean's earpiece. "Loki, Quebec, do you read me? Over."

"Quebec, Loki, loud and clear. Over"

"Loki, Quebec, Ahote, I repeat Ahote. Over."

"Quebec, Loki, Ahote confirmed. Out"

'Ahote' was the signal to confirm that the four guards on the outside of the ISRD were out of action and had been replaced by the two Dessert Phantoms and two CIA assets parading as SASS security guards.

Sean pushed the button on his throat mic. "Okay ladies, we're a go. I repeat, we're a go."

Twenty-five minutes later Sean and his team of black-cladded men fast-roped from the Seahawk onto the roof of the parking garage where the secret entry to the underground section of the ISRD complex was located. At the same time, 300 yards away, Dylan and his team of black-cladded men fast-roped out of the second Seahawk onto the roof of the ISRD building.

Rick and Samantha had taken control of security cameras ten minutes before the landing and were streaming 30-minute old video to the screens of the security guards inside the buildings. The two of them were now watching their computer monitors and listening for the signals from Sean and Dylan to flip the switches on the power supply and disable the alarm system.

The noise created by the helicopters was a big worry. They expected the security guards might want to come outside to see the helicopters and might notice the men coming down on the fast ropes. To take care of such an eventuality the two 'new guards' on roaming duty would position themselves at the front of the building close to the entry to take care of the problem.

The Seahawks hovered over the buildings for less than 20 seconds before continuing their journey east for a few miles, and then they would start circling.

Sean and Dylan were the first men of their teams to land. They ran to the entry doors on the top of their respective buildings shoved an electronic card, connected by a thin wire to a small handheld metal box, into the card reader slot next to the door, and waited. The rest of the team took defensive positions in a circular pattern around the door.

One of Dylan's men took position at the end of the roof looking down at the main entry. Shortly after, he saw the two security guards from the lobby walk out of the building and look up at the helicopters. One of them pointed at the helicopter directly above and said, "Those aren't ours, they're American.

He spoke into his throat mic, "Keeva, Jay, two spectators. Over."

Sean replied, "Give them ten secs, then take care of it. Out."

Jay raised his sniper rifle and got the first guard in his sights; he took a deep breath, let half of it out slowly and had started curling his finger around the trigger when he heard two faint plop sounds that almost sounded like one and saw both men drop to the ground. He looked up through the telescope and saw the two Phantoms, Abbadi, and Rayan, rising out of the shadows of the shrubs next to the front wall.

The minute it took for the algorithm to find the entry code, which would unlock the doors felt like an eternity.

"Keeva, Loki, do you read me? Over"

"Loki, Keeva, loud and clear. We're in. Over."

"Keeva, Loki, so are we. See you soon. Out."

Sean spoke into his throat mic again, "Romeo-Sierra, it's Loki, lights, I repeat lights."

Rick replied, "Keeva, it's Romeo, lights confirmed, I repeat lights confirmed."

Samantha pushed the button and a few seconds later the entire ISRD complex was engulfed in total darkness.

The team members lowered their balaclavas over their faces, night vision goggles over their eyes, and followed Sean and Dylan in single file down the stairs inside the buildings.

As Dylan and his team crept down the stairs of the main building, he posted a man on each level that gave entry to that particular hallway. He was going to take the ground floor where they knew a small hidden lift and stairs that led down to the subterranean levels.

When Abbadi and Rayan had stashed the bodies of the dead security guards in the shrubs, they went straight to the main electrical switchboard, which was located on the wall behind the security desk. They opened the box unscrewed the faceplate and cut all the wires. When the backup generator kicked in, no power would reach the building.

Sean and his men had reached the ground floor of the parking garage and went to the lift allocated to the ISRD staff. Sean again used Rick's magic door opener, and when the door slid aside, he poked his head in and listened carefully.

The two security guards controlling access to the tunnel leading to the underground facility were just one floor down, and according to the floor plans and body heat images from the drones, they were facing the lift doors.

Sean signaled Carter to follow him and to the rest of his men to stay down in their positions and then entered the lift. When he and Carter were inside, and the door started closing he whispered to Carter, "You cover everything from the center to the left, and I'll cover the right. When the door opens, and you see anyone going for a gun you shoot and keep on shooting until I tell you to stop."

Carter nodded, swallowed, and raised the silenced .45 Glock 21. He could feel the sweat on his face under the balaclava. Somehow he felt calm, almost relaxed; he didn't know how it was possible; he'd never fired a shot at another human being, but for the past seven months that was what he had trained to do.

For weeks, he'd been drilled endlessly in point shooting - a technique that required total focus on the target, not the sights of the weapon.

"Don't aim; there's no time, point and fire. It's that spilt-second that determines who remains standing afterward. Point and shoot, point and shoot. Don't think, just point and shoot." His instructors had drilled that into him – first with dry shots, then with a laser gun, and finally with real ammo.

"Don't aim. Orientate your body, then point and shoot; your body will do the aiming for you, just point and shoot."

The door opened, and everything went into slow motion for Carter, three yards away, slightly to his left was a man in uniform looking right at him, the man's eyes flared wide, a fleeting second of shock, before his right hand that held a gun started raising.

Carter felt the gun recoil in his hands twice; blood spattered against the wall behind the man, and Carter saw him and his chair flip over. He scanned further to his left, nothing, pointed back at the man and the chair and started shooting again.

"Stop!"

He looked to his right; Sean had his finger up. In front of Sean, three yards away was another splash of blood against the wall, and a man sprawled on top of a fallen chair on the floor.

"Cover the tunnel; I'll let the men know to come down."

Carter nodded. He couldn't get a word out. He turned to his left, holstered the pistol and slipped the Mossberg 590 Combat Pump-Action Shotgun from his shoulder and trained it on the entry to the tunnel, seven paces away.

Sean spoke into the throat mic, "Joe, Keeva, coast is clear. Quebec and Hotel in place? Over."

"Keeva, Joe, affirmative. We're on our way. Out."

Quebec and Hotel were the Phantoms. After they had cut the electrical cables, they ran over to the parking garage, entered through a side door, and joined the rest of Sean's team on the ground floor. They had to guard that entry while Sean and his men went through the tunnel to the underground levels of the ISRD.

Dylan had each floor covered. He was on the ground floor. He spoke into his throat mic, "Keeva team, confirm."

One by one the men on each floor replied they were ready. They had removed their night vision goggles as they were expecting people with flashlights, candles and even mobile phone lights in the hallways and rooms which would blind them if they had their night vision goggles on.

The doors through which they would enter were in the middle of the floor next to the lifts. The surveillance information showed that the security guards on each floor had cubicles about five paces away to the left of the doors where they were about to enter.

"On three," Dylan said and started counting.

Each of them had stuck a tiny device on the door lock in front of them which would explode and break the lock with a plop sound, nothing louder than a small pistol with a silencer.

"Three." Each one of them pushed the buttons on the remotes, and the locks were broken.

The doors on all six floors opened almost simultaneously, and the men slipped in. There was too much noise and talking going on; no one had heard the explosions. There were quite a few people in the hallways most of them had their cellphone lights on; there were also a few flashlights.

"This is a drill!" The six men shouted in Arabic. "Move back into your rooms and stay there until you can be evacuated. Everyone go now!" And just to make sure the staff followed their orders, they threw smoke grenades into the corridors.

It worked; people immediately rushed back to their offices and rooms and closed the doors to get away from the smoke. The hectic shuffling of people gave the men a chance to reach the cubicles of the unsuspecting security guards, most of who were on their cellphones trying to find out what had happened.

From the moment the six men stepped into the hallways, overpowered the six confused guards with etorphine darts, and hide their unconscious bodies beneath their own desks, was less than a minute.

One by one the men reported to Dylan as they completed their tasks and made their way down the stairs to the ground floor.

Daiyan Nasser, the Director of the Institute, was in his office, literally burning the midnight oil on a report for Xavier Algosaibi when he heard the helicopters. He stopped typing for a moment, frowned, and then went back to typing. He cursed when the lights went out. The backup generator would start in five minutes if the main power didn't come back on before that. He was tired; he leaned back in his chair and closed his eyes.

He sat up again when he heard someone shouting in Arabic, "This is a drill! Move back into your rooms and stay there until you can be evacuated. Everyone go now!"

A drill? What drill? I haven't been informed. He felt around for the handle of the top drawer of his desk, opened it, found the flashlight, switched it on, and found the keys to the bottom drawer where he kept his pistol.

Nasser was a scientist, not a hunter, or a soldier. He had a Ph.D. in Human Biology and protested when he was told that he had to have a gun when he took the job. However, after working in the position for a short while, it became clear why he had to carry a gun, and he had taken the time to learn how to use it.

Sitting at his desk, the pistol in his right hand, the switched off flashlight in his left, he saw light through his

The Wolves of Freydis

open door, coming down the corridor towards his office and he raised the gun. When he saw a shadow appear, he shouted in Arabic, "Who are you? What's going on?" At the same time, he pushed the button on the flashlight and, registering the masked face, aimed the gun at the figure.

Dylan had dropped to his knee when he heard the voice; his finger was tightening around the trigger when the sudden beam from the flashlight landed on his face. It threw his aim off by a tiny fraction of an inch, and the bullet hit Nasser in his right shoulder instead of his chest.

Nasser was thrown back in his chair by the impact of the bullet, and the gun dropped out of his hand on the floor. Dylan took three steps, kicked the gun away, and pushed his gun against Nasser's head. Two of his men arrived in the room; guns pointed at Nasser.

The element of surprise was still on their side. If Nasser had been able to fire off his unsilenced gun, they would have had a lot of unwelcome attention from the staff; thankfully that had been avoided.

"What's your name?" Dylan asked in fluent Arabic.

Nasser shook his head. "I'm not telling you anything. You can kill me. Go ahead do it."

Dylan picked Nasser's stronger flashlight up from the table, took a step back, and inspected Nasser's face carefully. "Dr. Daiyan Nasser, Director of the Institute." *How lucky can one get?*

Nasser groaned.

"Nasser, I would love to hang around, have a coffee, and chat about the work you do here at the Institute, but unfortunately, I've got a flight to catch."

Nasser bent over in his chair, gasping with pain as the blood seeped through his fingers.

Dylan nodded at one of his men, "close the door."

When the door was shut, Dylan took a roll of duct tape out of his side pocket, wrapped it around Nasser's mouth and head a few times, and then grabbed him by his wounded shoulder and started squeezing.

Nasser screamed and squirmed, but the sound was muffled.

"Now listen carefully, Nasser, I'm going to ask a few questions, and you'll answer quickly. I'm really in a hurry, so if you don't answer, I'm going to start shooting, left foot, then the right foot, then the left knee - you get the picture?"

Nasser looked up and raised the middle finger of his left hand to Dylan.

Dylan pulled the trigger, and Nasser's left foot jolted from the impact of the bullet. He screamed again.

"Do I shoot again or do you answer my questions?"

Nasser shook his head.

"Tell you what. I am going to spare your right foot and go for the left knee." Dylan pointed the gun to Nasser's knee.

Nasser's left hand came up as a sign to stop. He said a few muffled words.

"You want to talk to me?" Dylan asked. "Nod your head if I understand you correctly."

Nasser started nodding passionately.

"Good." Dylan took his dagger out and cut the duct tape from Nasser's mouth. "Now, where are Dr. Devereux, and her son?"

"On the – ah – on – the -" Nasser stuttered.

"You're wasting my time. I think its best I shoot you in the head and look for them myself." He raised the gun to Nasser's head.

"Fourth floor room 407." Nasser gasped.

"One man at the door, one man inside here, the rest

come with me when Loki is ready," Dylan said to the two men with him.

They nodded; one of them went to the door and told the three waiting outside what to do. The remaining man with Dylan took a roll of duct tape out wrapped it around Nasser's mouth and head and tied his feet and arms to the chair with cable ties.

Dylan walked to the bookcase, played the beam of the flashlight over it, saw the little wheels at the bottom and pushed the bookcase to the side revealing the doors to the lift and the stairs behind it.

To the day of his death, Nasser would wonder who these men were and how they knew about that concealed door.

Dylan spoke into his throat mic. "Loki, Keeva, can you read me? Over."

"Keeva, Loki, loud and clear. What's your situation? Over."

"Loki, Keeva, all secured. What's yours? Over."

"Keeva, Loki. Same. Ready when you are. Over."

"Loki, Keeva, got the big fish, had a quick chat, Charlie wants to go to room 407 fourth floor. Repeat, room 407 fourth floor. Over."

'Charlie' was Carter's codename for the mission.

"Keeva, Loki, confirm 407 fourth floor. Over."

"Loki, Keeva, down in a minute. Out."

Sean and Dylan looked at their watches at almost the same time. They had 11 minutes left.

Chapter Sixty

FREYDIS! I REPEAT FREYDIS!

The four occupants of the small conference room in the White House were silent; it was as if they were taking turns to breathe as their eyes fixed on the screens in front of them. They all looked at the clock on the wall, 11 minutes left; when they heard Dylan's voice, they all leaned forward.

"Loki, Keeva, got the big fish, had a quick chat, Charlie wants to go to room 407 fourth floor. Repeat, room 407 fourth floor. Over."

They could not hear Sean's reply, but they knew what Dylan's message meant.

"Loki, Keeva, roger, down in a minute. Out."

The President whispered, "By God, they're going to get her and her son and make it out of there."

General Crawford and Bill Griffin nodded quietly.

Irene took a sip of water, cleared her dry throat, closed her eyes, and prayed in silence. *Please God let it be so.*

The images on the screen became fractured and then disappeared; the audio broke up, The President looked to the others with concern.

General Crawford raised his finger slightly, "Don't worry, Dylan and his men have gone down the stairs; we won't hear them again until they come out above ground."

The President let out a sigh of relief, but still found it nerve wrecking to lose contact with the soldiers.

The capturing of Daiyan Nasser was a big windfall, which they had not bargained on. They knew all about him and knew he would be a great asset if they could get to him, but the chances of finding Nasser on the premises after midnight were so remote they didn't give it much thought. They didn't even know that the room on the floor plans with the entry to the stairs, which accessed the underground facility, was actually Nasser's office. Nevertheless, Dylan was a seasoned clandestine operative and knew that things did not always go as planned, and knew how to adapt and adjust rapidly. He immediately knew what a big catch it was when he recognized Nasser's face in the beam of the flashlight.

The Intel gathered from the Ground Penetrating Radar, body heat detection cameras, and the electrical structure showed that all doors leading to sleeping quarters on the underground floors were closed and automatically locked at 10:00 pm. The doors leading to offices and workspaces were always locked; entry and exit were always by swipe card only.

When the power was cut off, all the doors below ground remained locked, assuring that, unlike the levels above ground, no people were in the hallways.

When Dylan and his team had secured the six floors above ground, they would join Sean and his men below. Four men were assigned to each of the three floors where the sleeping quarters were - levels four, five, and six. Two two-man teams on each floor would work their way through the sleeping quarters from opposite directions, interrogating occupants, to find out where the American woman and her son were held.

However now that they knew where Mackenzie and Liam were, the men only had to keep a lookout for unwelcome visitors.

The alarm system went down with the power, but the problem was everyone above ground had cell phones and was calling out for information; there was nothing the extraction team could do about it. The helicopters would be on their way back to the Institute soon, and the Saudi Police would probably be closing in already.

"We've got 10 minutes," Sean said to Dylan when they met on the fourth floor. "Carter and I will go to 407, and I'll let you know as soon as we're in. Have two of your guys ready to come and help if need be."

"Roger. You and Carter get moving I'll take care of the rest.

Dylan turned to the three men with him. "Jay, you and Kevin go down, one each to levels five and six. James, you stay with me."

Carter and Sean were already at the door of 407; Sean placed the silenced explosive device on the lock, stepped away, pushed his back against the wall and flipped the switch on the remote control in his hand.

Mackenzie was tossing in her sleep. Nothing helped her relax; her dreams were tangled messes of long corridors and overhead neon lights that cast cold white light against far-reaching black shadows.

"Liu?" she called out in her sleep, "Liu, I can't see you."

Something woke her from her restless sleep; an unusual noise perhaps? Something or someone was moving in the next room. "Liam? Is that you?"

A shadow detached from the walls, "I'm here, Mackie." But the shadow grew longer and longer as it stretched out into the corridor.

The door is open, she realized. "Liu? Seema? Who's there?"

Mackenzie felt stifled, unable to breathe, and realized the shadows were closing in on her. One of them leaned over her, and she screamed when she saw a faint light.

Sliding out of bed she tried to switch on the bed light, but all remained black, just as black as her dream, but one of the shadows was real, she positioned herself between it and Beth.

"Go away! Get out of here!" She shouted.

"Shhh! Mackie, it's me."

Terror struck into the depths of her being, "Don't call me Mackie; I don't know you. Get out!"

A flashlight suddenly lit the tiny room; the figure was not just a shadow, and it spoke to her, "Mackie, it's me, Carter."

"Carter!" Mackenzie's eyes flashed fire in the dim light. "Where in hell have you been? Damn you!" She yelled and burst into tears, her body shaking wildly. "You're not dead? This isn't – a – dream?" she whispered through her tears.

Carter moved rapidly across the intervening space and gathered her in his arms. He had been preparing for this moment for months, weeks, days, hours, and all of a sudden he had no words.

Carter held her tight, "Shhh, I'm alive; I've come to get you and Liam."

"Oh God Carter, I don't believe it, you're - you can't -"

"Oh Mackie, my Mackie, I never gave up."

He held her close until a voice said, "Dad?"

"Liam! Oh my, God, you've grown so tall." He held out his arm and gathered him in with Mackenzie.

Sean stepped forward from the door. They were wasting precious seconds. "Come on, let's go."

"Wait," Mackenzie ran back to her bed and gathered up a bundle.

"What's this?"

She handed Beth to Carter, "Beth. Beth this is your Daddy I've been telling you about."

Carter was struck numb as he stared down at the tiny form. "Good Lord!"

"Come on Carter, move it, we're running out of time." James urged.

Carter grabbed a blanket off the bed with one hand; Beth tucked securely in his other arm and gave the blanket to Mackenzie to wrap around herself. He gave one more quick look at the tiny face in his arms. "Beth," he muttered.

"Sean, get Liam!" Carter said.

Sean picked Liam up and ran out the door, turned left and headed for the stairs, followed closely by Carter, Mackenzie, and James.

Sean and Dylan spoke into their throat mics to their teams. "Start evacuation. Repeat start evacuation."

The confirmation came in from the team members.

When they reached the door to the stairs, Mackenzie shouted, "Wait! Have you got Liu?"

"Who's Liu?" Carter asked.

"Dr. Liu Cheun, the Chinese language specialist, you know her. She was abducted and brought here as well."

Sean stepped forward, "Do you know where they're keeping her?"

"Yes, she's on floor 5 in room 510."

"Are there any others here that you know of?"

"I don't know; there could be -"

"Got that Sean," Dylan said. "Chinese woman, Dr. Cheun, 5th floor room 510." Dylan and his team had the shortest distance to cover to the assembly point on the roof. "You keep going I'll take care of it."

They both looked at their watches, 4 minutes.

"Roger." Sean looked at Carter and Mackenzie, "Let's go." He didn't wait for them to acknowledge, he turned and started running up the stairs with Liam in his arms.

"Jim, you go up to the ground floor," Dylan said to James.

James nodded and turned for the stairs.

Dylan spoke into his throat mic contacting Jay on the fifth floor. "Jay, Keeva, I'm on my way down. Go to room 510; get the door open. Chinese woman to evac. Over"

"Keeva, Jay, roger, on my way to 510."

When they reached the entry to the tunnel on the first floor below ground, Mackenzie looked back and stopped. She panicked and shouted "Carter will they get Liu? Please tell me they will get her. We can't leave her here."

Sean stopped, moved Liam over to his left shoulder, grabbed Mackenzie's shoulder with his right hand, staring firmly into her eyes, "Mackenzie, we will get her out, you have my word, now please we must go."

They all started running again. In the tunnel in front of them, about 30 paces ahead two men were making sure the way ahead was clear; behind them were two more covering their rear.

Flying down the stairs to level five, Dylan wondered, are there others here we know nothing about? Hell, if there are how are we going to airlift them? Maybe call in another chopper?

He shouldered the door leading from the stairs to the level five hallway and sprinted to room 510. He arrived just in time to see the silent flash of the explosion on the door lock; he shoved the door open.

In the glow of the flashlight, he discerned a form in the bed against the left wall. Moving quietly, he put a hand on a shoulder whispering, "it's okay, I'm not going to hurt you; I'm here to help."

He felt the body stir and turn, a Chinese woman frowned as she opened her eyes, no panic, "Who are you?"

"I'm an American soldier, here to get you out of this place." He knelt down beside her keeping his hand on her shoulder. "The rest of my team already have Dr. Devereux and her son. We are going to airlift you to a safe place and then to the United States.

"I - I - don't - believe it. How - how -?"" She started crying.

Dylan took her hand and pulled her out of bed and close to him. "It's ok. Don't worry; it's all over, and you're safe. Now, quick, throw on some clothes."

She nodded, immediately understanding she stepped back from him; pulling off the black nightgown, revealing she was naked. With unselfconscious haste, she reached for underwear and dropped the black jilbab she had been wearing for so many months over her head.

Dylan turned his head away, slightly dazed by her speed and lack of self-consciousness; he put it down to shock on her part, but what he'd seen was beautiful - something he would not forget.

Without looking back, he said, "Please, hurry, we have to run."

A few seconds later she stood next to him.

Suddenly he leaned over and gave her a hug. "Let's get you out of here."

He shouldered the Hackler and Koch UMP45 assault rifle bent down and lifted Liu's light body into his arms and started running.

Jay followed close behind, covering the rear.

The eyes of the occupants of the Situation Room in the White House flared wide when the video screens and sound started coming alive after an agonizing seven minutes of silence while Dylan and Sean went off the air.

They heard Sean's voice first. "Team, Loki, Echo one in two minutes. Move out. I repeat Echo one in two. Move out."

They were on the ground level of the parking garage. There were four flights of stairs to climb to reach the empty parking space on the roof. The sounds of sirens on approaching police vehicles were clearly heard.

In the ISRD building 300 yards away, the staff had been congregating in the passages again; they were going to be in the way when the team had to run down the hallway to the staircase.

When Andre saw the people gathering in the hallway, he didn't hesitate, he tugged a flashbang out of the pouch on his side, moved into the hallway, and shouted in Arabic, "Bomb!" He pulled the pin and tossed the flashbang down the corridor and to the men in the room behind him he shouted, "Ears!"

Dylan with Liu in his arms arrived in Nasser's office just in time to see the reflection of the blinding flash through the open door and heard the explosion. The light and deafening sound of the flashbang would have disorientated the people.

Dylan didn't slow down he kept on running down the hall to the door leading to the stairs, that would take them to the roof. He, Liu and John were followed by Andre and Kevin. James and Jay were ahead of them weaving their way through the sounds of screaming staff, some sitting, and some lying on the floor, all of them deaf, blind, and dazed.

When Dylan reached the stairs, Liu shouted in his ear. "Put me down! I can run!"

Dylan did so saying, "Go up, all the way to the top. Just follow the men in front of you." He slowed down a bit, pushed the button on his throat mic and spoke, "Team, Keeva, Echo two in one minute. I repeat Echo two in one." He looked up; Liu was four steps ahead of him, catching up to James and Jay.

The President, General Crawford, Bill Griffin, and Irene O'Connell had one, no actually two burning questions; was everyone okay? Did they get Mackenzie and Liam? But they were remote spectators; they had to wait - more anguish.

The voice of one of the CIA undercover agents in the guardhouse at the front gate came over on Sean and Dylan's earpieces.

"Loki, Keeva, Foxtrot one, do you read. Over?"

Sean replied. "Foxtrot one, Loki, loud and clear over."

Dylan replied. "Foxtrot one, Keeva, loud and clear over."

"Loki, Keeva, Foxtrot one, unfriendlies half a mile away. Clearing out now. Over."

"Foxtrot one, Loki, confirmed. Clear out now. Out"

Foxtrot one and two, the CIA undercover agents,

sprinted out of the guardhouse to the back of the building and a pedestrian gate. They cut the chain with bolt cutters and by the time they'd run across the street towards the buildings behind the ISRD, the first black and white double cab police vehicle had crashed through the main gate. Ten more followed, all with whining sirens and flashing lights.

James and Jay were on the roof and ran to the perimeter, taking defensive positions overlooking the front of the building. They could hear the choppers approaching. Looking down from the wall they saw the police cars arriving, men with guns drawn, jumping out, and taking up position behind their vehicles waiting for the command to rush the building.

Jay spoke into his throat mic to the chopper pilot.

"Echo two, Jay, can you read me? Over."

"Jay, Echo two, loud and clear. Over."

"Echo two, Jay, many unfriendlies, keep low when you come in. I repeat many unfriendlies keep it low. Over."

"Jay, Echo two, roger. Coming in low. Out"

Liu appeared in the opening of the door on the roof, stepped out, moved to the left, and sat down with her back against the wall as she was instructed.

Dylan, John, Kevin, and Andre appeared ten seconds later. They spread out and squatted behind parapets. The chopper was about 200 yards away to the west, approaching from the back of the ISRD building.

Sean and his group were all on the roof of the parking garage. Echo one, their chopper, was close. He spoke to the pilot telling them they were ready. There was no helipad, but the deserted parking area was ideal for the chopper.

No police vehicles were approaching their area, all the noise, and flashing lights were happening 300 yards away at the ISRD building. From his position, Sean had a clear view across to the front of the ISRD.

"Keeva, Loki, do you read? Over."

"Loki, Keeva, loud and clear. Over."

"Keeva, Loki, everyone there and ready to go? My group is ready. Over."

"Loki, Keeva, same here. Over."

In the White House, the President looked around at the faces of his three companions; they were all smiling. When he opened his mouth to ask the question, they all held their thumbs up; The President closed his mouth. It meant everyone was alive; Mackenzie and Liam were with them.

"Keeva, Loki, I just hope your visitors out front don't get it in their heads to attack the building. Over."

"Loki, Keeva, I am monitoring them. If they move, I'll launch a few flashbangs at them. Over."

"Keeva, Loki, roger. Out."

The chopper touched down on the roof of the garage; Carter, Mackenzie, Liam carried by Roy, and Beth, who was wailing loudly in her father's arms, were the first in. Then Sean started signaling the rest of the men, one by one in rapid succession, to go. He would be the last one into the chopper.

Over at the ISRD, the police commander shouted orders over the megaphone. Dylan and Jay would be the last men into their chopper. Dylan checked to make sure everyone was inside.

Andre touched his arm and shouted, "They're getting ready to shoot at us."

"Okay. Let's see if we can cure their itchy trigger fingers."

Dylan and Jay grabbed the loaded flashbang launchers next to them and fired the first grenades down on the police.

They reloaded and fired again; each of them fired a total of three grenades in quick succession.

After the first two grenades had exploded, the police task force was in shambles. When the next four explosions came soon after, some of the least stunned officers started running – away. Others, too disoriented to run, crawled under their vehicles; those closest to explosions were rendered deaf and blind and were screaming.

Dylan and Jay grabbed their equipment and sprinted to the chopper, keeping their heads low as they approached under the rotors.

As Dylan entered, he quickly scanned his team making sure everyone was there. He saw Liu; she was shaking and staring out in front of her in a daze. He took the open seat next to her, put his arm around her shoulder and said, "Hi, my name's Dylan. Are you okay doctor?"

She slowly turned her head to look at him, obviously in shock. "It's Liu; my name is Liu, not doctor." Her eyes began to focus again, and she smiled, "and yes I'm okay; no wait, I'm so much more than okay." She smiled at him, and tears began streaming down her cheeks. "Thank you. How can I -?"

"Shhh, just sit back and relax for now," Dylan smiled, "we have a long trip home, and a lot of time to talk."

Liu leaned her head against Dylan's shoulder and closed her eyes as the chopper lifted off the roof. It was the first time in many months she felt safe. There was a little smile playing on her tear-washed face.

Sean pushed the button on his throat mic, "Quebec, Hotel, Loki, do you read? Over?"

"Loki, Quebec, loud and clear. Over."

"Quebec, Hotel, Loki, thanks, guys. Great job. We'll talk soon. Over."

"Loki, Quebec, our pleasure, talk soon. Out."

The Echo one chopper banked to the right and headed west.

Sean spoke into the throat mic again.

"Keeva, Loki do you read?" Over."

"Loki, Keeva, loud and clear. Freydis! I repeat Freydis! Over."

"Keeva, Loki, Freydis! I repeat Freydis! Out."

Freydis was the code word that meant the hostages were evacuated, everyone was safe, and they were on their way to the warship in the Red Sea 70 miles away.

In the White House the President was on his feet and so were Irene, Bill and General Crawford. They were hugging each other. "Thank God," The President whispered with deep emotion choking his voice.

On the ship, Samantha grabbed Rick by the back of his head, pulled him to her and laid a long, lingering kiss on him that made his toes curl and left him breathless.

Liam's mouth was agape as he looked at his dad's blackened camouflaged face, black uniform and weapons and the men in the helicopter dressed the same as his dad.

Beth's eyes were open; she had stopped crying and now was staring up at Carter. It was almost as if she was studying her father's face, he stared back down at her in amazement, "Mackie this is incredible, she's utterly beautiful, I just can't believe it."

Mackenzie, had her arm hooked through Carter's, and she smiled at him, "Probably no more than I can believe you're here, and we are going home."

Chapter Sixty-One

ON THE PHONES

Epic scenes of elation erupted on the deck of the warship after Echo one and two landed and the four hostages and their rescuers set foot on the ship at 1:45 am. Carter, Mackenzie, Liam, Beth, Liu, and James were quickly surrounded by the rescue team, which included Rick and Samantha, the commander of the ship and the intelligence officer.

Carter held his daughter in his arms; despite all the noise, she was calm. Liam was the proudest boy on the planet as he stood between his mom and dad. When Mackenzie saw Liu, she ran to her, and the two women embraced each other, laughing and crying.

James saw the bundle in Carter's arms and approached. "Carter, what's that? It looks like you're holding a baby."

"That's exactly what I'm holding, Jim! This is my daughter; Beth! Can you believe it?"

"Oh my God! Carter, Mackenzie! You - you - have a daughter?" James stuttered. "Mackenzie!" He stepped forward and hugged her and then leaned over to Carter to get a glimpse of the little one's face. "Carolyn and I volunteer to be the godparents!" He chuckled.

Carter just nodded; tears were streaming down his face. Mackenzie smiled as she watched him, not yet believing he was here holding Beth in his arms.

The rest of the people on the deck had formed a semi-circle around the group and started cheering loudly.

A few minutes later the commander of the ship managed to herd them all into the mess hall where hot food and drinks were awaiting them.

Two physicians and other medical staff who were on standby, escorted Mackenzie, Liam, Beth, Liu, and Carter down to ship's hospital for a checkup and treatment if necessary, before they would be transferred to their next destination, Tel Aviv.

They still had a lot of traveling to do before they would set their feet back on American soil. The President and General Crawford wanted the group to be out of the area and safe as quickly as possible before they contacted the Saudi officials.

The entire group of 18 people was scheduled to be airlifted by an MV-22 Osprey at 3:00 am to Tel Aviv first. From the ship's position to Tel Aviv was 646 nautical miles, less than three hours for the Osprey, which had a cruising speed of 241 knots. They would land in Tel Aviv at a secured military airbase known as the Lod Airbase, the military part of Ben Gurion International Airport.

From the Lod Airbase, they would be transferred to a private jet, in which they would make the 12-hour flight directly to DC.

The Wolves of Freydis

It was 7:00 am in Riyadh; the private jet had just reached cruising altitude and had set course for Washington DC when the President of the United States greeted King Al Saud.

The King was immediately on alert when he was told who was on the phone. A few minutes into the conversation the King was fuming with rage, not against The President or America; in fact, at the end of the conversation, he thanked the President for bringing the matter to his personal attention. The King was infuriated by the discovery of the treachery in his midst. When he heard the names Xavier Algosaibi and Ibrahimi El Fadl he felt the dagger of betrayal in his back and went quiet, as he comprehended that what he felt was in reality, only the tip of the dagger.

When the President suggested the King have an audience with the US Secretary of State, Joshua Bartlet, he accepted. Bartlet, The President explained, would fill the King in on all the details. Al Saud knew he was running out of time and had to act swiftly.

When Bly answered the phone and heard Carter's voice, she shouted, "Ahote, come quickly; it's Carter!" Ahote must have broken a speed record to get to the phone. Bly put the phone on speaker and said, "We are all ears, Carter!"

"Bly, Ahote, it's good news we've got them! They're alive; they're here with me. I - I -" Carter's voice faltered as he started crying. "We - we are - coming - home."

Bly and Ahote grabbed each other and started dancing and shouting. Carter could hear Bly calling out "I knew it! I knew it! The wolves told us; they told us!"

Ahote was the first one to get a grip and said, "Carter can we talk to Mackenzie?"

"Yes, of course, she is right here. But before I -"

Carter didn't get to finish his sentence; Mackenzie had grabbed the phone and shouted, "Bly! Ahote!"

Carter started laughing when he heard Bly and Ahote's shouts of joy when Mackenzie told them about Beth.

Carter smiled and sat back, looking at Liam, who was fast asleep. He looked at Mackenzie's beaming face as she was talking on the phone; Beth slept peacefully in his arms. He carefully moved the soft baby blanket away from her face and drank in the infant's face; he just couldn't get enough of his red-haired sleeping beauty.

It was 4:30 pm in Boston when the bell on the front door of the Andersons house chimed. Steven, and Ray their son who was home on leave, were engrossed in a program on the National Geographic channel; it was Mary who opened the door.

"Good afternoon Mrs. Anderson, I don't know if you will remember me? I'm Irene O'Connell."

"Yes, I remember you, Irene," Mary was instantly on alert. The one and only time she met Irene was when Irene met her, Steven and Ray at the airport in DC and accompanied them to a private jet, which flew them to Israel. It was not a good memory.

Irene immediately detected the fear on Mary's face. "Mrs. Anderson, please don't worry; this time, I'm the bearer of very good news," Irene said with a smile. "May I come in?"

"Yes, please; come in," Mary invited, leading the way to

the living room where Steven and Ray were. Their reactions were no different to Mary's when they recognized Irene and remembered the heartbreaking circumstances when they last saw her.

Irene knew she had to get the news out quickly. She didn't take a seat. "I have the most wonderful news ever," she drew a short breath, "Mackenzie and Liam are alive and on their way home."

Steven sat forward, "Say that again, Irene."

"Mackenzie and Liam are alive, Steven, and they're on their way home."

Mary's voice quivered, "Alive? Mackenzie's alive; and Liam too?"

Irene nodded. "It's a very long story, and The President himself wants to see you and tell you all about it, but he insisted I come and tell you first. He knew it would be impossible over the phone."

Mary's voice was hesitant, "Are they alright?"

"Yes, Mary, they're both just fine," Irene was nodding firmly.

"What about Carter? Is he alright? Does he know?"

"He's absolutely fine too, and he knows, he's with them right now."

Mary turned to Steven and Ray. Like her, tears were rolling down their cheeks. The three Andersons reached out and held each other.

"I can't believe this," Steven whispered. "How is it possible? Is it really true?"

"They're really alive, Irene?" Ray asked in a wavering voice. "You're sure?"

"Yes, they are alive," Irene said as she wiped the tears from her eyes.

It had been decided not to tell them about their granddaughter; that honor and privilege belonged to Beth's parents, and her proud brother, Liam.

"How can you be so sure, Irene?" Steven asked.

Irene smiled and said, "I'm going to phone her right now, and you can talk to her, and Liam, and Carter." She took her satellite phone out and pushed the buttons.

It was 11:00 pm, two hours before the private jet from Tel Aviv was scheduled to land in the high-security area of the Joint Base Andrews. The still shell-shocked but ecstatic Andersons were led into the Oval Office by Irene to meet with President Grant.

The President welcomed them and asked them to take a seat then sat down with them. He already knew they had spoken to Mackenzie and Liam, and that she had told them about Beth, the latest addition to the family. He tried to imagine the conversation, *Yes Mom, we are alive and well, it's real, and you can believe it. You won't know Liam; he's grown so tall, and guess what? You have a granddaughter! Her name is Beth!* The President could only imagine the joy.

He cleared his throat; "I've asked to meet you to share some information with you, share in your joy, and to explain a few things," He continued and gave them a brief summary of the operation and how it was executed.

"Mr. President, can you tell us more about where they were and what happened to them?" Steven asked.

The President went into more detail and answered as many of their questions as was possible without breaking security protocols.

"Mr. President, why were we not told sooner?" Mary asked.

"Yes. With all due respect Mr. President, why was it necessary to withhold this information from us?" Steven added.

The President nodded. "Unfortunately, painful as it must be for you to know you were kept in the dark, it was absolutely necessary for their safety. I want to apologize for that, however, for what it's worth, we only discovered about nine days ago that they were alive and where they were being held."

Steven leaned back, visibly relaxing.

"The main reason we couldn't tell you earlier was because it would have placed them in too much danger. Only the rescue team was allowed to know. If that information had leaked out before they were rescued, their captors would have killed them," The President paused for a moment and continued. "I apologize again; I can only imagine the hell you must have been going through the last ten months. All I can say is - it's over. They are alive and well."

Steven smiled, looked at Mary and Ray, saw their smiles and nodded. "Mr. President you have our eternal gratitude for bringing our children back to us. We'll never forget it as long as we live. There could never be a more perfect day in our lives."

"Thank you, I appreciate that, but I only gave the orders to rescue them, the recognitions should go to your son-in-law, Irene here and the others who never stopped believing and never gave up," The President replied.

The Andersons and Irene were invited to travel on Marine One, The President's helicopter, with him to Joint Base Andrews. Fifteen minutes after their arrival, the private jet landed and taxied into the hangar.

The President and Irene stood to the side and watched

as the Andersons engulfed Mackenzie, Carter, Liam, Beth, and Liu in their arms.

A few minutes later, Liu took a few steps out of the family circle and walked over to Dylan. He smiled happily as he put his arm around her and looked down into her shining face.

Chapter Sixty-Two

IN THE NEWS

Despite the lateness of the hour, Steven and Mary had insisted that Carter, Mackenzie, Liam, Beth and Lui all stay at their house, at least for the night, and they had all been glad to accept. Everyone was exhausted from being up most of the previous night and had slept most of the day.

The next evening Carter, Steven, and Ray sat quietly enjoying a glass of whiskey in the den at the Anderson's house. The women were in the kitchen preparing a light dinner, and the men had gathered in the den to watch the news. Liam was enjoying the privilege of sitting on his father's lap after missing him for so many months, and Carter had reluctantly surrendered Beth to the arms of her Grandfather.

"… and in world news tonight, some major, and surprising, events in Saudi Arabia. For the report, we go now to our correspondent on special assignment, Robert Evans. Bob, we understand there are some remarkable events taking place over there."

"That's right, Cindy. From what we have been told, there was a raid on the Institute of Scientific Research and Development yesterday

that lead to the discovery of a plot to bring down the House of Saud and resulted in the release of hostages that were, until now, being held without anyone knowing about it.

"Upon receiving the information about the treachery against the House of Saud, King Al Saud gave orders for the arrest of local businessman and former General Intelligence Presidency employee, Xavier Algosaibi, and had Ibrahimi El Fadl – current deputy director of the General Intelligence Presidency detained as well. If what we have been told is true, this is a conspiracy at the highest government level. At the moment, interviews with the two men are being conducted, and officers continue to investigate the information that led to the discovery of the plot. We'll have more for you on these as further developments arise. Back to you, Cindy."

"Thank you, Bob. We look forward to those updates!" The TV news reporter refocused on the camera to address viewers. *"And in news back on American soil, earlier today Dwayne Miller, CEO of the American company Competitive Response Solutions, and one of his board members, Nate Gordon, were arrested on charges of treason and espionage, and we are told there could be further charges filed. The homes of Miller and Gordon, as well as the offices of Competitive Response Solutions were raided and searched, under warrant, by the FBI after they received information about treasonous actions by the two men and the company. Many staff members were detained as well, but we are told most of them are being interviewed and released."*

"Thank you for that report, Cindy," the news anchor said. *"We now have an update on the Vice-President's condition. As we reported yesterday, the Vice-President collapsed while attending a meeting at the Whitehouse. It appears that he suffered an incapacitating stroke and is currently in intensive care at a secure and unknown location. His condition is serious, and although he has improved slightly over the past 24 hours, his spokesperson has said his campaign for the Presidency has been suspended."*

"Well, Scott, it looks like we won't have a 'President Robertson' coming out of the next election."

"No, Cindy, we sure won't. But, we do wish him a speedy recovery and …"

Carter turned the volume down as he sat up. "It looks like we're going to see some justice done in the world."

The Devereux's spent the next week in Boston with the Anderson's. As much as Carter wanted to scoop his family up and take them to the safety of Freydis, he knew it was important for Mackenzie to re-connect with her family, and they with her. Liam, ecstatic to be back at home with his father and grandparents, didn't seem to be any the worse for his experience. Mackenzie was physically and emotionally exhausted, and it took her time to recover from the ordeal she had been through. Frequently at night she broke down in tears; Carter held and soothed her, reassuring her that she and the children were safe and that they were all back together again. Carter had insisted that she take a nap in the afternoons with Beth, and by the end of the week, she was feeling more herself again.

The newspapers, radio, and television stations were flooded with reports from Saudi Arabia about the investigation into the conspiracy against the House of Saud.

Also, in the news was the investigation of Competitive Response Solutions. Given the numerous records and the international nature of their business, the completion of the investigation was expected to take at least a year if not longer. After that, the trials would begin, but it wasn't looking good for Dwayne Miller, Nate Gordon, and the other directors. There was no mention of the Vice-President.

In a chair in the office of Executive Advantage, he twiddled a pen in his fingers as he thought. *I took an oath to defend this country against enemies foreign and domestic.* He picked up the medical report on the Vice President and reviewed it again. His wrist and shoulder were healing nicely, but the man's mental state was completely another matter. According to the report, his behavior was like that of a caged lion and his communication skills had deteriorated to the profane and the absurd.

Returning the report to the desk, he stood and paced the office. *I took an oath to defend this country – Robertson is a traitor, a domestic enemy.* He carefully reviewed his strategy again. "I will honor my oath," he whispered, and he picked up the secure phone.

"Good evening, Sir," the young Secret Serviceman said recognizing the number on the secured phone.

"How is he this evening?" the caller asked.

"Profane, Sir. He doesn't appreciate the accommodations at all. He's still pacing like a caged lion."

"Let's see if we can make him a little more comfortable. Make arrangements for him to have a TV so he can keep up with what's in the news – he must want to know what is happening in the world."

Epilogue

It was late afternoon when Carter's plane approached Freydis for landing. Ahote, Bly, and Jeha were at the airstrip waiting for them. In the distance, hidden amongst the trees, Loki and Keeva with their four pups were also waiting. Long before Ahote, Bly or Jeha could hear or see it, the wolves' ears pitched when they heard the sound of the approaching plane, and they let out soft yipping sounds. They watched everyone get out of the plane and raised their noses to test the air, accounting for everyone, before they turned around and headed back to their cave.

With Liam and Jeha, it was hard to tell who was happier to see who; one ran around barking and jumping, the other ran around yelling and jumping. Mackenzie and Bly cried and hugged and cried some more. Carter and Ahote slapped one another on the back and laughed, then finally hugged one another.

Bly had prepared a lovely dinner for them all to celebrate the homecoming, and they sat down to enjoy the meal and have a long overdue visit.

Dawn was just lighting the sky over Freydis the next morning when Mackenzie placed the sleeping Beth back in her crib after feeding her.

After taking a long look at Carter who was, at last, looking rested and peaceful in his sleep, she peered into Liam's room; he too was fast asleep, smiling. Jeha was under the blankets with him, only her fluffy ears and face were showing. She pulled a coat over her nightdress, put wool-lined boots on her feet, and stepped out into the crisp spring air.

For a moment, she stood and gazed around remembering how she came to believe she'd never see her home ever again.

There was mist over the distant valleys and above, the snow-capped peaks of mountains that would not be bare before mid-summer.

As she walked, the sky changed from gray to pink, for her one of those magical colors she couldn't get enough of, then mauve and small clouds that were tinged with gold.

She headed for her special rock, a place where she would have a distant view of the world around her, a place where she would one day bring Beth to play in the long grass at her feet.

The sun was just hovering over the horizon as she pulled herself up on the large flat rock, sat, and waited.

Within minutes, Loki and Keeva arrived. Each of them moving quickly up the hill below her, their ears flattened as they raced; their tails out straight behind them. As they got closer, she could see their pink tongues lolling in their panting mouths before they finally leaped on the rock, greeting her with an enthusiasm she'd never seen before.

She threw her arms around them both hugging them as

The Wolves of Freydis

she ran her fingers through their thick coats, letting them lick her tears away.

"Oh my darlings, how would I ever have survived without you?"

Suddenly there was movement further down the hill and before she could draw a breath, four young pups arrived willing and eager to meet her.

She turned to Keeva and Loki; "Look how much they've grown!" she slid off the rock. Instantly she was bowled over by the enthusiasm of the four young wolves and found herself lying on the grass covered by furry, bounding, young bodies with long wet tongues as the pups rolled over and around her. Their excitement caused her to laugh until her tummy hurt; laugh as she'd not laughed for months. She laughed until she was sure the valleys were echoing her joy.

Finally, she pulled herself back up on the rock where Keeva and Loki joined her. She smiled; she was alone in the open air with the sun shining down on her, and a faint breeze carrying the scents of Freydis to her. She was with her wolves; they who'd kept her company in her dreams for all those months.

Slowly, as the sun rose, she was able to see the beauty of spring on Freydis - an eagle soaring high above on unseen air currents, the lime green of newly growing leaves on the trees, the sound and movement of small birds and animals in the undergrowth, and in front of her, the long grass turning gold as the sun rose and slowly warmed the Earth around her.

Next in the Carter Devereux Mystery Thriller Series

vinci-books.com/alboran

As an extinct empire resurfaces, Carter Devereux races against time to decode an ancient codex and save humanity.

The Nabateans, believed extinct for 1,900 years, now seek to reclaim their empire, and only Carter Devereux's knowledge of their secrets can stop them. As the Council of the Covenant of Nabatea pursues Devereux, he must unravel the mysteries of the Alboran Codex while evading their clutches. With the future of humanity at stake, Devereux is running out of time.

Turn the page for a free preview…

The Alboran Codex: Prologue

1897 BC—Twelve mighty princes

It was a time to celebrate. Today was Isaac's weaning, her firstborn's second birthday. He had survived the fragile stage of infancy and could now eat solid food rather than being breastfed. He would live a long and healthy life. But Sarah was quiet. She heard the music, saw the people eating, drinking, and laughing, but her insides were steaming — and had been for a long time.

Oh, how I rue the day I gave that slave woman to Abraham to produce an offspring for him. I was seventy-five and Abraham was eighty-five — how was I to know it was even possible to bear my own child at ninety? And now look at this. My slave is insolent, and her son thinks he is the heir. It must be Hagar who's putting him up to that.

She was startled out of her reverie by Isaac's wailing. Ishmael was dancing around the little boy, mocking and scaring him with a knife. *This is the final straw. This slave woman and her son must go. Now! Both of them. I've had enough of their impudence.*

She moved to pick up the terrified Isaac and place him on her hip, then turned and shouted at Ishmael, "You are fourteen years old. You should know better than to scare a little two-year-old. Leave Isaac alone. I never want to see you near him again! *Ever*."

Isaac's jeering smile disappeared from his face. He turned and with sagging shoulders walked away to find Hagar.

"This has to end today," Sarah said to herself. "God told Abraham to change my name from Sarai to Sarah? Abraham told me God said, *'As for Sarai your wife, you are no longer to call her Sarai; her name will be Sarah. I will bless her and she will give you a son by her. I will bless her; she will be the mother of nations; kings of peoples will come from her.'"* (Genesis 17:15-16)

Abraham saw the thundercloud on Sarah's face where she stood with Isaac on her hip. He excused himself from the men and walked over to her. "Sarah, what is wrong? This is a time to be happy and to be celebrating. Why the anger on your face?"

"When we were living at the well of Beer-lahai-roi, Hagar absconded, but then she came back. I don't know why she came back, but it would have been better if she had just stayed away. She is trouble and nothing but since she gave you that child," Sarah said.

"You know why she came back, Sarah. God told her to do so. She went away because you were treating her harshly."

Sarah's eyes were blistering when she answered, "Yes, that may be so, but look at it now. She despises me, and Ishmael is incessantly insulting and scaring Isaac. I've had enough," Sarah hissed. "Get rid of that slave woman and her son, for that woman's son will never share in the inheritance with my son Isaac." (Genesis 21:10)

"Sarah! I can never do that. Ishmael is my son. I can't send them away."

"God's promise was made to Isaac, not to Ishmael. Isaac is your only heir, not that slave's son," she snapped.

Abraham knew better than to argue with Sarah. Once she made up her mind, she became an immovable force. "Let's discuss this later," he said and turned away.

Later that afternoon, when the festivities were over and the guests had left, Abraham took a long stroll into the field. He had no idea what to do. Ishmael was his son, his own blood. How could he send him away? He climbed up a hill and watched the sun sinking below the horizon in the west. The desert was silent; it was as if everything in nature stopped and went quiet to watch as the sun slowly disappeared.

Then he heard the voice of God. *"Do not be so distressed about the boy and your slave woman. Listen to whatever Sarah tells you, because it is through Isaac that your offspring will be reckoned. I will make the son of the slave into a nation also because he is your offspring."* (Genesis 21:12)

It was dark when Abraham returned and began preparing. Early the next morning, he called Hagar and Ishmael to his tent.

It was with sadness he said, "Hagar, God spoke to me about you and Ishmael, and you can no longer live with us. You and Ishmael must go away from here and find another place to live."

Hagar was shaken. "How can you do this, Abraham? This is our son. He is *your* firstborn. How can you just cut us off from you? What will become of us? How can you throw your own blood away?"

"Hagar, I have asked God to bless Ishmael and He said to me, '*And as for Ishmael, I have heard you: I will surely bless him;*

I will make him fruitful and will greatly increase his numbers. He will be the father of twelve mighty princes, and I will make him into a great nation.'" (Genesis 17:20)

Hagar had tears in her eyes as she looked at Abraham, but she knew this was how it was to be. Nothing would change his mind.

In silence, Abraham took the skin-bags with food and water and set them on her shoulders. He looked to Ishmael and handed him a small wooden box wrapped in skin. "Ishmael, keep this with you always. It contains God's promise to you."

Abraham wiped the tears from his eyes, took a step back, and said, "He who has protected and blessed me will bless and protect you."

Hagar and Ishmael went away into the Desert of Beersheba. They wandered without direction with nowhere to go, and finally the water in the skin-bag was gone. Hagar had squeezed the last few drops onto Ishmael's cracked lips. "My son and I will die in this wilderness."

She was weak and parched when she placed Ishmael in the shade of a bush, walked a bowshot away, sat down, and moaned softly. "I cannot watch the boy die."

"What is the matter, Hagar?" (Genesis 21:17)

The voice startled her. "Am I hallucinating?" she whispered to herself.

But then the voice was there again. *"Do not be afraid; God has heard the boy crying as he lies there. Lift the boy up and take him by the hand, for I will make him into a great nation."* (Genesis 21:17)

And then the voice was gone and the desert silence returned.

She was bewildered. *What... who was that?*

Her head cleared as she took a deep breath. Looking

around, she saw what seemed like the rim of a well. *That was not there before. Or was it? Why haven't I seen it?*

She stood and walked to it — it *was* a well. And there was water in it! Then she remembered Abraham's parting words to her and Ishmael.

"*It must have been the angel of God who spoke to me just now,*" she thought.

She cupped her hands and drank, then filled the skin-bag and ran back to her son. Propping his head, she helped him drink. His whimpering stopped, and he looked around.

Hagar spoke softly to Ishmael. "My son, your name means '*God will hear*' and today God has heard me. I am the daughter of the Pharaoh of Egypt. You, Ishmael, are a prince; you are of noble descent. I will get you a wife from the house of the Pharaoh, and you are going to be the father of a great nation. It will be as God has promised to your father, Abraham; twelve mighty princes will you beget."

1774 BC—He was gathered to his people

Ishmael's hair and beard were white as snow, his eyes were hazy, his hands were shaking, and his skin bore witness of 137 years' of desert life. His breathing was labored when he spoke to his wife.

"Aisha, my days have been numbered; my time to be gathered to my father, Abraham, and my ancestors has come. You must send a message to my children to come to me without delay." Aisha nodded and left to summon the messengers.

A few days before the full moon, Ishmael's twelve sons, Nebajoth, Hadad, Dumah, Adbeel, Mibsam, Tema, Naphish, Mishma, Jetur, Massa, Kedar, Kedemah, and his daughter, Basemath, also known as Mahalath, who was married to Esau, the son of Isaac, stood around his bed. They were sad. It was obvious that their father had reached the end of his days. (Genesis 25:12-16)

Ishmael's voice was soft and gruff as he spoke.

"My days on the earth have come to an end. God had blessed me as He had promised my father Abraham, your grandfather. God has given me twelve mighty princes and a beautiful princess, Basemath.

"God made His promise to your grandmother, Hagar, before I was born. It was by a fountain of water in the wilderness, on the way to Shur, when God's angel said to her:

"I will multiply thy seed exceedingly, that it shall not be numbered for multitude. Behold, thou art with child, and shalt bear a son, and shalt call his name Ishmael; because the LORD hath heard thy affliction." (Genesis 16:10)

"And he will be a wild man; his hand will be against every man, and every man's hand against him; and he shall dwell in the presence of all his brethren." (Genesis 16:12)

Ishmael took a deep breath, a sip of water, and continued, "And that is how it was. I am Ishmael - *'God will hear'* - and I have been a wild man. Everyone was against me, and I was against everyone. But despite my wild nature, God has kept His promise and blessed me.

"I was a boy of fourteen when my mother and I arrived in the Desert of Paran. We had nothing, only water and a little food. I am now 137 years old, and my twelve sons are ruling my kingdom from Havilah to Shur." (from Assyria to the border of Egypt)

He lay back on his bed and closed his eyes. His children stared at the old patriarch, the strong man, the archer, the man who knew the desert, the warrior, and the conqueror;

the man who formed them and set them in their ways. What was it going to be like without him?

Slowly Ishmael opened his eyes again. "You must all now go outside and wait there. I will call you in one by one so I can give you my blessing, starting with Nebajoth. Then when I die, you must bury me next to my mother, Hagar, in Makkah."

All of them except Nebajoth bowed and left.

"Come closer, Nebajoth," Ishmael whispered.

Nebajoth went to his father's bed and knelt. Ishmael placed his right hand on Nebajoth's head and said, "Nebajoth, you are my firstborn, the sign of the strength of my youth, shining in honor, outrivaling in power.

"Your grandmother was a princess from the house of the Pharaoh. You are a Prince, and you will be nobody's slave.

"You will draw water from the desert, trade from the east to the west, and you will become the father of a great nation."

Nebajoth had to lean in close to his father to hear his faltering voice.

Ishmael continued, "Under the bed is a small box wrapped in skin, given to me by my father, Abraham. It is now yours. Keep it with you always. You and your offspring are the heirs of the promise in that box."

Tears were streaming down Nebajoth's face when he left Ishmael's tent.

One by one, the rest of his children entered and received their father's blessing.

"Ishmael lived a hundred and thirty-seven years. He breathed his last and died, and he was gathered to his people. His descendants settled in the area from Havilah to Shur, near the eastern border of

Egypt, as you go toward Ashur. And they lived in hostility toward all the tribes related to them." (Genesis 25: 17-18)

Modern-day Paris, France

It was 11:05 when the electronic double doors slid apart. A woman stepped into the opulent chamber ten stories below the house located on the bank of the River Seine in the 3rd *Arrondissement* (district) of Paris. She wore no jewelry — her white dress trimmed in gold was more than enough to strike a stately figure — the epitome of elegance.

As she made her way to the round table in the middle of the room, everyone admired her athletic body and unflawed features. No one knew how old she was, and no one would ask, but she didn't look a day older than forty. Graziella Marie Nabati's life, filled with the privileges of money, not only granted her an extended middle age, it also gave her the best possible education and a healthy lifestyle. It was not arrogance that she radiated, it was confidence — the absolute conviction that the world around her had been organized exactly the way she wanted it. It bestowed on her a graceful *sang-froid* that made her peers pale by comparison. Her dark-brown eyes were sharp and piercing, and her dark hair was cut in a voguish bob that dropped to her strong jawline.

She was beautiful — very beautiful — in the same way an iceberg is beautiful, and equally forbidding.

When she arrived, the eleven people already seated at the enormous round oak table in the middle of the chamber all stood, bowed to her, and in chorus said, "Behold the daughter of Hagar of whom God said, '*I will multiply thy seed exceedingly, that it shall not be numbered for multitude.*' The mother of Ishmael of whom God said, *'I will make him into a great nation.'"*

Graziella bowed in acknowledgment and took her seat. Everyone followed suit. Her smile was as cold as it was seductive.

In the center of the table was a small gold monument, about ten inches high —a miniature roundtable with three gold swords as legs. Atop rested a small wooden chest roughly the size of a modern-day shoebox.

The chamber was circular, about ten yards in diameter. The four pillars looking as if they held the ceiling up were covered with inscribed gold plates. The floor was covered with a made-to-specifications Isfahan rug, the elite of Persian carpets, with silk foundations and silk inlaid kourk wool pile, displaying a Garden of Paradise pattern in the center. The paintings on the walls continued the Garden of Paradise theme of the floor rug with a lavish display of water features — canals, ponds, fountains, and waterfalls. There was a particularly striking painting of a bottlenose dolphin surrounded by other marine mammals of the Cetacean order, including porpoises, whales, and dolphins.

The chamber below Graziella's house was part of *les carrières* de Paris, better known as the Paris Catacombs — also at times referred to as "The World's Largest Grave" because of the more than six million bodies that have been buried there over the ages.

The catacombs were created when rich limestone deposits were discovered below the Left Bank many centuries ago, and the limestone was excavated and used to build the city. In some places, the diggers delved up to ten stories underground, etching out massive cavities and tangled tunnels spreading over more than two hundred miles.

In ancient times, these quarries were on the outskirts of the city. But over time, as the city of Paris expanded, it eventually covered the top of the old labyrinth, until almost half of the modern-day metropolis was located above the mines.

During the eighteenth century, when Parisians had a problem with overcrowded cemeteries, the authorities ordered all city graveyards be dug up and the skeletons dumped in the underground tunnels. Millions of skeletons were moved, broken up, and stacked there like firewood.

In 1788, after the riots in the *Place de Grève*, the *Hôtel de Brienne*, and *Rue Meslée*, the bodies of those dead were also dumped in the catacombs. In 1871, *communards*, members of the Paris Commune, killed a group of monarchists there. The French Resistance used the tunnel system during World War II. The Nazis established an underground bunker below *Lycée Montaigne*.

In 2004, police found a movie theater in one of the caverns. It was fully equipped with a huge viewing screen and seating for an audience. There was projection equipment, film reels, a fully stocked bar, and a restaurant with tables and chairs to cater to the attending people. Who was responsible for it and how it was powered remains a mystery.

To this day, large parts of the elaborate labyrinth remain unexplored, unmapped, and mysterious.

Grab your copy...
vinci-books.com/alboran

About the Author

JC Ryan is a bestselling author renowned for his intricate espionage, archaeological thrillers, and conspiracy mysteries. With over 30 acclaimed novels, including the popular Rex Dalton K9 Thrillers, Rossler Foundation Mysteries, and Carter Devereux Mystery Thrillers, Ryan has captivated readers around the globe.

Drawing from his diverse professional background—as a military officer, lawyer, and IT manager—Ryan creates compelling narratives that skillfully blend historical accuracy with thrilling adventure. He is celebrated as a master storyteller, known for crafting riveting plots, meticulous historical details, and engaging, multidimensional characters. Ryan's meticulous research lends authenticity and depth to each story, immersing readers in richly constructed worlds filled with intrigue, suspense, and adventure.

Fans of David Baldacci, Lee Child's Jack Reacher, Tom Clancy's Jack Ryan, Nelson DeMille's John Corey, Vince Flynn's Mitch Rapp, Mark Greaney's Gray Man, Gregg Hurwitz's Orphan X, Robert Ludlum's Jason Bourne, Daniel Silva's Gabriel Allon, Brad Taylor's Pike Logan, Brad Thor's Scot Harvath, James Rollins' Sigma Force, Steve Berry's Cotton Malone, and Dan Brown's Robert Langdon will find JC Ryan's novels equally compelling and unforgettable.

When not writing, Ryan enjoys spending time with his college sweetheart, whom he married in 1978. They are proud parents of two daughters, have two sons-in-law, and are grandparents to two grandchildren.